BLOOD

OF

TROY

Also by Claire M. Andrews

Daughter of Sparta

BLOOD OF TROY

A DAUGHTER OF SPARTA NOVEL

CLAIRE M. ANDREWS

LITTLE, BROWN AND COMPANY

New York   Boston

Copyright © 2022 by Claire M. Andrews
Map copyright © 2022 by Maxime Plasse

Cover art figure © Cristian Baitg Schreiweis/Arcangel Images; background © Chantapa3624/Shutterstock.com; sparks © fotograzia/Getty Images; spear © Alex44ARH/Shutterstock.com. Front cover design by Amanda Hudson, Faceout Studio. Cover copyright © 2022 by Hachette Book Group, Inc.

Little, Brown and Company
Hachette Book Group
1290 Avenue of the Americas, New York, NY 10104
Visit us at LBYR.com

First Edition: September 2022

Little, Brown and Company is a division of Hachette Book Group, Inc. The Little, Brown name and logo are trademarks of Hachette Book Group, Inc.

The publisher is not responsible for websites (or their content) that are not owned by the publisher.

Library of Congress Cataloging-in-Publication Data
Names: Andrews, Claire M., author.
Title: Blood of Troy / Claire M. Andrews.
Description: First edition. | New York ; Boston : Little, Brown and Company, 2022. | Series: A Daughter of Sparta novel | Audience: Ages 14 & up. | Summary: "As the kingdoms of Greece clash on the shores of Troy and the gods choose sides, Daphne must use her wits, her training, and her precarious relationship with Apollo to keep her queen safe, stop the war, and uncover the true reason the gods led her to Troy"—Provided by publisher.
Identifiers: LCCN 2022005043 | ISBN 9780316366748 (hardcover) | ISBN 9780316366960 (ebook)
Subjects: CYAC: Trojan War—Fiction. | Mythology, Greek—Fiction. | Brothers and sisters—Fiction. | Secrets—Fiction. | LCGFT: Novels.
Classification: LCC PZ7.1.A53274 Bl 2022 | DDC [Fic]—dc23
LC record available at https://lccn.loc.gov/2022005043

ISBNs: 978-0-316-36674-8 (hardcover), 978-0-316-36696-0 (ebook), 978-0-316-52856-6 (int'l)

Printed in the United States of America

LSC-C

Printing 1, 2022

FOR CHARLOTTE,
WHOSE CREATIVITY IS AN INSPIRATION

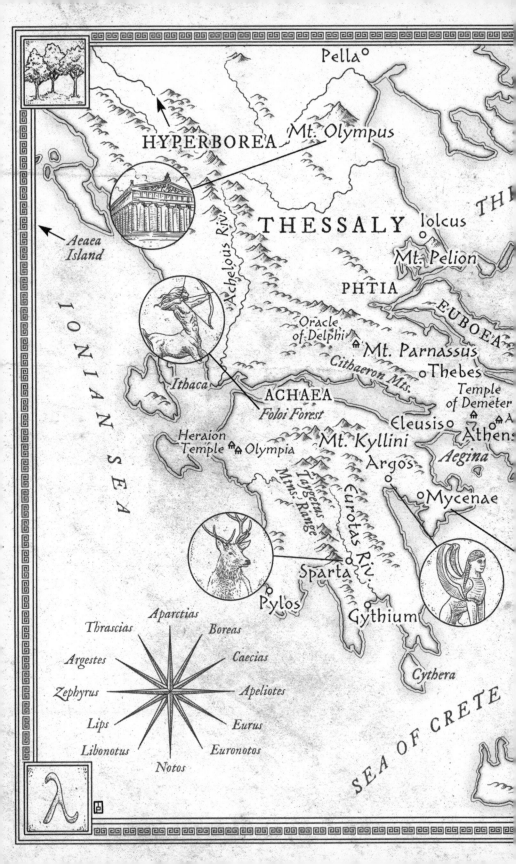

Pella

HYPERBOREA Mt. Olympus

Aeaea
Island

THESSALY Iolcus THI

Mt. Pelion

PHTIA EUBOEA

Achelous Riv.

Oracle
of Delphi Mt. Parnassus

Cithaeron Mts. Thebes

IONIAN SEA

Ithaca

ACHAEA

Foloi Forest

Temple
of Demeter

Eleusis Athens

Heraion
Temple Olympia Mt. Kyllini Aegina

Argos

Taygetus Mtns. Range Eurotas Riv. Mycenae

Sparta

Pylos Gythium

Aparctias

Thrascias Boreas

Argestes Caecias

Zephyrus Apeliotes

Lips Eurus

Libonotus Euronotos

Notos

Cythera

SEA OF CRETE

The Hellespont

SEA

Lemnos

Hephaestus's
Forge

Troy

Mt. Kazbek

Lyrnessus

THEMYSCIRA

Lesbos

Pergamon

Entrance to
the Underworld

Chios

ASIA
MINOR

AEGEAN SEA

Icaria

Delos

CYCLADES

Naxos

MESOGEIOS

CRETE

Heraklion

Karpathos

Kasos

ASSYRIA

Knossos

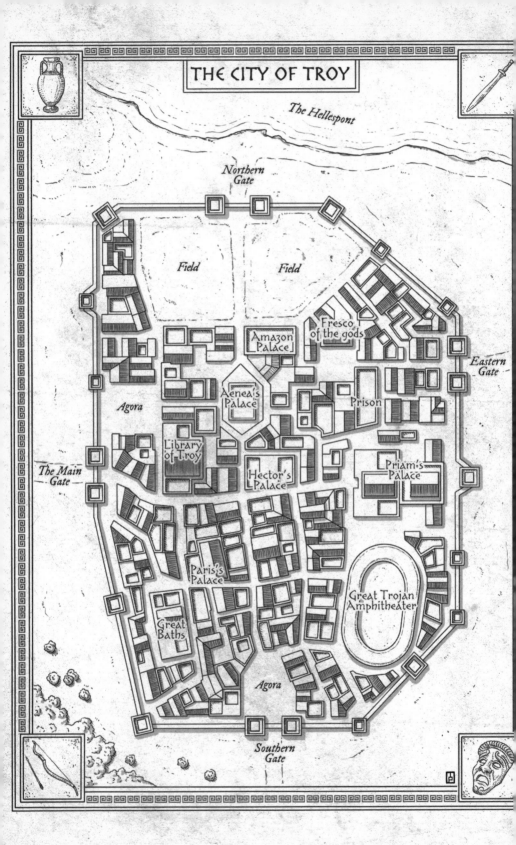

THE CITY OF TROY

The Hellespont

Northern
Gate

Field

Field

Fresco
of the gods

Amazon
Palace

Eastern
Gate

Aenea's
Palace

Prison

Agora

Library
of Troy

Priam's
Palace

Hector's
Palace

The Main
Gate

Paris's
Palace

Great Trojan
Amphitheater

Great
Baths

Agora

Southern
Gate

No man or woman born, coward or brave, can shun his destiny.

—Homer, *The Iliad*

Part One

Sparta

CHAPTER

I

Spartans are made of metal and fire. Their every instinct, every drive is solely focused on war and protecting their kingdom at all costs. They value nothing more than victory.

Where once I aspired to such greatness, now I have tasted its folly, for I have experienced death in ways no other Spartan has.

I try to remind myself of this fact as Paidonomos Leonidas marches up and down the line of Spartiates, my kingdom's most elite warriors. We're being paired up for practice. A frown furrows my brow. I, along with the other women and *Mothakes*—outsiders with no prospects—were forced into our own line. The Spartiates are being handed the prime weapons, while down my own line, our swords and spears are on the verge of crumbling in our palms.

The *paidonomos* stops before me, his face as unreadable as ever. His hands are fisted at his sides, shoulders ever so slightly hunched. "No weapons for you, Diodorus," he says before pointing to a familiar head of curly black hair in the other line. "You've spent too much time behind a shield. It makes for a rusted blade."

Without needing further direction, Lykou and I march to a corner of the arena, taking up our fighting stances. Last summer we sparred in similar positions, twirling spears around raging bonfires and dancing around unsaid feelings.

My friend chuckles. "This feels painfully familiar, doesn't it?"

"Because we're always paired up?" I return his laugh. "I'm sure it will feel *painfully* familiar as I'm swiping your legs from beneath you."

Soon I'm eating my words as, head over heels, I'm flung across the grass.

I soar across the depths of Tartarus once more. The scent of seawater fills my nose, ruby eyes swarming my vision. All my training on how to brace for such a landing flees my mind and I land hard enough to steal the air from my lungs. Aching, I climb to my feet. I don't miss Paidonomos Leonidas shaking his head in disappointment, nor the confused glances of the other Spartans who are sparring around us.

Lykou doesn't give me a chance to catch my breath. He charges me and I have only a moment to dance from his reach. I could have grabbed him by the arm and used his own speed against him. I could have even tripped him. Yet my head is so clouded that all I can think to do is dodge his attacks.

Lykou holds nothing back as he clips me in the jaw. I barely remain on my feet.

Images of Nyx standing above me flicker in and out of my vision. Her claws dig deep into my spine.

I don't duck in time to avoid my friend's next swing. A fist catches my temple.

"I'm going to enjoy ripping you apart." Nyx drags me to my feet and slams her forehead into mine. "And then, when I'm finished, I'm going to find your brothers and do the same to them."

The stadium spins. The memory of Nyx's assault is so fresh the stars still flash behind my eyes. I raise my arms to block Lykou's punches, gritting my teeth. His knuckles dig so deep that my bones sing.

"Enough!"

The *paidonomos*'s barked order is sharp enough to stop all movement across the *gymnasion*. When Leonidas addresses Lykou, the others reluctantly continue their brawls.

"Leave us, son of Xanthippos," he says, nodding to my friend.

Breathing ragged, Lykou takes a step back and bows low for the Spartan general before turning on his heel.

"You know the rules of the arena as much as any, Daphne Diodorus." His voice is stern, but not angry. I cannot meet his too-knowing gaze. He points to the entrance. "The moment you step beneath that archway, you leave your personal feelings behind. You are not to be weighed down by trivial concerns or familial worries when training here. That is the surest way to get injured."

The bruises already forming on my arms affirm as much. "Yes, sir."

Paidonomos Leonidas grabs me by the shoulder, forcing me to turn toward the other sparring matches. Waving an arm to them, he says, "You earned their respect last year when you won the race. You brought our kingdom a year of wonderful harvest and fortuitous alliances."

Gritting my teeth, I nod.

"Now go and choose a weapon." He claps me on the back. "Not a spear. With your head in the clouds, you'll knock out your own teeth before the end of the day. Pick a weapon that will distract us both."

Leaving him, I press through the crowd of sweaty Spartans toward the row of gleaming swords. Shame threatens to overwhelm me as I pass the line of sparring warriors. I should be practicing, fighting among them. I've let Nyx haunt me for long enough.

I don't notice the hand latched around my wrist until my arm is nearly ripped from its socket.

"What happened back there?" Lykou demands, spinning me around.

"Nothing." I yank my hand away and cross my arms.

People watch us from around the stadium. When I glare in their direction, they quickly turn to their weapons and opponents. Their eavesdropping couldn't be more obvious.

My friend's dark eyes narrow. "Don't lie to me, Daphne. I deserve better than that."

He does deserve better than my hedging. His handsome face is pulled into harsh lines. I can almost still see the wolf in his features.

With the gods waiting at all times to drag me again into their games, every moment I spend with Lykou is another chance for them to ensnare him as well.

"Truly," I lie, unflinching as I hold his gaze, "I didn't sleep well last night."

My words sound wooden and forced even to my own ears. Lykou steps close, dropping his voice.

"This has to do with *them*, doesn't it?" His eyes are imploring. "Apollo turned me into a wolf for the entire summer. Artemis turned your brother into a deer. You *died*, Daphne. You actually died to fix their mistakes."

How could I forget? The memory of that death haunts me. The emptiness, the weightlessness of my body as I fell through space and time, even if it was only for the barest of moments, jerks me awake every night.

All for *them*.

The gods are reckless with their power. Last summer, when they commanded me to find answers, I didn't trust them, especially not Apollo, who was sent on the mission alongside me. But something precious was stolen from them, and they needed me to learn where it was hidden.

These stolen items were the Muses. And as the caretakers of the Garden of the Hesperides, the power of Olympus became a wild rampant thing with them missing.

One by one, I brought the Muses back to Olympus, and the power of the gods returned.

But not before I faced down the Muses' kidnappers—the gods Ares, Hermes, and Nyx.

The last claimed my life. I struck her down with one of Artemis's arrows. Yet like me, she eluded true death.

The gods have no idea where she is. Nyx could come after the Muses, or me, at any time.

"It's not that simple," I say to Lykou, raising my chin. "The gods own me."

I swore myself to Zeus as protector of Olympus. When the gods need me, I am at their disposal, and with Nyx still very much alive, that time might come sooner than I like.

Lykou reaches for me again, this time to brush a lock of hair from my face. His voice is soft, coaxing. "The Daphne I knew was beholden to no one, even the people who love her the most."

I cannot take the disappointment clouding his face. "The Daphne you knew died."

There is no lie in my words.

I don't look at Lykou again as I march toward the racks of weapons.

I stumble as I reach the row of blunted swords. Not because of them, but instead because of the goddess of the hunt lurking in the shadows of the *gymnasion's* entrance.

Artemis winks and crooks a finger to me.

The gods are finally calling in my blood debt.

CHAPTER 2

Sunlight spills across the forest floor, alighting our path. Artemis expertly leads me through the trees, her steps as lithe and silent as a panther's. I swallow any friendly conversation I might've made. I don't miss the golden arrow gleaming from the quiver on her back.

"Still bearing a grudge, I see." Artemis pulls aside a branch for me to pass. Her lips curl into a feral grin.

"It's impossible not to when I'm reminded of your Curse every time I bathe." Even now, the Midas Curse pools on my abdomen. The molten gold, a living tattoo, makes my skin itch wherever it travels. The sting of her arrow slicing across that very spot a year before still causes my hands to tremble.

"Are you not grateful? It saved your life." She inclines her head, considering me as she walks. "Many times, in fact."

The Curse was once both a punishment and insurance, retribution for my insolence toward the gods and to assure I succeeded in their mission. It nearly killed me, once.

My hands curl into fists. "I have no need of it anymore."

She releases a small, girlish giggle. "Oh, I'm sure you'll have need of it again soon enough."

I'm prevented from asking what she refers to by the sudden firmness of the ground beneath my feet. My sandals thump across marble as Artemis continues down a long, open hallway, one side looking out to vast mountains with shimmering palaces perched on each peak. We pass a dozen marble columns as we continue down the hallway, between each a glimmering fresco.

"This is your palace," I realize, dragging my fingers across a fresco that details a black horse rearing in Artemis's hidden glen. The next is of a white stag frolicking across a midnight sky. Another is of a bear with a small cub beside a lonely spring. The bear has an arrow through its neck, blood pooling into the water. "Are these your victims?"

Artemis nods. Something akin to remorse flickers in her eyes.

I consider the empty palace, bereft of personal effects. Hermes once said that Artemis prefers the forest to Mount Olympus. I wonder what the other gods' palaces are like. An image of fountains overflowing with wine crosses my mind when I think of Dionysus, and the lavish silks and furs that must adorn every surface of Aphrodite's palace. Weapons, cold and gleaming on a pale marble wall, rise from the depths of my memory, and I keenly remember the way Ares's fist cracked across Ganymede's body. That must have been the god of war's palace. No amount of curiosity could draw me to those dark hallways ever again.

Golden brown hair atop her head in a tight bun, Artemis has dark green *peplos* bound on each shoulder, and across her midriff is a leather cuirass and on each arm are leather greaves.

"Are you preparing for war?" I ask, nodding at the battle attire.

"I'm always prepared for anything, or anyone"—her hand lifts to the silver grip of her bow—"that might want to do my family harm."

I cross the threshold of the airy pantheon and surprise makes me take a step back.

Where once three of the marble thrones were empty, now only two remain vacant. There are no signs of Hermes or Ares, the bloody traitors who cost me my life last year, and now, unlike then, Poseidon sits atop his pillared throne, considering me with hooded eyes and pursed lips.

He is tall and broad like his stormy brother. Dissimilar to the bronze curls of Zeus, Poseidon's hair is flaxen and shaggy, bound to his brow by a band of turquoise stones fashioned like stars. His skin is paler even than Hades, king of the Underworld, with a strange blue tinge.

Swallowing, I allow him nothing more than a cursory glance before raising my chin and marching to the center of the pantheon. Dionysus lifts a *kylix* toward me from his ruby throne, grinning widely. To his left, Demeter and Aphrodite sit in astute silence. Beside them, Athena's face is as unreadable as ever, and opposite are Hades, Hephaestus, and Hera. The latter's bitterness toward me has not lessened, evident in the withering glare she spears me with.

I don't understand why she dislikes me so much. Perhaps she hates all mortals, and I just happen to be in her presence more than others.

My gaze is drawn inexorably to the god of prophecy, Apollo. Something I cannot, will not explain courses through me at the sight of him. It itches like an insatiable hunger and yet holds me back all the same. His bronze hair and tan skin and handsome face are just as I remember—though his hair is a touch longer than last summer, curling gently atop his broad shoulders. My throat is suddenly dry.

Apollo offers me nothing but a small, bland smile. Absolutely meaningless.

Hurt flickers in the back of my mind. Artemis takes her place beside him, hopping nimbly atop her high throne.

I never noticed it before, how their power fills the space and fights for dominance. The smells, the crackling of energy, and the shift in the very elements around me. The roses of Aphrodite fill my nose as Dionysus's wine coats my throat without me even taking a single sip; Demeter's aura of a warm summer sun heats my skin just as the cool sea breeze of Poseidon fights to chill my bones.

The king of the gods' face is unreadable. As stern as ever and a slightly aged version of the son I grew to love last summer, Zeus rests his chin upon a fist, though it is Aphrodite who breaks the silence first.

She waves a hand before her face with a pinched grimace, then says, "Do all mortals smell as bad as her, or just the Spartans?"

A blush rises up my neck. I smell, no doubt, like the sparring ring. Sweat and dirt cling to my arms and cheeks. I can't even look at Apollo.

"Shut up, Aphrodite," Artemis snaps. "Not everyone can magically make themselves smell like roses."

A sharp laugh bursts from Hera. Her ebony hair is plaited over a shoulder with purple ribbons that match the vibrant shade of her silk chiton. "Did she hit a nerve teasing your precious Spartans, *Orthia*?" Her grin is feral. "Or are you likewise insecure about the smell of horseshit that follows you around?"

"Perhaps what you are smelling is hard work," I say, words spilling from my mouth before I can think twice about them. "Something you wouldn't know a thing about."

Lavender light begins to pulse around Hera, her face pinched with fury.

Undaunted, I continue. "Have you brought me here for anything in particular"—I throw Aphrodite my most withering glare—"or just to critique my personal hygiene?"

"Oh, discussing your lack of personal hygiene would take us all day, darling." Aphrodite's smile is saccharine.

"Enough." Poseidon's rough voice startles me. I jump, meeting his piercing, gray eyes. "We haven't got an eternity to listen to this nonsense."

"You're lucky to have any time at all," I snap, once again speaking before I can consider my words. "Any time you have is thanks to me."

Silence stretches across the pantheon. A chill creeps up my spine as my stomach churns. I shift on my feet and silently implore Apollo to meet my gaze but it remains on his hands, which are hooked over his knees.

Coward, I want to call him. His silence is all the proof I need that I made the right choice turning him away.

The quiet is broken by a bark of laughter. Dionysus claps his knees, roaring so hard his wine is flung across the white marble floor. Poseidon glares at me. Apollo's face is suddenly pained, but his father merely chuckles.

Zeus claps Poseidon on the back. "See? I told you that she has her father's tongue."

My mouth snaps shut. "My father?"

He waves aside my question impatiently. "Neither here nor there. Forget I brought it up."

"I'll forget if you tell me who he is."

"Liar," Hera says.

"Rude," I say with mock afront. "I'm the embodiment of honesty."

"As stubborn as her damn father," Hera exclaims, waving a tan hand through the air.

"If you tell me exactly who that is, maybe I can rectify my behavior." I give her a smile as sweet as pomegranate juice.

Dionysus chuckles into his goblet. Hera's power crackles around the pantheon. Like static, it raises my hair, itching my scalp. Sweat rolls down my spine. She could level me with a single thought. They all could.

As coolly as I can manage, I say, "You brought me to Olympus because Nyx is still out there, correct?"

Zeus nods. The hearth in the center of the pantheon crackles and Hestia feeds it another stalk of wheat.

My gaze flicks to Apollo through the smoke swirling atop the hearth. Irritation eats at me; his lips press harder together. He knows just how dangerous Nyx is, and how very much alive she still is. Together, we foiled her efforts to steal the power of Olympus, but we also both failed to kill her.

Hera leans forward, violet-painted nails digging into the arms of her throne. Her lovely face holds nothing but contempt. "Are you afraid? Yes. That is exactly as the bitch would have you. You foiled her plan, and so as punishment, she wants you to fear her for the rest of your life."

I bite my tongue to keep from retorting. When I finally harness my fury, I wave an arm to the assembled gods. "Do you truly think that she won't come for you again?"

"She would be a fool to do such," Athena says, followed by a chorus of agreement from her kin. Her owl, Glaukopis, chirps on her shoulder.

"I think Daphne's fear should serve as an example." Hades gives me a small nod. "After all, she is the only one among us within the last century to personally know Nyx's wrath."

"Which would make any mortal more paranoid," Hera says, confirming my theory that she holds a similar disdain for all mortals. She crosses slim arms over her chest and leans back, sniffing.

"What my uncle says is true." Apollo finally speaks up, straightening under the full might of Olympus's attention. "She knows Nyx's machinations. Daphne is the only among us to have tangled with the goddess of night and survived."

My spine straightens. I want to give him a grateful smile, but he still won't look at me.

Hades interrupts my thoughts by adding, "And all of us know that Nyx is nothing if not relentless in her wrath."

"Be that as it may"—Zeus cuts his son and brother a silencing glance before returning his attention to me—"if Nyx is indeed fool enough to strike Mount Olympus, this time we will not be sitting idly. Your warning is heeded, young Daphne. As my son says, Nyx's wrath is nothing new to us and we are prepared to smite her back to Tartarus."

"Because that worked so well the first time," I mutter.

Dionysus, leaning back with a goblet balanced on his chest, guffaws. "I like this one, Apollo. Why do you not bring her around more often?"

Because I'm the one who refused him, I do not say.

A peal of thunder forces the god of revelry to clamp his lips firmly shut, though his eyes wrinkle at the edges with mirth.

"We have a task for you," Zeus says, voice rumbling around the pantheon.

"Oh?" I ask dryly.

I don't fail to notice the tic forming in his jaw. "There will be an *agon* in Sparta to be among Helen's personal guard."

A frown pinches the space between my brows. "This is the first I've heard of it."

In a society as fiercely competitive as Sparta, *agon*s are as often and expected as the seasons. Though, never one with a prize so significant.

"I may or may not have given the *anassa* an idea while she was daydreaming." Aphrodite waves a hand through the air.

"Why do you care about mortal games?"

"Not out of boredom, I assure you," Zeus says. "We want you to win it."

The pinched line between my brows threatens to become a permanent feature. "Why?"

Zeus ignores my question and points to Hephaestus. "We will outfit you with whatever you need."

"I need nothing from you to win. What I need is to know why." I square my shoulders.

Poseidon rises. "You will hold that insolent tongue and do as you're told or—"

"Or what?" I cut him off. "You'll turn one of my brothers into a fish?"

"Daphne, please." Hades's gaze is pleading. "Be reasonable. Do we ask anything of you without purpose?"

"Why am I not allowed to know what that purpose is?"

"Because I damn ordered your obedience, you foolish mortal," Zeus barks, slamming a fist into the arm of his throne hard enough to make the entire pantheon tremble. Dark storm clouds roll in from behind him, shrouding the entire sky. The gods glance among one another. Wind whips around me, yanking my hair from its braid and threatening to toss me aside.

Hestia looks up from where she sits beside the hearth. She raises both hands, undulating them in a gentle wave motion and stopping them before her chest, palms facing toward her brother. Zeus's face softens and the clouds rapidly recede. Poseidon's fury has not lessened, though. The anger on his face is enough to make me tremble. With a snap of his fingers, he could level all of Sparta.

Apollo rises and my breath catches. He walks slowly toward me—eyes unreadable but never leaving my own—before moving to stand at my back. Surprise flickers in my chest. Despite whatever it is between us, his presence is a comforting warmth. He meets Poseidon's gaze evenly, frown for frown.

"You proved yourself last summer," Zeus says with a sigh, leaning back. "And as such, I would wish for no other to personally protect my daughter."

"Your daughter?" I inhale sharply. "Anassa Helen is *your* daughter?"

I've heard the rumors, just as everyone in Sparta has, but had given them no worth. Stories of Helen's mother, Queen Leda, seduced by a god. Two of Leda's children blessed by Olympus and two the image of a mortal king. How the stories forced the queen into hiding the moment her daughter ascended the throne five years ago.

Hera's expression has darkened considerably. I didn't think it possible for the glower to carve deeper into her face. The glare she gives her husband could melt stone. Even Hades cringes when he glances Hera's way.

Zeus ignores his wife. "We have reason to believe that Helen could be in danger. Menelaus has called all the Achaean kings to Sparta for a conclave. After the *agon*, all the rulers of Greece will descend upon my daughter's palace like locusts. Protect her, and your family will know wealth, power, and prestige beyond your wildest dreams."

His offer means nothing to me, but I cannot deny the need to protect Helen. I chew the inside of my cheek while in my mind a war brews. I press, "Have you heard something that makes you believe that she will be in danger at this conclave?"

Zeus considers me a long moment, but it is Athena who speaks. "We've been unable to enter the Mycenaean palace for a number of years, particularly the bedchambers and council chambers, which leads us to believe there are other Olympian powers at play here. Only recently did we hear whispers of the conclave."

This only fills me with a hundred more questions. "How is that possible? Why would Helen be in any danger from an Olympian?"

"What a fool." Hera's eyes roll up to the clouded sky.

"She is my daughter," Zeus says, as if the answer were obvious. "And *your* queen."

"And you're the one who foiled Nyx." Hera's lips curl back.

"She will want revenge, Daphne," Demeter says, face pained. "Against you and Olympus. We don't know where or whom she will attack first. The Nyx we knew centuries ago was nothing short of vengeful, cutting down anyone she thought stood between her and her vendettas."

"She will rain darkness upon Sparta until nothing remains but bones," Apollo says, voice harsh.

Gaping, I turn to him. My heart pounds in my ears, so loud I do not hear anyone's next words. This time when I look at him, he doesn't tear his gaze away. I cannot read what his eyes say, what his lips will not.

The gods continue conferring around me. I may have defeated Nyx before, but that was due to nothing but sheer luck. I was dying, broken in body and full of a venom with no cure. If it hadn't been for Artemis's silver bow, Nyx would have continued on her path. And if it hadn't been for Apollo's golden bow, my soul would still be in the Underworld. A silver bow to take life, and golden to bestow it. Only once, though.

Now both are as useless against a god as a mortal weapon.

I merely wounded Nyx, and she left to lick her wounds and bide her time. To continue to plot Olympus's downfall, and unleash calamity upon the mortal world.

I have no desire to be another pawn in the gods' games, but I cannot refuse the order to protect Helen. Not when her life could be at risk because of my mistakes. I may be a *Mothakes*, not a true Spartan, but Helen is still my queen.

I take a knee, bowing low to the earth before Zeus. "Your daughter will be safe under my protection. I would lay down my life for the Anassa of Sparta."

Apollo shifts behind me.

"Of that, we have no doubt," Demeter says softly. The stunning goddess of the harvest blesses me with an encouraging smile.

I look to each of the gods, my gaze resting the longest on the empty seats. "And if they come after me? Hermes, Ares, and Nyx? Will you protect me?"

There's no response.

Not waiting any longer for an answer, I stand and raise my chin high. With a curt nod, I spin on my heel.

Lykou asked what the gods still hold over me. I, like Spartans, am made of metal and fire, but even a raging kiln can only take so much before its fire is extinguished. When I turn for one last look at the god of the sea, Poseidon's gaze meets mine.

I still answer to the gods because not even Sparta could withstand the wrath of Olympus.

CHAPTER 3

Excited chatter greets me when I walk into the Diodorus household. The day has passed, and Nyx's night has risen, making me shiver as I cross beneath the painted doorway.

My adoptive parents exclaim when they see me, waving around chalices overflowing with wine.

"Where have you been?" my mother, Révna, demands, rushing past the roaring hearth to fold me into her arms.

"Leave the poor girl alone. She must have been preparing." Ephor Apidanos Diodorus is suddenly behind her. As one of Sparta's longest-reigning magistrates, my father has perfected the art of masking his expression. I've never been able to read his face.

My mother's arms are thin and comforting. I lean into her embrace just a little bit more than I normally would. The goddess of luck must have been shrouding all of our shoulders when Ligeia brought my brothers and me to Sparta. Had we ended up at any other household, our lives would be so different.

"Preparing for what?" I ask.

Révna's arms drop as a collection of surprised and confused faces turn to me from over the flames of the hearth. Alkaios has come for dinner, as he does most nights, with his wife and twin sons. Ligeia's carrying a tray of fruit and cheeses. My handmaid lowers the tray, letting me pluck a handful of feta. Pyrrhus stands behind her, mid-reach for the grapes, with a bewildered expression.

"You didn't hear?" he asks. He's grinning now, a contagious smile I want to return with every fiber of my being, but he could only be referring to one thing.

"Obviously not." I cross my arms.

Pyrrhus can barely contain himself. "There will be an *agon*. Tomorrow."

"Another? I feel like there's a new one every other day." I reach for another piece of cheese to avoid my brothers' gazes. They can always tell when I'm lying.

Pyrrhus's chest puffs out. "To be among Helen's personal guard. They announced it just after you left the arena this morning."

"You left?" Alkaios's eyes see too much. "We usually have to drag you away."

Since my dance with death, I've been preparing for my next tangle with the goddess of night.

"Do you realize what this means, Daphne?" Pyrrhus asks, grinning.

I shake my head. "Another excuse for Spartan men to postulate like a bunch of peacocks?"

He shakes me hard enough to rattle my teeth. "This is my chance at redemption."

"Wha-what?" I blink.

"This is how I get my honor back," he says, dropping his voice low with a furtive glance around us. "No one will care that I am the Deserter of *Carneia* if I win this title."

Joy blooms inside me, warm and fierce. This is exactly what Pyrrhus needs to remove the dark mantle shrouding his future. His reputation has decidedly soured since that fated festival last year. Despite me salvaging our family's honor, many still resent him for failing to show up to the race. Some whisper that he did it on purpose and that he sought to bring ill-fortune to the armies.

"Only one can win, though." Ligeia's good eye is on my face, missing nothing, her other clouded and gazing far away.

That joy sputters as quickly as it rose. The gods want me to win the *agon* as well, which would mean not only stealing that victory from Pyrrhus, but also his chance at redemption.

"Will you enter the competition, too?" he asks.

I blink. In another lifetime, I would never steal this from my brother. I wouldn't even think of it. But the gods commanded me, and the fate of Queen Helen—and all of Sparta—could be at risk. All our fates decided by this single *agon*.

"And let you sweep the floor with me in front of all of Sparta? Never." I squeeze his arm and force a smile. "Tyche favors you."

His eyes shutter, darkening. "I don't need the gods to help me win."

Pyrrhus turns, prattling with Alkaios about what he can expect tomorrow, how he's been practicing every night for a chance like this.

It truly is the opportunity he's been training endlessly for. He's carved himself into one of the greatest soldiers Sparta will ever see— if the kingdom will ever forgive him enough to recognize that.

Not only will I have to try to steal this victory from him, despite everything he's done to earn it, I might not even be successful. He might wallop me into the earth and spit in my face for even trying.

My stomach churns. I couldn't eat, even if I wanted to.

But I know I should force myself to despite the queasiness rising in my belly. My hand passes over the feta and instead reaches for the plain bread. Ligeia's brows rise. Damn Olympus, she really misses nothing.

With no desire to field her questions, I leave my family to their excitement. I don't choose to sleep in the garden, night after night, simply because my body rejects the comforts of my bed. Rather, my body craves the god who once laid on the earth beside me.

The specter of Apollo's warmth harangues me, dragging my thoughts back to him and his secrets, Zeus and his power, and finally Nyx and her wrath. Fear curls in my belly, threatening to make me sick.

I fight sleep for as long as I can, going over *dory* swings and battle formations. I can fight it for only so long. Nyx's claws pull me into the deep throes of nightmares as surely as the beast Cetus pulls great ships into the dark depths of the sea.

The giant stone stands of the *gymnasion* arc into the sky around me, filled to bursting with Spartans. They thump their feet and pound their chests, screaming and yelling until their throats must burn, all to support their friends and kin.

Dawn has barely spilled across the sky, and already hopeful competitors crowd the pitch of grass and sand. All of them I recognize from my training and, I'm glad to see, quite a few women are among them. From raised seats in the center of the stands, the entire royal family has come to watch.

Helen, beautiful as ever, wears a long red chiton, and gold silk is braided into her chestnut hair. Beside her, Menelaus glares down at the competitors, wearing Mycenaean gray. To Helen's left are her twin brothers, Pollux and Castor. I wonder if Castor can recognize me from where he sits as the *Mothakes* who stole his victory last *Carneia*.

The crowd sure does.

"*Mothakes, Mothakes, Mothakes!*" they cheer, thumping their seats in rhythm as I stride across the grass toward the growing crowd.

Catching the stag, though with Artemis's divine intervention, seems to have won me a lot of favor.

I move to Pyrrhus's side, cheeks burning. I don't think he's noticed me yet, his focus on the other men walking toward the line of competitors, some looking like they would rather disappear under a rock, and others preening more than peacocks. He shifts on his feet, gaze sweeping in my direction. My breath catches and he stiffens.

A maelstrom of emotions flash across his face. A hollow ringing fills my ears as a tic forms in his jaw. I offer him a close-lipped smile, everything screaming in me to run for the stands. If he wins this competition, maybe we could work together to protect Helen during the conclave.

His face shifts, a reflection of a deer in his eyes.

No, I will not draw him further into the games of the gods.

A trumpeting of horns precedes the herald striding across the grass. We turn along with the other competitors to face him.

"Sister," Pyrrhus says from the corner of his mouth. "Why are you here?"

To protect Helen at the behest of the gods you despise.

"To make you look better when I inevitably lose," I lie between my teeth.

I've been doing a lot of lying to the people I love most, lately.

"How uncharacteristically pessimistic of you." He looks over me, frowning. "You said you wouldn't enter in the *agon*."

I cannot meet his gaze. Instead, I look to the crowd, waving my arms and grinning. The crowd roars anew, many standing and cheering.

"Looks like they already have a favorite," Lykou says, striding up to us.

He offers me a warm smile, our spat yesterday forgiven but not forgotten. He told me that he, too, still feels the horrors of last summer inflicted upon him. That he can still taste the blood of Minos's soldiers.

I take his hand, giving it a firm squeeze. "Here to beat Pyr and me senseless?"

"You, perhaps." He laughs. "But I've seen how hard your brother has been training these last few months." He nods to Pyrrhus. "We might come to regret this in the morning."

I already do.

The *kerykes* climbs atop the wooden dais, the red cloak stretching behind him. The herald's skin is weathered and scarred from years of service to Sparta. I and about fifty other competitors await instruction. We don't have to wait long before his words echo throughout the enormous stadium. His booming voice is the reason he was chosen to be the *kerykes*.

"Spartans," he roars and receives a cheer from the stands in response. "Are you ready to test your mettle? To put your strength and courage to the test? Only the greatest among you is worthy to protect our *anassa*."

Another roar soars through the audience, so loud they must hear it all the way in Crete. Spartans are a people born and bred for battle, and they live for very few things more than an *agon*.

"First we will test your precision," he goes on, "and only twenty of you will move on."

A frown creases between my brows as I consider what the test will be. Likely something to challenge our skills with a spear or bows.

"Next, we will test your strength. Only ten of you will advance."

I purse my lips. So, something that will pair us off. A duel of sorts.

I'm somewhat rusty as of late with a knife, finding myself unable to pick them up after that fateful night with Minos and the sons of Ares.

A shiver wracks my spine as an image of their faces flashes before my eyes. Of their claws reaching for me and of Theseus's death. We'd been so close to succeeding, only to have my friend's life stolen at the brink of victory.

Lykou squeezes my hand hard enough to drag me back to the present.

"And last, we will test your courage."

The cheers around the stadium must be heard all the way up in Olympus now, Spartans roaring for all to hear just how courageous our people are.

The *kerykes* waves an arm to the end of the stadium. Behind the herald, Spartiates raise ten golden hoops into the air at varying heights. Some are larger than a horse, while others are no wider than my fist.

Next, servants come forward bearing stands of spears. We accept the weapons and march in perfect unison toward the red line painted across the grass, standing in a single-file line with Pyrrhus before me and Lykou after.

We need no instruction. The first, unlucky competitor strides forward. He stands thirty yards from the first hoop and, without taking aim, throws. To the surprise of no one, it goes wide. Growling, he marches to the next, and then the next, before missing all of the hoops. I cluck my tongue. What a fool.

The other competitors fare much better. We're raised with the *dory*, the weapon of choice for many Spartans. The spear's reach is longer than the sword, the wood heavy and thick enough to shatter most metal. For many soldiers, the *dory* is a mere extension of their arm.

When it's Pyrrhus's turn, he proves as much. His aim is true and finds the center of every single hoop. The applause he receives is still begrudging. He'll have to do more to earn Sparta's respect—and forgiveness.

I'm next. I walk stiffly to the line and heft my spear. The wood is lighter than the ones used for duels and the bronze butt is removed. I balance it in my hand and stop at the marker for the first hoop. It's the widest of the bunch but also the farthest. They would never make this too easy. I reach the spear back as far as I'm able. The muscles in my arm are clenched and my other hand points toward my target.

The cheers are nearly deafening, almost impossible to ignore. I take a deep breath, focusing on the dark center of the golden hoop. The breeze makes it sway.

On my exhale, I let the spear soar. It flies across the space and through the hoop, tip planting firmly in the grass beyond. The next eight hoops are much of the same, each finding their target with easy precision. The sun has risen just beyond the field, making it harder and harder to aim.

With my tenth *dory*, I reach back, left hand pointing to the center of the smallest hoop a nearly impossible distance of forty yards away.

The last time I fought with a *dory*, it found its target in Nyx's heart.

Her shadows reached for me, blurring the edges of my vision. They coiled through the air, my spear flying straight through them.

The white dory, *Praxidikai, as Apollo named it, pierces her chest. Victory surges through me in a great rush. The ringing in my ears is snuffed as a smile curls her lips. Nyx rips the spear from her body without so much as a grimace and, as easily as if a mere splinter, snaps it in two.*

A shudder quakes my shoulders just as I throw.

The spear glances off the edge of the hoop.

A groan echoes around the stadium. Cursing under my breath, I return to my place among the other competitors. Luckily, only Pyrrhus has a perfect score so far, but ten others have similar scores to mine, and there are still five more to go. At least I have the goddess Tyche's favor right now.

I advance to the next round by the barest of margins. I imagine the gods watching from atop Olympus and cursing my foolishness. I will have to forget Nyx and the horrors she inflicted if I'm to succeed. The memories will only get in the way. I shake my head, thoughts of Apollo and his family eddying around.

Ten circles are drawn in white chalk around the arena. The *kerykes* commands us to stand in a line. Hands behind our backs and shoulders straight, none of us react as he marches up and down, examining the competitors. I bite the inside of my cheek but command my face to show no expression, praying to Olympus that I'm not paired off against Pyrrhus.

The herald stops at my feet, looking me up and down with a disdainful expression. No doubt he resents that a *Mothakes* is allowed to compete, despite the love the public has shown me after last summer.

His pale eyes flick to my brother and his lips curl upward. Sweat drips down my spine. His eyes turn to my right, and he grins even wider. He dances for a moment, surprisingly light-footed despite his immense size.

"You two." He points to someone down the line from me. "The far corner."

He's paired me off with the largest man in all of Sparta. Leandros stands a good two heads higher than me, his shoulders twice as wide. The muscles in his arms and legs are likely strong enough to crack my skull wide open. I've seen him knock a man unconscious with a single punch.

With a smile so sweet it could choke, I turn back to the *kerykes*. His grin vanishes. The fool has no idea I've taken down creatures twice Leandros's size and walked away.

Without looking back, I march to the waiting duel circle. Leandros follows, footsteps so heavy I swear the ground shakes. The air is ripe with heady anticipation as we face each other from either side of the circle. The big oaf doesn't bother to move into position. He stands, rigid and wide, staring me down through his long, oily black hair.

The Minotaur lurks in the shadows of my mind, a great dark beast made of shadows. His rancid breath makes my stomach churn.

"He's dead," I whisper to myself, shaking my head. "I killed him last summer."

The reminder fills me with at least a semblance of calm. With a swift breath, I bend my knees and raise my fists, turning sideways so that Leandros can see as little of me as possible.

"First blood spilled decides the winners. No cheats," the herald calls. "No dirty tricks. Win with strength and dignity, Spartans."

A warm breeze stirs the air, scented with lavender, cedarwood, and the sea. The gods watch.

A *salphinx* echoes across the arena. The horn's call hasn't even ended before I leap across the space.

Leandros charges me. I duck to avoid his swing and his fist sings through the air above my head. I'm sliding across the sand right between his legs.

It would be a cowardly move to kick him in the most sensitive place, but I'm half tempted.

He spins around, faster than should be possible for a man his size. I duck again beneath his punch and ram my fist into the tender skin of his armpit. Leandros howls, turning. I stumble backward to avoid his kick. Rolling across the sand, I pounce to my feet.

He's considering me now. I hop from foot to foot, never stopping as I do the same for him. The sun beats down on us, crisping my already tan shoulders. I could play dirty and throw sand in his face, but I have something better in mind.

I sprint toward him again. When he swings for me this time, I grab his arm as it soars past. It flings me to the other side of the circle. He turns, squinting in the light of the glaring sun. When he swings toward me again, he completely misses. I'm already around him. He turns, but the sand catches his feet and he falls to his knees. My own knee cracks his nose, spraying his blood across the sand.

Raucous screams echo throughout the arena. Grinning widely, I hold my arms aloft. Their rumble grows ever louder.

"Mothakes! Mothakes! Mothakes!"

For the first time in my life, I'm not ashamed of the title. For the first time in my life, it fills me with pride.

CHAPTER

4

The final challenge will be held first thing tomorrow morning. The remaining competitors, Lykou and Pyrrhus included, are sent home to rest and prepare.

My brother does neither.

He paces across the jade-tiled floor of our father's courtyard. The hearth in its center spits with low flames, and it bathes Pyrrhus's tan skin in amber light.

"Sit, Pyr," Alkaios says from where he reclines on a cushioned *kline*. He pats the seat next to him. "You earned the best marks of the whole lot of them. You've earned yourself a moment of respite."

"Besides"—I pour my brother a glass of wine to distract myself—"fretting about tomorrow won't make Eos awaken any faster."

I should learn to heed my own words. I have half a mind to join my brother in his pacing.

Our parents and Ligeia have long gone to bed, and Alkaios joined us as he does most nights.

The rift that was present between Alkaios and me ever since my birth has finally started to close. When I returned to Sparta last summer, I told him everything that had happened. Of my journey across Olympus. The things I had to do, the people I killed in order to bring Pyrrhus home and rescue the Muses. Everything but the final life I took: my own.

Since then, he's looked at me anew. Like he's actually proud of me. I can't help but worry, though, that it isn't with the love for a sister, but rather with the respect of a fellow soldier.

"What I don't understand," Pyrrhus says, voice so loud it makes me jump, "is why my sister had the gall to even compete when she knew what was at stake for me."

"Pyr, I..." I struggle to think of any excuse. I should have prepared one. "I didn't think I would stand a chance. I just can't resist a competition."

"Are you truly that selfish?" Pyrrhus shoves himself straight. "Or just a fool? Of course you can win. You've fought gods and monsters, Daphne."

Pushing away from the hearth, he storms into the night. Over his shoulder he calls, "Good night, Alkaios. I expect you to be there when they crown me in the morning."

My older brother and I sit in silence for a long time after he leaves. I'm pulled from my tumultuous thoughts by his gentle voice.

"If you win tomorrow," Alkaios says, "it will destroy him."

"I know." My voice is barely even a whisper. Guilt tears holes through my gut.

"They commanded you to enter, didn't they?" He jabs a finger at me. "Why would the gods want you to compete?"

I raise a nonchalant shoulder. "Perhaps they are bored and in need of some entertainment?"

"You won't tell me because you don't know," he says, and then cuts me off when I open my mouth to protest. "Not truly."

My jaw snaps shut. I press my lips together.

"Wherever the gods meddle, chaos is sure to follow," he says, softly this time. He turns, planting his hands on either side of the hearth, leaning so close to the fire the heat must be unbearable. "The old Daphne would cut her nose to spite her face if someone tried to control her."

Perhaps I obey because my queen is worth more to me than my pride, or maybe I'm just tired of fighting.

Death may have taken the battle from me.

I can't meet his gaze. "I'm tired, Alkaios. I should rest before tomorrow's challenge."

My brother, with cold, cold eyes, says, "No amount of sleep will help you feel better about yourself. Betraying your brother, stealing his chance of redemption, just to impress the gods."

I stand. "I seek to impress no one but myself."

"Another lie." He shakes his head slowly. "I was a fool to ever feel proud of you. You saved Pyrrhus not out of brotherly love, but to make a name for yourself."

Cold as death, I meet his gaze.

"You are nothing more than a *Mothakes*." Lips curled back, he continues, "And no one will remember Daphne, the *Mothakes* of Sparta."

I stumble from the courtyard toward my garden, the exhaustion like a hazy fog, and stride face-first into the god whose arms I crave the most.

"Apollo." I step back and cross my arms, fighting to keep the pertinent scrunch of my nose from appearing childlike. "Did Zeus send you here to chastise me for my near failure today?"

"Poseidon did mention that you were a poor choice to protect Helen," he says. Moonlight frames his face, making it impossible to read.

I fiddle with the sleeve of my chiton. I can never keep still around him. "Did you happen to tell him where to shove that opinion?"

"No." His mouth quirks to the side, as if holding a grin at bay. "But I should have."

He extends his hands and two glittering, golden vambraces appear in his palms.

I rock back on my heels. "What are those?"

"Armor made by Hephaestus. They will make you faster."

"I'm already fast."

"Stronger."

"I don't need them." I press my lips in a line. "I don't need your help."

The vambraces disappear in a blink. He sighs, scuffing a toe in the dirt. "Stubborn to a fault. You haven't changed at all."

Maybe I have changed. You just wouldn't know because you haven't seen me in a year, I don't say aloud. Instead, "Maybe you just bring out the poor attitude in me."

"There are many things I bring out in you, I'm sure." A low chuckle. His gaze dips to my mouth. My lips part in response.

To change tactics, and the direction of my own thoughts, I ask, "Why do you still cower before your father? Was rescuing the Muses not enough to get you in Olympus's good graces again?"

"It will take much more than that to atone for my sins," Apollo says, voice gravelly.

"And what sins are those?"

"If I told you, we would be sitting here listening to me talk for a century, at least." His gaze is still trained on my lips.

An overwhelming urge sweeps over me to pull him close and brush my lips against his neck. *Help me forget your sins*, I would say. *For what I want to do is perhaps among them.*

"I'm sure your father has even more sins to atone for than you." I cross my arms, more to keep them from reaching toward him than anything else.

He misses nothing. "After all that we did, all that we've shared. You still hold yourself back."

Why do you not give in to the fire between us? he does not ask.

Because I don't want to get burned would be the simple answer.

"You're the one who stayed away," I snap.

His hands shake at his sides, and they bunch into fists. Voice hoarse, he says, "I was respecting your wishes. Because you told me you didn't love me, Daphne."

I say, "Yes, because I'm nothing more than a pawn to your family. Because, as you've said, we have shared so much and yet you still keep secrets from me. Because, despite me dying to save you and your family, Zeus couldn't even give me the name of my father." My voice has risen to the point of yelling, sharp and abrasive to my own ears.

Apollo opens his mouth to protest but I cut him off with a harsh sound and continue.

"Because I don't think that what I feel for you can overcome all the hurt your family has caused mine. Your sister turned my brother into a deer, and that animal madness still lurks inside him. One of you killed my mother." I stride forward, my arms aching to hook around his neck. Instead, I stab a finger into his warm, broad chest. "All the ruin your family has wrought over the centuries, and even now they use me in their games. After all I did for them. For you."

Before I can blink, Apollo swings an arm around my waist. A gasp steals past my lips. He pulls me close, hips to hips, chest to chest, so close each breath molds our bodies tighter together. The early summer heat has slicked my skin with sweat, my legs clinging to the powerful warmth of his thighs.

"I could never forget holding your lifeless body in my arms," Apollo says, voice soft and bitter. He gazes at me, his face a mixture of anger and frustration. "The way my heart shattered as you hit the ground."

I swallow, throat dry. "That pain is not enough."

Something shutters in his gaze and, a grim expression slamming down on his features, he asks, "Then what is?"

I trace his face with my eyes, not trusting my hands. They clutch between our chests, his hard warmth digging my wrists between my breasts. His features are so familiar to me and yet foreign. Those sharp lines of his face, his clean-shaven tan jaw, and his depthless cerulean eyes. My lips are drawn to his like a moth to a flame. I angle my chin high, ignoring the rough cut of Apollo's lips and the way my body aches at the memory of them pressed against my own.

"Honesty," I say softly, dragging my gaze from his lips to his eyes.

His mouth presses together in a firm line, as though he can physically keep his secrets from being revealed to me.

"That's what I thought." Jerking from his grip, I stumble away. "Is this actually why you've kept your distance all this time? Because you can't be honest with me? I don't understand what you could have done that was so terrible you'd keep it from me. I know about your dead lover Koronis and I know your stories as you've told them. What else could your family have done? What could my father have done? Why keep it and his name from me after all that I have sacrificed?"

Apollo's arms slowly lower. He takes a step to me, but stops when I back toward the house. He laughs, the sound soft and bitter.

"We have maintained our seats atop Olympus for a very long time, Daphne." He releases a shuddering breath and shakes his head. "We achieved our power through bloody plots, and we sustain that through even darker means."

He jabs a finger at the Midas Curse now coiling around my upper arms. "If I tell you, if Artemis hears me tell you any of my father's darkest secrets, not even I can protect you."

"Is this why you won't tell me?" I rip at the Curse. My skin tears, nails digging deep, but the gold remains, immobile and unharmed. "Then remove it. Have Artemis take it back. I don't need its protection anymore."

"I can't." His shoulders slump. "She can't. Zeus ordered her to keep it there. For your protection."

"Tell him to take it and shove it up his ass." A strangled noise claws from my throat. "And, again, I don't need your protection. I don't need any of you."

Apollo's face is twisted with pain. "I can leave, too. If that's what you want."

His voice is almost hopeful, but does he want me to ask him to stay or leave?

"If you won't be honest with me, then yes. I want you to leave." I arch a brow. "You didn't have a problem staying away before." For nearly a year. "It shouldn't be a problem now."

"I stayed away because you told me to." His words are guttural and low.

"I didn't want to be your lover." My fingers curl into tight fists, nails digging into my palms. "I never said I didn't want to be your friend. And friends are honest with each other."

The friend I made across Greece, who held me on cold nights when the fire couldn't. Who healed and laughed with me.

"You cannot have it both ways." Apollo's voice rises, loud enough to echo into the night. "We were never friends."

"So I was nothing more than a weapon." I nod, scuffing the dirt with my foot.

When he doesn't immediately deny it, I continue, throat burning, "I will win this *agon*. I will become Anassa Helen's bodyguard. I will do it without your help and I will do it to prove that I am more than some blunt blade for Zeus to use to beat back his enemies."

I turn my back on him fully now and step into my bedroom. Tomorrow, I will win the competition to protect my queen. The gods may treat me like their weapon, but I will prove to the world that I am so much more.

The brazier in my room is full of cerulean ashes when I wake. I frown and drag a finger through the incense's remnants. I've never seen blue ashes like this before.

Ligeia isn't home to ask about them when I drag myself from my bed. Dread, like a sickness, creeps over me. I'm slow going, methodical even, as I pull my hair into a taut braid and tighten the knots of my woolen chiton. The vambraces are atop the foot of my bed.

They definitely weren't there when I fell asleep, meaning Apollo returned sometime in the night. I throw a blanket over the glittering armor and leave.

The sky is tinted lavender when I finally march to the stadium. It is unusually quiet when I arrive, and the air is rich with heady anticipation. This is the most exciting competition Spartans have seen for a hundred years, and the people wait with bated breath to see who will be the victor.

Before I can walk beneath the curved entrance, a pair of soldiers stop and guide me to an outer portico. I'm the last of the ten remaining competitors to arrive. The others are being stripped down and their naked bodies painted red and gold. Pyrrhus offers me nothing more than a curt nod as his arms are lifted and his chest painted with a giant, golden *lambda*. Silently, I will the Midas Curse to hide before my own clothes are taken away. With my back to the wall, it slinks to the bottom of my foot.

The chill morning air raises goose bumps on my arms and legs. Servants brush red and gold swirls across my clavicle, abdomen, and back. I do not blush as my naked body is bared for all to see. We all regularly train naked, and there is nothing here that any of these people haven't seen before.

When Lykou marches forward, though, heat still rises in my cheeks at the sight of his red-glazed chest. He truly is the most handsome man in all of Sparta.

"What do you think waits for us in there?" He looks me over, a small smile pulling at his lips. His dark hair threatens to fall in front of his eyes. I can see the hint of scars around his neck, puncture wounds no bigger than my thumb. He doesn't have to tell me what they're from. The memory of the Sphinx digging her claws into his neck will be with me for the rest of my life.

"Something to test our courage, apparently," I say.

Whatever courage I have left. Bitterness coats the back of my throat. Lykou's dark hair is wet, perhaps from an early morning swim, and I itch to tuck it behind his ears. But I don't. I won't hurt him again.

He reaches out instead, brushing callused fingers across my own scars. "Will we ever return to normal?"

Despite the dozen or so people milling about around us, and the indecency it threatens, I pull Lykou in for a hug. His body is warm, firm, and familiar against mine. I whisper into his dark curls, "We will."

He plants a small kiss at the base of my neck before releasing me. The soldiers march in again and hand the other competitors a strip of cloth with instructions to cover our eyes. A helmeted soldier shoves a length of the dark blue-and-silver cloth into my own hand; I wordlessly wrap it over my eyes. Properly blinded, we're all marched from the tent. I know when we cross into the stadium by the sudden eruption of screams around us.

The scent of vanilla and saffron tells me the soldier still guides me. His firm hands grip me by the shoulders, jerking me around and then holding me in place. We must be in a line, a starting point to something. The cheers suddenly dim.

"Welcome, Spartans, to the beginning of the end," the *kerykes*'s booming voice calls out.

The blinds are suddenly ripped from our heads. With mine, a couple strands of my hair come out and I wince. We're indeed at a starting line, and before us stretches an obstacle course. Toppled columns and sand extend across the once-pristine stadium. At the far end, a single golden hoop is raised high into the sky.

Fully armed soldiers wait amid rows of spears. The points of arrows glint from the corners of my eyes and I have no doubt that their instructions are to properly wound. These are no blunted weapons.

Queen Helen stands and raises her arms. "My Spartans. Bring me that prize."

A *salphinx* sounds and I leap forward.

CHAPTER
5

My bare feet thunder across the sand. I pay no heed to the other runners, my attention focused solely on the challenges before me.

Whistling arrows miss me by a hair's breadth. I twist out of the way of a spear, spiraling through the air to avoid its pain-lanced touch.

Landing in the grass, I'm sprinting before another volley of arrows can find their mark, knocking my nearest assailant from his feet and stealing his sword in a single movement. Another sword arcs through the air in an attempt to catch my midriff. I slide across the ground, the blade hissing above my face.

I'm racing across the earth, the golden hoop now only fifty yards from my reach. On either side of me, competitors dodge traps. The crowd thunders all around us, filling the stands with their raucous cheers and stomping feet.

Grass gives way to treacherous sand, slowing my footsteps. It's an extra effort to not fall as the sand clutches at my feet. Another assailant swings a *dory* in my path, and the sand stunts my jump, the iron tip catching my wrist hard enough to make me yelp.

Nyx sneers and stomps on my arm. A short screech escapes me, my wrist threatening to snap between her heel and the cold stone floor.

The memory of Nyx's assault is so fresh, so tangible, I nearly scream again. I can feel her heel digging into my wrist as I race across the sand. So helpless then, but not helpless now.

I lithely dodge the next attack, leaping aside as a soldier jabs the *dory* through the air. I catch the weapon mid-swing, using the man's weight against himself as I tug it from his grasp. I sweep the man from his feet before he can blink, and then I'm on the move again. My legs burn as I bound over the sand.

Nyx grabs me by the frayed remains of my chiton. She drags me to my feet and slams her forehead into mine. Stars flash behind my eyes before she flings me across the room again.

Only thirty more yards to go, I stumble as I reach the last of the sandy expanse, nearly tumbling into the grass at its edge. The memories are so vivid. I can almost feel Nyx's forehead cracking against my own again, can almost see the stars that flashed before my eyes.

Another assailant steps forward, bow at the ready. I dodge the arrows he shoots my way, diving behind broken pillars and boulders, using any defense possible. His onslaught slows me, the stream of arrows relentless. I don't dodge one quickly enough, the arrow grazing my other wrist as I dive behind another pillar.

Another bolt of lightning streaks across the sky. I catch sight of Lykou, in the body of a wolf, leaping for the neck of the centaur. White teeth flash with dark-red blood before my bag weighs me down. I'm pulled into the deep water of the swamp. Even beneath the murky water, the screams and shouts, the rumble of angry thunder, and Apollo shouting my name echo dimly in my ears.

I'm fighting for breath, drowning as surely as I did that summer in Foloi Forest. I'm panting, my skin drenched in sweat—or is that swamp water? I can't distinguish memory from present, gasps wracking my frame. Lykou barrels past my hiding spot behind the pillar.

If he wins, the gods will have no qualms controlling him to meet their agenda. With a growl, I throw myself to my feet, surging after him. We dodge the arrows as one.

I slide between the bowman's feet, letting Lykou catch the brunt of his aim. There is one more racer, just ahead, dodging attacks smoothly. Pyrrhus leaps for a rope dangling from the ceiling, swinging across the tops of spears. I don't have time to marvel at how effortlessly he moves as I jump for my own rope.

I swing across the spears. The weightlessness makes me gasp, and I nearly lose my grip.

My panic doesn't have even a moment to register before the centaur yanks me by my hair. A strangled scream escapes me. I'm dangling in the air.

I let go of the rope. My body soars through the air and lands just on the edge of the rocks. I spy Pyrrhus's red hair five yards before me. Arrows bounce around us and one hisses past my thigh, slicing my skin.

Nyx towers above me. Her smirking face fades in and out of my blurred vision.

This is no mere memory. She's here. In this arena.

My body trembles so hard my teeth rattle. I can almost feel her claws, shredding my skin and bones.

I see you, Daphne.

"You failed to kill me once," I whisper. My chest rises and falls with rapid breaths, and yet I can't seem to fill them with enough air. A choked scream lodges in my throat. "You will fail again."

I search the arena. Her ruby eyes elude me.

But I can feel them. Watching and waiting for me to stumble.

I won't give her the satisfaction. Shaking my head, I hurtle around the obstacles. A volley of arrows rains down around me.

I wasted too much time. Pyrrhus is too far ahead. I should have accepted Apollo's damn vambraces. Any extra speed and strength are necessary now.

Growling, I tumble into the field of spears. I dodge their lances. Some are embedded with thorns and jagged edges. My arm brushes one and my skin tears. A yelp escapes me. I'm jumping back and forth, following the blur of Pyrrhus just ahead. My legs and lungs burning, I shoot forward as if launched from a bow.

I'm coming for you.

"I hope you do," I hiss under my breath. "So I can really kill you, Nyx."

Her cackle, like the crackling of a fire, must echo around the arena.

I force myself to run faster. All my strength focuses on my thundering legs.

Pyrrhus is mere yards from the hoop.

It is too high for even my strongest jump to reach. Angling my body, I veer toward a fallen column. I leap, landing on the column. Sprinting up its marble length at an impossible speed, I let my body soar.

Just as Pyrrhus's fingers graze the hoop's rim, my entire body crashes into it. Wrapping my arms around the cold metal, my body plummets to the ground. I hit the earth hard enough to knock the air from my lungs.

Stars litter my vision and the ocean's roar fills my ears.

Lykou skids to a halt beside me. He says something, but his voice is too far away.

On unsteady legs, I stagger to my feet. My mouth hangs open, eyes wide as I watch the audience surge from the stands toward me like an enormous wave. The roaring isn't in my ears. It's them.

They scream my name, leaping from the stands. I spy my parents, faces glowing with pride. Lykou, grinning widely, takes my hand and raises it to the sky. I raise the other, lifting the hoop toward the heavens. The crowd parts before Helen, who strides forward, holding a cloak the color of blood.

She drapes it around my shoulders and whispers in my ear, "I'm looking forward to seeing you in the palace, Daphne."

She disappears into the crowd with Menelaus; the people of Sparta surge forward. They clap me on the back, shake my hand, and hug me tight. Lykou's hand has dropped to my naked hip, and I let it sit there, the joy overwhelming me. Until I see Alkaios's face in the crowd.

His narrow face is pulled into a stern frown with not even a trace of pride. He's not looking at me. I follow his gaze until my eyes catch the glare of another.

Pyrrhus stands above the crowd. His entire chest heaves, tan face dark with fury.

In his expression, there is no happiness for my victory. Only anger that I've stolen his.

CHAPTER
6

Celebrations go late into the night. Ephor Apidanos Diodorus invites the entire city to our home to celebrate my victory. Our courtyard is so crowded, I cannot even see the jade tiles of the floor. The hearth in the center roars happily, sparks filling the sky, and the ever-flowing wine is bountiful. Despite the happiness in the air and wide smiles of my parents, a palpable chill has settled in the air.

Ligeia mingles among the crowd, pouring wine while her face is plastered with a fake smile. Pyrrhus stews by the hearth with Alkaios lingering beside him. I cannot hear what my brothers say to each other; the darkening of Pyr's expression is all I need to know that it isn't something that I'd like. Lykou leans against a wall, face tipped toward the sky.

I walk up to him and offer a tentative smile. "You put up a valiant challenge, my wolf."

"I'm not the one who you should be trying to appease, Daphne."

He continues staring at the sky, eyes black in the dim light. "I only entered the race to impress you."

I swallow. There is no heat in me to match that in his voice. Not anymore. I want to tell him that his affections are misplaced, but can't find the words. Lykou shoves away from the wall and strides across the room. I reach for him.

"To the House of Diodorus," Apidanos says, saving me from hurting Lykou, and raises his cup high. My adoptive father is a tall, lanky man with dark hair and deep frown lines, but the smile he has tonight is the brightest I've ever seen. "Our honor as sharp as a *xiphos*'s blade, thanks to our daughter, Daphne."

My cheeks burning, I raise my own cup to match his. "What strength I have is due to you, dear Father."

The words are nonsense, of course. Everyone knows I am a *Mothakes*.

Révna, dressed in her finest blue *peplos*, adds to the toast. "Where once we wished for the marriage of great wealth for you, now we need none." I refrain from rolling my eyes. "We could not have asked the gods to bring us a better child."

I glance quickly to my brothers, their faces unreadable.

My father roars, "To Daphne Diodorus, Shield of Helen!"

"Daphne Diodorus, Shield of Helen!" the partiers respond.

Despite my embarrassment, pride blossoms through me. My smile is genuine as I gulp down the contents of my cup and accept another. I earned this victory, and I didn't need the gods' help to do so.

My smile falters. One goddess had been there, in the arena. Her laugh that echoed around the space, the words she whispered into my ears—those were no memories. Could Nyx be here right now, too?

I spin around, searching the crowd. The goddess of night, with thick dark hair and ruby eyes, eludes me. Nyx bides her time.

My brothers still sit by the hearth. I slide between people, dodging elbows and hips. Pyrrhus sees me first, glancing up just as I break from the crowd. With a wordless sneer, he stands and leaves. Alkaios catches my wrist before I can follow.

"Don't," he says, voice rough. "You've done enough."

I jerk from his grip. "I had no choice. The gods commanded me to protect Helen."

"You should have let him win," Alkaios says, shaking his head, "and protected Anassa Helen together."

I scoff. "It's not that simple."

"It's never that simple for you." He looks down his narrow nose at me. "An impertinent brat to the very end."

He follows Pyrrhus, leaving me with a chill that no fire could abate. Apidanos slides between people, coming to wrap an arm around my shoulders. His eyes crinkle in the corners when he smiles. "You have proven yourself once again, Daphne. May your brothers learn from your example."

"Please don't compare them to me." I accept a *kylix* of wine and down it in one gulp. "They're not too fond of me at the moment."

"The love of siblings forgives all slights, eventually." The *ephor* looks to where my brothers had just been and frowns. "When you were all much younger, I used to take you all to the Eurotas. Do you remember?"

"Barely."

"I taught the three of you how to swim there." Apidanos, eyes as blue as the river he speaks of, turns his gaze skyward. "You took to the water much more quickly than either of your brothers, and Pyrrhus hated you for it." My head snaps toward him and he continues, "Pyr could barely even float. One day when the skies turned dark and the Anemoi fought, the water was suddenly too rough for even you. You fought and fought, but were pulled inexorably down the Eurotas."

"I don't remember any of this," I admit, voice soft.

47

A wan smile tugs at his lips. "That's because you were unconscious when you were pulled from the water. Pyrrhus dove right in after you and was dragged beneath the current again and again. Révna was frantic, thinking that we'd lost both of you. The Eurotas would not truly harm either of you, though. Gasping and spitting out water, Alkaios suddenly emerged with you both tucked beneath each of his arms."

My heart clenches. I open my mouth to ask for more, but my father shakes his head.

"Alkaios needn't have worried. As I said, the Eurotas would never allow you to be hurt. Not while the gods watch over you. I could not hold Pyrrhus back when he thought you were in danger. And Alkaios jumped in after you both without me ever noticing." He squeezes my shoulder. "That love is in them both still, just masked by hurt. Sparta has broken them, as it does far too many men."

My father leaves me sifting my thoughts like sand between the fingers. I have no taste for the wine or food. A small touch on my waist makes me spin, but nobody stands behind me. Then a gentle hand teases my curls hanging down my spine, deft fingers tripping through my locks.

"It is dangerous. You coming here." I turn to face Apollo. Despite my ire with him and his family, I cannot help the smile that pulls at my lips.

He's disguised himself well. His hair is no longer the burnished bronze I loved running my fingers through, but instead matches the black tresses of the Spartans milling around us. He's a tad shorter than normal, so now he doesn't tower over the mortals and draw attention. His voice is the same, though, and his blue eyes earnest, as he says, "I needed to congratulate you. My father is very pleased."

I raise my chin, smile slipping. "I hope Poseidon is stewing somewhere in the Aegean."

"Always." His laugh mingles with my own. "I cannot stay long or they will notice me. Meet me in the garden once the party is over?"

My core stirs with intoxicating heat. I ignore it and pull my face into a stern frown. Perhaps I am giddy with victory, but I allow, "I can spare a few minutes. If you're even a moment late, I'm going to bed." At his wicked grin, I add, "Without you."

He winks, then turns into the crowd, disappearing from sight.

"The god of prophecy is becoming reckless." Ligeia's musky sandalwood scent wafts over to me, despite the press of the crowd.

I spin. "How do you manage to sneak up on me every time?"

"It is quite easy when your thoughts are in the clouds like Perseus astride Pegasus." She grabs me gently by the upper arm, her hands warm and leathery. "I am proud of you, my *kataigída*."

"Thank you." I bow my head.

With two firm fingers below my chin, she raises my head. Her eyes, even the clouded one, are steely when they meet mine. "Before, you did as the gods commanded to save Pyrrhus. To what end are you now serving them?"

How much can I tell her and how much does she already know?

My voice is low so no others can hear when I reply, "To protect my *anassa*. The gods fear for Helen's safety."

Her lined lips purse. "I'm sure protecting his daughter is well within Zeus's considerable capabilities. No, this is about something more. Keep your wits close. The gods will chain you up in their secrets and tricks if they can." She pats me on the cheek. "Apollo would upend the world for you, Daphne, and the gods will not take kindly to that."

She moves on to talk to my brothers. I ignore the trepidation stirring inside me, firmly shoving it down to the pit of my stomach. Still, it lurks and fills me with a queasy sickness. The wine I indulged in only moments before threatens to rise in my throat.

Many more cups of wine later, the revelers have finally begun to herd themselves home. Lykou disappears, and my parents are too deep into their cups to notice as I dip from the room. The celebration has gone on so long that even Eos starts to rise, painting the horizon lavender. I tread barefoot across the silent garden.

Apollo's hair is bronze once more, his normal height returned.

Perhaps it is the wine, perhaps it is the memory of him, powerless and human from last summer, but despite all that has transpired between us—the death and secrets—everything in me screams to hold him.

I wrap my arms around myself and notch my chin high. "I await your father's praises, and Poseidon's apologies. They were fools to ever doubt me after—"

"Last summer?" A small, almost tentative smile pulls at the corner of Apollo's mouth. "Fools indeed."

He steps forward, a cool breeze carrying his cedarwood scent over to me. I breathe it in deeply through my nose.

"You asked for honesty, Daphne," he says, taking another step. "I can give it to you."

"For a price?"

"Everything has a price." He reaches out, brushing a curl behind my ear and making my heart trip. "Ask me a question. Any question. I will answer it for you if I can have but one, single kiss in return."

One question for one, single kiss. Hunger pools in my core like liquid fire. The fire of my fury fights for dominance in my mind, reminding me of his secrets. We gaze at each other, my chest rising and falling with rapid breaths.

"Why, Daphne?"

Panic seizing me, I spin around.

Pyrrhus stands at the edge of the garden, the rising sun painting the furious lines of his face with pale light. His hands are bunched into fists.

"Nothing happened," I promise, despite the heat in my face proclaiming me for a liar.

"Why do you even still talk to him?" he asks again between gritted teeth.

"I don't—" I stumble, cold sweeping over me. "I don't owe you any explanation."

Rage flares across his face, there and then gone only a moment later, but tangible enough to get me to step in front of Apollo. My hands likewise curl into fists.

"He is dangerous, Daphne," Pyrrhus says, voice so low I barely hear him. "Or did you forget what his sister did to me? What *he* did to Lykou? What his family did to our mother?"

I could never forget. No response is forthcoming, my tongue tied behind my teeth. All I can do is level my brother with a baleful glare.

"You're better than this," he spits, voice rising dangerously loud. He marches forward, steps jerky.

"Careful what you choose to do now, young buck," Apollo says with lethal quiet from behind me.

Slowly, I turn to see the barely concealed fire in the god's eyes. Terror dashes across my chest. In my mind's eye, I see Lykou's transformation again, hear the curse Apollo inflicted upon Theseus.

Pyrrhus is too lost in rage to care. "Or what, *bdelyròs*? You'll turn me into a deer again? Do you truly think my sister will forgive you so easily next time?"

He reaches out as if to yank me away. Before I can think, I take a step back. My brother blanches.

Without turning, I say to Apollo, "Leave. My brother and I must have words. Alone."

As tangible as a hand on my shoulder, Apollo's presence vanishes from the garden, leaving just Pyrrhus, myself, and the swaying flowers around us. They reach for my ankles as I stride toward my brother, as if Demeter begs me to stand still. Olympian presence harangues me always, even when I'm trying to prove that the gods don't control me.

He knows that, too. His face is pinched, blotched with furious red. "They cannot keep their claws from you."

"Apollo left when I asked," I say, my eyes imploring. "He will not turn you into an animal."

His voice low, he says, "What will he do when he tires of you?"

Silence stretches between us, heavy and cold.

"He should fear what I'll do when I tire of him." I force a hollow laugh.

"This isn't a game. Maybe for them—it always is for them—but not for you."

"I know." My lips pinch together. "I'm no fool."

He nods. "That's right. So why play along with their games, Daphne, unless you have something to gain?"

I blink, taken aback. "What are you implying?"

Despite our equal height, my brother looks down his nose at me when he asks, "What did you offer Apollo in return for winning the *agon*? Is that why you were with him in this garden?"

Betrayal, like none I have ever felt before, hits me as keenly as a slap across the face. "How can you even ask that?"

I would have expected this from a random Spartan, perhaps even Alkaios last year, but not Pyrrhus. Not the brother who cradled me even as our father disowned us all on the day of my birth. Not the brother I journeyed to Tartarus and back to save.

"You think…" I swallow, struggling to find the words that voice my hurt. "You truly believe that I would barter my own body to win that tournament? To steal your victory, your chance of redemption? I may have won at their behest, but I did so without their help."

"Liar," Pyrrhus says with a snarl. "I saw you leap for the hoop. You could not have flown through the air like that without their help."

It takes every ounce of my patience not to slap my own brother across the face. I take a deep, shaking breath. "I won fairly."

He steps close, looking me over with unconcealed disdain. "Did you?"

I was fast. Too fast. "Don't let your jealousy blind you. There will be other opportunities for your redemption."

"For you to steal as well?" he snaps.

"You're acting like a child," I say, my voice like the lash of a whip to match his.

Silence, like the dreadful calm before a storm, settles between us. He opens his mouth, closes it as if tasting the words for himself, before finally saying, "Tell yourself whatever you need to. You and I both know that, no matter how you might try to spin it, there was a small, insurmountable part of you that entered to feel that rush of victory."

He leaves me then, standing alone in the garden. My breathing is heavy but controlled. No tears spill from my eyes.

Because, though I don't want to admit it aloud, some part of me did crave that victory. Not for the gods, but for myself.

From the corner of my eye, movement attracts my attention. On the edge of the garden, shadows flicker. My hand immediately snaps to the knife I keep atop my thigh at all times. I'm tensed, blade raised and ready to spring at the goddess of night... But, instead, three others step forward.

The Moirai, the keepers of destiny and children of Nyx, glide toward me. They are not the crones the stories paint them to be. One is young, far younger than I, with poppy curls and pale skin. One is older, maybe twenty years my senior, and regal in bearing with tan skin and sleek brown hair. The third, of age with me, is the spitting image of their mother. I have no doubt who these three women are.

"Our mother sends her regards," the oldest says. Her eyes, like Nyx's, are ruby pools. "We have words of portent that need to be shared."

CHAPTER

7

Dread curls in the pit of my stomach. Nothing good ever comes with knowing your own future.

"The predictions of the Fates can cause madness, no matter how trivial they may seem," Ligeia once warned me.

I square my shoulders and turn to the Moirai. "What if I don't want to hear said wisdom?"

"What you want is no longer of concern." They draw closer, legs moving in perfect unison until they are within arm's reach.

The Fate's words make my pulse leap. I splay a hand over the Midas Curse between my breasts. "Whatever you tell me, you tell Olympus as well."

"Our words are meant for your ears alone." The poppy-haired Fate's mouth curls slowly into a smile. "Artemis will hear nothing through your golden curse. Not unless we will it."

A myriad of emotions flutter through me. Relief and fear jostling for dominance.

"Congratulations on your victory," the youngest says. "Or should we instead offer our condolences?"

The oldest Fate reaches out, her hand stopping just before her fingers can brush my face. "You have experienced our gifts before, Storm of Olympus. Prepare yourself."

I don't have even a moment to suck in a breath before her finger touches my brow. Just as with my time with Prometheus, the ground is swept from beneath me. But where his visions were choppy, disjointed, and swiftly moving, I am now pulled slowly, floating on a tide until my feet find steady ground.

I stand in a field of blood, corpses stretching for miles and miles. The winds whip around me, singing a haunting dirge off the walls of a city beyond. The bodies are burdened by armor from all corners of Greece. A blood-splattered Spartan helmet lies at my feet beside a Tenedos axe, and just beyond are Athenian swords and Mycenaean spears.

The youngest Fate steps forward next and takes my hand. Her grip is like an iron manacle, holding me in place despite her small size.

Where my hair whips in the wind, hers is completely still. "I, Lakhesis of the Moirai, impart upon you a warning."

I want to beg her to stop talking. Before I can, she waves her free arm to the desolate battlefield. "There is a great war on the horizon, like none Greece has ever known. All the kingdoms from every corner of this world will take part and stake their claim. Should you fail in the task assigned to you by the gods, that which you love most will meet its end right here on this battlefield. The Sparta you know will be gone forever more on the bloody fields of Troy."

"Troy? We will go to war with Troy?"

I spin to see the third and final Fate.

She nods, grinning widely. Her teeth are small, yellow with rot. "Yes, and they will welcome their own destruction with open arms."

The oldest Fate's hand now rests on my scarred shoulder. "I, Klotho, ask you to protect Troy, when you inevitably fail to protect your queen."

"I will not fail," I bite out, baring my teeth. My hands curl into tight fists. "And I would never betray my kingdom for Troy."

"That's what you think now, but betrayal is in your blood," a lilting voice says with a soft laugh. The third, so like her mother. "I, Atropos the Undeniable, will say this only once. Kingdoms may fall and monarchies may tremble before you, but none more so than the gods. You, *kataigída*," she says the name like a hiss, "will be the ruin of Olympus."

She flips my hand over, revealing the curved scar Nyx left upon me so many moons ago. It glows a brilliant red, brighter and brighter until my eyes water.

"Stop." I clench my eyes shut. The red pierces my eyelids. My entire arm feels as if it might burst into flame. "Make it stop!"

"Only you can do that," the Moirai say in unison.

"I said stop!" I rip my hands from theirs so hard I stumble.

The red blinks from behind my eyelids, the world suddenly dark. When I open my eyes again, the Moirai have disappeared, but their words still linger in the cool night air.

The Sparta you know will be gone forever more on the bloody fields of Troy.

CHAPTER

8

D espite the crescent moon hanging in the sky above, the Spartan palace rings with hollow birdsong. It seeps about the dark corners and narrow hallways. Birds don't sing like that in Sparta during the night. This is a warning.

Mindful of the queen sleeping in the room behind me, I follow the noise with a dagger in each hand. It trickles, covering the sound of my wary footsteps. The shadows grow with each movement. My breath catches. Nyx is here in the palace.

My grip is suddenly slick on the weapons. I will not show her any fear.

The birdsong dies. It's choked off as abruptly as it started.

I step into the throne room. A moan tangles in my throat.

Bodies are strewn everywhere. Blood pours between the square tiles, painting a deep red labyrinth on the floor. The kings from all the corners of Greece lay in pieces.

I don't understand how I could have failed already. The conclave only just started. The men arrived yesterday. Their laughter had filled the entire palace only moments ago.

"You failed them," a voice says, as melodic as I remember.

In the center of the dead stands a single woman.

Nyx turns, teeth gleaming. Blood, the same color as her eyes, is splattered on her face.

The scent of lavender is overwhelming now, making my eyes water. How did I not notice it before?

"I'm here to protect my *anassa*." I raise the dagger. "Not them."

"You truly know nothing of war. Despite all your fear of it." She flicks a wrist and her nails curl into long claws, pointing at a man clutching a black lion shield. "You think your queen won't be punished for their deaths?"

The man has long, curly black hair. Half his face is a mess of claw marks. That was not his cause of death, though. No, that fault lies with the sword protruding from his chest, hilt engraved with a *lambda*.

"I should have heard the fight," I say under my breath. I spin, the bodies blending together. "I should have heard the screams."

"Unless you were too distracted by Apollo." Nyx's laugh is malicious.

"Get out of my dreams." I sneer. We've done this dangerous dance in my sleep too many times to count. "Get out of my head."

"Make me."

I blink and she's leaping across the space. Her talons stretch for my face. I raise my blades. Not quickly enough.

She pierces my arms and chest. A scream bursts from me. Each touch is a lance of fire. Her body collides with mine and we slam backward onto the floor.

"You won't be enough to protect her," Nyx says fiercely. Her teeth are so close to my neck her breath stings my skin. "Not when all the Achaean kingdoms are demanding her head."

She raises one hand and yanks me by the throat. I can't breathe. Her claws pierce my skin and my blood joins that already staining the floor.

"One by one, they will arrive." She squeezes tighter. "And one by one, they will fall."

Her shadows fill my vision. The room fills with black.

"And you will be unable to stop it."

My eyes flutter shut.

The weight lifts and I throw myself up with a short scream. I clutch at my throat and kick away the furs of my bed. I fall, knees colliding with the floor hard enough to make me gasp.

The Sparta you know will be gone forever more on the bloody fields of Troy.

"No," I say. "I will not let that happen."

No one is here.

I fall backward and clutch my head in my hands.

If what Nyx has shown me and what the Moirai say is true—and the goddesses have never been known to lie—then my role as Helen's bodyguard is twofold: protect my queen and prevent a war. I should have known that was the Olympians' fear the moment they mentioned the conclave. Like a thorn in my heel, their infinite secrets make my blood boil.

My bedroom is quiet, no sounds even from the rest of the house. My floor is cool, a balm against my flushed skin. My fingers curl into claws of my own, digging into my scalp hard enough to drag me back to the present, and further from Nyx's nightmares.

I don't understand why the gods concern themselves with a mortal war. Perhaps they fear the people will love them less, and so their power will weaken. They may also have received visions from the Moirai as well. Whatever their reasons, they must revolve around both Troy and me.

They'll never tell me. Even Apollo, with all his professions of honesty, has his tongue held by his father. The goddess of truth must have abandoned Olympus long ago, because not a single god on that mountain would recognize honesty even if slapped in the face by it.

That might not be too far from what happened, I realize, inclining my head. The goddess of truth, Aletheia, was created by Prometheus. She might have been exiled from Olympus when her creator was banished to Mount Kazbek.

Ligeia stomps into my room and snaps open the curtains, revealing a cloudy day beyond my father's walls.

"Quit your sulking," she says, laying a tray of grapes and cheese on my bed.

"I'm not sulking." I stand, reaching for the cheese. "I'm imagining what shade of purple Hera's face would turn if I slapped her."

Ligeia inhales sharply. "That kind of sacrilegious talk will get you and everyone you love killed."

That might happen anyway.

... When you inevitably fail to protect your queen.

My hair is a curtain of knots and dirt around my face. I brush it back with an irritated hand, watching as Ligeia busies herself around my room. She's done this since I was a child, ensuring that I don't sneak out the back door toward the Taygetus forest when I should be somewhere else.

She needn't bother this time.

You, kataigída, *will be the ruin of Olympus.*

I will protect both my queen and Olympus.

At least, I will try to, even if it means dying again and again.

"I fear for you."

My gaze snaps up.

Ligeia says, "My sight, it only goes so far with you."

"What do you mean?" Curiosity blankets any dread I might feel toward her words.

"You disappear. Your future. It just drops, as if falling into an abyss."

Or walking into the Underworld. Perhaps dying, despite coming back, has affected her abilities.

My eyes meet her cloudy one. "Are you touched by the gods, as I am?"

"I prayed to Demeter for guidance. I did not know which path to take." She inclines her head to study me. "She gifted me with the future. But my other eye...Hermes took my sight in that eye, in exchange for another sight entirely."

"That rotten bastard always seems to give with one hand and take with the other," I say as I pull on my fighting leathers. "I'm well rid of him."

Ligeia barks a laugh. "The messenger god is not still in Tartarus, dear one. Mind your mouth when his name is in it."

I chuckle. "I have more daggers to leave in his back should he try anything."

Ligeia pats me on the cheek, no doubt recognizing the resolute setting of my shoulders. "Eat quick and head to the palace. Anassa Helen waits for you."

Sparta is already bustling as I make my way up to the palace atop the hill. As a militant city, my people are always ready for war. Nervousness and excitement fight inside me, numbing my steps. Vendors crowd the streets, people head out to the surrounding fields for sowing and *gymnasion* for training, and soldiers march by. The people I pass nod with respect. I am no longer one of the *Mothakes*. No longer just the girl who snatched up *Carneia*.

I am Daphne Diodorus, Shield of Helen.

A breeze stirs my hair as I look up at the palace. It sits atop the acropolis in the Eurotas Valley, overlooking the entire city with a long, winding road up to the front gates. The former Anax Tyndareus, Helen's father—or rather adoptive father, I guess—built a tall wall around the palace. Though he excused it as a last means of defense for his family should Sparta ever be attacked, I overheard my father say that it had actually been built to keep out the gods themselves. Having learned the truth of Helen's heritage, I now wonder if a wall could ever be tall enough to keep out the king of Olympus.

The longer I stare up at those walls, the more I wish to tear them down. Not to destroy what lies within, but to prove how capable I am. Under the doubts that plague me, the girl who marched up the mountain with Apollo and stared down the Minotaur without flinching must still be in there somewhere.

Hands fisted at my hips, I continue marching up the hill, gaze pinned to the sandstone wall. The soldiers at the entrance don't stop me as I pass. Everyone in the city bore witness to my victory, yesterday and last summer. Everyone knows of the *Mothakes* Diodorus. Before I can enter the palace, a familiar face appears in my path. I halt, doubt rising in me despite myself.

Grinning, Paidonomos Leonidas says, "Welcome, Diodorus. The *anassa* is eager to meet you."

His scarred shoulders shine in the rising sunlight as he turns to lead me into the palace. I follow, making an effort to keep my mouth closed. It is an incredible effort as I take in the palace I had only heard stories about.

So different from the palace of Knossos I explored only a year before, Sparta's palace is warm and welcoming, bustling with friendly servants and surrounded by lush gardens. There are no frescoes on the wall, though. No art of any kind. Sparta has never had the time for such frivolities.

Leonidas leads me to a garden in the back of the palace, with tall trees and a pond wide and deep enough to swim in. Helen sits at the shore, watching swans swimming past with her feet dangled in the water. Her daughter, Hermione, wades in the shallows, plucking reeds and weaving them together into a yellow crown.

Helen looks up when we start around the pond, a bright smile blossoming on her stunning face. Chestnut curls drape over her tan shoulders, split by strands of gold and fire. Her eyes are a startling gray, and her smile, kind yet brimming with secrets, reminds me so much of Artemis I'm almost breathless. Sisters, I remember then. Helen is a half-sister to Artemis—

And Apollo.

Helen stands, every movement filled with an ethereal grace that isn't entirely mortal. "You may leave us, *Paidonomos*. Take Hermione to Korinna. I believe she's in the kitchens."

Leonidas bows and, with a quick wink to me, plops the sodden toddler on his shoulders and turns from the garden. Helen walks slowly around the pond toward me, still smiling.

"You won *Carneia* last year," she says, pointing at my chest. "What happened to the *dory* I gave you?"

Praxidikai. Snapped in half like a mere twig.

"I left it at home," I lie smoothly. I can't exactly tell her that it's currently rotting in pieces in the depths of Tartarus. Patting the sword at my hip, I add, "It was more for ceremony anyway. Not actual combat."

"Indeed." She looks me over and, though I did not stumble at all over the words, I suspect that she does not believe me. She angles her head. "Come. Walk with me. I will give you a tour of my prison."

I nearly trip. "Prison?"

She waves to the wall with a frown. "Yes. What is a queen kept in a palace, to do nothing but oversee ceremonies, other than a bauble to be protected? I am nothing more than a hoarded treasure."

"You are far more than that to me, my dove."

We both jump as Menelaus strides into the garden. No warmth radiates from him as he wraps an arm around Helen's waist. "Don't be so melodramatic."

He places a firm kiss on her cheek before turning to assess me. I feel naked beneath his stare, measuring every inch of me. I hate it.

"Your father gives me quite the headache. I can never guess which way he will vote," the king finally says. "Or should I say, your adoptive father? You're a *Mothakes*."

I force myself to nod. "Indeed I am. And I'd like to think my father quite predictable."

Menelaus turns to face me fully. "Oh?"

"He takes his role as an *ephor* quite seriously." I stand straighter. "Everything he does is for the people, not himself."

"Yes, Apidanos Diodorus is a charitable man. Tax cuts left and right. Voting for the exact measures he knows will keep him in favor of the people." Menelaus cuts a hand through the air. "That charitable nature is probably why he took you in."

I open my mouth to affirm, but he cuts me off. "Though that's not entirely true, is it? My sources say that you were brought to their doorstep by an oracle. A sybil even, and she prophesized that you and your brothers are the gods' chosen."

My throat is suddenly dry. "You've done your research."

"Of course. I'd look into anyone spending as much time with my wife as you will be. Your brothers, too. Alkaios, bless him, has proven nothing so far in his short career as a Spartiate," he goes on. "More rigid than a column, and more bland than water. He'll be lucky if the people fall in love with him enough to elect him to take up your father's seat." The king's eyes are as cold and pale as ice. "And Pyrrhus? He's lucky to still have his life after what he did last summer. Forfeiting our people's future to indulge in a few extra cups of wine."

My nostrils flare, every fiber of my being screaming at me to defend my brothers, yet I hold my tongue, literally clamping it between my teeth so hard warm blood floods my mouth.

"And you?" Menelaus looks me over again, gaze lingering on the blonde curls escaping my braid. "The Shield of Helen? We're sure to see what kind of trouble you'll bring my people."

Not our people. *His* people.

Because, even though he is not born of Sparta, he has more of a claim to this kingdom than I will ever have. Despite all I have done to save it.

A storm stirs in my chest, a tempest begging to be unleashed.

Helen places an elegant hand on her husband's shoulder, nails digging into his dark blue *peplos*. "Paidonomos Leonidas was looking for you, my love. You shouldn't keep him waiting."

Menelaus glances between me and his wife before, without even a word of farewell, he strides from the garden.

"Believe it or not," Helen says, gazing after him. Sadness presses into her lovely features. "He's much friendlier than his brother."

I blink, but she doesn't give me the opportunity to press. With springing steps, she leads me from the garden and back into the palace.

"The palace is much more active today for a reason," she says. "We're preparing for the arrival of many envoys over the following weeks, starting with my dear husband's brother, Agamemnon, in fact. Hopefully the big clod brings my sister with him this time." She waves a hand to the servants that we pass, all dropping into low bows until we're out of sight. "I can't even imagine how crowded the palace will be then."

The conclave. I pretend to appear surprised and murmur, "I'll have my work cut out for me, that's for sure."

"That's an understatement if I ever heard one before," Helen says. "Agamemnon has been itching for war, any war with anyone, since he took power. And my husband is all too happy to oblige in order to curry my kingdom's favor."

The hair on my arms rises. She chews on her lip and glances around the empty corridor. The statement seems to fill her with as much ill ease as it does me.

"But I do not agree," she continues. "Sparta has been entrenched in bloodshed for too long. I would do anything to keep another war from taking the lives of my people."

War is all Sparta has ever known. I never thought a queen of Sparta would be such an idealist. She hurries on, leaving me to wonder just how many of my assumptions have been foolish.

"Your room will be attached to mine," she says, voice breezy, as if she wishes to move on from our previous talk. "I have already sent for your belongings to be brought up to the palace."

Helen points to a set of stairs that lead downward, the shadows climbing from their depths. I shiver. "That way leads to the cellars and prison cells. I'll probably ask you to steal some wine and figs for me from time to time."

We pass a wide archway next and walk through, crossing a great megaron with silk *klines* and a deep-set hearth in the center. Tiles of polished amber stretch across the ground, some worn by the passage of time. A fresco, painted to match the Taygetus mountains overlooking the city, stretches from wall to wall, making the space feel much more open than it is. Giving an unsuspecting guest a false sense of security, I'm sure. I don't fail to note that it is the single piece of art in the entire palace.

"This is where we greet esteemed guests and host banquets," Helen says, pointing to the mahogany thrones on the far side of the room. "You will stand there, to my right."

We continue through the palace, and she points out the bathing chamber, resplendent with a great pool, and the armory, sure to rival any other in the entire world.

"So what does your paramour think of your new promotion?" Helen teases.

I stumble and hide it by dragging my hand along the wall. "I don't have a paramour."

She raises a brow. "No need to hide Lykou Xanthippos from me."

I blink. "How did you—"

"Know that you and Lykou are romantically intertwined?" Her smile is cheeky. I open my mouth to argue that she couldn't be further from the truth, but she cuts me off. "I did my research. You think I wouldn't look into the girl who showed up my brother at *Carneia* last year?"

People have long assumed that Lykou and I were a bonded pair. And in a way, we are. Lykou no doubt still hopes we will be in more ways, someday.

Yet the love he has for me will never be returned. At least not how he would like it to be.

"What other kings can we expect to arrive soon?" I ask, changing the subject and following into her rooms.

A warm breeze stirs the silk curtains separating her room from another garden outside, bringing with it the scent of cedarwood I know too well. A trace of Nyx's lavender also stirs the air, making me itch to reach for my dagger. Helen doesn't seem to notice the suspicious glance I shoot around the room.

"Too many." She throws herself onto the luxurious red furs of her bed, lying on her back so that her hair tumbles over the side. She begins ticking names off on her fingers. "Phthia, Ithaca, Sicyon, Ormenius, Argos, and Athens, among many more."

My heart stutters. Athens. Theseus's father will be here. Seeing his face, no doubt near identical to his dead son's, will be a foreign type of agony. I swallow, forcing myself to nod as Helen continues.

Thinking of the Moirai's words, I press, "The Trojans as well?"

"How astute of you."

They could be bringing war right into this palace, while Helen welcomes it with open arms.

She flips over onto her stomach and throws a furtive glance around the room. "Are we alone?"

"I believe so." Though just because I can't see or hear anyone else, that doesn't mean that the gods don't listen nearby.

The Midas Curse threads along my scalp, meaning that Artemis definitely listens. When the Curse is particularly active it usually means that her ear is pressed against my heart. Her eavesdropping makes my skin crawl and my teeth grind. I want to rip the Curse from my skin.

"You won't tell anyone what I said earlier, will you?" She bites her lip. "About war and my people."

Quietly, and with complete honesty, I say, "You are my queen. If keeping your secrets is what I must do to protect you, then I will take whatever you say to my last burning pyre."

She considers me, rising slowly to sit cross-legged on the furs. Her impossibly beautiful face is strained, as if doubts war within her. What she must see in mine smooths her features.

Helen's voice drops to a whisper as she finally admits, "I cannot understand why Menelaus invited the Trojans. He said this would be a summit, a treaty of sorts, except we have no issue with the Trojans, nor any of the other kings."

I grip a wrist behind my back. "You are the Anassa of Sparta. You should be told these things."

She grins. "I can tell that you and I are going to get along fabulously." The smile slips a bit. "But no, I am nothing more than a crown to Menelaus, the keys to the Spartan kingdom, so to speak."

I balance between pressing further and leaving well enough alone. From Helen's earnest expression, the loneliness that dances in her eyes, I know she craves the question hanging on the tip of my tongue.

"Why do you say that?" I ask finally.

Helen's gaze fixes on the throws, fingers picking at the auburn fur. Bitterness laces her reply. "Because I am second to a foreign *anax* in my own kingdom. That is all women are to ever be, it seems. Second to the men who own them." Her gray gaze flicks to mine. "Until you, that is."

I resist the urge to take a step back from the unspoken command in those eyes.

"You're owned by no one, Daphne."

Not entirely true, I think to the gods no doubt watching this exchange, and incline my head. "I am at *your* command."

"You are," she allows. "Why did you enter the *agon*, Daphne? Everyone knows your brother sought to regain favor in Sparta and you stole that away."

I ignore the guilt that itches at me. This question is as much a test as everything else Helen has said leading up to now. Watching for my reaction when she tells me of her confinement in the palace, how Menelaus sees her as nothing more than an ornament, and of her dreams for a peaceful Sparta.

I could say something like that I was helpless to the whims of the men around me. Soon, my father would force me into a marriage of my own choosing, to be used simply to bring more Spartans into the world. Or that my brother will have other chances to bring honor to his name, but my time was drawing short. Or even something closer to the truth, like that the gods visited me and commanded me to enter.

Instead, I say, "Because there is no honor greater than being your Shield."

Helen places her hands on her chest, long elegant fingers gripping the fabric of her chiton. Her pulse flutters rapidly at the base of her neck. She opens her mouth, then closes it, before whispering, "What of being my friend?"

My mouth pops open. "Your friend?"

"That's what I said." She rises, striding toward me. Her golden *peplos* swishes with each step, brushing my legs when she stands close enough to grab my hands. Hers are so soft, like silk, unblemished by the world. "I can't have someone so close to me, every day, every night, unless I trust them."

"And to be your friend is to earn that trust?"

Helen nods.

"You're the queen of Sparta," I say. Tremors of trepidation shake my hands. I pull them from hers. "You should have more friends than I could even dream up."

"A throne is a lonely place." She glances in the direction of the megaron, as if she can see through the walls. "Made even lonelier by the seat beside it."

There's more she's not telling me. Not yet, at least.

"Will you be my friend as well as Shield, Daphne Diodorus?"

"I would be honored." One of the first honest things I've said to her so far.

She doesn't seem to notice, beaming and bouncing on her toes. "Sparta has no clue what is coming for it! You and I are going to be so much trouble."

"Trouble I can provide." I add to myself, *Intentionally or not.*

"Menelaus is going to be so cross," she coos, chattering happily about all the riot we will cause and not looking in the least worried about the king of Sparta being angry with her.

As I let her lead me from the room, my mind is a whirl that eddies with every step, my thoughts drawn inexorably to the kings who will arrive at the palace.

I may have gained the position I fought and trained for years to achieve, but that doesn't mean I can stop honing my skills, nor let my senses dull. I cannot allow Helen's passive acceptance of an army of foreign kings descending upon Sparta let me fall into a false sense of security.

Are they the danger my gods feared, or do they foretell of a war to come should this conclave fail?

CHAPTER
9

With almost childish glee, Helen instructs me to follow as she explores the lush gold and green city. Each day, we follow the twisty Eurotas, delve deep into the Taygetus forest, and pull our cloaks tight as we explore shadowed alleyways and the crowded agora.

No doubt we drive the other guards mad, but Helen delights in this game. Eluding any claim to her that Menelaus has. They are his guards, after all, she tells me one day. And myself? The Shield of Helen was her idea, brought to her in a dream. No doubt the same dream Aphrodite referred to only weeks before.

Menelaus orders even her own child, the toddler Hermione, to be taken from her day in and day out. The pain in Helen's eyes is tangible. And each day, my distaste for the man—this foreign king who causes my queen so much pain—festers and grows.

Too much trouble, though, and our reins are yanked back.

"Please," Helen says. "We only ask to go to the Sanctuary of Artemis Orthia to pray for our men."

The queen kneels at her husband's feet. The sight makes my skin crawl. Her tone is lovely, like a lyre's final ring, and her head rests across Menelaus's knee. Her mahogany curls spread across his lap.

I stand at the megaron's entrance with my hands behind my back. His guards, wearing cloaks of both Spartan red and Mycenaean gray, flank me. Another two of them stand on either side of the king's throne. Watching me.

He rubs his fingers through her strands of hair, his face pinched in thought. "The way you flaunt your blatant disregard for my rules hurts me, my dove."

His hand tightens, pulling her head back and baring her neck. Her eyes twitch, the only sign of the pain he must be causing her.

I itch to withdraw my dagger and slice the hand from his arm. The gazes of his guards are a heavy weight. I bite down on my tongue.

The queen draws a star on his thigh with a narrow finger. "Please, my darling."

"Why would you want to go anywhere when I offer you all you could ever desire right here?" He angles her head up so she's looking in his eyes. "You have everything you could ever want right here."

"I wish to talk to Artemis." Her eyes are imploring.

"Who are you going to meet there?"

"Nobody." She grimaces as his hand tightens on her hair. "I only wish to ask for her favor during the conclave."

"A likely excuse. You've grown rather skilled at lying since Ephor Diodorus's daughter joined your guard."

I shift, tension gathering in my shoulders.

Menelaus's other hand cups her chin, thumb grazing over Helen's lips. "Do not cross me again, my dove."

With a jerk, he releases her. She falls backward, catching herself before tumbling down the dais's steps.

Eyes stormy with unsaid rage, she inclines her head. "Thank you."

I let her lead me from the megaron, and not a moment too soon. Any longer watching him jerk her around, and my dagger might have ended up in the base of his spine.

Helen is silent as we ride through the city. She fiddles with the reins. Her voice firm, she says, "Careful how you look at my husband, Daphne."

My head snaps toward her.

She adds, "Your dislike of the man is too obvious."

I can't deny it, though I should. "Am I so easy to read?"

"Call it intuition." Helen doesn't meet my gaze and kicks the sides of her horse, spurring the mare onward. "If he notices, too, not even I can protect you."

The road to the Sanctuary of Artemis Orthia is winding and high, on an acropolis above the Eurotas's reach when it floods every spring. We're flanked by four of Menelaus's guards, who watch us both wearily. If we elude them again, it will be their backs whipped at dawn.

Helen dismounts and strides inside without a backward glance at Menelaus's guards. The men aren't allowed inside. The priestesses of Artemis Orthia say that if a man steps across that threshold, they will be struck down by divine arrows. No man has been brave enough to challenge that claim. After witnessing the coldness of the goddess of the hunt as she turned my brother into a deer last summer, I don't doubt the claim, either.

The temple is dark inside, a stark contrast to the bright, elegant simplicity of Demeter's in Eleusis. The walls and columns are made from carved wood, great trees atop stone pedestals with varying likenesses of the goddess of the hunt carved into them. The walls are painted with black deer and nymphs. Helen's face is upturned to the staggeringly high ceiling, painted a dark green. "I once considered priesthood." Her voice is so quiet I almost don't hear her.

"Why didn't you?"

"I had a dream, of a lovely child with brown hair and gray eyes the same as mine." Tears form in the corners of her eyes. "I dreamed of Hermione. Besides, it would have simply been trading one life of servitude for another."

I struggle to find the words at first, but then I admit, "I considered it once, too."

Twin priestesses hand us daggers for offerings; as one, Helen and I slice our palms and let the blood drip into the clay bowl at the base of the statue in the center, a stunning likeness of Artemis carved from a single, great tree. The statue points to an arrow, her face pulled into a frown of consternation and a diadem atop her brow.

We're given red bandages to wrap our hands and I allow Helen space as she kneels before the statue. Helen whispers to the goddess's wooden feet, and I turn about the small space. Priestesses in red sweep past to make sure the guards do not even peek inside. They sing a song of hunting and the forest, loud enough to drown out Helen's prayer.

A wave of warm power creeps over my skin. It presses against my core.

Under my breath so that Helen and the priestesses do not hear, I say, "I thought this was your sister's temple?"

"She's here, too." Apollo wears the red cloak and *kalyptra* of the priestesses, but his presence is unmistakable. "Besides, she can share."

He does not lie. Artemis's power emanates from the statue. When I peer closely at her face, it winks.

"Helen will hear what you say to me."

Glittering light trickles down from the ceiling, dotting Helen's brow and landing on my outstretched hands. "No, she won't."

"Good to see I returned your powers just so you could use them so flippantly." I reach for a sprig of laurel and rub the leaves between my thumb and forefinger. "Why are you here?"

"The kings will be arriving soon." Apollo watches Helen. "She needs protecting."

I let the leaf go as if burnt. "I already plan on doing that."

A light begins to glow from the corner of my eyes.

Apollo holds out the same golden vambraces he offered before the final challenge. "These will help."

I should have taken them before the *agon*. I nearly lost because of my fear.

I will not be afraid this time. And yet...

"I don't need them."

The vambraces disappear. "I can help."

I refrain from grinding my teeth. "I don't want your help."

"Why are you so stubborn?"

"I don't know, Apollo. Why are you so secretive?"

"With good reason, Daphne. I've told you this countless times."

I chew the inside of my cheek. "I still don't entirely trust you."

Not just here and now, but at all times. Even after we've saved each other's lives multiple times.

Apollo's arms drop to his sides. "I will not hurt you, Daphne."

"Your past says otherwise."

"Last summer, I thought your distrust misplaced." Apollo brushes his knuckles across my cheek and my breath catches. "Then I heard of the circumstances around your birth, and of Ligeia's stories. You were born to hate the gods."

I clench my teeth, willing my heart to slow its stampeding as he continues, "And then you learned of Koronis, my greatest regret." He looks up, eyes meeting mine. "You didn't even ask my side of the story."

My stomach twists. Maybe that is why he won't look at me sometimes. Why he's so cold one moment and then cannot keep his hands from me the next.

Perhaps my heart wasn't the one broken, but instead it was his.

My voice is gruff. "There are no good reasons for keeping secrets from the people you profess to have feelings for."

Breathing hard, we stare each other down for a few moments, silently willing each other to break, to submit. But both of us are as unbendable as columns of marble.

A horn at the city gates makes us both look up. The number of notes makes my stomach twist.

Helen leaps to her feet. Her face drains of color. In a blink, Apollo's gone.

"He's here already," she says and turns to me.

Agamemnon.

I begin walking toward the entrance, but her hand snaps out to latch on to my wrist.

"One last game?" Her voice is pleading. "Let's leave the guards behind."

They would never deny their queen. The priestesses give us a pair of red cloaks and veils. We leave our horses and walk down the backside of the acropolis, making for the Eurotas. Apollo's touch still lingers on my cheek.

When we reach the river below and the cover of the shrubs and trees that grow high there, blocking the guards above from our sight, we share a grin.

"Menelaus is going to lose his mind," Helen says with a breathless laugh.

"Perhaps he'll finally learn that, as the queen of Sparta, you answer to no one." I untie my sandals.

She gives me a curious, unreadable look before kicking off her own shoes to start wading across the river. Anglers along the banks stare as we pass, making us both giggle even harder. Their faces would be less incredulous and more horrified if they knew our true identities.

"I'm sure he'll forget all about us with his brother arriving," Helen says, as if assuring herself.

The water reaches our waists. I steady her with a hand and we climb out onto the opposite bank in silence. We head for a serpentine trail up the hill behind the palace, our heavy breathing suffocated by our tumultuous thoughts. Before we can pass beneath the arched back entrance of the palace, Helen again grabs my wrist.

She pulls me close, whispering, "I told you before to watch your face. Be even more careful around Menelaus's brother. Agamemnon's temper is worse than my husband's."

I only have time to nod before she tugs me into the palace. She tears the clasps at her shoulders as she walks, letting the priestess's clothes fall. Her lithe body, naked for all to see, cuts a quick figure to her rooms.

"Korinna," Helen yells, striding to her royal suite. "Bring me a green silk gown and the ochre."

"Why that color?" I ask, handing her the gold bangle she loves to wear each time she sits before an audience. It is two intertwined snakes with emerald eyes.

She takes it and brusquely shoves it up to her bicep. "Agamemnon hates green."

A laugh escapes me, but I keep a careful eye on the servants spinning around Helen, wrapping the dark chiton around her frame. A golden *meander* decorates the hem. They clasp it atop a single tan shoulder with an emerald larger than my fist, and weave a fishtail bread with the diadem atop her brow, baring her long, elegant neck.

"Are you ready?" A wicked smile pulls at her lips, the one I've come to recognize as the kind that leads to trouble.

I follow her to the megaron and take the space she indicated only weeks before as she sits upon the throne. She crosses her legs, eyes dark. I stand akimbo behind her, hands always within reach of my weapons. A frowning Menelaus enters next and takes the seat beside Helen. He spares her and me nothing more than a cursory glance, his attention focused on the arched entrance to the megaron.

My heart thunders in my chest. Not for fear of my queen's life, but of the man soon to make an appearance.

Agamemnon, King of Mycenae. He is said to be terrible to behold, and even worse to battle. His temper unruly and his lineage cursed just as Menelaus's is.

The Brothers Atreus, they call them. Bound forever in blackened blood by the actions of their father, Atreus, who murdered his own brother's sons and served them up to him in a stew.

Or so the stories say. I glance at Menelaus. Stern, heavy-lidded with dark brows and even darker hair. I cannot help but wonder how this cool, calculating man will compare to the raging fire of his brother, and how much of what they are is shaped by the curse hanging over their heads.

The guards at the entrance straighten, heralding the Mycenaean king's arrival. Tension begins to knot my shoulders.

Agamemnon strides across the amber tiles, a red cloak streaming behind him. His soldiers, a dozen of them, follow in quick succession bearing swords and shields painted with maroon rampant lions. His wide mouth is split by a broad smile, displaying crooked yellow teeth.

I blink, mouth popping open. The man from Nyx's dream. With a blade in his chest.

Agamemnon, King of Mycenae, flashes the room a charming smile. Too charming. Like the look of innocence a beggar child gives you while his friends rob your purse. My blood curdles.

"Brother!" he bellows, holding his arms aloft. "Where is the wine?"

Servants hurry over with trays laden with cups. Agamemnon takes one in each hand and downs them in quick succession, then grimaces.

"I forgot how foul the wine is here," he says under his breath, just loud enough that we can hear him from the dais. He pounds his chest. "Not quite the warm reception I expected, Menelaus. Where are the dancing women? Why is there no boar already roasting on a spit? Is this how you would treat your favorite brother?"

His only brother, actually.

Menelaus stands, hand flexing and unflexing behind his back. "We did not expect you for another week."

Foolish to admit the failings of our city. Menelaus should let Helen speak. She would never have made such a slight.

"Then your spies are failing you, dear brother," Agamemnon says, eyes gleaming.

An insult to Sparta and our army. Words will be had tonight with the scouts along Sparta's roads. Lives will no doubt be taken as a warning. I swallow, throat dry. Hopefully Alkaios isn't among them.

"Come now," Helen says, standing and walking toward her brother-in-law. She peeks around him to the entrance. "Have you brought my sister and niece with you?"

When Agamemnon shakes his head, disappointment floods her features. "No. Clytemnestra stayed home like a good wife and sees to Mycenae in my stead. Besides, these talks will bore her to an early grave."

"Oh?" Helen raises an eyebrow.

"Yes, yes." Agamemnon waves an irritated hand to the nearest servant, who rushes over with more wine. "Nothing but discussing trade."

"So many Achaean kings here for mere trade talks?" Helen asks pointedly.

The elder Mycenaean stills, cup of wine raised to his lips. His eyes narrow. "You're rather nosy, sister."

I take a step forward despite myself, face carefully blank, watching his free hand and the guards around him.

"Of course I'm curious," Helen says with a dismissive wave. "You and your brother are bringing a whole army of kings to my doorstep. Any reasonable person would ask why."

"As a woman," he says, sneering, "even as Anassa of Sparta, it is not your place to be curious. Your place is in the bedchamber, and the bedchamber alone."

The shift in the air is palpable. As if the sun in the air above us has turned its direct focus on this Spartan palace. If I could cut out his tongue without losing my head, I would. Cut his head from his shoulders for disrespecting Helen.

Sweat slicks the back of my neck. A dull roar builds between my ears. My rage is matched by the Spartan guards around us. They glare at this foreign king, this *suagroi* who dares to insult our queen.

The storm inside me is quickly extinguished by Menelaus stepping between his wife and brother. He grabs Agamemnon by the shoulder.

"Must you two always bicker like children?" He indicates a side entrance as he says, "Shall we discuss our other guests in private?"

Grinning salaciously at Helen, Agamemnon lets his brother lead him from the megaron. Spartan and Mycenaean guards follow. Helen watches their retreating backs with curled fists. Before I can say anything, she spins, marching from the room with a straight spine. I can do nothing but follow.

Helen's room echoes with the childish giggles of her daughter.

Hermione dances on her toes, waving a doll in each hand as she spins and twirls. Helen claps, grinning broadly. It is the first time I've seen her smile since Agamemnon arrived this morning.

The smile vanishes when her daughter asks, "How long is Uncle visiting for?"

Helen stands, picking at her white gown. "Not too long, dearest."

Looking over at the queen and her daughter, doubt sweeps over me. Perhaps I should have accepted Apollo's help. When all the kings of Greece come for Helen, I don't know if I'll be enough to protect them. Especially not when I'm weighed down by fear. I resist wrapping my arms around myself.

My thumb catches on the bandage tied around my hand. It's still wet from the Eurotas. I peel back the cloth and my mouth pops open.

My palm is completely healed. My breath catches. That's impossible. I remember clearly the sharp sting of the priestess's blade.

"Why couldn't Uncle bring Cousin Iphigenia with him?" Hermione's voice is the sharp whine of a princess used to getting whatever she wants.

"Because there will be too many people here for her and your aunt," Helen says, the words wooden. "Perhaps after the conclave your father will let us go visit them in Mycenae."

The princess's eyes—so similar to her mother's—light up. She clasps her tiny hands in front of her face. "Really? Daddy says I'm never going to leave Sparta."

Helen's smile is pained. "You are a princess, my darling." She tenderly brushes Hermione's hair from her rosy cheeks. "You can do whatever you want."

The hunger, the longing in Helen's gaze as she turns to the garden and wall beyond says otherwise.

The Queen's smile is falsely bright. "What about you, Daphne? Did Ephor Diodorus ever take you anywhere?"

"My father hasn't left Sparta in more than forty years." I toss a handful of flowers at the princess's feet. "But that doesn't mean I had to stay here. I've been to Crete and Eleusis, Thebes and Foloi Forest."

Hermione gasps. "Will you take me to those places, *Mana Mou?*"

Helen kneels and catches her daughter with a sharp laugh, burying kisses in the child's wild, brown hair. "I'll take you anywhere you want, my darling."

"Don't say things you don't mean."

Menelaus marches into the room. He's flanked by his guards, the very ones we left at the Sanctuary, and his face is cold and detached. Dread floods my limbs, numbing my fingers.

"What does he mean?" Hermione's voice takes on a piteous whine. "Will we not go on an adventure?"

"Not tonight, pet." Menelaus waves to Helen's handmaid. "Take her to her room."

The princess begins to cry. Korinna scoops up Hermione and carries her from the room. Her wails fill the halls. Their hollow sadness wrenches my heart. The way Helen's face twists with pain lets me know that her own heart cracks.

"You didn't have to hurt her feelings like that." Her voice is rough and bristling with unspent anger. Her hands clench atop her thighs.

"What a pretty little fool you are," Menelaus says, walking slowly about the room.

I fight to keep my tongue under control. He pulls the curtains that separate the room from the garden beyond, drawing them closed. The moon and stars disappear. The remaining handmaids light the oil lamps in every corner.

When they finish, he turns to them. "Leave us."

I move to follow, normally dismissed at the same time, but a pair of guards block my path. Their faces are cold and emotionless.

"No. You stay." He points to my chest, then to the space beside my queen.

With stiff legs, I march over to where he indicates.

"You were both reckless today." He pushes the sleeves of his *peplos* up and ties them atop each shoulder. "I hope you enjoyed your moment of fun, fleeing my guards at the temple."

Shivers that have nothing to do with the sudden drop in the room's temperature wrack my frame.

"You flagrantly ignored my rules," Menelaus continues. "Abandoned the guards I keep for *your* protection." He holds out a hand and a servant places in his palm a black, coiled whip. "You disrespected not only my throne, but me, your king."

"You will not touch my *anassa*." Without thinking, I step in front of Helen. I stare down the whip. Dread pinches the back of my neck.

Menelaus's answering smile is laced with cruelty. "Good. You know who will pay the price."

"No!" Helen leaps to her feet. "She only did as I commanded!"

She tries to shove me aside, but my feet are planted. I notch my chin high. If the whip isn't for me, he would turn it on her. I can't allow that.

"I will not remove you from your post," he says to me, ignoring Helen. "No, the people and *ephor*s will not have that." He lets the tail of the whip fall to the floor with a soft click. "One lash for each guard."

My ears begin to ring. The guards stride past. Helen cries out as I'm shoved past her and flattened against a wall. The guards take each of my wrists and smash them above my head. The Midas Curse flares, covering my entire back. Any relief I might have felt at the golden barrier vanishes when the men dig their fingers into the fabric of my chiton.

The Midas Curse is forced to flee when they shred the fabric along my spine. A gasp steals past my lips. I clench my teeth to keep any other noise from escaping me. The curse pools at my belly, the only comfort Artemis can offer now.

"Five lashes," Menelaus says, voice remorseless.

Helen begins to scream. There's a scuffle behind me and I turn just as a pair of Spartan guards haul her backward. Before I can yell at them to let her go, the whip sings through the air.

Its sting is belated, like an afterthought. Then it begins to burn, a line of fire across my spine. I press my cheek against the stone wall, desperate to absorb its chill. The whip is passed off to a guard and I clench my lip between my teeth, panting. It cuts through the air and slices my back.

Under my breath I say, "Don't let him—"

Another lash. Lightning begins to crackle along my spine.

"Don't let him know, Artemis," I whisper. Sweat beads on my brow.

A fourth line spreads like wildfire. My nails dig hard enough into the wall to crack.

"Don't tell Apollo." My knees shake, threatening to buckle.

"One more," Menelaus says. I don't dare to turn. "For my honor."

His lash is the worst. It stretches across my shoulders and catches in my hair. Darkness flares in the corner of my eyes.

"He'll kill them all," I whisper, then fall to the ground, knees slamming on the hard floor. Finally released, Helen is at my side in a moment, clutching desperately at my arms.

"You're a monster," she says to her husband, voice a low growl. "You're not the man I loved."

"No," he says simply. "I'm not."

A choked sound catches in Helen's throat.

"I'll expect you at my side when the kings arrive." He brushes his hands on his thighs, as if removing them of my filth. He gazes down at us, utterly remorseless and unfeeling. "Let this be a lesson to you. Both of you."

He leaves us huddled on the floor. Shame begs me to curl into a ball on the floor and hide my face from the watching guards. Helen weeps as birds call outside the room, wild and frenzied. The noise fades away, my ears ringing so loud I can hear nothing else.

I will make Menelaus pay. Even if I lose my own head on my path to retribution.

CHAPTER

10

There is a great war on the horizon, like none Greece has ever known. All the kingdoms from every corner of this world will take part and stake their claim.

I don't have time to plot my revenge against Menelaus.

Each night, Nyx haunts my dreams. Each morning, the Moirai's words echo through me like a dirge, harkening the end of Greece and a war I can only hope to stop. And each day, I dress in my shined battle leathers, hissing as they cling to my still-healing back, sharpen my blades, and don the Shield of Helen cloak. Fate may try to take my kingdom from me, but I will not let her take my queen.

Odysseus of Ithaca arrives first. His skin is dark, his hair long and curled, and his face, though only ten or so years older than mine, is immeasurably wise. It's smooth-paned and his voice is soft.

He bows low before my king and queen. "Greetings. It has been many years since I last saw any of you. Sorry to say it, lads, but Helen is the only one who remains the same. As lovely as ever, while Agamemnon over here looks like a fig left out in the sun too long, and Menelaus a grape that has pruned."

I fight against the smile pulling my lips. Helen's laugh is genuine.

"Welcome, Anax of Ithaca," she says. "I am not ashamed to admit that you're the one person I was looking forward to arriving."

The slight isn't missed by anyone in the room. Odysseus's gaze flicks to a glowering Agamemnon and back.

Odysseus sweeps an arm behind his back and bows again. "Then I will make sure that my time here is spent complimenting you while also rubbing your husband's back so I don't find a knife in mine."

He leaves, his small battalion of soldiers following to his suite. Smart of him to arrive first. Pretty soon there will be no more rooms available for kings and the rest will be forced to camp out in the megaron. I purse my lips. Perhaps my father should curry favor by offering his own home to the arriving lords. I will send him a note this evening.

Achilles of Phthia arrives next, his battalion small but still powerful. He brings with him only ten men, each armed to the teeth and towering over everyone else in the room. The Myrmidons, they are called. Warriors said to bathe in the blood of their enemies and leave nothing to chance.

His bow to Menelaus is almost mocking, low and with a smirk. "Anax of Sparta. I will not take up your time with introductions. My men will make camp outside the walls. I will see you this evening for the banquet, but we will otherwise wait for all the other guests to arrive."

They cut a quick exit from the megaron, and that evening Helen and I stay up late, perched high on the wall, to watch them train outside. The night sky is clear, the full moon illuminating the grassy plain in which the Myrmidons train. Achilles spars with three of his soldiers at once. His movements are as fluid as the sea, as assured as pouring rain. He disarms one with a neat trick, before dropping low and swiping the legs out from underneath the other two.

"They say his mother is a sea nymph," Helen whispers, her eyes wide as she watches Achilles continue to practice. "And that she tried everything to make him immortal when he was a babe. She would anoint him with ambrosia each night, and one time tried to place him in a fire as if to burn away his mortality."

"What?" My mouth pops open. Gently, I shift on our perch to get a better view, conscious of how my leathers tug at my tender back. It's mostly healed, the welts no longer visible save for the one across my shoulders. "That would kill a child."

Helen nods. "I didn't see any burn scars on him, so I doubt it is true. They also say that she dipped him in the River Styx to make him invulnerable."

"Ligeia, my maid, told me that rumor." Now that I think about it, I don't remember seeing a single scar on the man when he was in the megaron, either. If the story is true, I should have dunked myself in the Styx when I had the chance. "Perhaps the ambrosia worked."

Ambrosia, a food of the gods. Stories say that it can bestow immortality, but the effects are unwieldy. Sometimes, it does not grant eternal life. Instead it snatches it away.

If war does indeed break out following this conclave, I might actually find out if the mighty Achilles is as immortal as the rumors profess.

Another figure catches my eye. Even in the moonlight, his copper tresses are unmistakable. "What's my brother doing with them?"

"Pyrrhus probably fits in better with the Myrmidons than with the Spartans," Helen muses, pursing her lips. "Have you not spoken with him?"

"When have I had the chance?"

"Fair enough." Helen watches my brother, sparring and laughing with one of Achilles's men. "Menelaus told me the other night that your brother is aimless and...on the brink of banishment."

I snap toward her. "Why?"

"He misses training and refuses the *paidonomos*'s instructions. Sparta is only as strong as its soldiers. Any loose stone and an entire temple could fall." Her dark brows furrow. "I'm sorry, Daphne."

I hadn't even realized until now that my eyes were watering. My vision fogs, and I climb down from our spot on the wall.

Pyrrhus no doubt blames me for his current predicament, and I cannot fault him for it. Not only did I snatch his victory not too long ago, but many, many more years before that I stole his mother from him as well. So much debt I have for my brother, and no matter the lengths I go to, I can never shake myself of it.

Next, with a hundred men each between the two of them, Alcimedes of Locris and Ajax of Salamis arrive a week after Achilles, with booming voices loud enough to shake the earth. Both tower above everyone else in the room, tall as horses with arms thicker than my skull. King Nestor is next to arrive with his two sons. Both of the younger men are scrawny, thin-as-reeds versions of their barrel-chested father. Nestor still bears the scars of his famed adventures with Iason of the Argonauts, and Heracles. Ligeia's stories of this great king were always Pyrrhus's favorites.

Many more kings and envoys arrive after that, nameless because they are lost in the seemingly endless list of guests, until the envoy of Crete strides into the megaron.

The princess of Crete, flanked by twelve guards, holds her head high and an expression of utmost wisdom that I know too well and admire. Her raven hair is piled high, just as when I first met her, held back with a diadem of pink pearls fashioned like falling rain. She carries swords on each hip, and her curved lips are painted red.

"Ariadne," Helen cries, leaping to her feet and rushing to the princess. Shock wars across the Cretan guards' faces as Helen envelopes their princess in a great hug. I walk slowly after her. And pray to all the gods watching from above that Ariadne does not reveal me.

I wonder if she will even recognize me, or if she considers me to be an enemy now. I killed her brother last summer, and she might even know that I'm responsible for her father's death as well. She only spares me a cursory glance and returns Helen's embrace.

Odysseus, who's been standing in the shadows for the arrival of every king, steps forward with a hand over his heart. "Had I known that you would be joining us, Ariadne, I would not have been so selfish when selecting a room. You may take mine."

"My thanks, Anax of Ithaca." Ariadne nods and, so quick I barely notice, winks at me. So, she does recognize me, at least. "I hope you have room for a last-moment addition to our number. I have brought my cousins."

She waves behind her and it takes every single ounce of my control to keep my jaw from dropping to the floor.

Dionysus, wearing a teal cloak and shimmering silver armor, steps forward. He cuts a hand behind his back and bows. "Dion of Phrygia."

And then Apollo, resplendent in a red chiton trimmed in gold and an *axine* strapped to his back, bows next. The double-headed axe looks sharp enough to chop off a head with a single swing. "You, lovely Anassa of Sparta, may call me Apollodoris."

So subtle. I roll my eyes. I want to bite off both of their heads.

Confusion wars on all faces in the room save Ariadne and the gods, who exchange mischievous smiles. Without thinking, I step between Apollo and Helen.

"I am going to have to ask you to leave," I say, the firmness in my voice startling myself, "unless you remove that weapon from your back."

Apollo's grin is wicked. "Care to remove it yourself?"

My nostrils flare. He is playing this game in front of everyone here?

"You may use one of the adjoining rooms attached to Ariadne's," Menelaus says, standing at last.

Servants bearing trays of wine and grapes swerve through the crowd of kings. With an eager smile, Dionysus dives after them. Ariadne takes Apollo's wrist and drags him away before I can question him.

"What was that about?" Helen asks out of the corner of her mouth, offering a pinched smile to Nestor as he passes.

I have no answer for her. Pressing my lips into a firm line, I trail Apollo across the room with my eyes.

Odysseus confers quietly to our right with Achilles. The Ithacan's face is smoothed into a placating smile. Ajax interrupts them by clapping the Ithacan on the back.

"A miracle to see you off your meager island, Odysseus." Ajax's voice is loud enough to be heard outside the palace. "What did Menelaus have to bribe you with to come here?"

"Yes," Achilles says, voice dark. "What did the Spartan king have to give up in order for you to join us? Last time I saw you was at your wedding, where you promised, loud and clear, that you were never going to leave your wife unless held at knifepoint."

"I see no knife." Ajax pretends to look Odysseus up and down. "Do you see one at his neck?"

"No, perhaps Menelaus has it pointed somewhere else. Somewhere more valuable."

"Or maybe his wife just kicked him from the bed."

Odysseus coughs, choking on his wine.

A red cloak moves in front of me, a voice cutting off my eavesdropping.

"It's rude to spy." Apollo grins crookedly.

I scoff. "You're one to talk."

"The Trojans will arrive at any moment." Apollo hooks his hands behind his back. "Artemis's dryads have been watching them ever since their ship landed in Gythium."

My stomach drops. I immediately search for Helen. She's disappeared into the crowd. I move to look for her, and Apollo catches my wrist.

"No need. Dionys—Dion watches her."

I jerk my hand away with a furtive glance to the men around us. None seem to have noticed.

"I told you I didn't need your help," I hiss under my breath.

"You said you didn't *want* it, actually."

"And you ignored my desires. As usual."

Apollo's gaze strips me. "Then tell me to leave. Tell me you don't want me here."

"I—"

"Tell me"—he draws a circle on my palm behind our backs—"and I'll leave."

My cheeks are overly warm. "You're insufferable."

His heat—his power—fills the limited space between us, making it hard to breath.

He brushes a curl from my brow, fingers warm against my cheek. "Tell me."

I lean away, despite every fiber of my body wanting to fold into him, and a hiss escapes me when my armor pulls at the welt that has yet to fully heal. I roll my shoulders, trying to keep the leather from tugging at my skin.

Apollo's dark brows furrow. "What's wrong with your back?"

Artemis heeded my wishes and didn't tell him about Menelaus's punishment. Explains why my king is still alive.

"Nothing," I answer, too quickly. "I just strained it yesterday."

"I can heal you." He reaches out.

I should let him, but he might notice what is actually wrong with my back. I sidestep his reach.

"Whether you need or want my help, it's all the same." He steps forward, so close our chests touch with every rapid, furious breath. "I'll be here."

I open my mouth to tell Apollo where to shove his concern, but his gaze snaps toward the entrance, stealing any words I might have thrown in his face.

"They're here," he bites out.

"Who?"

"Started celebrating without us?" a melodic voice asks.

All heads turn to the two men standing beneath the arched entrance. Drums thunder and the strings of a lyre snap.

The Trojans.

The men stride into the room with measured, proud steps. Jolts of anxiety ricochet through me. Without a backward glance at Apollo, I dip into the crowd to where Helen's gold diadem rises above the men.

The Trojans, from what my father has told me, control trade in the east. Their placement on the Hellespont allows them to receive everything before we do. Horses, spices, fabrics, weapons...even knowledge. The kings have no doubt drawn the Trojans into the fold this summer to discuss better trade for the Achaeans, but what do we have to leverage against one of the greatest cities in the east?

"We assumed you would be tired of revelry," Ajax says with a sneer, voice gravelly. "Word is that Trojans spend more time drinking than thinking."

"What's wrong with that?" Dionysus mutters, suddenly behind me.

Agamemnon's chest puffs out, face already flushing an angry smear of red. Something about these Trojans has him defensive, piquing my curiosity. He, like Odysseus, has said nothing about the other arrivals.

The ugly head of doubt roils inside me. I look to Apollo, and he, too, watches Agamemnon's face with a deep frown.

"We are here to talk trade, not insults." The younger of the two says, burnished gold hair a contrast to his deeply tanned skin.

The Sparta you know will be gone forever more on the bloody fields of Troy.

The Moirai's prophecy tumbles through my mind. Are these men harbingers of war?

Odysseus speaks before tensions can rise further. "Priam of Troy has so many sons, and I haven't had the chance yet to visit your fair city to meet them all. Let us hear your names."

One Trojan with black hair and deeply tanned skin steps forward, bowing to the assembled kings. "My thanks, kings of Ithaca, Sparta, and even Mycenae, for welcoming my brother and me. Paris speaks too freely sometimes. Ephor Diodorus has already offered us rooms at his spacious home down in the city, and we have accepted his offer." Helen and Agamemnon whip toward me, pinning me to the floor with their eyes. They turn again to the Trojans as the man speaks once more. "I am Hector, Priam's heir. Ignore Paris's tongue. He's still a young pup tripping over his own ears."

"I know exactly what you mean, Prince Hector," Odysseus says, eyes crinkling at the corners. "My own pup, Argos, does little thinking, but a lot of barking."

They shake hands, both men grinning. Behind Hector, his brother huffs a golden curl from his face. Where Hector is dark, Paris is blazing light; just as Artemis is the cool moon to Apollo's raging sun. Both men are just as beautiful and thickly muscled.

Paris's blue-green eyes, which he tries to hide behind the golden bangs that refuse to shake from his face, are all for Helen. He's hungry, leaning forward as if yearning to reach for her. I would slap his hand away before he even tried.

Caught lovers, especially between enemy kingdoms, are an assured way to start a war.

If Helen notices, she doesn't let it show. Ignoring Paris, she returns to the dais and calls to Ariadne, "Princess of Crete. If you're not too weary after your journey, would you care to join me in the garden this evening?"

Before Ariadne can reply, a horn rings out through the afternoon sky, turning all our gazes toward the city's gates. Helen throws her husband a questioning look, but neither says a word, quickly heading back to their thrones.

"Return this evening, our guests," Menelaus says, voice a touch more high-pitched than usual. "We will have a feast to celebrate your arrival."

Despite Menelaus's words, nobody moves to leave the megaron. The lords and kings stand aside, all waiting and watching the arched entrance with abject interest. Even Apollo's face is pulled into a confused frown, something that stirs a wave of anxiety deep in my stomach.

Whoever marches through Sparta's gates managed to not only elude Sparta's spies, but also the eyes of Olympus.

I stand akimbo, hands within reach of my weapons, and force my breathing to soften. I suck in my lips to cease their trembling and glare at the shadows seeming to grow from the entrance.

Heavy footfalls echo down the hallway toward us. To arrive so quickly after the horns, whoever it is must have ridden hard through the city, not stopping for guards or pausing to find their way. They knew exactly which road to follow to reach the Spartan palace. Either a friend or a too-knowing enemy walks toward us.

My jaw drops when he enters, long brown hair plaited down his back. The stubble of a beard grazes his pale skin and his eyes, wild and gray, find mine the moment he enters the megaron.

He strides across the amber tiles and takes a low bow before the dais. My heart thunders in my chest like a stampede of centaurs.

"Sorry for my delay, Menelaus," Theseus of Athens says, gaze returning to mine. "But even death couldn't keep me away."

CHAPTER

II

Theseus collapses in the dirt, eyes locked on mine. His blood pours into the earth. I roll across the sand and kneel by my friend's side. I flip him onto his back, ready to stanch the wound in his gut.

He chokes slightly, his eyes desperate, begging me to reverse this. The warm pool of blood beneath him stains my knees.

I stagger, reaching for the back of Helen's throne before catching myself and cupping my hands behind my back.

"But even death couldn't keep me away," a very much alive Theseus says. His eyes lock on mine, face unreadable, before turning to my king and queen.

"I see that you are no less melodramatic since last summer, Theseus," Helen says, frowning.

Apollo's normally tan face has blanched. From the corner of my eye, I watch his hand inch toward the sword at his hip. The Spartan guards around us take notice, too. They straighten, eyes zeroing in on the god who doesn't quite fit in. I silently will him to look my way, and his eyes flick toward me. I give him an infinitesimal shake of my head, praying to Tyche that the guards don't notice my movement. His hand instead rests on his hip, just above the sword, and the guards relax. Slightly.

"Well, I've never quite been able to resist an audience," Theseus says with a great laugh. His voice is different. I cannot place it. Deeper. Older.

"We are grateful you could make it." Menelaus inclines his head. "I'm afraid that there are no more rooms available and you will have to share the megaron with some of the other kings."

"You wound me," Theseus says, but laughs again. "I take no offense so long as I can indulge in a cup of your finest wine."

The mood in the room seems to lighten. A false light, if I have any say. After weeks of banquets, the kings have long grown tired of roasted boar and too-sweet wine. The songs are always the same, and by now the dancers are long tired and the guests bored with what little entertainment Sparta has to offer. We are a kingdom known for battle, not parties.

Never more evident is our lack of ability in entertainment than it is this evening. The night is filled with a simmering sense of false calm, made worse by the newest arrivals. The nervous trepidation of the gathered kings sets my teeth on edge.

Paris and Hector talk quietly with Achilles on the far side of the room, with Odysseus standing far too close to not be eavesdropping. Theseus cracks his cup against Agamemnon's, making the great kings both roar with laughter as wine spills all over their feet.

With a nod to Dionysus to make sure he's watching Helen, I cut through the crowd. Theseus's dark hair reflects in the firelight from the hearth. I follow his bobbing, laughing head. He leads me in a circle around the room, quickly greeting each of the kings, then leaving.

Muttering under my breath, I change course. I know where he will go next.

Theseus stops at the banquet table and lifts an overfull goblet of wine.

"Perhaps you should wait until after you've eaten," I say, coming up alongside him. "We both know that you're a lousy drunk on an empty stomach."

"I ate before I arrived." He lifts the goblet and drinks heartily.

Theseus, eyes blank and blood dripping in the sand, lays at my feet.

"It's good to see you." My voice trembles. "Alive."

His fingers are bare when he lowers the drink, rings left in death. "Hades sent me to help you."

"Theseus!" Menelaus beckons from across the room.

Theseus winks. "I'll find you later."

I watch his back, crossing my arms.

Apollo steps up beside me and I whisper under my breath, "What is he doing here?"

"I don't know." Apollo is still pale.

My stomach drops.

Apollo opens his mouth, but Theseus's booming voice cuts him off.

"I am pleased that you remember me from last summer, Anassa." The Athenian smiles up at Helen. "At Minos's banquet, correct?" His eyes flick to me and back.

"How could I forget the prince who spilled his wine all down the front of my gown?" There's an unmistakable bite to Helen's words. She doesn't trust him, either.

Apollo coughs and walks over to them. "Is your father, Aegeus, unwell, Prince Theseus?"

"My dear father died quite recently." Theseus sounds the opposite of brokenhearted about it. His mouth is forced down into a frown, as though he would rather smile. Nothing in his face reflects the comradery that the pair built up last summer. "He fell from a cliff into the sea."

Or he was pushed.

"I'm very sorry to hear that," Apollo says, voice stilted.

Theseus shrugs. "A bit macabre, but I always felt that he was too old to spend so much time on those cliffs anyway."

He walks away again, clapping Odysseus on the back. Apollo's shoulder brushes mine. We stare daggers into the Athenian's spine.

"Something is wrong with him." Tension radiates from Apollo.

"I'm sure being dragged from death changes a person." I twist a length of my chiton. I would know.

"Prince Hector," Agamemnon booms, attracting my attention. He raises a new cup. "Join me for a drink."

The Trojan prince's face is unreadable as he walks over, steps slow and deliberate. As if he knows he walks into a trap. He claps the Mycenaean on the back and accepts some wine. "We're not beginning negotiations already, are we? You must know that anything I say with a belly full of wine cannot be held against me. Though I think you may be far more inebriated than I."

The surrounding kings all chortle. Nestor whispers something to Ajax. I shuffle closer to attempt to catch their words.

Agamemnon's face flushes an ugly magenta. "I can hold my drink far better than any man here."

"Say that to the wine staining your sandals," Hector says, voice teasing yet sharp.

"That would be Theseus's fault." Menelaus's deep voice cuts through the ensuing laughter. "I had my dear brother here call you over to ask of your father. Why did old Priam send you and not come himself? We are all kings here."

Does the Trojan king not trust us? is what Menelaus does not ask.

My shoulders tense. Conclaves are infamous throughout history for stirring trouble. New alliances are formed, battles break out. A single wrong word and an entire kingdom could collapse.

"Our father—" Paris starts, but Hector cuts him off.

"Our father is older than any man here," Hector says, looking each of the surrounding kings in the eye. "And governs five times as many people. He sent Paris to get a taste of rule, and I because he is not afraid to share the burden."

"So what you're saying is that he is afraid to leave his people behind?" Theseus asks from the other side of the hearth. There's something off about his smile. Something wicked and twisted that I never noticed before.

I try to meet Apollo's gaze again, but his focus is on the Athenian. Dionysus and Ariadne whisper in the back of the room. Their eyes are for each other, and each other alone. I watch as he brushes a lock of her black hair from her brow, the gesture tender. An unfamiliar ache forms in my chest.

"What my brother is saying is that," Paris sneers, "our father is too busy to stoop to petty trade squabbles."

Hector grimaces, gripping his brother hard enough on the shoulder to make the young man flinch.

A fervid whisper grows among the gathered kings and princes, making the hair on the back of my neck rise. Helen stands on the outskirts, and I slink between kings and envoys toward her.

Odysseus places himself firmly between Hector and Agamemnon—he must have a wish to meet with the god Thanatos—and raises his arms. "Must we bicker already? We will get nowhere with negotiations if we insist on petty squabbling." He looks Agamemnon meaningfully in the eye. "Let us enjoy tonight at least before we descend into our animal counterparts."

"What animal would you be, Odysseus of Ithaca?" Apollo asks, loud enough for all the whispering lords to hear.

"And I!" Dionysus raises a glass.

"I would be a crane, to fly myself far from this wretched place and back to my wife," Odysseus replies, voice light. "I imagine you, Dion, would be a wasp, considering the way you gravitate to the wine."

"A fair assessment of my friend. I imagine myself to be a python," Apollo says, returning Odysseus's laugh.

"A python would be more subtle with his movements." Odysseus assesses the god I know so well. "Though much less fair."

The mood has lightened, the other men moving from where they once crowded the hearth. Apollo winks at me above their heads.

I roll my eyes and refrain from telling him under my breath—as a god would be able to hear—exactly what animal I think he is. Something that meddles and puts its nose where it doesn't belong.

Ariadne steps before me, cutting the god from my sight. She looks me over from toe to curly head. "Some new scars, I see."

I blink. "I'm sorry. About your father, I mean." I stumble over the words because, to be honest, I'm truly not sorry.

Ariadne doesn't betray even an ounce of emotion, her face still. "Dionysus told me everything. What my father did. Who he supposedly killed."

We both turn to look at Theseus, laughing with Ajax and Patroclus, who arrived with Achilles. Minos killed the Athenian. Or so I thought.

Theseus's laugh is hearty and deep, so similar to the man I knew last summer, yet the way he holds himself, the way he speaks, still makes me itch to reach for my sword.

He looks over at us and grins. The smile is pointed and feral, making my heart hammer against my ribs.

"He's changed," Ariadne says with a frown. "And impossibly alive."

Theseus's father had yet to announce his son's death, or at least word of it had yet to reach Sparta. Stories of Prince Theseus claim he's still in Thebes; I can't tell the truth without implicating myself. As if anyone would believe the story anyway.

If I close my eyes, I can still remember the sound of Minos's death. The squelch of blood and bone. I shudder.

"Do not apologize for killing Minos." She raises her chin. "I should have done it and cursed myself for all eternity as a kin-killer to stop the evil he was spreading."

I'm saved from forming an awkward reply by Helen, returning from where she'd been conferring with her husband, greeting the Cretan princess with another hug.

"How is it that you're even lovelier than last summer?" Helen holds the princess at arm's length to look her over. "Rule suits you."

"I am but a mere emissary." Ariadne straightens her dress. "My sister Phaedra has taken Crete's throne."

Helen looks over Ariadne's shoulder at me. "Have you two met before?"

I open my mouth to spill some bald-faced lie, but Ariadne cuts me off, raising her *kylix*. "Your Shield was kind enough to find me another glass. Agamemnon knocked my last one from my hand."

Helen sighs. "He's such an oaf."

Absently, I nod. My thoughts are still on Theseus. Perhaps Hades truly did send him.

Paris's gaze trails us as we circle the room, as well as the stares of Apollo and Theseus. I watch as Menelaus notes all three men and frowns. If he thinks that they lust after his wife, this could turn deadly fast. Wars have been started over less.

My throat is suddenly dry. "Perhaps we could show Ariadne your garden now?"

"A brilliant idea, Daphne." Helen tugs on Ariadne's hand. "Let's leave this sorry lot behind. I'm much too tired of men."

I follow the ladies into the growing night, entirely aware of the gods in Olympus watching our every step.

CHAPTER

12

The next morning, Menelaus and Helen wage a war of their very own. The birds outside scatter with frightened screeches as the two take their argument to the gardens. I follow, nearly tripping over a tree root in the process. My vision is foggy, a yawn threatening to rise up my throat. Sleep evaded me last night, so instead I stood in the corner of Helen's rooms, cloaked in shadow and watching each entrance.

"You're not going to attend these discussions and that is final." Menelaus cuts a hand through the air.

Helen looks about ready to spit fire. I could have sworn wisps of smoke curled from her ears and her father's lightning flashed in her white teeth. "You don't tell me what to do in my own kingdom."

"You will stay here. You will stay quiet." Menelaus jabs a finger toward the earth. "And you will listen to me."

"I have to do none of those things," Helen says, voice like the lash of a whip. "I am a daughter of Sparta, and we do not cower behind foreign kings."

They stare each other down and I would rather be anywhere than here. Even the labyrinth beneath Knossos couldn't compare to this. I shift on my feet, biting my lip, and Menelaus's gaze snaps my way as he notices me standing there for the first time.

His lips pinch together, making him look all the more like his brother. "Don't you have other places you can be right now?"

Don't you have a kingdom to rule rather than a wife to control? I want to snap in response.

Instead, I say, "My place is behind my queen."

"Will you stand behind the bed as I fuck her as well?"

I recoil as if slapped.

"When did the Menelaus I loved turn into such a monster?" Helen marches right up to his face and jabs him in the chest. Her entire body trembles with fury.

He ignores her, his hands curled into fists as he looks at me. "If you want to watch Helen, then watch her in this garden. I had better not see her in the council chamber." He turns to his wife, sneering. "If I see you there, your pretty little bodyguard will find herself lashed until all the blood drains from her back."

A rumble echoes, heralding the first of summer's storms. And Zeus's ire.

As if sensing the divine monarch's presence, Menelaus's gaze snaps to the ever-darkening sky before shaking his head. "That is final."

Without another word, he storms from the garden. Dust stirs in his wake.

Rain begins to fall then, catching on my eyelashes and shoulders. Any words of comfort I could spare for Helen are immediately swallowed by a clap of thunder. We sprint for her rooms, and Helen catches herself on a marble column as she slides through the archway.

"That rutting bastard." Panting, and ever lovelier in her fury, she says, "If I cannot go to that council chamber, then you will in my stead."

I take a step back. "I cannot. I have to stay here and watch over you."

She rolls her eyes and waves to the guards stationed in each corner of the room. "I'll be just fine."

Before I can protest, she grabs me by both shoulders. "As my protector, I need you to be my eyes and ears as well. I don't trust these foreign kings, or even my husband. Tell me what is said."

"Will they even let me in?" I thumb the hilt of my dagger.

She raises her chin, smiling impishly. "You'll find a way in."

I release a shuddering breath. To protect my queen...or my kingdom. I bite my lip.

She shakes her head. "Gods, you're protective. Flattering, but I command you to go to that council chamber."

Commands I cannot deny—again.

She adds, "Tell me *everything*."

My thoughts are a maelstrom as I march stiffly down the dark hallways to Sparta's council chamber. Irritation digs into my spine like little thorns. If Apollo really wanted to help me, he would be in Helen's room, standing guard while I follow her orders.

The council chamber entrance is unguarded. All the palace soldiers are already in the room, monitoring and waiting for any king to make a single misstep.

Quiet as a mouse, I slink over to a shadowed corner behind Patroclus, the most reserved among the crowd and the least likely to cause a stir and get me noticed. Theseus is opposite me, with Apollo and Dionysus in corners directly opposite us. Despite the safety of my position behind Patroclus, I walk between kings and lords toward the god.

"Have you talked with him yet?" I whisper to Apollo as I pass. "Or Hades? How can he be here?"

"Not yet," the god says under his breath.

I cluck my tongue. "Too busy interfering here?"

"Too busy keeping a war from breaking out in the middle of this conclave while you and Helen leer at the sparring men."

"Just ask Hades." I refuse to look him in the eye. "Can't be that hard for you to drop in on him in the Underworld now that I've restored your magic." I tilt my head, watching Theseus. "Shouldn't be hard for you to go anywhere, anytime, now."

"Why do I feel that you are not just talking about traveling to the Underworld?" He grips my wrist.

I'm not entirely sure. The words spilled from me before I could stop them. Perhaps I'm still angry that he stayed away all that time. Even though, as he's said so many times now, that was my choice.

Hector interrupts our quiet squabble by asking Menelaus, "So you called us from the opposite end of the Aegean without any thought to what you might offer us?"

Several kings cough and shift on their feet.

"If we're being blunt," Agamemnon says, hands curled into fists on the table before him. "We called you here because your monopoly on resources will not be tolerated any longer."

"Is that a threat?" Paris's face darkens, but his brother rests a hand on his shoulder.

"Why should we care? Threat or not." Hector looks to each of the kings surrounding him without a trace of fear. "We do not price our goods outrageously. Troy has always been open and up front about trade. My father assumed this would be a meeting of equals to discuss the troubles from last summer, and how our kingdom could help all of yours. But Sparta seems relatively untouched by the plights of crops around Greece."

Demeter's last gift to me for saving Olympus, still ebbing in the fields surrounding Sparta. Many other kingdoms suffered terrible droughts when her power floundered last summer. Some have yet to recover. Some kingdoms have disappeared entirely.

"And how is it that Troy never succumbed to such a plight?" Nestor glares across the table.

"Perhaps we never offended the gods as you have," Hector's words are echoed by a clap of thunder outside that makes the corners of his mouth turn up.

"Are all of Priam's sons as arrogant as you?" Agamemnon asks, almost dismissively, before turning the subject. "We are not here to argue, fellows. We are here to come to an accord."

"Why dance when we can simply get to the point?" Theseus asks, voice cutting above all our heads. He meets my eyes with a grin and turns to Paris. "Is it true that your parents left you on a mountainside, hoping that you'd die?"

Paris glares. "Isn't it true that the goddess Athena cursed you?"

"Well." The Athenian inclines his head, the movement so foreign it makes me blink. "Athena has always held grudges."

"Might I suggest not stirring the ire of the goddess of wisdom today?" Odysseus steps forward. "Or ever?"

Theseus flashes a bared-teeth smile in challenge.

A smile so unusual on his face it makes my skin crawl.

"If I wanted to listen to kings posture and preen like swans, I would have stayed home," Ariadne says, cutting a hand through the air. "Let's get to it. The kings here are jealous of your father's wealth, Prince Hector, and seek to level the playing field. What would your father want in return for a more beneficial trade?"

Apollo presses close behind her, watching Theseus from across the table. The god squints, likely trying to understand the otherness that seems to emanate from the Athenian with every breath.

"My father would like your allegiance," Hector says with a cocky slant to his lips. "And your promise to never engage in an alliance that might endanger his people. Enemies circle Greece. It is only a matter of time before one of them descends upon us."

"Spoken like somebody who has already been courting allies elsewhere." Theseus looks down his nose at the young prince. My friend was many things, but he was never condescending. I rest a hand above the dagger at my hip.

Odysseus pinches the bridge of his nose and releases a great sigh. "It seems we will get nowhere with you stirring trouble day and night, Anax of Athens."

"Indeed," Menelaus says, my king finally speaking in his own council chamber. Despite my ire with the man, my chin raises reverentially at the command in his tone. The power he wields as each of them bite their tongues. "Perhaps we should spend another night thinking on what we all want for our kingdoms. We can present our cases tomorrow morning. Tonight, we empty my stores and cellars."

"You heard the man"—Agamemnon waves a meaty hand—"off with you all."

I do not fail to notice, as I return to my queen, that the men finally left at the command of a foreign king and not the one who rules this very palace.

The music drawls above the crowd, and wine is kicked back eagerly. Only half of the kings are in attendance at tonight's banquet. The others remain outside the palace, venting their frustrations with an ever-training Achilles. My stomach is uneasy as I watch over all of them, searching for anything that might lead my kingdom to war.

Nestor and Ajax, almost inseparable, confer in a corner on the opposite end of the room. My feet itch to walk over and eavesdrop, but I can't leave Helen's side without her permission. I clasp a wrist behind my back and dig my nails into the tender skin.

"Theseus longs for war," Apollo says, stepping up beside me. "My father tells me that Athens is in no position for it, though. Athenian forces have been dwindling for decades, Minos having sacrificed most of the kingdom's able-bodied men."

"Did you get a chance to talk with Theseus?" I ask, to which Apollo offers only a curt shake of his head. "What did Hades have to say about one of his charges roaming freely? Shouldn't Theseus still be in the Underworld?"

"Hades had Thanatos look for the Athenian in Elysium," Apollo says, and I smile. That is exactly where in the Underworld I imagined my friend would rest. "His soul was still there."

I feel not even a glimmer of surprise. Instead, fear is what races up my spine. My voice trembles, despite my forced levity as I say, "That wasn't too hard, was it? I bet it took Agamemnon longer to get his feet scrubbed this morning than it took to give your Uncle Hades a visit." My gaze again drifts to Ajax and Nestor in the corner. "Can you hear what they are talking about?"

"Ajax has agreed to put his men behind Nestor's should this conclave turn violent," Apollo says, so softly I barely hear him.

A chill sweeps over me. "Now I understand why they've chosen the rooms closest to the Spartan armory. I'll have to tell Helen."

Perhaps she can assign more guards to the armory, and extra eyes on the suspicious kings.

"They're not planning anything, though?"

Apollo shakes his head. "Not yet."

"Has Dionysus heard anything?"

He chuckles under his breath. "He's been too distracted by a certain Cretan princess to do much spying."

The god in question is missing, no doubt chasing Ariadne around like a puppy.

"Does he not realize how much his love will hurt her?" The words are painful, but they tumble from my mouth.

Apollo stiffens beside me. His power is anything but still. It pulses, erratic and unmistakable. I drop my wrist and grab his own.

"Stop. They will notice."

His power snaps back, and he takes a step away from me. He doesn't remove my hand, though.

The weight of his gaze forces me to finally turn to him. His cerulean eyes are deep as the Aegean.

"Do you think I would hurt you?" he asks.

I blink. "Isn't it inevitable?"

"Isn't it inevitable," he repeats, and something buried deep inside me, something I cannot name, cracks.

I open my mouth to explain, apologize, deflect, I don't know. Anything to ease the pain that flickers in the back of his eyes.

"Ajax is speaking to Menelaus now."

My mouth snaps shut and I turn to where the pair of kings confer across the room. "What are they saying?"

"Menelaus wants to know where the rest of Ajax's men wait." Apollo inclines his head, but his gaze still rests on me. It trails down my neck. "Ajax just lied. He told Menelaus that they are in Gythium, but they are actually in the Taygetus forest. Artemis has them surrounded by her nymphs should they try to move against the city."

I purse my lips. If I reveal Ajax's duplicity to Helen, it could cause even more trouble.

As if reading my thoughts, Apollo says, "Let Artemis handle them. Focus on the enemies here."

I know I should tell him of the Moirai's prophecies. That what we are doing now, trying to stop a war, might be for naught. He should

know that the Fates have condemned his destruction and his family's—
at my hands. I curl a fist against the Midas Curse circling at the base of
my spine.

If I tell Apollo, though, I tell Artemis and consequently all of
Olympus. Zeus would kill me the moment he hears that the Moirai
have fated me to be his downfall.

I bite my lip.

"What aren't you telling me?" Apollo leans closer.

I hesitate, but I can't keep it from him. "The Moirai visited me," I
say, mouth quivering. Something gathers in the back of my throat.

Apollo follows my gaze. Paris stares morosely into a cup of wine.
He looks up to where the Spartans sit, his gaze resting on Helen a
moment longer than it should.

"Since when does Daphne of Sparta give a damn about fate?" His
voice is teasing, but his face serious.

I lift a shoulder and admit, "The Fates knew exactly what to say to
get under my skin."

The god's expression is unreadable. "What did they tell you?"

I press my lips together. As if that might keep the last prophecy
from revealing itself. He will press until I break if I let him. "If you can
keep secrets, so can I."

His eyes are dark with unsaid words. Sharp laughter drags our
attention away.

I shift on my feet and change the subject. "Can't you just, I don't
know, magic some sense into these men?"

His mouth curls into a rueful smile. "Magic some sense into
them?"

"Yes. For someone who can hear men across the room, you sure do
ask me to repeat myself a lot."

He chuckles and the tension between us from moments ago dissipates. "All that time together and you still don't understand my

powers. I can't just magic away any strain, or some sense into these men, as you put it."

"There you go, repeating some more."

"No, I could try, but human nature can't be controlled like that." He nods to the kings eating and talking below. "I could root out any potential dangers, sure. I could curse all of these men to return home and forget all of this happened. But war is a disease." Apollo raises his chin and turns to the crowd. "And these men are ripe with hunger for it."

"They will find another way." My palms are sweaty. That's what they wanted all along. They don't want peace. This is just an excuse to start a war.

The god nods. "And we need to give them none."

I nod to Odysseus, talking quietly with Hector. "The Ithacan doesn't seem to want war."

"No," Apollo says in agreement, shaking his head. "He is favored by Athena. She's no doubt told him the cost of this conclave and warned him what will happen should the talks fail."

More meddling gods. "Why do I suspect that Eris is here, stirring trouble?"

Wherever chaos walks, the goddess Eris is sure to be leading the way.

And Hermes, too. I peer into the faces of all the men crowding the room, searching for any hint of the god of tricks. His isn't the power I sense here, though.

The megaron just reeks of smoke.

Menelaus watches the Trojan, gaze as wary as my own, throwing a possessive arm over Helen's seat and thrumming his fingers on her arm. She stiffens infinitesimally, but resists pulling away and continues to watch the men banter below the dais.

A soft sigh escapes Helen, and she leans over to her husband. "My love, Hermione exhausted me today. May I retire early?"

Her voice is breathy to appease him, but her face tight. It no doubt angers her to have to ask to leave in her own palace.

Menelaus gives her a curt nod without looking over, a cold dismissal. With a hooked finger, she indicates for me to follow and my red cloak swishes behind me as we flee the audience chamber. Paris's gaze follows our every step.

Instead of returning to her rooms, Helen leads me down a narrow corridor to a different part of the surrounding gardens. Lifting her finger to her lips, Helen waves me toward a tree on the far side. We press to the shadows and creep around the tree, where a gap in the wall reveals the moonlit ground beyond.

The rain from earlier has made the ground muddy, so each of our steps stick. A partridge's call echoes through the night, letting me know that Artemis watches our backs.

"Where are we going?" I finally ask.

"To get a closer look at our dueling kings. My father always said that men lose their masks when they're threatened with getting their feet wiped out from underneath them."

We creep around a corner of the wall, and I silently both curse and thank the gods for the lack of guards stationed around the palace. Helen presses against the wall, resting her head back and breathing deeply. With a minxlike smile, she inclines her head to the corner before us. I lean past her to take a look.

Achilles, death incarnate with every breath, sweeps the legs out from under a man not ten feet from where we stand. The laughter of the surrounding men echoes into the night. Patroclus claps him on the back and hands the king a *dory*. Achilles turns, sweeping the spear. I inhale sharply as Pyrrhus steps forward next.

Spear meets spear with the crack of lightning. They dance, dodging blows and leaping back. Pyrrhus rolls beneath Achilles's swing. He springs to his feet and lances forward in a single movement.

Achilles easily dodges my brother's attack. "You are slow tonight, Spartan."

"He's no Spartan," says a soldier, making me grit my teeth. "They call him a coward *Mothakes* in the streets."

The men around them, Spartans, Myrmidons, and Ithacans alike, roar with laughter. Every part of my body coils at the feral look Achilles gives my brother. His grin is primal.

He leaps across the space between them. Pyrrhus hardly has time to dodge before Achilles sweeps the *dory* wide. Fast, so inhumanly fast, are Achilles's movements. My brother ducks, feet catching in the mud, and he falls. Like an animal homing in on its prey, Achilles pounces on him. Each *dory* is kicked aside and the two roll across the ground. There's a roar of pain from my brother that makes me want to leap around the corner and throw myself at the foreign king.

"He yields, Achilles." Patroclus yanks his friend back by the cuff as a mother wolf would do to her cub.

Achilles merely wipes the dirt from his bare chest. "Your form is poor today, Pyrrhus. Sloppy."

Even in the moonlight, my brother's face flushes a dark red. "I slept badly last night."

Achilles merely shakes his head. "Not an excuse."

"Is that how your sister trounced you so soundly?" another bystander asks, his voice raising the hair on the back of my neck. "That pretty little thing who shadows your queen? They say she saved your skin last summer, and made you pay for it this summer."

"Leave Daphne out of it," Pyrrhus says with a growl.

Theseus merely cocks his head. "How pathetic you must feel, bested by your younger sister."

I want to run over and break his nose.

Pyrrhus sneers, spitting at his feet. "My sister could—"

Theseus throws his head back and laughs at the moon. "I know exactly what your sister is capable of."

"What do we have here?" Apollo strides up to the tense circle of warriors. His eyes find mine, even in the dark, and my heart skips a beat. He tosses his sword neatly from hand to hand. "Who do I have to bribe here to let me have a turn?"

Before I can watch more, Helen tugs on my dress. "We must return. Menelaus will be looking for me."

Hopefully, Dionysus has kept the throne room from bursting into a wild fight in our absence. I throw one last glance toward my brother before climbing down from the wall. Pyrrhus claps Achilles on the back, leaning in to whisper something my mortal ears could never hope to hear.

We return to Helen's rooms just as Menelaus strides through the doorway. He looks between us, brows narrowing. "Why are you two out of breath?"

Helen raises her chin. "I asked Daphne to show me some defensive maneuvers should someone be stupid enough to kidnap me."

Menelaus's laugh is biting. "Should anyone come close enough for you to need those tricks, your bodyguard will find herself without a head." My stomach flips. He waves to the doorway through which my room beckons. "Leave us, *Mothakes*."

Bowing stiffly, I do as he commands.

CHAPTER

13

The tension in the air is so thick, you could slice it with a dagger. The kings crowd the table, elbows out and no thought for the others around them. Taking as much space as they can.

Ariadne has sidled up beside me, quiet as an adder. She looks me up and down. "Did your queen send you, or did Apollo ask that you come?"

Heart thundering in my ears, I watch the simmering men around us. "The former."

She nods, turning. "She's wise. I don't trust what will be said here, either."

Before I can ask why, Menelaus's voice cuts through the air.

"Perhaps we may behave as adults today." He looks to Theseus, then Hector, and also his brother. "Or perhaps we can all return to our wives and I may return to herding Spartans."

A tentative roll of laughter echoes around the chamber. A truce, for now.

"Now let us try again," Menelaus says. Beneath his hands, a map is painted onto the table. Greece stretches across its surface. He jabs a finger into the far right corner where Troy sits. "Hector. You said your kingdom wanted allies. We can do that, but Achaeans do not ally themselves blindly. We will make this allegiance, but will do so as if we are trading goods and services. I did not ask Ajax for the loyalty of his navy without offering the loyalty of my foot soldiers in return. My brother provides trade and goods, Nestor provides weapons and amphoras."

Hector crosses his heavily muscled arms. "And what do you propose we offer you?"

"We can offer you all that, and more"—Menelaus holds his arms open—"for more favorable trade."

"My father's prices are fair," Paris says.

Murmuring rises from the kings. They don't like the youngest of our number speaking so boldly. Ajax, red in the face, rests a hand on the knife at his hip. Dionysus sidles up beside him and offers a cup of wine. My eyes widen. Whatever the god says makes the king's hand fall away. He accepts the cup and takes a long swill.

"Yes." Menelaus nods. "But we would like more than fair. We want ideal."

Odysseus, who has been unusually silent this entire exchange, raises a hand to toy with his beard. Theseus, beside him, suddenly grins, making the hair on the back of my neck rise.

"Are you saying that we are not worth better prices?" He steps into the light. "That you would offer our enemies to the south and east better rates?"

Odysseus steps forward and I straighten. These discussions are about to get more interesting.

"That is not what our friend Menelaus asks, nor is it what Prince Hector implies." He stares down the Athenian. "What Menelaus wants to ask, and is perhaps being too subtle with it, is if Priam would be willing to drop the tax upon Achaean ships as they travel up the Hellespont to the east."

"What would we have to gain from that?" Paris asks, and his brother cuts him a dark look. The younger prince wisely bites his tongue, but has already revealed the Trojan weakness. The Hellespont.

"Perhaps Odysseus is wise to dive right to the point." Menelaus nods to the Ithacan. "We Achaeans would like your father to drop the tax on our ships. In return, we promise a thousand ships to your aid should war ever stir in the east."

Paris ignores the dark look from Hector and asks, "And if war comes to Troy from the east, and we haven't dropped the Hellespont tax? Will you abandon us?"

Theseus's teeth shine in the torchlight as he says, "Perhaps we'll simply wait and enjoy the spoils of your downfall."

I step forward to wipe that smug look from his face. Someone grabs my wrist behind my back. My head snaps up and I meet Apollo's gaze. Tension radiates from him in waves.

"More threats?" Hector raises his dark brows. "I guess the Achaeans have never been known for subtlety."

Agamemnon gives an exaggerated sigh. "We're back to this? How subtle would your father feel a knife pressed to your throat is?"

"My father," Paris bites out, "does not take idly to threats. Keep them up, and the tax upon the Hellespont will never be removed."

I assess the younger Trojan prince anew. He looks down his angular nose and meets Agamemnon's eyes with not even a trace of fear. His feet widen almost imperceptibly and his hands drop to his sides. Preparing for a fight.

Standing in front of me, Achilles moves to match the Trojan's posture and I do the same. My gaze flicks to the entryway beside me. I'm ready to return to Helen's room at a moment's notice.

"There will be no need for violence in my council chamber," Menelaus says, voice low and lethal. "The kings here have all drawn up a list of potential trades for your father to consider, in exchange for dropping the Hellespont tax."

Paris straightens. "And should we refuse?"

Menelaus meets his gaze evenly. "That is entirely up to you."

"Entirely up to Paris?" Helen scoffs, throwing herself onto her furs and reaching for a precariously balanced bowl of grapes. She pops one into her mouth and says around the food, "He gives that child too little credit. Hector and Paris knew when they arrived that the Hellespont would be a point of contention. It has been for a hundred years. They're not going to be intimidated by Achaeans. They have the entire world behind them, and the gods' blessing." She flips onto her back. "They say the walls around Troy are impenetrable and taller than mountains. Only a god could have made them so."

"You've never been to Troy?"

"I've only ever been on a boat once. We traveled to Crete last summer." Her gaze is distant as she looks up at the sandstone ceiling. "It was wonderful. The sea was lovely."

"Why did you marry him?" I ask, and immediately regret the question. Too forward. We're not such close friends yet.

Without hesitation, she answers, "Because Menelaus was the first person other than my brothers to make me laugh." She rolls again onto her stomach. "I was thirteen when I met him, and he five years older, when he came for Agamemnon and Clytemnestra's wedding. The other men just gawked and ogled. I was heir to the greatest army in Greece. Five years after that, we were married." She flicks a nonexistent piece of lint from her sleeve. "And another five after that and he hasn't made me laugh ever since." She sighs and throws herself from the bed. "Call Korinna. I need to get dressed."

"I thought you were going to sit this banquet out?"

Her smile is sly. "And miss seeing the Trojans throw my husband's offer back in his face?"

A forest-green silk chiton is wrapped twice over her lithe frame, accented with golden eagles, swans, and the *meander*. The silk sighs with each assured step as she leads me to the megaron, chin held high and shoulders squared. A warrior in her very blood.

The final banquet is subdued when we arrive, despite Dionysus's best efforts for a raucous celebration, I'm sure. The music has yet to start, the servants milling about with empty trays. Kings stand in stiff silence and boars roast atop the hearth. Waiting to see if this will be a celebration or a blood-letting.

Sure enough, Dionysus sashays into the room, wearing a too-long maroon chiton that threatens to tangle around his legs. He winks at Ariadne, who raises a *kylix* in response.

"The tension in the room is so thick, I could choke on it," the god announces. "Loosen up your tongues with some libations."

He swings an arm, wine spilling in a semicircle around him. There's a flare of power, so subtle it could be confused with an errant breeze. Kings surge forward, collecting two cups each and downing them in quick succession.

Dionysus's coy smile could rival the Sphinx.

The air seems to still. Footsteps echo down the long corridor leading to the megaron. The Trojans step into the sweeping hearth light, wearing their leathers atop dark blue chitons, taking wide, swift steps across the room.

Dressed for battle, they stop a few feet from the dais. Each rests a hand on their swords. Helen's face is unreadable.

Menelaus's voice, booming and gravelly, asks, "And what do the sons of Priam have to say for Troy?"

Hector meets his gaze evenly. "Troy accepts the offer of the Achaeans. The tax will be lifted."

A great sigh passes through the room. Menelaus nods, eyes stony, and the music starts. A joyous melody trills through the air from a spirited musician. No doubt they had no wish to witness the bloodbath that could have occurred should the Trojans have refused my king.

Apollo catches my eye above the now raucous crowd and raises a cup. A war deterred.

For now. The prophecies of the Moirai are not so easily dissuaded.

Jubilant laughter echoes around the great chamber. The men clap one another on the back and begin to feast. I ignore an offered platter of meat and figs, attention focused on Helen. With a great sigh, she stands from the throne and descends into the crowd. I'm forced to follow, hand on the hilt at all times. This is to be my future. Helen's shadow, not just her Shield.

Ajax stops us with an outstretched arm and I flinch. I should chop the limb from his body for being so assuming in Helen's own palace.

He doesn't even bow. "Where is the lovely *anassa* off to now?"

Helen stiffens. "Why do you care, Anax of Salamis?"

"Just want to make sure you don't do anything"—his gaze peruses her body in a way that makes my skin crawl—"foolish."

"The only foolish one here is you," Helen says, stepping toe to toe with him. She looks him up and down for a mere second and steps past without another word.

She gives the other kings we pass nothing more than a courteous smile until she reaches the Trojans. The men around us seem to quiet, waiting again for some explanation.

"I'm glad that we could come to an accord." She crosses her arms. "I would have hated for our two kingdoms to be enemies."

Hector raises his brows. "Frankly speaking, your highness, we both know that any animosity wouldn't have been contained to just our two kingdoms."

"No," she agrees. "Our allies are far and wide."

"As are ours."

She relaxes her arms, letting one drop to her side as the other accepts a *kylix* of wine. "Tell me more about Troy. I doubt the stories do it justice."

Paris clinks his cup against hers. "Depends on the stories. But I cannot go about spilling all of my city's secrets."

Helen's lips take on a coy slant. "Can I bargain for some, then?"

"I'm afraid my brother and I have done enough bargaining this day, as far as Troy is concerned." Hector comes up behind Paris and claps his brother on the back. He gives the younger prince a meaningful look. "Don't spill too many of our secrets while I go find Achilles."

Helen and Paris stare each other down over the rims of their cups after Hector leaves. Paris turns to me. "You're the famous Shield, aren't you?"

"None other," I reply, bowing slightly. "Though I think calling me famous would be a bit of a stretch."

"We're staying with your father in town." Paris waves a hand toward the entrance. "Ephor Apidanos stopped us on our way in and offered some rooms. It seems that a little bird told him of a shortage here in the palace."

Helen, raising a brow, turns to me.

I bite my lip. "Well, I didn't want you to have to sleep on a cold floor."

"Agamemnon would have made a mockery of our suffering, I'm sure." He inclines his head. "My thanks."

"You should have seen Daphne last year during *Carneia*," Helen says. "She runs faster than a deer."

My cheeks must be magenta by now, they burn so hot. "If that was truly the case, I would have beat the deer to the forest and not the other way around."

"Do you run, Helen?" Paris asks, voice high with eagerness. "They say that the women of Sparta are even faster than their men."

"Well, I won't argue with that assessment," she says, with a demure glance down to her feet.

He leans in, cupping his mouth and whispering, "Between us three, Spartan women and Trojan men would be a well-matched pair. Your strength and our smarts, together as one, and we could rule the world."

A startled laugh escapes Helen. "Are you flirting with me, young prince?" Her face is the image of mock solemnity. "A dangerous thing to do in another king's palace."

Paris does not look away. "This is your palace, not his."

My eyebrows rise high as my hairline. Silence stretches between the pair as they appraise each other. Helen's entire chest lifts with each breath, a blush painting her lovely cheeks pink. I huff, blowing a strand of curls from my own cheek, startling them both.

"Well, Prince. This conversation has certainly been eye-opening." Helen looks anywhere but at Paris. She waves over a servant for another cup of wine. "I really must find Odysseus. I want to ask him how my fair cousin Penelope likes Ithaca."

Paris opens his mouth to reply, but she's already spun away, emerald chiton flaring behind her. We find Odysseus conferring quietly with Ariadne and Dionysus in a corner of the room. Agamemnon's booming laugh snaps all their heads up.

Ariadne rolls her eyes. "Must men always need to be heard from every corner of Greece?"

"Only when they're insecure about other, *smaller* things," Helen says with a wicked laugh.

"You two are going to make me insecure about the tone of my voice now," Odysseus moans.

Helen sees right through him. "You would never fret over such an inconsequential thing."

Despite the celebration, something is missing from the party. I look around, frowning. Nestor and Ajax clink drinks as Achilles and Paris discuss a fresco. Theseus laughs with Agamemnon.

The Theseus of before was cocky, his movements languid as if he had all the time in the world. This Theseus holds himself straight, almost on his toes, and moves too swiftly, hands always within reach of his weapons and his gaze pinning everyone he speaks to. As if on the hunt.

The Theseus of last summer fought with an axe. This one carries a sword.

With fingers bare of the rings he always wore, he pinches his chin, squinting at the Mycenae king's next words. Theseus never fiddled with his face before.

This Theseus is an imposter. Trepidation shudders gently through my body.

Helen turns to me. "Shall we return to my rooms? I want to catch Hermione before her nursemaids bring her to bed."

As we're leaving the megaron, something burns in the base of my spine. I turn and catch a blackened gaze.

The imposter watches us leave, mouth open and hungry.

I don't have to wait long for Helen to fall asleep. The moon is full above the palace, filtering in to paint the floor and walls silver. I'm on the hunt, my footsteps quick and silent, as I stride down the corridors toward the megaron once more. With three guards posted at every entrance and window of Helen's rooms, I shed the cape of trepidation that follows me and don a mask of deadly intent.

Drunken snores echo across the banquet hall, interrupted by farts and sleepy muttering. Dionysus slipped a little drop of Lethe into the cups being served. Oblivion paints the kings' unconscious faces. When they awake, they will remember nothing of their dreams.

Hand on the hilt of my sword, I step nimbly between each sleeping man. Their guards, likewise drunk, rest against the walls and steps, heads hanging back and drool slipping from the corners of their mouths.

I search the prone forms crowding the amber-tiled floor. Odysseus and his men lay near the exit, and the Ithacan king's arm is draped across his rising chest. I step around them, careful not to accidentally nudge an arm or leg.

The hearth in the center of the room still blazes, warming my cheeks and bathing the room with an orange glow.

I can make out all the faces in the room, and not one belongs to Theseus.

My heart skips. I tighten my grip on the hilt of my sword. The shadows on the far right of the room beckon to me. That corridor leads back to Helen's room. I quicken my steps.

If I left Helen to search for Theseus, only to have him circle back and take her from beneath my nose, I'll—

My arm is nearly yanked from its socket as I'm hauled around a corner. My body slams into a wall, forcing the air from my lungs. A shadowed face looms before me. Before I can scream, a hand slaps over my lips.

Theseus towers over me. His smile is wide and wicked. "Looking for me?"

I nod against his hand before yanking my head away. I hiss, "How are you alive?"

"Maybe I never died at all," he says, voice deepening with each word, sharpening and twisting. He grows even taller, his hair straightening. The moonlight peeks through a window, illuminating a face from my nightmares.

"I've been waiting a long time to kill you," says Ares, the god of war.

CHAPTER

14

Fear grips me tight by the throat. "How is this possible?"

"You returned the Olympians to the height of their power." Ares's hand—the one Lykou ripped off last summer—is encased in molten black metal and caresses my neck. Sweat slicks down my spine. I doubt I will get the chance to dagger him again. "And that includes me."

Oh gods. If Ares was masquerading as Theseus, Nyx and Hermes could have been playing anyone the entire time.

I try to tear away, but his fingers suddenly tighten on my throat. My breath abandons me. With impossible strength, he lifts and slams me into the wall. The palace seems to shake.

I claw at the hand holding me. Stars form in front of my eyes.

Ares leans close, sneering. "I will enjoy every second of watching you fight for your life."

I jam my thumbs into his eyes. My nails dig in, cutting deep.

He roars, dropping me. I gasp for breath and shuffle away on the floor as fast as I can. He stomps toward me, ichor dripping down his face. His eyes are already healing and they zero in on me with murder in their dark depths.

"What is going on here?"

I climb to my feet and spin, dagger raised. Odysseus stands there. Moonlight frames him, painting his face in shadows. As subtly as I can, I sniff, scenting for the lavender of Nyx. Only the sea and the sour tang of olives emanates from Odysseus as he steps toward us, genuine confusion flickering across his features. He turns to Ares, once more in Theseus's form.

"The young woman seemed lost," he says, holding his hands out, placating. The metal hand has been replaced by one too devoid of calluses and scars to not be an illusion.

"In her own palace?" Odysseus raises an eyebrow. "Seems unlikely."

"I don't care what you believe or don't believe." Ares-as-Theseus sneers, dropping the friendly facade. He considers Odysseus, a large vein in his throat pulsing. Finally, he inclines his head and says, "I will see you both on the morrow. Athenians know when to take their leave." He glares at Odysseus. "Even if those of Ithaca don't."

He strides past us into the megaron where soldiers and kings snore.

Heart thundering in my chest, I turn to my would-be savior. "My thanks."

Odysseus shrugs. "It seems like you handled the situation just fine, but I thought it best to interrupt before things got too heated."

"Had you arrived earlier, you would have saved me a massive headache." Though not too late to see Ares in his true form.

Any mortal would be horrified right now. Perhaps Odysseus isn't quite mortal, either. My brows narrow with suspicion. He couldn't be Hermes. The smell isn't right. Besides, Hermes wouldn't have stopped Ares from ripping my head from my shoulders.

"As always, your wise counsel is appreciated." I move to step past him and return to Helen's chambers, yet Odysseus grabs me firmly by the wrist.

"What did he want with you?" he asks, eyes stormy even in the dim light. No, not another godly deceiver.

I should cower beneath the gaze of a king, but I've never even bowed my head to a god.

"What do all men seem to want?" I raise my chin. "To control women."

I yank my wrist away and sprint to Helen's rooms.

I slam into Apollo's firm chest the moment I barrel through the doorway.

He lets me drag him into the garden and says, "Your face tells me that there is much I need to know."

I hiss, "He's here. Ares is here."

Apollo's face blanches. "What?"

"He's Theseus." I grab his upper arms, nails digging into his dark tan skin. "He's pretending to be Theseus."

Before the god can react, a deep voice fills the garden. "We have to do something."

Both of our heads snap upward. My hands grip Apollo's hard arms and he drags me into a dark corner.

The voice continues on the other side of the wall. "There is nothing left for us to do. They agreed to the proposal."

"Then make a new offer," the deep voice—Agamemnon—replies. "One they cannot accept."

"This is why you cannot secure bargains for Mycenae, brother." Menelaus's unmistakable voice echoes through the night. "You have no tact. No strategy."

"And you bend too easily," Agamemnon says with a snarl. "Has hiding behind Sparta's army made you so weak?"

I angle my head to hear better. The Brothers Atreus must be passing on the other side of the wall. Their voices are barely above a whisper, but the silent night makes their words flitter high into the sky.

"We must be careful." Menelaus's voice is rough. "We cannot incite a war with Troy blindly. We need to find a way to rally our allies against them."

A war. Even though the Trojans agreed to the Hellespont agreement.

"Then we fabricate an excuse." Ares's voice—unmistakable, coated in death and decay—is coaxing, filling me with an icky sweetness. I'll kick myself from here to the Underworld for not recognizing it sooner.

Apollo stiffens, his arms tightening around my waist as he holds me in the darkness.

"We cannot let them leave," Ares continues. "We need Priam to declare war. It is the only way."

A moment of silence passes. I lick my lips.

Finally, Agamemnon says, "If we cannot get Priam to declare war, we will declare it on them."

"But the Hellespont—"

"Damn the Hellespont," Agamemnon snaps. "We can fabricate some other excuse for capturing the princes. They attacked you, they assaulted your wife, they insulted the gods. Anything. Priam isn't here, and the other kings in this palace are just biding their time waiting for a war."

My heart thunders in my chest, so loud it must be heard by Hades. I hold my breath and wait for my king to call out his brother's madness.

Finally, with a silky smoothness that makes the world fall from beneath my feet, Menelaus says, "If we're to capture them, we must be quick about it. No loose ends. Kill the *ephor* and his family."

The Trojans are staying with my father. He means my family. My heart leaps into my throat.

Agamemnon says something else that I cannot hear, but the last of his words are unmistakable. "I will send Ajax and his men to capture them. Nestor will distract Odysseus. You prepare a cell. The deed will be done before the moon sets."

The pair have moved on, past my line of hearing. Apollo's supernatural hearing can still catch their words, and his skin grows paler by the second.

"You must warn your father," he finally says. "The soldiers will be at his home soon."

I grab Apollo's arm and dig my nails deep into his skin as I hiss, "Go to Ligeia. Warn her. I need to tell Helen."

"Helen?" Apollo likewise catches my wrist. "Why bring the queen into this?"

"Because her husband threatens to drag my people into war," I say, raising my chin. "And she could be the only one who can stop him."

CHAPTER

15

Birds screech outside Helen's rooms, their calls piercing the inky darkness that blankets the night. A hawk and partridge create a frenzied symphony so insistent I can hardly think.

Hurry. Hurry. Hurry. Artemis seems to speak through their cries.

When I hurriedly tell Helen what I heard in the garden, her eyes glaze over with pain. That pain crumbles in the next breath, resolve taking its place. She sits among her furs, fingers digging deep into the plush fibers.

She grits her teeth. "We have to get the Trojans out of the city."

I blink. "Shouldn't you talk to your husband first?" And urge him from this madness.

Helen shakes her head, sending her chestnut waves tumbling, and throws the furs from her legs. "He won't listen to me. Never has. He has dragged the good name of my kingdom through the muck for long enough. I won't let him bring war to our doorstep."

She yanks a worn chiton from a chest and throws it over her

shoulders, dragging her hair atop her head in a hasty bun. "We must hurry and warn them. Your family will be implicated as well."

A fact that I am—too keenly—aware of. My heart thunders in my chest, palms laced with sweat.

"We must be quick." I collect my weapons, strapping them to my body. "But first, a plan."

"I have one." Helen raises her chin. "But do you promise to protect and serve me, no matter the cost?"

Even if it costs me my family, she doesn't specify.

I have no choice but to say, "I already have."

Helen leads me to the gardens, throwing one last glance to the window behind which Hermione sleeps. A pained expression passes my queen's face, there and gone in an instant, before resolve settles once more onto her beautiful features.

We leave via the same fortuitous gap in the wall, and as we round the corner, my stomach somersaults. Achilles and his men are not here, not sparring as they have been nightly. What—or whom—has pulled them away? Either they are helping Agamemnon's plot or are being distracted elsewhere.

We take our hidden path that leads to the city. We slide down the rock embankment, pebbles gathering in our sandals. Helen tumbles once and I catch her. We're already running on before either of us can catch our breath.

A hawk screams high above us, and I yank Helen behind a bush. Just in time, we press against a root-covered rock. A dozen horses thunder past, riders wearing Mycenaean boar's tusk helmets. Agamemnon's men have already been dispatched.

"We must hurry," I hiss and drag Helen away from our hiding spot.

My father and mother, Ligeia, and even my brothers could be caught in Agamemnon's machinations. Hopefully Apollo warned them in time.

My family's faces flash before my eyes as we sprint through the brush. The riders will no doubt take the winding road to my parents' house, but a more direct path cuts through the fields. The wings of Hermes do not ease my passage, though. We trip and tumble each step of the way, luck against us.

The earth comes up to meet me, rocks digging deep into my knees and palms. Gritting my teeth, I haul myself to my feet. Helen surges forward. She races across the field, me at her heels. We break through the first line of houses, our sandals slapping the streets. A thunder of hooves heralds the arrival of Agamemnon's men somewhere behind us, so similar to my chase through Foloi Forest, the centaurs out for my blood.

We turn a corner, one last street to go until we reach my home. A hand hooks on to my arm, yanking me hard into a wall. Another hand slaps over my mouth as Helen is likewise dragged into the shadows beside me.

"Shh," Lykou says, gently releasing me. "It's just me."

I spin to face my friend. "What are you doing? I have to get to my family."

"They're safe." Lykou looks to Helen, being held by Apollo. "They're in my house with the Trojans. It will only be a matter of time before Agamemnon's men start going door to door."

I whirl on Apollo. "You dragged his family into this as well?"

"No, I did," Lykou says, hauling me by the arm into the building. "We only have a few moments before all of us are skewered on their spears."

We hurry into the shadowed kitchen of his home, both of our families and the Trojans pressed around the table in the center. A collective gasp escapes all of them when Helen enters the room.

All, except the Trojans.

"Your husband has put all of our lives at risk." Paris strides forward, going toe to toe with Helen.

I shove myself between them, glaring down my nose at the prince. "Your quarrel is with Agamemnon."

"And we came here at the behest of his brother. Assured that we would be safe." Hector shakes his head. "Spartans are always itching to draw blood. Wanting war after war to sate their bloodlust."

"Neither man is Spartan," I bite out.

"We accepted Menelaus's offer," the Trojan continues. "We were prepared to drop the Hellespont tax."

"Apparently, that is not what they truly want," Paris mutters under his breath.

"You can seethe all night," Helen says, voice sharp. "But I'm here to right the wrongs of my husband. I'm here to help you escape Sparta without bloodshed, if you promise not to retaliate against my kingdom."

"Or what?" Paris draws his sword. "You'll turn us over? We might as well take you hostage right now to assure our own escape."

"Only a fool would threaten the queen of Sparta under the noses of her own soldiers." I draw my own sword. "Especially ones from Sparta. I will cut you down before you lay a hand on her."

Lykou draws his *dory* beside me, crouching and pointing the spear at Hector. The elder prince raises his palms placatingly.

"My brother spoke in anger." Like facing a wolf, Hector slowly draws his own sword, then places it on the table between us. "We would very much appreciate your help in escaping."

He gives Paris a reassuring nod, and the younger man places his own weapon on the table.

"Don't cross us twice," he says, his voice hoarse.

"A threat I will not even deign to take seriously." Lykou turns to

Apollo. "How do we get them out of the city? Menelaus will have already sent men to the gates."

"The river." All of our heads snap toward my father, who steps forward. Apidanos is wrapped in a dark cloak, black curls mashed to the side of his face as if he had been dragged from bed. "We will travel along the Eurotas. It will protect and carry us to the coast, and Menelaus's hounds cannot track us if we make sure to stay by the water."

"Peneios?" Apollo looks my father over and a wide grin splits his face. "It cannot be! You wily bastard! My father thought you had left us for the southern continent."

My mind is blank as I look between the god of prophecy and my adoptive father. "Peneios? As in the...the river god?"

With my words, a light seems to grow behind my father's eyes. Cerulean and blinding like a sudden dawn. Ephor Diodorus nods, his face solemn. "I was ordered to stay here. To watch over the gods' chosen. You hadn't yet arrived, my dear Daphne"—he walks slowly around the table, raising a smooth hand to cup my cheek—"but when Ligeia brought you and your brothers to me, I knew."

My mind is awhirl. "But how? Why?"

"*Who* ordered you to stay here?" Apollo's frowning now, all mirth gone from his face.

"A story we have neither the time nor the strength for." Apidanos—no, Peneios—drops his hand and turns to the small group. "We must move fast. There will be boats waiting for us."

"The river isn't deep enough for boats," Lykou protests.

Peneios waves a hand. "The Eurotas is as deep and swift as I will it."

Lykou helps his parents pack their bags, and the Trojans keep watch for the soldiers that are no doubt looting my father's home.

Peneios turns to my mother. "I'm sorry, my love. We must leave Sparta behind or they will kill us both. I cannot protect you from the dark forces that drive them."

To Helen, I say, "It is not too late. You can still return to the palace. Menelaus likely doesn't even know you're gone."

A stubborn gleam fills her eyes. "I will see these Trojans to safety."

I want to throttle her. "Go back to the palace, *now*."

A crashing sound echoes through the night. A door being kicked in. Yells echo outside.

"We don't have time for this," Apollo says roughly, guiding us toward the back garden. Screams outside dampen his next words. "We need to leave now or even the queen will lose her head."

The house next to ours erupts with screams.

A deep voice echoes into the night. "The Trojans have dishonored your king and queen. Find them!"

Ares.

Lykou and I lead everyone as quietly as possible between buildings, sliding our bodies through cracks in walls. It is less than a mile from here to the Eurotas, but every step feels like a thousand years between here and the river. Lykou's mother sobs from the back of the group. Lykou's expression is unreadable; the Trojans' faces are stormy, no doubt pulled between fear and rage. Helen keeps tripping behind me as if Sparta reaches up and grabs her ankles, begging her to stay.

We reach the last line of houses, perched on the edge of the Eurotas, and I catch Helen by the wrist. The others continue past us, hopping into the waiting boats.

"You can still return to the palace," I say, voice ragged as I nod to her home, which is a dark shadow on the horizon above us. "Return to your daughter."

She glances at me, face haloed by the golden firelight flickering from the palace above. She takes a step, then another.

I want to shove her. "Go. Go now!"

She takes another step. A yell snaps us both around.

"They're on the river!" a Mycenaean soldier yells and points from a dirt plateau above us.

Cursing under his breath, Apollo shoves the first boat into the current. Lykou's sobbing mother and father hold each other, my parents with them as Lykou guides the boat down the river. My father turns just before they pass a corner, glowing a vivid blue and waving a hand to us.

"See them to Gythium." Helen takes a step back from me. "And from the port city, find them a ship to Troy. I can buy them some more time."

The Trojans hop nimbly into the second raft. Apollo moves to shove it into the current, yanking me along. I jerk my hand from his grasp.

"Wait." I look to Helen. "My place is here. Protecting you."

Before she can take another step from me, a figure cloaked in black emerges from the bushes behind her.

"They're here!" Ares-as-Theseus yells. "And so is your queen!"

I only have enough time to raise a dagger. His sword shatters it with a single blow. I roll away from his next swing.

Helen has the good sense to run behind Apollo, who raises a sword.

My heart shutters to a stop, but I don't have the luxury of hesitation. I pull out my *dory* next. He dives forward, aiming for my rib cage. I bat his swing aside. We dance around each other.

"The queen is here!" soldiers call from the bushes around us.

Ares's voice above all the others cries out, "Anassa Helen has betrayed Sparta!"

"You better get in that boat, Helen," Apollo whispers from behind me. "Or they will kill you."

"They won't kill their own queen." Helen steps forward. "Stop this madness and do as your *anassa* says."

"My *anassa*?" Ares sheds Theseus's skin. It ripples away as he stands to his full height, a wicked grin slowly splitting his face. An ethereal red glow spreads from behind him, pulsating in time to the thunder of my heart. Blood drips from the god of war's hands as he towers above us. "You never want to tangle with her."

Fear, cold and quick, grips me by the throat.

Apollo steps past me, imbued with a golden glow. He and Ares alight the riverbank.

"Get Helen in the boat now." Apollo's voice is gruff. He holds his sword aloft, pointing it at his brother's face.

"The river won't keep her from me." Ares circles Apollo, stepping closer and closer to Helen.

I take my queen's hand and drag her away. "If you don't climb in that boat, Ares will kill you."

Her face is a deathly pale, horror filling her eyes as the god of war steps ever closer.

Ares drags his sword up and down Apollo's, making the metal screech into the night. "You think you can take me on, brother?"

An arrow hisses. It skids beside my feet. Another volley follows. Hector raises his shield and they thud against the surface. "They're escaping!"

I nudge Helen and she falls into the boat. It groans as I shove it across the sand. My muscles burn, protesting against the weight of all three of them. My curls flutter against my cheek as an arrow hisses past my face. It imbeds itself in the wood.

Swords ring into the night. Ares dives past Apollo toward us.

With one last push, the boat is free of the beach and the current sweeps it away. I leap in, the entire boat tilting. Water splashes our legs. A dull pain ricochets up my spine. A yelp escapes me, and I double over.

"Daphne!" Helen screams.

"Hold on!" Paris grits his teeth and steers the boat deeper into the raging Eurotas.

I turn, my entire body aching with the effort, and find a bent arrow beside me. The gold of the Midas Curse shines through a new hole in my leathers.

Apollo roars my name from the shore. Before I can look back, we're swept around a corner. The gods' glow dims, the crashing of the river drowning out all other noise. Helen grips my hand so tight my bones protest. Hector and Paris struggle to steer.

A branch reaches up from the depths, snatching the oar from the older brother. Our boat starts to spin. It tilts, more water splashing in. Helen screams. I wrap my arms around her, holding her against me as the river threatens to tear us apart.

"Do not fight the Eurotas, Daphne." A voice, melodic and familiar, sings through me. My father's voice. *"Trust the river."*

The boat is spinning faster now. Paris's oar is torn away. The world around us is a dark blur and I'm drenched, waves of icy water pouring over us all. I try to scream, but water rushes into my mouth. I cough, choking, and more seems to flood in.

A sudden impact jars me. My bones sing, and we're all flung forward. I keep my arms locked around Helen as we tumble into the river.

Hope flees me in a colossal wave. The emptiness it creates is flooded with more water, the river dragging me down, down, down.

I kick, but Helen is a leaden weight, limp in my arms. Her body drags me into the dark abyss of the Eurotas. My throat burns. I release one final scream and the river comes crashing in.

CHAPTER
16

They will welcome their own destruction with open arms.

A gull screams directly into my ear.

I throw myself to the side. One of my arms is weighed down, though, and I can only pull myself so far. Sand plasters half of my face, my hair a wicked tangle of knots and branches across my battered shoulders. I open my eyes, blinking against the sudden rays of dawn.

Blearily, I turn to look at what holds me to the ground.

One of my arms is still firmly wrapped around an unconscious Helen.

I yank myself free and push her onto her back. The steady rise and fall of her chest pulls a relieved sigh from my lips. I rake my fingers through my curls, dragging them from my face so I can assess her wounds.

She appears unhurt, a miracle from Olympus no doubt. The bird screeches again, whipping me around. A seagull flaps its wings, hopping on the sand around me. Just beyond it, Paris and Hector groan, dragging themselves up the beach. Hector vomits, an entire lake's worth of water escaping his poor stomach.

Beach.

I blink and stagger to my feet. A gasp escapes me.

"How are we—" I raise a hand to my mouth.

To my right, the Eurotas pours into the sea, glittering and stretching across the horizon.

"A last gift to you, my child."

I spin, kicking up sand that sticks to my drenched legs.

My father stands in a boat as it slides up the beach. Lykou hops out and helps his mother. Peneios, god of rivers in Greece, gives my own mother a hand as she climbs from the raft.

Helen coughs. I drop to a knee and ease her into a sitting position, clapping her back until she spits up a lungful of water. Her chiton clings to her frame, and I peel off my cloak, wrapping it around her shoulders. It does little to cover her, as the red fabric is shredded in many places. She still pulls it tighter with shaking fingers. I squeeze her shoulder before again climbing to unsteady legs.

I stagger across the sand toward where Peneios watches me. "Why didn't you tell me who you are?" I ask, my voice rough.

"What would it have gained?" Peneios looks to the Trojans beyond me. "I'm sorry I was not able to save your boat. Other powers greater than my own were at work last night."

"What of my brothers?" I search his face, but it is carefully blank. "Your sons. Will they be safe, or will they be hunted down?"

Peneios blinks. "Your brother Pyrrhus was among the soldiers searching for us last night. He will be fine."

"And Alkaios?" I spit a mouthful of sand. "Will he and his children be hunted down as traitors as well?"

"No," Helen says, stumbling up beside me. "At least not outright.

Menelaus will try to use them to find us. Ephor Diodorus has had a target on his back for a long time, anyway, and my husband will use that as leverage. Help them hunt us, or die."

"My brothers will choose death before betraying their own family," I say, though the words sound sour in my mouth.

"Are you so sure?" Helen inclines her head to me, searching my face, before turning to my father. "Learning your true name explains your hold on power, Ephor Diodorus."

"Trying to grasp the machinations of the gods is like trying to stop the tide." Ligeia limps toward us, an arm flung over Lykou's shoulder. "The same could be said of any of the gods."

Apollo. I turn toward the river, tracing its swell inland. Hopefully Ares hasn't killed him. The thought of him dead threatens to fracture something within me I long thought tucked away.

I return my gaze to Ligeia and tilt my head in my father's direction. "Did you know who this man truly is?"

She barks a laugh. "Of course."

I nod, gritting my teeth. To be the last to learn anything is... infuriating. "I guess that is neither here nor there. What we need to do now is find our next steps."

Helen appraises me. Even still drenched and bedraggled, her face is lovely and her eyes clear. "We find the Trojans a ship home."

"I concur." Hector has come to stand beside Helen. He grips a bicep, a stream of blood running through his fingers. "We must also make a plan for you, your highness."

Helen blinks. "I will go home, of course."

"To death," Peneios says gruffly. "Certain death. Your Spartan heritage will not protect you from the wrath of the Brothers Atreus."

"Hermione." A sob escapes Helen, and she cups her mouth. "I can't just leave my daughter. I would rather die than abandon her."

"She is safer without you." Hector grimaces, releasing his arm and rolling a shoulder. "Menelaus would no doubt use your influence as an excuse to hurt her. Without you, he can claim her completely as his daughter."

Another sob breaks free of Helen. Tears roll down her cheeks, cutting streams in the dirt and sand.

"The Trojan speaks like a king." Peneios appraises Hector. "And true. Hermione is safer without you, Helen. The Brothers Atreus are not the only ones seeking vengeance now. The god Ares will kill both you and her if it meant inciting the war his goddess desires."

"Where will I go?" Helen turns tear-filled eyes toward me. "What will I do? What is the point of living without my daughter?"

I pull her close, wrapping my arms around her shoulders. Great, heaving sobs wrench her entire body. I rest my chin on the top of her head. "You will survive for her."

"And Troy will take you in," Paris says. He cuts off Hector's protests with a wave of his hand. "An answered debt for saving our lives."

"Troy?" Helen looks up, her cheeks red and splotchy but still impossibly lovely.

Paris nods, his face earnest. "To Troy."

Our bedraggled group staggers down the beach. From the Eurotas, we're only a few miles from the port city of Gythium. I don't think I'll ever understand how the magic of the gods works. Between Peneios's control of the river and Olympian intervention, only a day has passed since we left Sparta, judging by where the sun rises on the horizon.

Before we can stumble into the city, my father stops walking. He plants his feet firmly, an arm wrapped around my mother's shoulders. He waves the others ahead of us.

"This is where we must part, my dearest." Sadness swells in the deep lines of his face.

"Come with us." My voice cracks. "The Trojans will surely take you all in."

"There is no place in Troy for me." Peneios grabs me by the shoulders. "I am a god of Greek rivers. My place is here, where my power is strongest to protect your mother and Lykou's family."

I grind my teeth. "No. You belong with me."

"You are well versed in battling alone. You do not need me." He turns around. "Tear my *peplos*."

"What?" Of all the absurd things I've heard today…

"Tear it. Directly down the middle. There is something I must show you."

I do as he says, shredding the black fabric. A gasp claws from my throat.

A moving tattoo—like the roosters and snakes on Hermes, and the vulture emblazoned across Ares's chest—is drawn across my father's back. A map, but not of mountains, cities, or temples. Blue lines, undulating and twisting, reach from his shoulders to the backs of his thighs. Rivers, streams, and lakes.

"This tattoo," Peneios says, "is a token of an old age. A relic, if you will. Keep track of the gods that have these, and those that don't."

"Why? What do they mean?"

He turns back around without answering, nodding to the waiting group behind me.

"We'll miss you, Daphne," Révna says, my mother's eyes shining with tears.

"I will see you again," I say, lips trembling.

"No, you won't." Ligeia comes to stand beside my adoptive parents. "But you'll see *me* again. Someday."

An ache forms above my heart. I look between my handmaid and Peneios. "Have I earned a name yet?" I raise my chin. "The name of my true father."

"Not yet." Peneios shakes his head and that ache grows sharp. "Not unless you wish to die."

"What do you mean?" My hands tremble.

Ligeia points to the Midas Curse atop my clavicle. "There are many things Zeus would kill you for knowing. Find a way to remove the Curse, and all your questions will be answered soon enough."

With a last hug from each of them, my mother's scent of lilacs mingling with the earthen musk of Peneios and the sandalwood of Ligeia, I turn to the waiting group. Lykou's sobbing mother breaks from the others with her husband, following my adoptive parents into Gythium's surrounding forest.

Lykou matches me step by weary step into the city. The Trojans and Helen are too recognizable, so they wait on the outskirts while Lykou and I secure our passage. My friend's handsome face is drawn with pain as we walk along the harbor, skirting piles of fish and sea sludge.

"How many more times must we flee by ship at the gods' behest?" Lykou asks, more to the sea than me.

"Hopefully only once more." I hail down a sailor to ask for directions, then say to my friend, "You do not have to join us, Lykou. You can go with your parents and mine. Make sure they find a new home somewhere safe."

"Your father—that god will make sure they are safe." Lykou cuts a hand through the air. "I will protect my *anassa* to the end." He looks sidelong at me. "And you."

I don't press for more. We find a ship to take us at least halfway, to the island of Scyros, and from there hope to find passage to Troy. We cannot afford to wait in Gythium for a better option. Messengers from Sparta will be here by this evening, and by tomorrow the city will be crawling with Achaean soldiers.

We sneak our fleeing royals aboard the ship as the sun begins its descent beyond the horizon, just before the captain's sailors release their oars into the deep green harbor. I don't stay to watch my home drift into the distance. Instead, I tread lightly down the sodden stairs of the ship.

Helen sits on the floor in a shadowed corner, knees tucked against her chest. I ease myself down beside her. A single sob escapes her before she buries her head in my chest and curls into me. I wrap my arms around her trembling shoulders.

The sea coils and splashes against the bow of the ship around us. Nothing needs to be said between us, our grief shared. Grief for a life earned and forever gone.

CHAPTER
17

I fall asleep holding Helen, but when I wake, my arms are empty. The ship's salt-crusted floor is no longer beneath me, and the sea air no longer sticks to my skin. I wake to brilliant white light and silk curtains.

Artemis reaches down to help me to my bare feet. I grimace at my reflection in the cold marble floor. My hair is a tangled rat's nest, with reeds poking from the knots and mud clinging to my face.

"Always getting into trouble," the goddess of the hunt mutters.

"And always cleaning up after Olympians," I shoot back.

Her answering smile is crooked. She points to the hole in my leathers, the Midas Curse shimmering through. "You're welcome."

Grumbling under my breath, I follow her to the pantheon. Dread echoes my every step on the way there.

Angry voices greet me before I even step into the wooded throne room. A fire crackles, smoke singeing my nose.

In the center of the space, Hephaestus pounds a great hammer into an anvil above the hearth, spitting sparks into the dawn sky. Around him, gods balance weapons and argue. Athena and Hera are in each other's faces, both dressed in shimmering battle leathers. The Queen of Olympus's leathers are painted amethyst, and Athena's are a dark blue. Poseidon, with his fists on his hips, towers over the working Hephaestus. Zeus and Hades argue in a corner, the latter's wife quietly conferring in an opposite corner with her mother. Dionysus sits by himself, staring morosely into a cup of wine.

They all ignore us and continue their petty arguments. From the opposite end, Apollo strides through a pair of thrones toward me.

"You're alive!" The happiness in my voice startles myself.

A small chuckle escapes him. "Of course I am. Ares has always been more bark than bite."

There's a dark bruise on his sharp jawline, and a gash that slices his left eyebrow in half. His palms are sticky with black blood—no, ichor. Checking for other wounds, I pat his body and pull down the top of his chiton, revealing the pale brands the centaurs gave him last year.

"You kept these?" I let go of his clothes. "Can't you heal them?"

His gaze is unreadable. "When you've lived as many lifetimes as I have, scars are a memory not easily erased."

Swallowing, I change the subject back to the god of war. "Where is he?"

Apollo shakes his head. "Only the Fates know."

The gods have ceased their chatter and bickering, looking upon us with a mixture of disappointment and even fury. I cannot bring my gaze to meet Poseidon's, shame eating away at me as my failure echoes with the steady drum of my heart.

The gods all turn as one, taking their seats around the pantheon. A chorus of rulers so similar to the menagerie of kings that crowded Helen's palace.

"You can all fix this," I say, marching forward. I curl a hand over my heart. "You can use your gifts."

"We can't, Daphne," Apollo says softly, head hanging.

"Make the kings forget and go home. Return Helen and me to Sparta." I wave to the world below the pantheon, covered in roiling clouds. "I gave you all your powers back. Use them."

"It is beyond our power, girl," Aphrodite says. She hugs her chest and begins to pace. "We cannot wipe the memories from a hundred people at once. We are powerful, but nothing like that. Each action has a reaction. If we wipe all the minds but forget one, they will all remember eventually. And the war will begin anyway."

"But we did everything we could to *keep* Troy from going to war."

"You had one task," Zeus says, a rumble of thunder growing above us. "Protect Helen. And you managed to drag my daughter into a war instead."

The Sparta you know will be gone forever more on the bloody fields of Troy.

Something cold and hollow thumps in my chest. "But we freed the Trojans. They agreed to not fight with Sparta, and to dropping the Hellespont tax."

"You're not so stupid as to believe the Achaeans ever gave a damn about that tax," Poseidon says. I turn in his direction, my face growing hot. "Or were you and Apollo too distracted in each other's arms to realize that the whole debate was a ruse? A mere diversion while the Achaeans plotted to incite a war with the greatest kingdom in the world."

The whole thing just doesn't make any sense. The Achaeans would be throwing away all trade with the eastern continent, and for what? Only the gods can say, and I doubt if I ask they would tell me.

I try anyway. "What do the Achaeans have to gain from a declaration of war? The cost should they lose is too damn high."

"Obviously, there are darker powers at play here." Athena thrums her fingers on her blue-painted vambraces. "Ones that give the Achaeans reason to believe they would actually win the war."

Apollo speaks up. "Ares was there. No sign of Nyx and Hermes, but Ares stirred up trouble just fine without them."

"Which brings me back to my other point." Poseidon turns to his nephew, upper lip curling beneath his shining blond beard. "Were you so distracted, yet again, by the entice of a woman that you put the safety of our entire family at risk? Did you learn nothing from last summer?" His smile twists with cruelty. "Or was her rejection not clear enough?"

"Let Apollo live, Uncle," Artemis protests, but he silences her with a severe look.

"Do you not tire of protecting him?" The god of the sea straightens. "Of spending all your life watching your brother's back?"

Artemis isn't cowed. She raises her chin, straightening, and tosses her mahogany hair over a shoulder. "That's what family is for, which you would know if there was a single loyal bone in your body."

"You don't get to lecture me about loyalty, Artemis of the Arcadia."

Curiosity flickers through me, but it's quickly snuffed by a flash of lightning above. All turn to Zeus again, his gaze fixed on Apollo and me.

"You have failed, Daphne Diodorus." His words are cold and edged with finality, brokering no argument. For how could I argue, when he goes on. "You have sentenced your people to needless death at the walls of Troy, and my daughter among them. Helen should have stayed in the palace that night, leaving you to guide the Trojans to safety."

Despite the thunder rumbling above, I say, "I dare you to tell her that yourself. She gets her stubbornness from you."

Silence echoes now in the pantheon, broken only by a chuckle from Dionysus. Zeus's tan knuckles blanch as they grip the arms of his throne, the dark marble fracturing beneath his grip.

"As I said"—he stands, each word like a clap of thunder—"you have failed in your task of protecting Helen, even with our help."

My next words are a death sentence. "Then don't you mean that *we* failed to protect Helen?"

Pain, like none I have ever known, shoots through me. I scream and crumple to my knees. My back arches as lash after lash of lightning hits me. Rain begins to fall in the pantheon. It drenches me, and each drop is another stab of light and pain. I scream again, the cry tearing my throat apart. Dimly, as though down a deep, very dark cave, Apollo roars my name.

Behind my clenched eyelids, a flare of golden light bursts around me. Finally, both pain and storm stop. My hands sing as they clap the marble and I tumble forward.

My chest heaves, but no air will come in. Each breath sends a spasm throughout my entire body. Apollo rests a hand on my back, and the pain ebbs, unforgivingly slow.

"When you're done lapping your own sweat from the floor, rise." Zeus's voice is like rocks colliding.

My fingers curl into fists against the cold marble. I shove myself to my feet.

"Well, that was delightful," I mutter, smiling sweetly.

Zeus's scowl must be ingrained in the very lines of his face. "You are lucky we still owe you a debt, young woman."

And don't you forget it. I will my face into an unreadable mask, once again the Shield of Helen and nothing more.

"We will gift you with another chance," Hera says, gaze icy as always. "And you will continue in your task of protecting Helen. At any cost."

She stands, followed by the other gods. They each pick a side of the pantheon, the gauze and silk and leathers of their clothes sighing as they choose sides. Athena and Poseidon join Hera, while Aphrodite,

Artemis, and Demeter stand opposite. Hades and Persephone join Zeus in the center, with the latter giving me an apologetic look.

"Are you"—I swallow, at a loss—"really picking sides in a war where the life of Zeus's daughter is at stake?"

"There is more at stake in this war than Helen's safety," Hera says with a sneer.

"Then why are you divided?" I cross my arms. "You are gods of Greece! You shouldn't want the Achaeans—your people—to go to war!"

"What Hera means to say," Dionysus drawls, still reclined on his throne, "is that some of us are not willing to put their egos aside for even the slightest moment, while the rest of us have a true understanding of what is at stake here."

Hera blushes a furious red. Before the queen of Olympus can spit sparks, Zeus looks to Apollo.

"Come, son." He gestures to his right, where Hera stands. "Join your family."

Apollo's warmth leaves my side as he walks, movements stiff, around the hearth and stands beside Artemis.

Opposite Hera.

"I will not tolerate insolence," Zeus warns, "from either of you."

"I think we've stated our case quite clearly." Artemis widens her stance, as if bracing for a fight.

"We will defend Troy." Apollo looks to me, a golden light framing his bronze curls. "Alongside Daphne."

"Her failure to protect my daughter has a cost," Zeus says, not even glancing to where I stand. "She will fight for Helen alone."

"No." Apollo stares his father down. "She won't."

"Then you leave me no choice."

I brace myself for his power again. He takes a careful step, then another, toward his wife. He stands shoulder to shoulder with her and

Poseidon, staring across the fiery hearth at the remainder of the gods. They take each other's hands. Apollo straightens beside his sister, growing pale.

"For your insolence"—Zeus looks from Apollo to me—"and her failure, I now bind your power."

A blast of silver light flares across the pantheon. It hits Apollo square in the chest.

A startled scream bursts from my lips as he crumples. The muscles in his shoulders and arms twitch, skin pulling taut. His head flings back, eyes and mouth clenched, as if he is fighting with every fiber of his immortal being against the curse now placed upon him.

Suddenly, he sprawls forward with a gasp. Now it is my turn to reach for him. I nearly jerk back at the feel of his skin. Where he is normally scalding to the touch, his back is now cool.

Shock grips me by the throat. "What did you do to him?"

"Apollo is now the weakest god of Olympus," Aphrodite says with a breathy laugh.

Artemis's lips curl back. "They've bound him."

"Is your ego so small that you would condemn an entire kingdom to ruin?" I hardly believe it's my own hollow voice that rings across the pantheon.

"This is not our doing," Zeus says, waving a hand through the air. "You brought this on Troy."

"Me?" I ask, voice sharp with indignation.

Zeus looks to me and raises a hand. Bolts of lightning dance between his fingertips.

I scoff. "There is no pain that you could inflict upon me that is greater than the shame I now carry." My voice rises with each word. "You don't deserve the throne you defile."

The king of Olympus has raised both hands now, swirling storms rising from his palms.

I glare down my nose at them and say, "I regret ever helping you last summer. You don't deserve the worship of mortals."

Before I can blink, his power blasts me from my feet. Pain explodes in me, racing like branches of crackling hoarfrost from my toes to each hair on my head. I bite down around any scream that may steal from my lips.

I will not give him that satisfaction this time.

I tumble through the air. My back does not slam into the marble. My head does not crack into the floor.

I thud into sand. My breath steals from my lungs in a gasp.

Stars dance before my eyes, twinkling across the light blue sky. Gulls scream around me. Groaning, I flip myself over and crawl farther up the sand.

"Daphne!"

I look up just in time to watch Helen sprint across the beach toward me. She slides to a halt, body slamming into mine with enough force to knock the air from my chest yet again.

"I feel like we've done all this before," I say under my breath.

The beach this time, though, is littered with pieces of ship. Helen's dark hair is plastered to her face, seaweed threaded in the strands. Down the line of golden sand, sailors retch seawater and curse the gods. Lykou, likewise drenched, helps Hector to his feet. Paris staggers toward us.

I look for Apollo, but I can't find him or any of the gods on the strip of beach. My fingers curl into the sand. Whatever they did to him, whatever it means to be *bound*, it can't be good. I release a shuddering breath.

"What happened?" I turn my face up to Helen, squinting beneath the blaring sun. "What happened to our ship?"

"We were cursed by Poseidon, obviously," Paris says.

"You don't remember?" Helen assesses me. "You must have hit your head quite hard."

"Our ship was captained by a madman is what happened." Lykou heaves slightly, clutching his abdomen. "He sailed right into that bloody storm. It chewed us all up and spit us out onto this blasted beach."

"Either madman," Hector says, limping up to us, "or gods blessed."

He looks inland. I follow his gaze, and a ringing starts in my ears. My mouth falls open and I reach a steadying hand to the ground.

Shimmering golden temples arc into the sky around us, before which black statues stand. The closest is a reflection of Apollo, standing proud and tall, a sword at one hip and a lyre atop the opposite shoulder. Across from his temple, Aphrodite's temple beckons. The statue of the ethereal beauty is an incredible likeness, the marble hewn so that her flowy chiton leaves nothing to the imagination of the lithe body beneath. Ten more temples stand behind them, and beyond, surrounded by a wall of gold and red, is the greatest city I've ever seen.

"Is that...?" Helen's mouth drops open, her eyes impossibly wide.

"Yes," Hector says, pride filling his voice. "Welcome to Troy."

Part Two

Troy

CHAPTER
18

W e drag our bedraggled selves from the beach. We don't walk
for long before cries resonate from inside the temples. A *salphinx* echoes into the cloudless day, followed quickly by the thundering of a hundred hooves.

Their wild ride kicks up so much dirt that it nearly blocks the city
from view. Or at least it would, if it weren't for the wall that towers
over a hundred feet high.

"Incredible," Helen says, looking up at Troy. Her focus quickly
switches to the horses barreling toward us. "Perhaps we should have
stayed in Gythium."

I share that thought. Would this war still loom on the horizon if
Helen had merely stayed behind? Agamemnon, Menelaus, and even
possibly Ares were driving for a war with Troy, no matter the cost.
I could have perhaps kept my queen safer in a life on the road rather
than at the hands of the men riding toward us.

Now I also don't have Apollo at my back. His steel would have been a comfort, his gifts a chance to turn the tides of war, and his presence...Despite everything, I would have welcomed him by my side. I can at least trust him to defend my back, even if not my heart.

We don't even pass the last temple, Hermes's statue watching from the doorway, before men and women begin filing out and the riders skid to a halt before us.

The horses prance, fighting their bits, as heavily armed men leap from their backs. The men's armor is a collection of iron and bronze scales, their arms and legs covered by maroon cloth. The nearest one lifts his helmet. His dark eyes land on the crown prince. "Prince Hector? We were not expecting you back so soon."

"A great many unexpected things happened," Hector says acidly.

The soldier's eyes pass over all of us, lingering on my sword and Helen's face. She takes my red cloak and pulls it up over her head. Too late, though. In his eyes, you can see the moment when all thoughts eddy out of his head. His face goes slack.

"Prince." He gapes. "Is that the Anassa of Sparta?"

There's a collective gasp from the crowd around us, even the sailors who ferried us across the Aegean. Lykou rests a reassuring hand on her shoulder, glaring at any man who dares to come too close.

"May Troy be more hospitable than my own kingdom," Helen says, lifting her chin.

Three more men dismount and offer their horses up to us. Lykou leads Helen to the closest pair, but I stop short of mounting my own. A leather and cloth contraption weighs down the horses' backs.

"What is this?" I ask, unable to keep the childish curiosity from my voice.

"Ah, yes. I forgot that Achaeans have yet to discover saddles." Paris puts his foot in a leather hook that dangles on his horse's side, using it to heft himself up. He waves to the contraption before pulling the reins tight. "We traded with the Eastern Continent for these. Very useful over long distances."

I don't point out that, to Achaeans, Troy is considered the East. I may have traveled every plain of Greece, but of the world I still have much to see and learn.

Paris claps the back of my horse. "Hop up. Your ass will thank you later."

My ass does no such thing. I find it harder to gauge my horse's rhythm with the contraption between me and its back, and my feet end up tangling in what the Trojan prince calls the stirrups the entire ride to the city. We ride up to the gates and my irritation gives way to awe.

The carved golden doors swing wide, revealing a marketplace larger than Sparta's palace and *gymnasion* combined. Fabrics, foods, weapons I've never thought possible are held up for us to see as we thunder farther into the glorious city. Buildings painted red, blue, green, and gold rise above us, decorated with a hundred frescoes and separated by cerulean fountains. I'm assailed with unfamiliar scents and colors, an entire new world within these walls.

We ride deeper and deeper into the city, ascending a towering acropolis atop which a palace sits. The dusty road gives way to white stone, and we grind to a halt before the green doors of the palace. I dismount carefully, then help Helen down from her own horse.

Before we can enter the palace, the doors groan open and a royal entourage sweeps through them—led by the ancient King Priam.

His face shares the wisdom of Hector and the gilded beauty of Paris despite what must be at least eight decades of time upon his shoulders. Even from where I stand, I can see the calluses dotting his palms from the twin swords that cross his back. These are a people who will protect themselves to the very end.

I lower my chin reverentially before kneeling. Helen continues to stand.

There's an elderly woman at his back, Queen Hecuba, as King Priam assesses Helen. His face inscrutable, he turns to his sons. "I take it that negotiations didn't go to plan."

"To say the least," Paris replies, bitterness unmistakable. Servants rush forward, bearing new clothes and large bowls of scented water. Paris and his brother shed their sea-stained cloaks and dip their hands into the water, flicking the drops on the sandals of everyone around them.

Priam looks to the growing crowd, his sons, and then us three Spartans. "Come."

At the single word, the crowd disperses with curious titters. Priam turns and strides into the palace, leaving us to follow in line. The Trojan palace is open and airy like those atop Olympus, decorated everywhere with fine art, unlike the dark halls of Sparta's own. Splashing echoes down a far hallway from what must be the famous baths of Troy, and birdsong like I've never heard before trills from the small gardens that open out over the city.

Trojan soldiers, bedecked in leather and bronze armor, follow closely on our heels. Their spears, much thinner than the *dory* of Sparta, point at our backs. I dare not reach for the sword at my hip, the only remaining weapon on my person after tumbling down the Eurotas and across the Aegean.

We're led to a large chamber. The floor is tiled with green and blue and gold, a map of Greece at our feet. The brown Cithaeron mountains where I faced down the Sphinx press beneath my heels when Priam holds up a fist, halting us in our tracks. He turns, emerald chiton swirling around his ankles.

"Tell me everything," he commands.

*   *   *

The Trojan princes spare no detail. Priam stands at a balcony, gripping one wrist behind his back as he overlooks Troy. Night has long fallen, and the sky is dotted with glittering stars. His city below is awash with flickering oil lamps and echoes with laughter and cheering. The Trojans are celebrating the return of their princes.

If only they knew the dark tidings Hector and Paris brought with them.

When Hector gets to the part where we finally washed ashore, Priam turns. His face is angled down, considering the tiled map beneath his feet. It stretches farther than Greece, with even Mount Kazbek looming in the far corner of the room. The aged king passes Prometheus's mountain, and stops at the mouth of the Hellespont.

His shined sandals dig into the blue tiles there. He cuts a frustrated hand through the air before hooking it again behind his back. "The gods taunt us. They aided in your sea crossing, but nearly got you killed in Sparta. The whole matter is clouded in the meddlings of the Fates."

They are selfish bastards, I don't say. *They care only for the worship of mortals and not of blood spilled on account of the wars they stir.* Except the few who stood apart, including Apollo. I can only guess what Zeus meant when he claimed to bind his son.

"We will need to call upon our allies," Hector says. He points to the space below Troy. "Rally them behind us to make the Achaeans think twice before declaring war on us."

"I don't know how long the gods held you in their power, my dear lad," Priam says, voice haggard and weary, "but the Achaeans have already declared war."

Helen's mouth falls open. "What are their reasons?"

Priam shakes his head. "They claim my sons stole you from the palace. That they killed the Athenian King Theseus while doing so. Menelaus says his honor is tarnished, and has called upon all the kings of Greece to serve justice."

Apollo didn't actually kill Ares that night, but I'm sure the god of war made it look like he did. The whole thing reeks of Hermes's and Nyx's trickery, and whatever other gods align themselves with them.

Hera, Athena, and Poseidon stood on the side of the Achaeans. Perhaps they also stand shoulder to shoulder with Nyx, though Zeus doesn't know yet.

"In fact," Priam continues, now standing in the center of the Aegean, "the Achaeans have begun their journey across the sea. A thousand ships, my spies say."

My stomach plummets to the depths of Tartarus.

"That's impossible," I whisper.

"Not impossible, but indeed unlikely." Priam glances up sharply, gaze narrowing as if noticing me for the first time. He looks me over, eyes lingering on the sword and my ruined leathers. "You're the Spartan soldier who helped my sons escape."

"My Shield," Helen says, stepping forward. "She is the one who discovered my husband's treachery."

Priam cuts her a stern, unforgiving look. "I would stay silent, if I were you, Anassa. I have yet to decide what to do with you." He returns his focus on me, mindful of my fingers now curling into fists at his harsh words to my queen. "But you. It would gain me nothing to return you to your *anax*. And my son's mention of Peneios is concerning, but would explain why the hand of Olympus hovers over us all."

If only he knew the depth of the truth to his words.

If only *I* knew.

He walks closer, sandals whispering across the fresco, until he stands toe to toe with me. He smells of spices I don't recognize. They make me uneasy.

Before he can speak and push me further over the edge, I say, "Whatever you decide to do with Helen, you must also do with me. I am her Shield, and I will remain at her side."

"Indeed." King Priam clicks his tongue. "I guess the choice is now Helen's."

Everyone turns in the room to look at her, waiting.

A queen to possibly her end, Helen raises her chin. "I have no place left in Sparta but, if you will let me, I will stay here and try to negotiate a truce with my husband. Barter for the safety of your people."

"Even if he demands your head?" Priam's words stir a maelstrom in my gut.

"That is something Agamemnon might ask. Not Menelaus." If Helen is afraid, she does not show it. "He will want to punish me slowly, painfully. Death is too quick for him."

I would die before letting anyone harm my queen. My friend.

"Spoken like someone who understands her husband quite well," Hecuba says, speaking for the first time. Her eyes, black in the firelight, are cold. "The *anassa* might be useful to our plight."

"We are in no true danger," Priam says. "Troy's walls are blessed by the gods themselves, stone by golden stone imbued with their power. There will indeed be blood on all of our hands no matter what we decide to do with Helen and her Shield." He shakes his head and walks again to the balcony. "I am not cruel, though. I did not raise Troy into the greatest city ever known by sentencing women to death because of the atrocities of their husbands. No, we will not abandon you to Menelaus's machinations, Helen of Sparta."

When he turns again, the aged lines of his face are deeper than before, trenches of exhaustion. "You will help us weather this storm."

*　　*　　*

Helen, Lykou, and I are led to our suite of rooms, resplendent with gold silk curtains, multiple lit hearths, and its own pool. The Trojan soldiers shut us in without a word, locking the doors with a firm click. The sound echoes in my ears.

"Both prisoner and political ally," Helen says, voice soft.

"At least we have a bathing chamber to ourselves," I say, trying in vain to lighten the mood.

"Good." Helen sniffs. "You need it."

"You're one to talk. You smell like a fish."

Our laughter echoes around the chamber, but there's a pained edge to it. Lykou doesn't join in our forced mirth. The stubble on his jaw pulls taut, a frown furrowing his face in deep shadows. His expression pained, he walks to a balcony and stares into the growing night, his back firmly to us.

Wordlessly, Helen walks to his side and wraps an arm around his waist. She gazes out at the ocean. As if she can see past the line of a thousand ships gathering far away.

"So we are either to give ourselves to my husband and certain death"—she sucks on her teeth—"or aid in the Trojan fight against them."

"You know that I cannot allow you to give yourself over to them." The gods would not allow it, either.

"*We* cannot," Lykou says, continuing to stare out into the night.

Helen turns, the dried seaweed still clinging to her hair. "It would be the honorable thing to do."

"Where is the honor in that?" I stand on Lykou's other side. "We can still fight for Sparta."

"The Trojans would never allow it."

"We can fight alongside both," I press. "We can refuse to spill

Spartan blood. Instead focus our help on taking down Agamemnon's or Ajax's armies."

"We shall have to see what the future holds for us, Daphne." She meets my eyes. "Know that I am grateful for you both. For saving my life. Theseus—or whoever that man parading as him was—had every intention of killing me that night."

"Or making it look like you killed him."

She nods. "It appears that we are nothing more than pawns in the games of the gods."

A role I'm all too familiar with.

The darkness on the horizon taunts us. Nyx waiting in the periphery as always.

I stare it down. I have bested the goddess of night before.

And I will do so again.

CHAPTER

19

I dream of blood and sand. Both coat my hands and knees, chafing beneath my armor. My helmet is heavy and too warm. Across a battlefield stained with gore, Pyrrhus waits. He balances a *dory* in one hand, then the other.

"See reason," I say. My voice is too small and insignificant. The screams of dying men surround me.

Pyrrhus seems to hear me above the din. He lowers the *dory*, but his face is still dark beneath the bronze Spartan helmet.

"You will be the ruin of Olympus," he says.

Bitterness, like old goat milk, coats the back of my throat. "We should be preparing for war."

"That's exactly what we're doing," Helen says, raising her chin for a better look at her reflection in the body-length bronze mirror. "Part of war is making allies."

She's dressed in a gossamer rose silk gown, with pink diamonds dripping from her braided hair like a cascade of flowers. She wrinkles her nose at the jewelry. By contrast, I wear a simple green *peplos*, bound at the waist with a silver belt. A breeze sweeps into the room, swirling both of our skirts and ushering us from the safety of our room.

Helen has given Lykou the day to explore the city. She thinks he should learn Troy's delights; I've told him to search for places to hide Helen instead. Should things take a more disastrous turn than they already have.

"I don't see how attending a play helps us make allies." I follow as she turns from the room, and we're quickly flanked by a trio of Trojan guards.

She drops her voice so that they cannot hear. "We must appear interested in their kingdom. Even if we would rather be twirling knives." She flicks a meaningful glance at the sword hanging from my hip.

I swallow back any tart replies. The city is loud with song and cheers. People crowd the alleys and streets, walking quickly for the theater at the top of the city. It's built into the wall, the seats steep and already crowded with excited Trojans. People from all corners of the world seem to have joined for the play despite the looming threat of war. They pass masks of all colors down the narrow line of chairs.

Seated across the theater from us, Priam bounces a child on his knee. Hector collects the boy from his father and hugs him to his chest. His wife sits on his other side, beautiful even from this distance in a bright yellow chiton. Around them, the common people of Troy laugh and cheer along with the play.

"The Trojans do not sit above their people," Helen says, watching them as I do.

"Lykou learned that the royalty of Troy only live in their palaces because Priam's grandfather built them specifically for the monarchy. Even then, I guess some of the princesses and princes of Troy live in more common homes," I say.

"Admirable." Helen's voice is soft and honest. "If I could tear down the Spartan palace and live among my people, I would gladly do it."

Paris sits beside a woman with wild hair and dressed in bright red.

"I didn't know Paris was married," I say to Helen.

The queen shakes her head. "His sister, Kassandra."

A child tugs on Helen's hand and points to a pair of actors wearing masks painted green and blue. "Those are sea nymphs."

"Oh yes," Helen says. The morning chill has prickled our legs and arms, but she seems to not notice. "Nereids."

Her face pulls tight as the little girl continues to cling to her hand. The child's hair is so similar to the tumbled brown curls of Hermione back in Sparta.

The Nereids sweep from the stage and are replaced by bulls, chasing actors dressed as butterflies until they tumble off the stage. The stands erupt in laughter. I can't even force a chuckle. My gaze is drawn to the wall behind us, and the armies encroaching far beyond it.

An actor dressed as Poseidon rides across the stage on a carriage drawn by Nereids. He waves, face pulled into a smile greater than I bet the real god has ever shared. Except perhaps with his many lovers. I barely refrain from crossing my arms and slumping in my seat. This is going to be a long play.

A fake Aphrodite, resplendent in a pink chiton and trailed by a seashell, follows Poseidon, but where the sea god leaves the stage, she merely dances around the center. Men whistle and cheer. An overly large bosom has been painted onto the goddess of love's dress.

"Ridiculous," Helen says, leaning backward. "How can Aphrodite stand to let them portray her like this?"

"I feel like Aphrodite probably likes being portrayed at all." Vain woman.

I'm eating my words, though, when the next scene unfolds. Ares, evident by the blood-painted fake swords hanging from his hips and helmet instead of a mask, lifts Aphrodite into the air with an arm around her hip and buries his face in her chest.

"Okay, I doubt she likes that."

The noises of their fake lovemaking grow more obnoxious by the second. The catcalls and whistles in the audience swell.

A hideous mask lets us know that Hephaestus, carrying a hammer and net, stomps across the stage. He throws the net over them.

"I catch you, Ares and Aphrodite," he announces. "This will never happen again."

"I would rather die than stay married to a monster," Aphrodite declares.

The audience murmurs their agreement.

"I'm inclined to grant your wish and kill you to end this matrimony, as only a god can kill a god," Hephaestus says, considering the pair. "But living with your sins will be an even crueler punishment than the Furies could dole out."

He rips the net from them. Ares flees and the crowd boos.

"Coward," they call him.

"Less spine than a jellyfish," one man yells.

I want to sink into my seat. The city should not call Ares's wrath upon them more than it already is.

Aphrodite flounces away but stops in the center of the stage. She holds a hand up to her ear, nearly hidden by the ostentatious mask covering half of her head, and then whatever she hears causes her to recoil. The actor begins waving their arms wildly, and down swoops Eros, his wings ivory and fluttering behind him.

"Ah, my favorite tale."

I nearly jump from my seat. Apollo sits beside me, elbows on his knees. Despite the mask covering his handsome features, I would recognize that voice even on a raging battlefield.

"Did Zeus hurt you?" I demand, keeping the touch of hysteria from my voice. "How did you sneak up on me? What did he mean that he was binding you?"

Apollo ignores my questions and nods to the stage. Eros is flying off at the behest of his mother. "There are so few stories of my family that end happily."

I pinch his leg and say between my clenched teeth, "Tell me what happened to you up there."

"My father bound my powers to his will," he says, turning. Something feral and dark flashes in his eyes. "I'm even more powerless than you saw last summer."

I swallow a petulant remark reminding him that I don't need his help, a lump forming in my throat. "How do you . . . undo it?"

"*I* can't." He turns again to the stage. His voice is suddenly lighter. "Did Ligeia ever tell you this story of Eros and Psykhe?"

"Of course. I'm not dropping this discussion, but will let you enjoy the play." I narrow my eyes at him. "Have your answers ready once the actors bow offstage."

He reaches over and pinches my chin. "If you can catch me first."

I hate how nonchalant he always is. I bat his hand away and return to watching the fake Eros.

Aphrodite's son swoops above three princesses, singled out as royalty by the *meander* on their dresses. He falters when he passes the third with red hair that falls past her knees. The extraordinarily beautiful Princess Psykhe. Instead of cursing her, as his mother demanded, Eros pricks himself with one of his arrows and falls hopelessly in love with the mortal girl.

Would Eros have loved Psykhe so much if he hadn't been struck by his own magic? Something, either regret or anger, twinges the back of my neck, making me straighten. I've heard this story many, many times before, but actually watching it paints a grimmer reality of the effects of Olympian magic. My hand curls into a fist atop my knee, where the Midas Curse has sheathed my entire thigh beneath the *peplos*.

If I ever meet Eros in person, I'll snap each of his arrows in half. No one, not even a god, should have the power to make someone fall in love against their will.

"I know what you're thinking," Apollo says. "Eros hates his magic just as much as you. That's why he imbues some of his arrows with hatred, not love."

"Is that supposed to make me empathize with him?" I scoff, shaking my head. "Both are taking away a person's free will."

Black shrouds are pulled over the actors' faces to symbolize the falling night. Psykhe is brought to Eros's palace, painted pillars of white pulled onto the stage, as they embrace. The princess cannot contain her curiosity, though. She must see her new lover for herself.

As Eros reclines on a bed, his mask hanging haphazardly on the side of his face and snores rumbling up the theater, Psykhe pulls up the shroud.

"That's not what happened," I murmur. "It wasn't curiosity that begged her to look. Her sisters tricked her into breaking Eros's rules."

A sharp laugh bursts from Apollo, making some audience members turn to give us disapproving glares.

"Forget what you know about our stories, my *kataigída*." He leans back on his elbows, and though I can't see his mouth beneath the mask, I imagine it curling in the corners with a grin. "They've been passed down countless times, in more languages than you can imagine. Each time, the tales change to suit the needs of the story's weaver. The only ones that know the truth"—his blue eyes bore into mine—"are us."

"Even Ligeia doesn't know the truth?"

He nods. "Even Ligeia. Everyone likes to think that the story they grew up hearing, the one their nursemaids told them so that they'd fall asleep every night, is the truth, but none of you know what really happened. Not really.

"You think the winners of this war will tell the truth about what happened? Do you think the Achaeans are telling their allies about how the Trojans agreed to lift the Hellespont tax but they conspired against them anyway?"

"No," I say softly. We turn back to the play just as the candle Psykhe holds up for light drips hot wax onto Eros's bare chest. The god leaps from the bed and flies away. In a burst of red smoke, Aphrodite appears at the edge of the bed. The princess must be punished; if she is to see him again, Aphrodite says after strutting around the stage with a gleeful mask, she must complete three tasks.

"Eros was beside himself," Apollo whispers, leaning close enough that his mask brushes my ear. "He had fallen so madly in love with the girl already."

"Because of her beauty?" I scoff.

"Because of her compassion." Apollo's elbow brushes mine.

His gaze is warm upon my skin. His thumb brushes my arm. I should stop him, swat his hand away or throw one of my snide remarks in his face.

"Shouldn't you be helping me prepare Troy for war?" I finally ask.

"Helen has the right of it. Appealing to the Trojans, playing the willing ally, will help you more in the long run. They won't want to be looking for your dagger while fending off Achaean swords at the same time."

Trepidation stirs within me, made worse by the hollow drums playing offstage.

"Aphrodite must truly be a beast if she couldn't just allow her son to be happy," I say, to distract myself.

Now it is Apollo's turn to pinch me. "Do you want Aphrodite to curse you? Take that back."

His voice shakes. The way his neck blanches beneath the mask gives me pause.

"The goddess of love is kind and thoughtful," I say, the words forced and clinging to the back of my throat. From what I've seen, she is anything but.

Below us, Psykhe is sent on a quest to complete three tasks. Sure enough, her compassion and kindness attracts many allies, and they help her complete them each time. The first is to retrieve the famed golden fleece. The actors set loose painted rams and sheep, then the theater erupts with laughter when the flock refuses to be corralled back offstage. A little lamb leaps into the crowd, and an actor loses his mask as he runs up the stands after it. Despite myself, laughter escapes me.

The second task is to sort an entire room of grain. Painted mounds of wheat are rolled across the stage. Psykhe begs actors dressed as ants to help her sort them, and feeling sorry for the sad mask the princess wears, they do it. I sigh, leaning back in my seat. There are a hundred different places I would rather be than here, watching actors dressed as ants stack grain. I shuffle through the formations *Paidonomos* might lead the Spartans into when they arrive.

"Pay attention before Priam notices. Trojans love their art," Apollo says, and I sense a mournful smile beneath his mask.

"That love is going to get them killed." I pat the sword hanging from my hip. "We should be training, not watching this debacle."

"It is because of this love that this kingdom will never fall. Not truly." Apollo waves a hand to the crowd. "They have more to protect."

Psykhe's last task is a trip to the Underworld. Ligeia told me the princess had been sent to retrieve water from the Styx, but in this version, she is sent for Aphrodite's famed beauty, held in a box by the goddess Persephone.

When she arrives at Hades's palace, black sheets are thrown across the floor and hung from the building behind the stage, and a table bearing food is brought forth. Persephone takes a seat at the end of the table, not even a fraction as beautiful as the true goddess. The actor playing Psykhe hugs their stomach, now wearing a mask with a frown.

"I am so hungry," they proclaim for the audience to hear. "I haven't eaten in so long, and this food tempts me like no other."

"Temptation is your hubris," a voice offstage says.

Persephone waves to the plates of food. "Please, eat whatever you like."

"No." I lean forward. "To eat food from the Underworld will bind your soul there."

Watching something inevitable, even if this version of Psykhe's story is likely far from the truth, makes my palms itch. I want to look away, but can't.

"This much of the story is true," Apollo says, as if reading my mind. "But Persephone did not offer the food out of unkindness. She had wanted to help a weary soul, but sometimes a god's best efforts of kindness are instead a curse."

Psykhe plucks a grape from the table and pops it into her mouth. There's a collective gasp from the audience.

Apollo is silent on my other side, focused on the play reaching its crescendo below, the music blaring all around. Startled birds soar from the surrounding rooftops. A dozen dancers twirl around a collapsed Psykhe. Persephone cackles above her, something the real goddess would never do. The image fills me with a bitter fury, lacerating my spine just like Menelaus's whip. These people should revere and love Persephone, not think she's cruel.

"Don't begrudge them for telling this version of the story," Apollo says out of the corner of his mouth. "They first heard it from the Mycenaeans."

"I'm surprised they want anything to do with Mycenae." I'm keenly aware of his leg rubbing against mine, intentionally or not. "Not when their king is bringing war to this land."

"That's because they still hope for a truce." Apollo's voice is cold, and the temperature in the air seems to drop despite the sun looming above us in a cloudless sky.

I rub my arms. "You don't think they will be successful?"

The god slowly shakes his head. "War is coming."

"You're so sure that war will still come?"

"Yes." His eyes bore into me. "It will bear down on Troy's gates sooner than we know."

Something hardens within me, unbreakable. I will defend Helen, no matter the cost. I won't let Troy use her in some misguided attempt at peace.

If the Achaeans hunger for a war, I will serve them up one more bountiful and deadly than Persephone's Underworld feast.

Eros rushes down. Now it's Apollo's turn to lean forward, elbows on his knees, an enrapt expression glazing his eyes beneath the ridiculous lacquered mask. His sudden attention captures my own. I mimic his posture, elbows planting on my knees, keen curiosity fluttering through me like a moth.

Eros dances around Psykhe's prone body. A chorus of mournful flutes echoes up the theater's stands.

"My beloved." The cupid sets aside his bow. "I beg you to refuse the hand of the god Thanatos."

Sure enough, an actor wearing the solemn gray mask of the god of death walks slowly to Psykhe's side. He outstretches a hand, ready to collect the princess's soul for Hades. A solemn lyre begins to play.

"Why now?" I ask, startled by the sound of my own voice. "Why are you suddenly here with me? In Sparta, I understood. You wanted to keep the conclave under control. But we failed and war will be here anyway. Here...what is here for you?"

"You are." Apollo's eyes bore into mine, stealing my breath. "You want me here. I want to be here. With you."

I do not—no, cannot deny it. Even though I should. My lips part. A lyre echoes above the crowd, playing a twisted melody.

A gasp from the audience spins me around in my seat.

Eros pulls a flower from the folds of his cloak, holding it aloft. Apollo's hands grip the folds of his *peplos* so tight his knuckles turn white.

"Perhaps I am not too late," Eros says, a sorrowful hymn echoing through the stands. "Perhaps this ambrosia can still save you."

He places the flower on the mouth of her mask.

The music suddenly lifts, trilling like birdsong. Golden silk curtains fall over the black. Bronze mirrors reflect sunlight upon the fallen princess. Psykhe leaps up with a gasp.

A *salphinx*'s call makes everyone in the audience jump to their feet. Helen likewise flings herself up. My heart hurls itself against my rib cage.

"What is happening?" Helen demands as guards grab her by the elbows.

I slap their hands away and thrust her behind me. My pulse is so loud it nearly drowns out the crowd streaming from the theater.

Helen looks over my shoulder. "Has my husband arrived?"

Not the Achaean army, she asks for. Only Menelaus.

The guards ignore her question. I don't dare withdraw my sword. They will skewer me in an instant. Now is not the time to become an enemy.

Apollo has disappeared, leaving nothing but his mask. It's cold to the touch but the smell of cedarwood is undeniable.

I follow on the heels of the soldiers as they lead my queen toward the palace. People stream from the theater in a mad rush. I cannot catch a single word anyone says. It's a panicked blur. My muscles are so tense they could snap like ice. Helen's wide eyes meet mine above the soldiers' leather-padded shoulders. Her chest rises and falls in rapid breaths.

Dread, a many-pronged fork, twists my gut with every step through the city.

We're paraded into the Trojan megaron, courtiers and nobles lining the massive room. Where a hearth splits Sparta's throne room, instead a many-colored rug is unfurled down the long space, like a wide hallway lined with dark blue marble columns that reach up to the domed gold ceilings.

An immediate display of Troy's wealth, should anyone forget that they are in the richest kingdom known to man.

We stand next to Hector, who's dressed in a silver and navy chiton, and panting from his mad dash across the city. His dark curls are oiled and eyes rimmed with metallic turquoise liner.

Lykou stumbles into my back, panting.

"I came as quickly as I could," he says between shallow breaths.

"They're at the gates," Paris, likewise flushed, murmurs from the other side of his brother. "Only a few moments more."

My heart pounds so wildly I feel ill. The *salphinx* calls a third time, the horn's song drawn out in three long blasts.

"From the north," Hector says, frowning.

Not Achaeans, then. My chest swells and to my side, Helen releases a short sigh of relief. Gently, like the grip of a baby, I pinch her elbow. Not much, but all the assurance I can offer in this crowded room, especially when my own anxiety threatens to eat me whole.

Priam was nothing if not industrious over the long tenure of his rule. Troy is the richest city in all the world, commanded by a king and queen universally loved, and to be inherited by over fifty children, all in attendance now.

If I succeed in saving this city. The Moirai's words echo in the back of my mind as I look over the many children of Troy. Their ages range from midthirties to toddler, the youngest being bounced on the knee of a wet nurse behind the throne.

To Hector's left is the young woman who sat beside Paris in the theater. Her full figure is wrapped in a red chiton threaded with golden birds and the sun. Her hair is dark, a black darker than even Nyx's, and tumbles down her back in tight coils. Her skin is the deep tan of her mother's, and when she looks my way, her light brown eyes do not flinch.

"My sister," Hector says, inclining his head to the woman when he notices my attention. "Kassandra."

She gives me the barest of smiles, before turning to Lykou and smiling wide. Her face blossoms into something impossibly lovely then. He ignores her.

Heavy footfalls echo from outside the megaron. My muscles tighten. My attention snaps to the entrance, hand resting on the sword at my hip. If these are allies of Menelaus, they will only claim Helen through bloodshed.

My hand drops, as slack as my jaw now hanging open, when a battalion of women stride down the long hall. Their sandals and uniforms and dark hair are dusted with sand from a frenzied journey, long swords and bows crossed over their backs. Twin cloaks threaded with the *meander* swing from the shoulders of the two women in the front.

The nearest woman drops to a knee, but not before the woman on her right flashes me a wink and bows as well, dark scarred shoulders catching the sunlight glancing into the megaron.

Hippolyta of the Amazons stands after who must be her sister, Penthesilea, rises with a reverential sweep of her hand. Around her waist, a golden girdle sits snugly.

"Great King Priam," Penthesilea, Queen of the Amazons, says. Her voice is deep and commanding. "The Amazons have heard concerning things. Whispers of war. Omens shared among priestesses."

"Well, your prophets may indeed be correct, and your arrival may be of great use to us," Priam says, leaning back. "But I do not breathe a sigh of relief just yet." His hand tightens on the arm of his throne. "To whom does the allegiance of the Amazons lie?"

"We come at the behest of the god Apollo," Hippolyta says, her grin so familiar. Her eyes meet mine. "To fight alongside Troy."

The city smells of citrus and cinnamon as Hector leads the Amazons through Troy's narrow streets toward the palace they will call home for now. The prince and Penthesilea talk in hushed tones in front of us, and my friend glances at me askance. Helen, Lykou, and I walk alongside Hippolyta behind them.

"By the time news reached me of the great champion in Sparta who became Helen's personal bodyguard," Lyta says, hooking her arm through mine, "I also heard of the *anassa* being seduced and spirited away by a Trojan prince."

A cold hand seems to grip the back of my neck. Hector spins around mid-sentence, and Penthesilea rests her hands on her hips, giving her sister a disapproving look.

Undeterred, Hippolyta continues, "Now, the Daphne I know would never let that happen. She would have killed that prince before he could even lay a hand on her. No offense, Hector. Your brother is lovely." She smirks at him, then turns back to me. "And she would have skewered both princes on her *dory* before either of them could get Helen out of the palace."

I look between Hippolyta and her sister, my shoulders slumping. "I generally hate pointing fingers, though it is safe to say that your father's machinations were largely at fault."

"I'm sorry," Helen says, shaking her head. "But can someone tell me how you two even know each other?"

Hector leaves us at the base of great stone stairs leading up to a palace in the north quarter of the city. Penthesilea ushers us into the palace before I can speak further, even though Helen's face demands an explanation now. I flash her an apologetic grimace before starting from the very beginning, from my journey across Greece last summer to the conclave and our wild flight from Sparta. Some things, such as Zeus's commands and the Moirai's prophecies that harangue me, I cannot bring myself to share. Not yet.

"Your father has been busy," I say to the Amazons, after telling them what all transpired in Sparta. I cross my arms, leaning against a column. "Ares incited this war along with Nyx, and likely Hermes as well."

"Well, the old bastard *is* the god of war," Hippolyta says, tossing her swords and a shield on her bed.

Ares is their father, though there is no love lost between the women and the god. I learned last summer just how much Hippolyta despises him. The Amazon hasn't changed at all since I last saw her outside of Foloi Forest. Her coy smile and dark eyes fill me with more relief than I've felt in nearly a year. Still the same Amazon who fought an army of centaurs and survived.

"Careful, Lyta," my friend's sister chides. "We don't want to paint targets on our own backs."

"I'm sure Ares has already painted them. Big and bold and as ostentatious as he is. Demanding attention like an annoying little—"

"Nonetheless," Penthesilea says sharply, raising her chin. She might be only a few years older than her sister, but her face is wise, with knowing eyes and a mouth that gives no secrets away. "We don't want to turn his anger on our soldiers."

"His eye was fixed on us long before I called him a bastard." Hippolyta strides over to her sister and queen, helping her pull the leather armor over her head. "Our father already declared his allegiance to the Achaeans."

The sun sets beyond Troy, painting the sky crimson. The city echoes with the ringing of forges and barked commands from Trojan generals. The city is finally preparing for war. Hippolyta turns toward me. "And Lykou? Did your wolf follow you to Troy?"

"Wolf?" Penthesilea and Helen ask at once.

The wolf in question raises a very human hand. "That would be me."

I grimace. "That's an even longer story. What is pressing right now is the fact that there are gods plotting against Troy."

Hippolyta rubs a thumb over the curved hilt of her sword and says, "The Amazons have long been allies of Troy. We would stand against the Achaeans on any battlefield. But to stand against the gods?" She straightens and squares her shoulders. "For the debt my people owe you for your help in returning the girdle, we will stand alongside you."

"How did you know that the Achaeans were on their way?" Helen asks.

Hippolyta doesn't break away from my gaze. "A certain gilded god is calling in all of Troy's allies."

"The god of prophecy may have many enemies, but he has twice as many allies." Penthesilea reaches into the folds of her cloak and pulls out something golden, brown, beautiful, and familiar.

A feather.

"He sent a gryphon to Themyscira. Along with this note." Next, she pulls out a crumpled scroll.

I've never seen Apollo's scrawl before, but I can tell at once it is his. The curves are bold and twisty, his message curt.

Troy calls for aid.

My heart swells with pride. Even with his powers bound by his father, Apollo has proven himself invaluable. Even with his powers bound, the god I grew to love last summer reminds me again and again what made me so weak as to fall for him.

Penthesilea spoke no lies. The horns bellow nonstop for the next three days. Troy's allies paint the horizon, arriving by foot, fleet, and stampede. The Lycians arrive that afternoon with fifty ships filled to the brim with weapons and food. The Phrygians arrive the next morning, with a hundred archers and two hundred cavalry. And the next day, the Thracians, Pelasgians, and Maionians are here in quick succession.

All allies carry a single piece of parchment painted with a golden sun.

Apollo.

I cannot imagine the rage that must stew inside Zeus at this moment, his favored son again spitting in his face.

Soon, the city of Troy teems with allies. The Thracians have begun digging a trench around the city, commanding the Lycians assist with fortifying the gates. Amazons have begun training with all the men.

Helen can do nothing but watch, however, and I am bound to her side.

She rises on her toes, peering down at the men and women sparring in the courtyard below our rooms. Hippolyta swipes the feet from under a poor Pelasgian. Helen and I both wince. The man only laughs and jumps back to his feet, ready for another walloping. I rest my elbows on the stone banister so I can see better.

"You wish you were down there," Helen says.

I turn to find her watching me. She flips her shining dark hair over a shoulder and points her chin down at the sparring ring.

"It would be pointless to say otherwise, apparently," I admit, watching the fighting hungrily.

"Then go," she says. "You followed me all the way to Troy. There's no point in standing at my back the entire time we're here. You'll be expected to fight, no doubt. Might as well learn as much as you can before then."

I'll have to fight.

Cold sweat trickles down my spine. Not at the danger, nor at the bloodshed.

At whose blood I will be expected to spill.

Spartans.

My knees wobble, threatening to buckle. I lock them and grit my teeth.

"I know what you're thinking," Helen says, searching my face. "It terrifies me in equal measure, too. We've watched Achilles and his men fight enough. You've trained alongside Spartans your whole life. We owe it to the people who are now protecting us to help them in any way that we can." She turns, resting her arms next to mine. "And that includes fighting alongside them."

"And killing our own." I grip the railing, nails digging hard enough into the stone to splinter them.

Helen nods, pressing her lips together before she says, "Lykou can take turns guarding me. I command you to go."

As if an invisible hand grips me by the shoulder, I turn and walk stiffly from her rooms. My feet drag with each step. Not because I want to resist Helen's command. This is the training I've hungered for, yet now the reality of it has settled in. I'm not just preparing to protect her, but also to kill my brethren.

I stumble, clutching at my stomach. I look back, debating returning to Helen, my mind already filing through a hundred different excuses. Shadows reach down the corridor toward me and a shudder wracks my frame.

The hand at my stomach curls into a fist. The Midas Curse pulses beneath my touch. Where I'm sure Artemis meant to comfort me, instead anger rises in my chest like the gale of a typhoon. I won't fail her family again, even if I partly blame them for the predicament Helen is in.

We're on the top floor of the palace, so I have to take four flights of stone steps down to the sparring ring, and also navigate the labyrinthine sprawl of narrow hallways. I turn onto the bottom floor, but realize immediately that I've taken the wrong stairs to the ring. I'll have to climb back up a floor, then take a separate set of stairs unless I want to navigate the roads surrounding the palace.

A soldier calls from down the hall.

"You, girl." He marches over to me, bedecked in the Trojan uniform. Underneath, his dark skin ripples with lithe muscles. "Where do you think you're going?"

Wariness sweeps over me. "To train outside. I've just taken a wrong turn."

His hand latches around my wrist, cold fingers digging into the tender skin below my palm. He smells like sweet spices. "If that's so, then let me see you there."

Before he can drag me along, I grab the hand holding me and spin. He yelps as I wrench his arm behind his back. I slam him into the wall and flip off his helmet, revealing a head of dark, wiry curls.

I rip my wrist from his grip. "I'm getting rather tired of you assholes trying to surprise me every damn day."

"Nice to see you again, too, Daphne," Hermes says.

CHAPTER
20

I hold the god against the wall with an arm pressing into the back of his neck. A dagger flicks to my other hand. I dig its tip into his side, right where I drove another blade less than a year before.

"Give me one good reason not to finish the job I failed to do in Tartarus," I snarl.

Hermes chuckles. "Well, you'll find that that one spot isn't quite so easily wounded anymore, now that you've returned the Muses."

His dark, wiry hair has grown out considerably, braided now and bound at the back of his head. His frame, broad and imposing, is wrapped in dark blue, rough-hewn fabric that matches the tattoos fluttering across his skin.

Before I can blink, he spins around. He backhands the dagger away and it clatters down the hallway. I duck beneath the swing he takes at my face and leap back from the knee that rises toward my midriff. My back collides with the wall.

I palm another dagger. But before I can leap across the space between us, Hermes lifts his palms.

His grin is tainted with wickedness. "Would you kill me so quickly?"

"Yes," I say without hesitation.

"I guess I should have expected nothing less from you." He blocks the hallway leading toward the stairs. "How about a truce, then?"

"And give you more time to betray me?" I raise the dagger. "Think again."

I leap forward. Hermes rolls from my reach. Nimbly, he snatches up my other dagger and twirls it between his fingers. We circle each other.

"What would you say to an alliance if I had something to offer you?" He looks me up and down. "A trade, per se."

I bark a laugh. "There are countless reasons why I would never align myself with you."

"Was it so terrible last time?" Hermes tosses the dagger from one hand to the other, feinting toward my left side. "I brought the first three Muses back to Olympus, remember?"

"Only because you stole them in the first place and didn't want to get caught!" I lunge, a test he easily dodges. "How are you even here?" Still facing him, I search the hallway for the gods who surely know of his whereabouts now. "How have you avoided their reach all this time?"

"I have my tricks." He grins, then disappears before my eyes.

"You always do."

A flutter of wings over my shoulder spins me around.

He leans a hip against the wall. "To prove I can be trusted, I shall offer you some advice for which I expect nothing in return."

"Gods always expect something in return."

He snaps his fingers. The dagger he held is now in my other hand

and we've switched places. His back is to the stairwell, again blocking my way out.

Hermes holds up both hands. "The days before the Achaeans arrive are officially numbered. Priam will find his allies have suddenly vanished, either swept into the sea or outnumbered by the Myrmidons leading the fleet."

My throat is suddenly dry. "You're lying. There's no possible way they could have traveled the Aegean so quickly. Not without..."

"The help of Poseidon? How long did it take you to get from Sparta to Troy?" He grins as my retort catches in the back of my mouth. "The same gods that help or hinder you do so as well for the Achaeans. This war will be but a mere game to Olympus, when instead they should fear it."

"Not all the gods," I say with a sneer. "Apollo wouldn't help the Achaeans."

Hermes merely shrugs, backing a step toward the stairwell. "He would if his father commanded him to. Or do you still truly think that Apollo would do anything for you? Do you not remember Koronis? I told you of her last summer."

The princess who spurned Apollo and her entire kingdom fell to ruin. I could never forget.

"Don't let your desire, or whatever it is your fickle mortal heart tells you you're feeling for that insufferable sunspot blind you."

"There's no desire left in me." I clench my teeth. "Not anymore."

"Don't lie to me, Daphne. I see right through all falsehoods." The grin falls from Hermes's handsome face. "And don't let your distrust of me keep you from seeing reason. Prepare your allies, Daphne. The Achaeans will arrive in ten days."

"I'll kill you if I see you again," I promise.

"Another lie." Hermes laughs. "No, you'll beg me to help you."

He tosses something to me. It whistles through the air. Without thinking, I drop a dagger in order to catch it. Uncurling my fingers, I find Hermes's pipes in my hand. Completely unharmed from when I threw them into the sea last summer.

When I look up, the god of cunning is gone.

CHAPTER
21

Begrudgingly, I tuck the pipes into the folds of my chiton and march up the stairs. I know not to expect Hermes in the palace again anytime soon. Even before he betrayed me, he had a habit of disappearing at a moment's notice—or, rather, in a flutter of wings.

"What a birdbrain," I mutter to myself, climbing the stairs and turning down the correct hallway to the sparring ring.

But, in the back of my mind, his words still linger.

Ten days. An impossibly short amount of time. When Apollo and I traveled last summer, before his powers began to truly wane, we crossed Greece in less than a week to reach Mount Kazbek. What have the Achaeans done to have Poseidon help them so?

My steps are urgent as I rush to the sparring ring. Whether or not Hermes has told me the truth, I must let the Trojans know. I march across the threshold of the training arena. The outdoor space is lined with racks of weapons, and packed with soldiers and warriors and nobles alike all preparing. So similar to the *gymnasion* I left behind in Sparta.

I stop outside the ring where Hippolyta currently trounces Paris. She flings the prince over her shoulder, and he slams hard into a wooden post.

Paris groans. "We're training. Not actually trying to kill each other, Princess."

"I see no reason for us to hold back." Hippolyta sniffs, tossing her braid over her shoulder.

"Trouncing the prince can wait," I call, jumping over the wooden railing. "I need to speak with you and your sister."

"You think you can just call a meeting with the Queen of the Amazons?" Hippolyta's grin matches mine. "What gives you that authority, Daphne?"

I open my mouth to retort. She leaps across the space between us before I can say a word. She catches me around the middle. We tumble into the sand.

I hook a leg around her waist and catch her hands in mine. I dodge the swing of her head, her dark hair stinging my eyes. With a grunt, I flip her over. I keep one foot hooked under her hips, ignoring the pain in my ankle as I rest the full weight of my body on top of her.

She chuckles. "I don't remember you using that move in Foloi."

"Not exactly practical against a centaur."

We circle each other, the movement so similar to what I did only moments ago in that hallway with Hermes. My back hits the railing. I should have monitored my surroundings better. *Paidonomos* would have made me run laps if I made that mistake back in Sparta.

Her fist flies toward my face. I duck.

Right into her next punch.

Nyx shoves my face into the corridor wall. A short scream escapes me. She slams an arm into the back of my shoulders, digging my chest into the wall and holding me immobile.

"The gods do not deserve your allegiance, my sweet. They do not deserve the powers of Olympus."

My teeth sing, and I stumble back. Blood fills my mouth. I shake my head and spit it at our feet.

"Maybe you should have waited until you were less distracted to challenge me, Daphne." Hippolyta's voice is crooning.

"Then she'd be waiting for all eternity," Lykou calls from behind me.

"I didn't challenge you. I wanted to talk to your sister." I don't turn from Hippolyta, whose legs have bent slightly, preparing to jump. "And you, Lykou, should be watching over our queen."

"She's in a private audience with King Priam. I wasn't allowed—"

"You should have waited outside the council chamber, then," I snap, turning. Never mind this nonsense. I should be telling Helen about the Achaeans.

Hippolyta's sandaled foot catches me square in the center of my back. I'm knocked into the wooden fence.

"You think you can stop me? I will stalk your every step, stall your every turn. The powers of Olympus have set like the sun, and I intend for them to never rise again."

I gasp for air. Shoving to my feet, I lean against the railing for balance and search the sparring crowd around Lyta and me. That may have been a memory, but that doesn't mean that Nyx isn't here, plotting my downfall alongside that of Olympus.

My fingers dig into the railing, splinters threatening to pierce the skin beneath my nails.

"Being distracted nearly got you killed last summer in Foloi." Lyta chuckles behind me, the sound far from mirthful, though. "Almost got you stomped on by a hundred centaurs."

"You never told me how they managed to capture you." I wipe sand from my lips with the back of my hand. It does very little. "It's only fair."

"I've seen you fight better than you just did, Daphne." Hippolyta tugs on her leather vambraces, likely ones meant specifically for training, judging by how worn they are. "So I will not comment on the mess everyone here just witnessed. But I will offer you a chance to redeem yourself. You are a capable fighter, and Sparta has trained you well, but not for war. They never train women for such things in Greece, even in Sparta. You might know how to best an opponent one-on-one, but I've seen you fight when surrounded by enemies. The distractions overtake you. You don't know where to focus, who to attack first."

A retort itches its way up my throat. But she's right.

My fear might kill me on the battlefield as swiftly as any enemy soldier.

Hippolyta softens her words with a smile. She tosses me a sword that leans against the fence, then picks up her own. "We will start with swords. Better to train with the shorter blade than the long *dory* a Spartan would normally use. Especially in a combat setting. Then once we've mastered the sword to my liking, I'll let you move back to the *dory.*"

The air in Troy is dry compared to the sticky heat of early summer in Sparta. The warm breeze kicks up the dust around us. Every muscle in my body aches by the time I limp from the sparring ring and up the twisting palace stairs. Delicious aches, but tender nonetheless.

I cross the threshold of my room and a blush rises to my cheeks.

Apollo leans against the far edge of the bath, his bronze hair framed by the setting sun behind him. Gold and red light fragments across the surface of the water, doing nothing to hide the sheer nakedness of him beneath it. In my mind, I don't bother ripping off my sweat- and sand-stained clothes. I leap into the bath fully clothed and smother the god with kisses. I press my hands against his warm shoulders and tuck my chin into the crook of his neck.

Apollo's voice cuts through my thoughts. "You're adorable when you're thinking too hard."

Despite the hunger coursing through me, I plant my feet wide and raise a dagger between us. The metal glints in the firelight. "When we fought Minos, what was the first thing I did after I made sure Lykou was alive?"

Confusion flickers across his handsome face, before his brows narrow. My other hand inches toward the knife at my hip as silence yawns wide.

Finally, voice hoarse, he says, "You grabbed your bedroll. It was stained with blood and you wanted to wash it out and—"

"I scrubbed a hole right through the fabric," I finish for him.

Still, I hesitate. Nyx has fooled me with illusions and shadows before. My caution must be written all over my face because he stills.

"You have no reason to fear me." Apollo shakes his head and climbs from the bath. He wraps a golden silk sheet around his tan waist, the fabric clinging to the wet, hard lines of his body.

"Of all the stupid things to say, that is the worst." I clench the hilt of my dagger. "Nyx has tricked me into nearly killing you before."

"Zeus bound my power, but I will try to show you." Apollo holds out a palm and light blossoms to life there. It sputters, flashing, then dies. "Nyx manipulates shadows. I manipulate light."

"That means nothing. She's ruthless. She knows your weaknesses, *my* weaknesses, and will stop at nothing until she gets what she wants, even killing me."

"See that wall out there?" He points to the glimmering golden wall that surrounds the city. "I built that wall myself. A drop of my ichor in every stone. Not to protect these people, but the secrets this city keeps. The closest I ever got to death wasn't last summer. It was when I nearly drained myself building that wall. Anyone with ill intentions for this city will be unable to step inside unless invited."

"If the magic of that wall is supposed to keep any enemies from stepping inside, why was Hermes here today?"

"What? Here? In the palace?" Apollo jerks as if stung, then his voice sharpens. The setting sunlight reflects off the muscled planes of his tan chest. "Did he threaten you?"

I drag my gaze from his chest. "He shouldn't be able to, remember? Hermes warned me that the Achaeans will arrive in ten days. Why is Poseidon helping them?"

"What are you talking about?" Apollo's frown deepens and he slices an impatient line through the air with his hand. "What lies did Hermes fill your head with?"

I ignore the urge to wrap my arms around myself. "He told me that the Achaeans are being helped by the gods."

"Poseidon is doing nothing of the sort. In fact, Agamemnon insulted Artemis by ransacking her temple in Sparta after you left, so my sister commanded nobody help him and his fleet cross the Aegean."

"But Hermes said—"

"You should know better by now not to trust a single word that he says." The silk sheet pulls taut against his wet skin as he turns, eyes narrowing. "Need I remind you of how he stabbed us all in the back?"

"I'm the one who quite literally stabbed him. In the back." I give an exaggerated sigh. "Not an uncommon thing in your family, I'm sure."

Apollo flashes me an impatient look.

I lean forward. "What does it feel like to be bridled like a horse by your own father? Can't feel good, I'm sure."

"Not completely tethered. I'm here, aren't I?" Not bothering to dress further, he plucks some grapes from a bowl and sits, dangling his legs in the water.

"Using the same magic that allows Hermes to evade your father?"

"Yes," he says curtly.

"But what about when I need you?" The question slips from my mouth before I can stop it.

He looks up. His face is almost hopeful.

I add, "On the battlefield."

I'll never admit out loud that some part of me might need him off the battlefield as well. If my words hurt, he does not show it, which only serves to sting myself.

He says, "I'll be there."

Something tugs within my chest. "What do Ares and Hermes have to gain from this war?"

Apollo's lips press together in a heavy line. A sure sign that he is biting back something. The same face he made many times last summer. That look is exactly why I can't cross that distance between us. Too many secrets.

"Give me a reason to trust you, Apollo."

He rolls a grape between his fingers, as if weighing how much he can tell me. "Those lines that were drawn up on Olympus? Those are merely for show. Hera, Athena, and Poseidon won't strike against Troy, but neither will they help these people. Troy is a valuable city to the gods." He meets my eyes. "Just as the Garden of the Hesperides is."

"Is there a source of Olympian power here?"

He shakes his head.

"What else aren't you telling me?"

"If I tell you the truth, he'll…" Apollo bites back a curse, hands curling into fists around the grapes. Red juice drips between his fingers. "Zeus would kill you before I even got out five words."

I swallow and lean back from the heated vehemence of his proclamation. I rest a hand against the gold circling my navel. Artemis can hear everything we say right now and therefore so can Apollo's father.

"I know I should be, but I'm not afraid of *him*." Only the woman who haunts my dreams every night.

He stands. "And that is why I'm afraid *for you*."

My breath catches.

He says, "Your courage will kill you."

We stare at each other a long moment. Apollo was my adversary once and possibly still is. My eyes rise from his lips to the earnestness of his eyes. He breathes hard, searching my face, before pulling something from the folds of his sheet. Silver catches in the fragmented moonlight. In his hand is a bangle, woven like vines around three golden stones. They begin to shine, glowing brighter and brighter until light fills the room and my eyes begin to water. When I blink, the light suddenly dims, disappearing in an instant.

He stands and walks around the bath. "I made this for you." His mouth quirks to the side. "Not those damn vambraces you turned your nose at."

I take the bangle from him. The metal is surprisingly warm, pleasantly so. When I turn it one way, the gold stones shimmer with pink and cerulean blue, and then green and lavender when I turn it again. "What are these?"

"They are made with an old power." He takes it from my hands and, as gently as one would with a newborn, clasps it around my biceps. The bangle holds firm, a sudden comfort, and the stones shift to a dull gold the moment it hits my skin. "Older even than Olympus."

"What do they do?" I rotate my arm, trying to make the stones glow again, but they remain astutely dark.

"They will protect you," Apollo says. Before I can tell him that I don't need protecting, he adds, "Even when you cannot." His face darkens. "When I cannot."

I want to argue and take off the bracelet, but the warm metal fills me with a quiet comfort, something I cannot name or place. Those stones, three of them hardly bigger than the nail on my pinky, speak to me of a time before I was born. A time when my ancestors were born of storms and ash.

My thoughts are now as wild as a tempest. I could lose myself in the eye of that storm, drift into its epicenter. Toward *him*.

"Promise me you won't be reckless," he says, a deep edge to his voice.

"And lie to you?" My voice shakes, and I force myself to step back. "Darling, I'm always reckless."

"Daphne?" Helen's voice rings from the doorway.

Apollo, the sodden sheet, and bowl of grapes all vanish. All that remains is a scent of cedarwood that harangues me, and the bracelet clasped around my arm.

"You won't believe what King Priam just told me. Apparently, my oaf of a brother-in-law ransacked the Temple of Artemis just after we left. He blamed her for our escape and so Poseidon has brought unseasonably dangerous storms to the Aegean in retribution. It will be months before they can cross the sea." More jubilant than I've seen her in weeks, Helen strides through the door, emerald dress billowing behind her, and wrinkles her nose upon seeing me. "Oh, darling. You look and smell ghastly. Why haven't you bathed yet?"

Lykou follows her through the doorway. His gaze flicks to the bracelet, up to my eyes, and he frowns. My wolf always sees too much.

Before I can protest, Helen begins pulling the sand-crusted ties of my uniform until it falls in a heap at my feet. The Midas Curse is the brush of a feather, squirreling away from her sight under the arms I cross over my chest.

Ignoring my huffed protests, she shoves me back over to the bath. As I climb into the water, she mutters behind me about wishing the servants would have left the grapes and, despite myself, a small smile pulls at my lips. I have zero doubt that Apollo knew Helen wanted them.

And so he took them.

I duck my head under the water just as a dark chuckle escapes my lips.

CHAPTER
22

Despite Apollo's assurances, I count down the ten days. I wouldn't trust Poseidon even if he promised me those storms himself. I climb up to stare at the glistening Aegean Sea on the horizon, searching for the thousand ships that creep closer. They bide their time, picking off our allies on the coast one by one. Each day, Priam receives another letter, another kingdom burned.

Apollo, though absent in body, invades my thoughts day after day. Each morning I wake, fingers reaching for his missing warmth. They curl into a fist. I haven't slept beside Apollo in a year.

Across the room, Lykou tosses and turns each night. He flings the furs from his bed in his sleep and his pillows shred between clenched fingers. Before I can ever wake him, he hurls himself up with a ragged gasp. If Helen finds our dual nightmares odd, she never says.

As a distraction, he and I throw ourselves into training with the

Amazons. Penthesilea is the reserved, watchful opposite of Hippolyta, but she will climb into the arena readily and at a moment's notice.

I'm sparring with both, twin swords in each hand. Helen watches the Amazon Queen—and myself—with hungry eyes. I raise my blade just in time to block a swing for my neck from Hippolyta as her sister lunges forward. I drop to my back and roll away from her next swing, leaping to my feet just as Hippolyta rams down her sword into the ground where I stood a moment before.

"Even a sparring sword can kill someone, Lyta," I say through a mouthful of sand. I look around the training arena. Nyx's shadows seem to crawl from every corner and doorway. I repress a shudder. "Maybe don't drive a sword into my gut before the Achaeans arrive?"

"You'll never learn without true fear," Penthesilea says. She tosses her sword neatly from hand to hand so I cannot pick which arm to defend against. "It is why my warriors have never lost a battle."

"Yet," I say. "The Amazons have never gone head-to-head with Sparta."

"If they all fight anything like you, we have nothing to worry about." Hippolyta spins away from my next swing.

"Don't be unkind," Penthesilea says, hardly sweating as she jabs, again and again, keeping me on my toes. "Daphne is a strong fighter. The Spartans have simply done her the injustice of never training with a battalion as we have."

"Penthe has a soft spot for you," Hippolyta says around a grin.

She lunges, and I take the advantage, driving into her unprotected hip with my knee. She turns, swinging wide. I duck beneath her arm and slap the flat of my blade against her thigh. Victory courses through me. Giddy, I bounce from foot to foot, waiting for her sister to continue the attack.

Penthesilea instead looks to the messenger now jogging across the training ring toward us. She is one of the Amazon's warriors, lean and built for running quickly over short distances. She leaps the fence with a deer's grace and presses her lips to Penthesilea's ear.

When the queen looks up again, her face is dark and stormy. She barks something to Hippolyta in a language I don't recognize before marching away, followed closely by two Amazons. I have no doubt that Penthesilea doesn't need the bodyguards and could easily defend herself.

"What spirited her away?" Helen asks. She's resting her chin in her cupped hands, elbows on the fence I'm now leaning against.

"Queenly duties." Hippolyta spins her sword around. "You know how that goes."

Helen's dark brows narrow, but she doesn't press further. She looks to the arched entrance of the training courtyard, painted green and blue. "Well, I'm quite bored with waiting around for the Achae-ans to get their ships in the water. Would you care to explore the city with me?"

And me by proxy, she doesn't add.

Lykou peels away from the group he trains with to follow as we leave the arena and delve into the colorful streets of Troy. His arm brushes mine, a comforting touch but nothing more.

The sound of clipping sandals follows us. Lykou and I spin around, daggers raised.

Princess Kassandra, dark ringlets spiraling behind her like a black, rumpled sheet, jogs after us. She wears a cerulean veil, open in the front and baring her lovely face, though the coverings are unneces-sary here, and stops short just beyond my reach.

"I heard you say you were going to explore Troy," she says, stutter-ing slightly. She must have been watching us train. "Would you care for a tour?"

She poses the question to all of us, but her rapt attention is for

Lykou. He either doesn't notice or doesn't care, dismissing her with a single glance and stepping even closer to me—and farther from the princess.

Helen appraises her. The veil no doubt means that Kassandra doesn't wish to be recognized, which means following us is exactly something the princess should not be doing. Helen gives the young woman a small, confiding smile. "We would love a tour."

Because Kassandra, a princess hidden away in a palace, is someone that Helen once was, too.

Shyly, Kassandra steps in front of us and begins leading the way down the city's winding streets. Her voice becomes more jubilant, unbounded, the farther from her father's palace we get. She points out various buildings, the public baths, the assembly, and many blacksmith stalls, their owners from all the reaches of the world. I keenly remember the last time my curiosity led me to a blacksmith stall, in Crete—Lykou started a brawl. I glare at him as we pass one, and he has the good grace to flush.

Something nameless passes through me the longer we traverse Troy. Spartans spend their every waking moment preparing for war, so unlike Trojans. Spartans live to fight, and Trojans fight to live, relishing in the joys of life. The sights fill me with warmth, not like the power of Apollo, but something akin to happiness. The feeling is so strong my fear of the shadows seems to, albeit temporarily, fade away.

Kassandra's voice is high-pitched and sweet, reminding me of a spring wine. Her arms point here and there, making sure we don't miss a single detail of her lovely city. We stop at the market, collecting food enough for an entire army just for the five of us. I'm handed a flatbread stuffed with onions, cheese, and spices I cannot name, so hot it scalds the roof of my mouth as I inhale it.

Rows of screech owls look down from the rooftops, watching us with too keen eyes. I can't remember what god they answer to. I should have paid more attention to Ligeia's stories. The wind sweeps through Troy, the Anemoi swaying the branches of olive trees on every corner and filling the streets with nature's song. Today, the sound is merry, almost high-pitched like birdsong. It tickles my neck as I cock my head to listen.

Kassandra notices my interest. "A design in all the buildings of Troy. There are cornices on every corner. Normally, this song, an easterly breeze, would mean many traders on the Hellespont, as they usually arrive when the weather is fair. When a storm is coming, the wind howls like wolves."

"Amazing." Helen peers at the corner of the wall nearest to us, where holes of varying sizes have been drilled through. "Who designed them?"

"My great grandfather, Tros." Kassandra glows with pride.

"The founder of Troy." Lyta continues walking, not caring about the structural wonders of the city.

A flute, clear and lovely, echoes above the wind's melody. I turn, looking everywhere for the unmistakable owner.

Not from the wind. Hermes.

He watches us, and no doubt doesn't want to be seen. But this is his way of letting me know that he still lingers in the city. Waiting for my defenses to drop. His pipes remain in our rooms up in the palace, tucked away at the bottom of a chest where I never have to look at them. I should have just tossed them over Troy's wall.

Kassandra chats excitedly with Helen and Lyta while Lykou and I march behind the trio. I glance over at my friend, but his focus is trained on the darkened doorways all around us. A bead of sweat slides down the back of his neck, and he reaches for the sword hanging from his hip. The food suddenly sours in the pit of my stomach.

I'm about to reach for his hand when Kassandra's sharp voice turns both of our heads.

"There are four gates to the city," she says as we pass one painted gold with lions and rays of sunlight. "This is the primary entrance, the one you took when you first arrived." She points north. "That is the trading gate, where wares from the Hellespont are inspected. To the east is another trader gate, and another *agora*, maybe half the size of this one?"

"Are they protected as the wall is?" Lykou asks.

"By the gods? Yes." Kassandra looks around nervously and pulls her veil tight. Her answer is a pinched, single word. "Or so the priests tell us."

She breezes through the market without stopping again. We follow and she points out more buildings. A library, gardens, the palaces of her siblings, and a field lined with trees, even within the city walls, just for Troy's famous horses and cattle.

She takes us down another street, lined with colorful doorways and fountains, until we reach a towering fresco. It depicts a place I know all too well—the pantheon. Each of the twelve gods sit around a single figure where the hearth is usually lit. Zeus bears an amiable and yet stern smile, a bolt of lightning clenched in his hand. His brothers sit on either side, Poseidon astride a dolphin and Hades with Cerberus at his hip.

Hera, Athena, and Demeter each have shrewd countenances, with their familiars—a peacock, an owl, and a thin, silvery snake—behind them. The other gods have taken their seats, but none catch my eye so much as Apollo. My gaze is glued to his bright eyes. Despite my resentment of the never-ending secrets broadening that rift between us, I want to reach out and touch the tan skin of his cheek.

"Isn't it magnificent?" Kassandra asks, misinterpreting our stunned gazes.

Helen gazes up at her father with a mixture of resentment and curiosity, her dark brows pulled together in a twisted frown. Lykou's frown matches hers as he looks upon Apollo—with not a shred of affection. Hippolyta stares up at her own father in dark silence.

Ares glares down at us, a black vulture perched atop his shoulder with its wings outstretched. The same bird is now emblazoned across his chest in red and black ink. But what happened to each of these animals to have them imprinted upon the gods' skin? Peneios warned me of the gods with the moving tattoos, like the ones Ares and Hermes have. But Demeter, Athena, and Peneios himself have them as well.

My gaze drifts to the woman standing in the center. At first glance, I thought she was Nyx, with her black hair and short stature, but her skin is a dark tan and her eyes a lovely green. She holds aloft a *pyxis*, a short, squat jar with a curved lid.

"Her name is Pandora." Kassandra runs her hands over the woman's sandaled feet. "I think the gods must have had this piece made to warn us of mortal folly."

"Or their own hubris," Lykou mutters.

Frowning, I look down at the flowers scattered across the ground at the base of the fresco, with coins and jewels sprinkled between in equal measure. Gifts to the Olympians.

Kassandra says, "There are temples to each of the gods outside the city, but not a single one within the walls. Every time my forefathers attempted to build one, some mishap or calamity happened. Once, an earthquake tumbled the brand-new columns of a temple dedicated to Aphrodite, and a fire immediately tore through a temple to Hades. My father told me that the earth opened wide right beneath a temple to Hera and swallowed it whole when he was a child." She waves to the fresco. "So this is how we pay homage here in the city." She brushes a hand on Apollo's sandaled feet, then snaps it back as if stung. "Even when we would rather do anything else."

I open my mouth to ask what she means when Helen exclaims

beside me. We turn as she bends, pointing to a broken piece. "That's a shame. How did that happen?"

"That's impossible," Kassandra says, getting down on her knees beside Helen. "This fresco was made by the gods themselves."

Just like the wall that surrounds this city. That explains the impeccable likenesses.

The piece Helen pointed to is a single square tile, a crack dividing it diagonally. I lean closer as she runs a nail along the break.

"Don't make it worse!" Kassandra slaps her hand away. "This entire fresco is over a thousand years old. It dates back even further than the wall."

"Touch my queen again"—Lykou's lips curl back—"and I will make you regret it."

Kassandra arches a brow. "You'll do what to me? Break my arm? Throw me to the ground? I'm not afraid of you in *my* city."

A tic forms in Lykou's jaw. He straightens and looks down at her, a flush rising up his neck.

At least someone can chew Lykou's ear off for his surly behavior. I leave them to their bickering and look more closely at the fresco. The crack Helen pointed to isn't the only one. In fact, upon closer examination, hundreds of minuscule hairline fractures run across the painting. I lean close, reaching a hand for the crack.

A scream snaps my hand back.

Hippolyta, Lykou, and I spin as one into defensive positions. A dagger is immediately in my hand. I was a fool to leave the palace without additional weapons.

More screams—pain-wrenching, clay-shattering screams—fill the air.

"We're defenseless here." Hippolyta looks to Kassandra and Helen behind us, their backs pressed against the fresco. "We return to the palace. Now."

Cries for help echo around us, men, women, and children yelling as one. From all directions.

"We don't know where the attack is coming from, or who it is," I say through gritted teeth. I bend my knees slightly. "We should stay put."

Shadows suddenly blanket us, there and gone in an instant. I look around wildly for Nyx, but her scent is nowhere near, and the sun shines once again. Hippolyta's face is drenched in darkness, then emblazoned with sunlight. A hollow, rhythmic thud fills the air.

We all turn to the sky just as women begin diving across it. The Erinyes, the goddesses of vengeance and fury, swoop overhead. Their cackles rise above the din of Troy's people.

And they aim directly for us.

CHAPTER 23

From their backs, great black wings stretch wide.

The Furies, three in all, swoop toward us, tucking in their leather wings to plummet faster than my eyes can track. They stop just short of us, diving behind a building.

More screams fill the air, cleaving my heart. Then, two Furies take flight once more. A woman cries for help as they grab each of her arms.

And then rip her in half.

The woman's blood rains down upon the city. *Salphinx* sing from every corner of the city.

"Oh, gods," Kassandra says, her face slack. "We're being attacked."

"Tell us something we don't know," Hippolyta snaps.

"We go," Lykou says, voice rough. "Now."

He leads us down the street toward a dark alleyway. The thumping of the Erinyes' wings seems to follow our every pounding step.

Smoke fills the air. Above the screaming, horns, and delighted cackle of the Furies, another sound I know all too well seems to swell.

The dirge of spears beaten upon shields.

Impossibly, the Achaeans are here.

Ten days, Hermes warned me. Apollo assured me he was wrong, but Olympus is blind to the machinations of Nyx, the goddess who wants to make a ruin of Troy.

We pound down the narrow streets. I hook an arm around Helen and steer her toward the shadows. I'm keenly aware, with every step, that the only weapon I have on my person is the dagger currently clenched in my fist.

The beat of wings presses closer. A yell shreds the air and a warm wetness rains down upon us. A choked scream breaks from Kassandra, and Hippolyta slams her into a wall just as clawed feet swoop down.

Without thinking, I ram my dagger into a foot. The Erinys screeches, a bloodcurdling sound that threatens to deafen me.

Lykou throws himself into Helen, shoving her around a corner just as another Erinys whips out a sword from her hip. The blade is crooked and barbed. A death on that blade would not be quick. It would be brutal and bloody.

I take up the rear as we thunder up a narrow street. Too narrow, I realize, for the Erinyes to follow by air. Their wings are too wide for the close buildings.

That doesn't stop them from plucking Trojans from other streets and ripping them in half above us. The cries of dying people ring out around us, their blood drenching my hair and clothes. A choked sob escapes Kassandra, her feet faltering. Hippolyta stumbles into her just as we reach the end of an alleyway.

I don't know where the third Erinys is, but the two blocking our path grin at us, fangs dripping with blood. Their wings pump the air, levitating them above the ground. Hippolyta and Lykou block our royals from the Furies, stepping to the front. I yank on Kassandra's and Helen's dresses, tugging them closer.

The two Erinyes ignore my friends, their dark eyes focused on me. More horns echo into the cloudy sky. Rain begins to pour, mingling with the blood on my skin, and running in rivulets down my face. I blink away the dark liquid.

They're dressed in black leather armor that glistens with blood. Their faces are a mixture of horrifying and lovely in equal measure, smooth skin marred with a deathly pale and red paint blazing from their eyelids. They carry barbed swords, and around each of their necks is a viper tattoo that incessantly coils.

When one speaks, her voice is smooth and heavy like honeyed wine.

"I, Megaera of the Erinyes, bear the Achaeans' message for you, Daphne Diodorus." She points a hooked, mangled claw at me. "You and your queen will never again be welcome in Sparta. You are no longer known as the Shield of Helen."

Her words bear upon my shoulders like a shroud of stone; I straighten them and raise my chin. "As long as my queen is in danger, I will always be her Shield."

They laugh, a mangled sound like tearing metal.

"And I, Alecto, bestow upon you a new name." The corners of another Erinys's mouth curl high enough to almost touch the edges of her eyes, baring hundreds of glinting, pointed teeth. "You are now Prodótis of Sparta."

The Traitor of Sparta.

A pain, keener even than the burning lance of venom, races down my spine and fills my stomach. I want to vomit.

"The Achaeans have arrived," Alecto says, beating her chest with a fist. "And they will have their vengeance."

The two sisters leap, taking to the skies. The third follows suit, and the thumping of their wings is eventually lost to the dull roar in my ears.

Hippolyta, breathing hard, clasps me by the shoulders. "We must return these two to the palace."

I nod, dimly aware of everyone's eyes glued to me. We jog to the palace, skirting the bloodier, more ravaged streets. It seems impossible, the amount of damage three women managed to cause, but I will never doubt the wrath of Nyx.

CHAPTER
24

W e arrive at the palace out of breath and coated in sticky blood that is not our own. The entire place is in an uproar, soldiers and nobles running about, but it is unravaged compared to the streets. The Erinyes seemed to have focused their ire on those around us. But, turning to look down at the city below, my breath is stolen by what exactly has caused such a stir.

No longer does the Aegean glisten on the horizon.

Sails, painted with the emblems of every kingdom in Greece, crowd the sea. The *lambda* of Sparta is painted in blood red on more than a hundred sails, matched in number by the lion of Mycenae in bright yellow. Each of the kings I banqueted with only a month before are making a steady course for Troy's beaches, led by Achilles's black sails.

My heart thunders in my ears. Hector marches from the palace wearing his armor, flanked by a battalion of his soldiers. His blue cape swirls behind him.

"All Trojans must come behind the walls," he says with the deep, unyielding voice of a commander. "Even those within the temples. I don't trust the Achaeans not to take whatever scraps they can find to use against us. These people do not answer to loyalty or honor. Only wealth and power. We will meet them in kind."

Spartan blood will be spilled this very day. The thought makes me want to retch, and not from squeamishness.

Hector's battalion follows as he begins down the stairs, more soldiers joining at each level, to the waiting horses below.

Penthesilea strides next from the palace, golden girdle shimmering around her waist, her sharp gray eyes landing on her sister. Hippolyta accepts the weapons her fellow Amazons hand her, strapping them to her body with quick efficiency.

"Where have you been?" The Amazon queen takes in the gore caking all of us. "What happened?"

Hector notices his sister and blanches. "Are you wounded? What happened to all of you? Get in the palace now, Kassandra."

"The Erinyes attacked us." The princess's eyes are wide and unseeing, arms wrapped around her quaking frame. "They ripped those people in half. Right above us."

Lykou, with a gentle hand at the woman's hip, nods to one of Hector's soldiers and the man escorts her away. The earth tilts beneath my feet, an image of a woman being shredded in half above me filling my vision.

"How did they evade Troy's scouts?" Helen breathes, tan face deathly pale as she watches the ships sail steadily closer.

"How did they get here in such an impossibly short amount of time?" I ask. Apollo assured me that Hermes had been lying, and that Poseidon wasn't aiding the Achaean voyage.

"Only the gods can say," Penthesilea answers, frowning at the encroaching army. She turns and snaps her fingers in my direction.

I take an unconscious step back as her soldiers stride toward me, placing in my hands a fresh set of leathers and an array of weapons. The leathers are painted Amazon blue and red, complete with high sandals and bronze vambraces. A helmet is passed over my head, so tight it hugs my face. My blonde curls are tugged through a hole in the top and bound quickly into a taut plait. Wordlessly, the Amazons walk around me, tying on the armor and strapping a sword to my hip.

"You are one of us now, Daphne," Penthesilea says, nodding at her warriors. "Though your training is yet to be completed, we accept you among our number in thanks for saving my sister in Foloi Forest."

Something warm and unnamed swells through me, briefly overwhelming the danger that looms beyond the city's walls. I turn to Lykou, who's still standing guard at Helen's side.

"You stay here with Helen," I command. Indignation at being ordered clouds his already tan face, but I continue, "In case the Erinyes attack again."

Helen straightens, nodding. "Lykou Xanthippos. To me."

Without question, my wolf walks to her side. My eyes meet his and I see no question in his gaze. Only loyalty to the end. Hopefully not to our deaths.

Ships in the distance now collide with the sandy beach. Men leap from them, storming up the pale stretch of land. The Myrmidons sprinting in impossible lengths. They breach the first temple in seconds. Trojans flee for the walls of the city. The first of Menelaus's ships lands next, horses thundering down the planks with a single chariot leading the way.

My chest constricts, fear binding my heart and lungs. I cannot breathe fast enough. The edges of my vision begin to blur, and then darken.

Helen grabs my trembling arms. She's not gentle about it, her nails digging deep into the tender skin. Something wordless passes between us. Nothing needs to be said. The command is there.

Survive.

I blink, stepping back into myself and straightening. I march alongside Hippolyta, still sticky with blood, and we descend the steps to war.

My breath shudders, arm trembling beneath the round shield I was handed as I passed beneath the golden gates. Civilians stream past us with terrified screams. Farmers herd their livestock into the city, threatening to trample the remaining people still running inside. Paris and his brother Polydorus help them all into the city as best they can, the last rays of the setting sun reflecting off of the golden wall behind them.

"Do not let them near the gates," Hector yells, thundering past on a black stallion. "Stay beyond the reach of our archers."

Penthesilea, astride a white horse, rides in the opposite direction with a sword raised above her head. "My daughters! Swords and shields high!"

Torches are lit along the line of soldiers, their flame warming my cheeks. The sun sets beyond the ships, and darkness settles upon us all with preternatural swiftness. There is only one goddess with the power to bring night upon us all so quickly.

And she's out for my blood.

Fear floods through me. The marching Achaeans swiftly cross the sand toward the Trojan army. The sun is blotted out by the shadows filling the sky; there's a chorus of gasps from the soldiers around me. Many throw prayers out to gods old and new, some I've never even heard of. The terror fragments, sharpening in my veins.

I stand with the Amazons, chewing on the inside of my cheek and watching the encroaching men I trained with. They stop fifty yards short of our army, carriages thundering before them with the Achaean kings standing tall and proud. Achilles is not among them, but this doesn't surprise me. The Myrmidon king had little patience for politics, even in Sparta. He will wait for the fighting to start.

Menelaus and Agamemnon come to the forefront as Hector rides out to meet them. A shuddering breath escapes me when my king's eyes pass over me. He doesn't pause, though, swiftly turning to the approaching Trojan prince.

The heir to the greatest city in the east meets Menelaus's gaze without flinching. Hector says, "Have you come to apologize, Anax of Sparta?"

"Apologize?" Agamemnon's thick lips curl back beneath his crimson beard. "We have come to take back what is ours."

"Helen?" Hector angles his head toward the great walls. "The proud *anassa* has more honor than you. She's earned a place here among my people."

"Not that traitorous whore," Agamemnon bites out. "The Hellespont."

A surprised laugh bursts from Hector, loud enough to be heard atop the wall.

Beside me, Lyta says, "They do not even attempt to bargain for the Spartan queen. No efforts for peace. Something festers and rots in the Achaean kings."

Not something. Someone.

Nyx no doubt whispers in their ears, haunts their dreams.

Hector waves a hand to the north, the glittering Hellespont beyond the line of hills there. "You think that anyone will trade with you ever again? If a single drop of blood falls on this field, the whole world will know the treachery of the Achaeans."

"Oh, they'll trade with us," Menelaus says. "They will even bow to us. If the gods demand it."

Battle drums begin to rumble on the far reaches of the field. The darkness swells again behind Sparta's allies, blotting out whatever remains of the sun. Not even a hundred torches could keep those shadows at bay.

"We will see just how gods-blessed the city of Troy actually is," Menelaus continues, voice like the hiss of a snake. He raises his *dory*, iron spearhead glinting. He points it at Hector and then, slowly, turns to the right.

To me. Shock grips me by the spine, claws digging into my bones.

"Prodótis of Sparta," he says, voice booming across the field for all to hear. "If you don't die tonight, then you will be forced to watch as I take everything and everyone you hold dear. I will slit their throats and throw their bodies from the walls of Troy."

Hippolyta's elbow brushes mine, the barest touch. She continues facing forward, glare pinned on the king raising his spear toward me. Another nudge on my other arm from the warrior to my right.

In an old language I don't understand, Penthesilea yells. I follow suit as her warriors rap their shields once, twice, a third time, before hugging them to our chests. The Amazons have my back always, no matter what poison Menelaus spews.

Arms shaking, he continues to point the spear at my chest. "You best pray to your gods that I do not meet you on the battlefield, Daphne Diodorus."

My stomach hollows out. Cold, like none I have ever felt, floods through me. Not at the threat, but the implication behind his words.

Your gods, he said. *Not* the *gods*.

Agamemnon raises a *salphinx* to his lips. Before the final note of its call rings, the Achaean army lurches forward.

A black wave of death and divine darkness comes to swallow me whole.

CHAPTER
25

With a roar that sings in my blood, Hippolyta leaps forward to meet the charging army. I run, sword raised. We fly across the sand.

I skid to a halt and throw up my shield against the black arrows raining down around us, their thuds against the leather surface felt in my very core. Tremors wrack my body. I can't move my legs.

Drums and horns echo around us, mixing with the screams of the dying. The stench of smoke and blood coats my throat. The darkness drowns out the fighting around us, the night swelling to a black so thick it blots out the stars.

I remain hunched beneath the shield. My breath escapes me in wild gasps.

Everywhere around me, Nyx appears. Her feet run past me. Her lavender scent clogs my throat. Her claws peel back my shield.

Hippolyta's scream, far beyond where I kneel on the ground,

jerks me to my senses. My fear will get me nowhere but the Underworld. I bested Nyx once before. I can do so again. I will not let her frighten me.

I roll to my feet, swallow the last of my fear, and settle deep into my greatest strength: my courage.

I am a Daughter of Sparta, the Storm of Olympus, and the Shield of Helen.

And no goddess will frighten me ever again.

I duck beneath the jab of a barbed *dory*, sliding across the sand. I slice my enemy's leg and stab him in the back as he collapses. The man chokes on his own scream.

I'm up and running before he's even hit the dirt. The Amazon banner flaps in the air and I make a beeline for it. As I watch, Hippolyta bends beneath the swing of a spear. I ram my sword into the next man's gut and shove him aside.

Agamemnon thunders on his carriage, cutting through Trojans with duel swords. His horse froths at the mouth, eyes wild. His own eyes light up when he sees Hippolyta.

He drops one sword and picks up a spear.

"No!" I scream. A rush of panic fuels my pounding footsteps. I've never run faster.

Agamemnon throws the spear.

I leap and grab Hippolyta around the middle. We crash to the ground, a rush of air passing above my head as the spear thuds beside me.

There are no Spartans on our side of the battlefield. Under my breath, I throw a prayer up to Olympus in thanks. Though, I can likely only thank Apollo and Artemis.

My next opponent is armed with a sword. Its reach is longer than mine, swinging a hair's breadth from my face. The Mycenaean hoplite roars, spittle flying between us. I knock his next swing away and throw one of my own. He bats it aside, slamming his shield into me. A yelp escapes me. I'm flung backward across the sand.

With a furious scream, I sprint for the line of Amazons, already forming an arrow formation on the northern front. Opposite a spit of barren sand, Agamemnon and his Mycenaeans charge straight for the gates of Troy. The hoplites form a line with two-handed spears and a battalion of soldiers behind them with short swords.

"Bring me Trojan heads," Agamemnon roars, raising his own sword high.

They charge and the Amazons drop their spears. Even as I sprint toward the oncoming collision of soldiers, I can see that the Mycenaeans have the women vastly outnumbered. Penthesilea's rage- and fire-filled scream echoes above all the others on the battlefield.

She leads her women with movements as fluid and assured as a snake, and the Amazons meet the Mycenaeans with as much force as a typhoon. They're flung backward, the women dodging blows and landing their own. Blood arcs through the sky and sprays the sand at my feet as I storm into the fray.

A spearhead dives straight for my face. I spin, sword flashing. It lodges into the arm of a man, and his scream rattles my eardrums. I wrench my weapon free and silence his cries with a slash across his throat. Better to die quickly than suffer the slow, agonizing death of bleeding out beneath a thousand feet.

Hippolyta collides with me hard, her shoulder thudding into mine. We turn our backs to each other and cut through a crowd of men. They keep coming, a never-ending onslaught. My breathing is ragged but I force myself on.

A horn peals in the distance, then another. Not Trojan, nor even Spartan. Perhaps Ithacan or Myrmidon. I cannot say when so many different kingdoms have rallied to tear down the city in which my queen seeks sanctuary.

Agamemnon's chariot thunders past, the wheels with spokes of pointed and jagged bronze to slice an enemy's leg before they can rip him from it.

"Retreat!" His scream rattles my brain. "Back to the camp!"

Lyta and I jerk to a halt. Bewilderment pulls her brows high and pops open her mouth. The shadows peel back, revealing the shimmering gold of the sun.

My surprise lasts only a moment before I'm sprinting after them. My blade slices into the slowest men's legs. Lyta tears after me and does the same, rounding a high dune of sand.

From the sea, a dozen ships are still out among the waves. The Cretan bull, in blue and red, is painted on their sails. On their backs, catapults hurl balls of flame into the tents. Flame tears across canvas-sided tents. Farther and farther out they drift, and a single woman stands at the bow of one ship shouting commands.

More Achaeans have rallied to the camp. A dozen of them start shoving a ship out to sea to give chase. Another ball of tar and flame blows through the entire hull.

King Minos, damn the man, ruled the Cretan Sea and Aegean with calculated control. No king other than Poseidon had such mastery of the seas. Ariadne inherited her father's naval mastery.

A *salphinx* bellows from the west, followed in quick succession by a symphony of more Achaean horns. The Grecians turn on their heels, sprinting with the last of their strength for the salt-crusted beach. They stream past Lyta and me, and we begin to slowly back away. Our swords are still raised, and though their attention may be turned toward the enemy in the water, no use having it returned to us.

More Achaean ships are thrust into the waves as all the kings rally to save face against the Cretan onslaught. Six of Ariadne's ships turn in a circular wave. Four, then two in each direction, volley the last of the balls of tar into the oncoming ships. A last ship then turns to follow Ariadne's and they cut through the waves.

A Trojan horn echoes above it all, calling for our return. Every muscle in my body aches. My thighs and arms quiver, barely strong enough to carry me back across the blood-drenched field. Above, the early rays of dawn peek high above our bruised and battered shoulders. I try to think of how long we'd been fighting, but cannot. All I can see in my mind's eye are the bodies I cut down. Their number is endless.

A great desire to throw my weapons to the ground and curl up in the sand sweeps through me but, gritting my teeth, I drag my feet the last twenty yards to the walls of Troy.

The gate remains obstinately shut. We're all splattered with blood and sweat runs rivulets through the crimson stains on our faces. I lost my helmet somewhere on the battlefield, but managed to keep ahold of my shield and sword.

A slap on my shoulder makes me jump. Hippolyta digs her fingers into my aching arm. She leans heavily on me, favoring her left leg. I never even noticed her wound while we fought.

"Only the first battle and I've already twisted my knee," she says, pain pitching her words high.

Only the first battle. We will have to do this again tomorrow. I sag.

Hippolyta must see the agony in my eyes. "This was a test. Both sides pulled at our threads, to find where our armies were woven the strongest. Now we know which kings have the weakest men. Which of the Achaeans are the bravest, and yet most foolhardy. And they know the same of us. They will regroup, deliberate, and plan their next attack." She digs her nails into my shoulder. "And we will do the same. Toss aside your weapons. Let the hoplites collect them while we assist our wounded."

Indeed, now that the Achaeans have fled the battlefield for their protected beach, the towering gates boom, swinging wide for our people to rush inside. Grimacing, I join Hippolyta as she strides to a pair of wounded Trojans. She limps slightly, but hides it well as she stoops to throw the man's arm over her shoulder. I do the same for the man's compatriot, a woman with a narrow gash down her thigh. We bring them to the waiting medics at the city's gates before striding back out into the bloody fold.

The sun is setting by the time I climb the thousand steps up to Priam's palace. My sandals catch on the lip of a stair and I fall forward, bruising my hands on the hard stone. The pain is an echo, a mere memory compared to the other aches throughout my body.

A tan hand reaches toward me, and I look up into Lykou's handsome face. "Thank you, friend."

"We are much more than friends," Lykou grunts, hauling me to my feet. "Even if you do not care to admit it."

I don't have the strength to argue with him, even though I should.

Penthesilea passes us up the stairs, hardly looking winded despite the killing spree she and her sister unleashed upon the battlefield. "Rest well, Daphne. We will meet with the other commanders at dawn. I expect you to my left."

She doesn't look back, continuing up and into the palace. I let Lykou lead me to Helen's and peel the sticky leather from my body. It falls to the floor just as Helen returns, a gasp leaving her.

"Let me help you," she says, with the commanding tone of a queen. Despite the impropriety, I let her—and Lykou—lead me to the edge of the pool. I do not step into the water, though, unwilling to taint it with the gore of war. I take the sponge and bowl of water that Helen carries over.

I will wash away this death myself.

They leave me to reflect and clean. I'm passing the sponge over my arms, trying to ignore the streams of blood—someone else's blood—down my skin, when the water suddenly ripples.

Ariadne, with a dancer's grace, balances upon the lip of the pool. She wears Cretan armor, a dark blue chiton beneath it edged with a silver *meander*. I don't recognize the scent of the god's power that brought her here. She is weaponless and stands with her arms akimbo.

She raises her chin high, and her black hair, streaked with sweat, clings to her neck. "I believe thanks are in order."

I arch a brow. "A simple thank-you wouldn't do justice."

"True."

I walk toward her through the water. "Why did you help us?"

"A debt," she says simply. A diadem dotted with purple gems sits on her brow.

"We should be enemies. I killed your father."

"My father may have been my blood, but he was cruel and thoughtless." She gazes out over the city below. "There was no love in him for me or his people. Only the throne." When she turns back to me, her eyes are dark and hard like stones. "Sometimes the ties of family are nothing more than imaginary threads."

I ignore the cold chill of foreboding that sweeps down my spine. "The Achaeans will be out for your blood."

She shrugs. "They can try. They have their own gods and goddesses at their backs, and I have mine."

An arm appears around Ariadne's shoulders, followed by a glimmering, silver-clad god. Dionysus, serious for the first time I've ever seen, gives me a solemn nod. "I've planted my feet firmly on the side of the Trojans, for better or worse." He turns to the Cretan queen, and his face softens. "We both have."

"Enemies of both Olympus and Greece," Ariadne muses. She kisses him firmly. "Sounds like an adventure."

"Give Apollo my regards," Dionysus says, grinning. "And tell Hera where to shove it."

The couple disappear in a blast of silver dust. Shaking my head, I return to my bathing ministrations, too tired to think on the bizarre interaction further and too confused to string another sentence along, even in my head.

Once I have bathed, eaten my fill of cheese, bread, and a meat I do not recognize, and changed into a loose chiton, I collapse on my bed and fall asleep instantly.

A feather-light touch along my arm pulls me from dreams of Eleusis. Theseus and the golden fields disappear, replaced by the soft furs and sheer curtains of my room.

"Did nobody tend to your wounds before you fell asleep?" Moonlight halos Apollo's head. "Remind me to chew out Lykou the next time I see that dog. You would have woken too stiff to even climb from your furs."

He brushes a tender thumb down my forearm.

"No." I catch his hand before it can move to my side, despite a bruised rib there silently yelling at me to let him continue. "Save your strength. Help the others who have worse wounds than I."

A tender smile pulls at Apollo's beautiful face. He brushes a curl from my brow. "You are too selfless for these mortals, and I too selfish to be a god." He presses a finger to my lips before I can protest. "The goddesses Akeso and Panakeia are already tending to the wounded."

I don't release his hand. "No."

"I cannot heal you anyway," he says gruffly. "Not with my powers bound. Let me take you to Panakeia."

He pulls his hand away and hooks it under my legs before lifting me. His chest is firm, and I must be utterly exhausted, because no qualms echo through my mind at tucking my chin into his arm.

He's wearing a red silk cloak, threaded with the silver moon and golden sun. I smile, the movement cracking my dry lips.

"Do you and Artemis pick out your clothes together? I bet she has the same cloak in green." I shift to stare at the tiled ceiling. "Was it your need to find the perfect outfit that kept you from helping in a timely manner?"

"I assure you this cloak is no more ridiculous than the cap that Hermes used to wear." Apollo matches my smile. "It had this stupid floppy brim and these fluffy white wings that would drop feathers everywhere. Zeus ordered him to throw it in the ocean after the messenger was caught spying on Hera for him because she found the feathers all over the floor."

"Quit deflecting," I say, poking him in the side. The steady rock of his feet makes my eyelids heavy. "Everyone between here and Mount Kazbek knows that you won't leave your palace unless the color of your cloak flatters your complexion."

Night, thick and impenetrable, blankets the hallway. Sleep tugs at me, Hypnos somewhere nearby drawing me into the lulling folds of dreams and a world where my bodily pains no longer exist.

"I'm sorry, Daphne," Apollo whispers. I crack my eyes open. His face is unreadable in the long shadows of the hallway. "I wish I could have been there to fight alongside you."

"Where were you really? Don't tell me I'm right and that you skipped the battle to fluff up your wardrobe."

"Zeus trapped me atop Olympus." Fury flickers on his face. "He tricked me. I didn't even know the battle began. Not until it was already over."

"That bastard." I sigh into his shoulder. It's getting harder and harder to stay awake. "Your family's secrets nearly cost me my life last summer. Did cost me my life, actually."

"I will never let that happen to you again," he says, voice rough.

I blink. "Even you cannot keep my mortality at bay."

"We'll see about that," he says, a mischievous glint in his eyes that does nothing to dampen the fire there, too. A challenge.

I let him hold my gaze until sleep claims me.

When I wake, Apollo is gone and I'm burrowed beneath my furs. The tension in my muscles has waned, but not disappeared entirely. There's a sharp piercing pain in one of my ankles, and my scalp feels as if it is on fire.

"Damn Zeus and his ego," I grumble around a yawn.

A curious scent makes my shoulders tense, sweet fruit interlaced with incense.

With a soft, sleepy sigh, I roll onto my side. Reaching for the blade beneath my furs.

My questing fingers come up empty.

A chuckle echoes through the room and my eyes open, finding Hermes sitting on the edge of my bed, one dark leg folded over the other.

"How did you know I was here?" His voice is like liquid mischief.

I stay as still as a deer in the forest. "Your scent. When you use magic, it gives you away."

"Curious." He bounces his leg, turning toward the balcony. "You and Apollo are absolutely *adorable*." The way he says the word makes it sound anything but. "That game you two play, pretending to not love each other, is just hysterical to watch."

I resist the urge to kick him. Barely.

"Speaking of snooping." I place a hand atop the Midas Curse pooled around my navel. "Artemis knows you're here."

"No she doesn't." He silences me with a bored look before I can argue. "With my Olympian powers back to their full height—thanks to you, I might add—I will remind you that I am the god of thieves, among other things." His gaze bores into my abdomen, as if he can see right through my dress to the golden skin beneath. "I'm quite capable of eluding Artemis's prying ears."

Slowly, I climb from the bed and turn to face him, backing toward my pile of weapons.

"You needn't bother, Daphne darling. I've hidden those away, too."

I grumble and he falls backward onto my furs, hooking an arm behind his head to prop it up. "I'm here for an apology, actually."

"An apology?" A startled laugh bursts from me, and I throw a quick look over my shoulder toward Helen's bed. Her soft snores still echo around the suite, and Lykou's bed is empty.

"For doubting me," he says, standing suddenly. In the blink of an eye, he's crossed the space between us. He raises a hand, grazing my jawline with the back of a finger. "Had you listened to me, the Trojans could have suitably prepared for the Achaean arrival."

"We managed." I jerk my chin from his touch. "How did you know that they would arrive so quickly? Are you still under Nyx's thumb?"

"My loyalties"—Hermes fiddles with my chiton's ties on my shoulder, thumb brushing the scarred skin there—"are bound to no one but myself."

"Then I apologize for nothing," I say, stepping again from his reach.

Hermes sighs, dropping his hand and turning to a plate of food either Helen or Lykou left out for me. He plucks up the feta, but I slap it from his hand.

"Not my cheese," I snap. "Eat the olives, if you're going to steal my food. I can't stand them."

"How do you not starve?" Hermes smiles around a mouthful of them. "Greeks cook them in everything."

I huff, crossing my arms. "There's no point waiting around for an apology, Hermes. You're not stupid enough to still expect one. What is it you truly want?"

He looks me square in the eye, dark skin reflecting the light of the oil lamps. "For you to survive this war."

That hard iron that I've built around myself cracks. "What?"

"Don't be too flattered." Hermes picks another olive and pops it into his mouth. "I have my own reasons for wanting you to live."

I glare. "Why does Nyx want me alive?"

He sighs, rolling his eyes. "I already told you. My loyalties aren't to her."

"Damn gods and their half-truths," I mutter, searching the room for a weapon, anything to bash this bastard upside the head.

I spy an oil lamp, but he catches my wrist before I can grab it. His fingers dig in hard enough to make me gasp. I tug, but his grip is inexorable.

"You'd be dead already if I wanted to hurt you, Daphne," Hermes says, his gaze tracking over me. "Let me help you survive this war."

My heart hammers at the base of my throat, breath held. "I survived my first battle just fine."

"Your fear nearly got you and your allies killed."

"Hippolyta fought just fine without me."

"That spear would have gone right through her throat if you had knocked her to the ground even a moment later." Hermes shakes his head. "And you wouldn't even be able to hold a sword right now if it wasn't for the goddess Panakeia."

I bite back my retort.

"I can train you," he continues, letting go of my wrist. "In all the arts of the world. The Amazon training is doing wonders for your abilities against multiple assailants, but that army out there"—he points to the dark beyond the palace, where pyres from the Achaeans glow in the distance—"they are being aided by forces even Zeus doesn't know of yet. They will bring down this city, wall be damned, and I cannot have that."

"How long have you been watching me, Hermes?"

He pretends to ponder this. "Since you stabbed me in the back."

"You were in Sparta all that time?"

His face is the image of innocence. "I meant nothing untoward."

"I bet you were even in my rooms," I mutter.

"Of course I was." His smile is smug. "Where do you think that blue incense came from?"

I want to slap that grin from his face.

"Relax," he says around another olive. "It was for your protection. The smoke kept Nyx from entering your house."

"I don't need your help." I bite out the words around bared teeth. "Leave, before I find another dagger to ram into your back."

Hermes shakes his head, dark braids swaying. "Your stubbornness has grown even less endearing, and I didn't think that possible. We'll see if you remain so stubborn after your next battle." He turns toward the balcony and, without another word, flings himself into the night. A fluttering of wings drifts on the warm air for a moment before the sounds of the city below resume.

CHAPTER
26

"The Cretans were quite a help yesterday," Hector says, pointing on a map to where Ariadne's ships once dotted the coastline. "Even if they're nowhere to be found now."

We gather with King Priam's counselors and eldest sons around a circular table in his council chamber. Beyond the room, the city rings with a howling wind. The Achaeans have abandoned their camp on the beach to wait on the banks of the Hellespont in case any ships still brave the trade thoroughfare. In vain, of course.

Priam, at the advice of his counselors, sent word ahead of time to his leading trade partners, though that means that Troy's resources will be extremely limited.

"Minos's daughter likely wanted to watch and see what the odds were before landing," Penthesilea says, pressing her knuckles into the wooden table. "And she saw that sticking a dagger into the Achaeans's backs was much more fruitful."

"Don't sound too impressed, Penthe. The Myrmidons didn't fight yesterday, either." Hippolyta crosses her arms over her chest.

I look to the battlefield sketched out before us, Hector's commanders shifting the scene to show from a hawk's point of view how exactly the battle went down.

Hector's men drove through the center of the Achaean fold, spearing through and dividing the enemy army. The Amazons and I had made quick work of Ajax's men, and then Agamemnon's, but the Trojans incurred many casualties on the opposite flank.

I purse my lips, watching as commanders point out the reason for such losses.

The Spartans. They had driven hard and fast, Menelaus at the forefront on his chariot. Priam's men note only a handful of casualties among the Spartans. A miracle, considering the bloodbath that had been yesterday.

"We need to do something about Menelaus," Paris says.

"Perhaps pit my warriors against the Spartans"—a grin splits Penthesilea's face—"and see if they like the taste of Amazon steel."

Dread fills my stomach, threatening to make me puke. A horn echoes in the distance.

"The southern gate," Paris says.

The Achaeans are rallying again.

"Let's see it, then," Hector says, standing straighter. "Amazons, take the field on the same side as Menelaus. My men will protect the gates."

Hippolyta leads her warriors out onto the still-bloodstained fold. I follow on her heels. My leathers are cleaned of yesterday's sand and gore, my sword sharpened and the arrows removed from the shield, but the helmet I'm handed reeks of sweat. I force it over my face, pulling my curls through the hole in the back.

Lykou marches alongside me this time. He wears Trojan armor. So unnatural on him compared to the Spartan leathers he grew up training for.

Hippolyta tugs down her own helmet, black braids swinging in a warm, southern breeze. Her own armor is threaded with a silver *meander*, and her belt is made of solid gold. I frown, recognizing the girdle from Foloi Forest.

"Your sister gave the girdle to you?"

Hippolyta grimaces. "After Agamemnon nearly killed me yesterday, my sister thought the girdle's protection would suit *me* best. She ignored when I pointed out that the girdle's magic comes from the same god that pits an entire army against us."

Hopefully the magic of her father can save us all on the battlefield—despite us all fighting against him.

My friend twirls her sword while looking over a shoulder and throwing me a wry grin. "Are you ready?"

"Never." I turn to Lykou. "Are *you*?"

"To kill my kin? Never in a thousand years." Pain flickers across his face, replaced in an instant with a determined frown.

Before I can reply, Achaean horns ring out across the field. The horses and feet of a thousand men kick up dust as far as I can see.

Just like before, my heart thunders loud enough in my ears to drown out the battle cries around me. Fear grips me by the ankles. I could almost choke on it. It's as potent as ever.

Hippolyta leaps forward. Her warriors don't hesitate to follow. They roar an Amazon call.

There are no shadows here. There are only soldiers. An army out to capture and potentially kill my queen. I clench my teeth. That will never happen.

I charge after the Amazons, a wild scream wrenching from the depths of my soul.

Spartans—my people—thunder forward, roaring in answer. I raise my sword high above my head, my muscles living flame as I speed across that last stretch of sand.

Spartans collide with Amazons with a crash that threatens to shake the earth.

The breath is stolen from my lungs as a man slams into my shield. I remain on my feet. He drives his *dory* for my chest, my face, my legs. I dance from his reach. Carnage echoes around us.

"*Prodótis,*" the man hisses, his dark hair peeking from beneath the Spartan helmet.

"Shield," I reply. I duck beneath his next swing and drive my sword forward.

He dodges my attack easily. A growl of frustration rumbles from the back of my throat. He swipes wide, forcing me to roll beneath the swing. Sand flies around us as I leap back to my feet. Just in time for the butt of his *dory* to land directly on my chest.

My breath eddies. I barely manage to keep ahold of my sword, stumbling backward. He advances, grinning.

I dash forward, leaping high. He raises his *dory* to meet my sword. I drop the weapon, grabbing on to the spear. The grin vanishes from his face.

Using my weight as I come flying down, I jerk the *dory* from his startled grip. I sweep his feet from beneath him, and with a wild scream, I ram the point through metal, leather, and bone. Right into the center of his chest.

He chokes on blood, spraying my face, only inches from his.

It drips from my eyelashes. My heart stutters, then stops.

I stumble backward, leaving the *dory*. My breath escapes me in rapid gasps, growing faster and faster until my lungs threaten to burst from my chest. A storm builds inside me, a tempest waiting to be unleashed. I can almost taste the static of lightning on my tongue, the roar of wind building in my ears.

I killed him. One of my own people. I stumble, keenly aware of the fighting continuing around me but heedless to the danger.

Perhaps I deserve death for my treachery and betrayal, of the people who took me in.

My knees wobble, threatening to buckle beneath me.

A scream directly to my right spins me around. I duck beneath a Spartan hoplite's wild swing, then run and slide across the sand, grabbing my sword and turning in the same movement. I slice wide, right through the man's leather armor and above his navel.

Blood spurts, then pours. The man grabs helplessly at the wound, collapsing on his knees.

A wave of lavender light blasts me from my feet, and I'm flung across the sand.

Hera strides toward me. I stand and raise my sword.

"Zeus will be quite cross with me for killing you." She cracks her neck, the noise audible even on the battlefield. "But better to ask for forgiveness."

She lunges, inhumanly fast. I barely register her scepter before it smashes into my cheek. Lights flash behind my eyes and my teeth sing. My head snaps back and I fall. Hera's scepter slams beside me, lightning fast, and I can only roll away before she pounds it again and again into the ground. The entire earth rumbles beneath her immortal strength. My mortal muscles are no match for her.

I'm on my feet, and only have time to raise my sword before her scepter sweeps between us and smashes the blade into pieces. I yelp, the blow making the bones in my arms sting. I fling the hilt at her head and she bats it away with a wild laugh.

"If I promise to only maim you, not kill you, will you stop moving?" She stalks forward, purple chiton billowing in the breeze behind her. "You're more annoying than a gnat."

Hera spins and kicks my legs out from under me. I hit the earth hard enough to knock the air from my lungs. She raises the scepter high and brings it down with all her strength.

A silver sword, curved like a crescent moon, meets it just above my face.

My thundering heart catches in my throat. Artemis, biceps flexing, raises the sword and the scepter atop it. Hera grimaces, teeth bared, as she fights to push down the goddess of the hunt's weapon.

"I don't know what my father sees in you," Artemis says. She lets go, and both Hera and the weapons fall forward at the sudden loss of resistance.

I roll away. Artemis collects her sword just as Hera springs to her feet. As she's about to raise her weapon again, the younger goddess lands a kick directly into the other's chest.

Hera snarls, "I can't wait to put you in your place, *Stainless Maiden.*" She sneers, then charges forward.

Their weapons meet in the air, and the force of the blow blasts sand all around in a curved arc. Their movements are too fast to track. Jabs, kicks, slashes, all in a matter of a few blinks.

A Spartan charges toward me.

"*Prodótis!*" he roars. Many heads turn in my direction.

A target is officially on my back.

I grab a fallen man's *dory* in my right hand, and another's sword in my left. The man charges me, and we meet in a flurry of movements. More men come running, weapons raised. I block and jab, fluid like the sea.

I can't move fast enough, their attacks coming from all sides. I spin on my heels, jabbing and slashing. My elbow catches the helmeted head of one, a lancing pain shooting up my arm. Without stopping, I slice the man from shoulder to hip, turning and ramming the next in the stomach with the butt of the *dory*.

His spear catches me in the ribs, tearing through leather and flesh.

I gasp, pain like a wildfire racing up my side. I don't let myself pause, angling my sword and slicing the man right across the throat. The one I hit with my *dory* has finally caught his breath, yelling and swinging for my legs. I jump, and in the same movement ram the *dory* into the side of his head.

I'm tossed from my feet by what feels like the force of an ox. Artemis and Hera, a whirlwind of swords, storm past. Men battling beside their duel fall beneath the goddesses' elbows and feet, screaming as they are stomped on and kicked with inhuman strength.

Artemis may be the goddess of the hunt and wilderness, but Hera is the Queen of Olympus for a reason.

I don't even see the elbow Hera throws at Artemis's face. She barely avoids getting her nose smashed when the queen's scepter hooks under her legs. Artemis falls and I cry out. Without hesitating, Hera drops to her knees and straddles the younger goddess, wrenching her face up to meet her own by yanking on a handful of Artemis's brown curls.

"I can't kill you," Hera says in her face. "But I'll make you regret the day you ever dared to stand in my way."

Her forehead smashes down into Artemis's nose. It crunches, black ichor spurting between them, and the goddess of the hunt collapses, still. Fury, like a rain of thunder, itches to explode from me.

The darkness swoops in despite the sun arcing high across the sky. I blink, looking up to the growing shadows. My stomach hollows out.

Through a crowd of soldiers, Ares marches toward me wearing

a bronze helm. His chest is bare, that red vulture tattoo flapping its outstretched wings with his every step. Chaos emerges around him. The eyes of Achaeans and Trojans alike go wide, the whites of their eyes glistening in the sun. Their movements are frenzied and without focus, slashing and hacking and chopping at random. They attack one another and themselves.

This is the power of the god of war. It is bloody and wild.

Hera laughs behind me. "My son. I knew you'd return to me."

"I'm not here for you, Mother." Ares's voice drips with malice. "I'm here to kill the girl."

"Zeus will be cross with me for not bringing you to Olympus for justice." Hera's smile is cruel, a twin to her son's. She takes a step back and gives me a mocking bow. "But I will gladly watch you kill this annoying mortal first."

"*Kuna*," I hiss under my breath. Turning to Ares, I hold my sword at my side, gripping the hilt tight with bloodstained fingers and tuck my *dory* beneath my other arm, bending my knees, ready to pounce.

His answering chuckle echoes above the screams around us.

There are no healing wounds or scars on his tan skin from his fight with Apollo. His hand is still gloved in black, the one Lykou bit off so long ago. Distantly, my own wounds protest, a trickle and sharp pain in my ribs.

"Might as well throw down your weapons," Ares says, grinning as he holds his arms wide. He stops five yards short of me, the darkness a barrier between us and the growing carnage of war. "They won't help you against my powers."

"I'll take my chances." I aim the point of my *dory* right between his eyes.

His knees bend, ready to leap the space between us, when a horn so familiar to my nightmares echoes across the field.

"You made many enemies last summer," Ares says.

The shadows dissipate, clearing to reveal Spartans and Amazons at one another's throats. But all fighting stalls, the people on the battlefield turning hesitantly toward the north.

Where a thousand horses thunder across the plains.

But there's no one astride them. The riders, bare chested and screaming with wild fury, are one with the horses.

The Kentauroi of Foloi Forest.

Before I can react to their arrival, Ares unleashes a wild roar. He clears the space between us with a single leap. His sword, made of solid black, aims for my head. I only have time to duck and roll from his attack. He advances, cackling. With each laugh, the lash of a whip cracks around us.

I barely reach my feet when he swings down for me. The Midas Curse leaps from my abdomen, and with a yell, I whip my hand out. The gold curse encases my hand like a glove just as the sword cleaves between my fingers.

It bounces off my palm, the blow reverberating up my arm. My bones cry out, pulling a pained yelp from between my clenched teeth.

Fury splits Ares's wild, frenzied face as a golden vein branches up the sword from hilt to tip. It shatters, glittering metal falling into the sand.

He drops the useless hilt, pulling a dagger from the air. I roll backward from his swing, stumbling over a body, and crash back. He leaps forward, arm back and ready to skewer me with the jagged blade.

Before he can kill me, a furious roar leaves him, pummeling me farther to the ground with its force.

An arrow has pierced his chest, followed in quick succession by two more. He staggers back. Black ichor beads from the wounds, veins standing out against his skin as he looks above me.

Where Apollo advances, another arrow nocked into his golden bow. Something warm and unnamed swells through me.

He wears golden armor, bronze curls free in the whipping wind. He closes one eye, the other fixed on the goddess of marriage. "Now, my memory isn't what it was a couple of centuries ago, but I believe Zeus told you to leave Daphne alone."

Hera blanches, taking a step back, and disappears. Ares yanks an arrow from his chest with a growl, the wounds sealing themselves up almost instantly. Apollo turns the arrow on his brother.

"And you'll get not a single step closer before I cut her head from her shoulders," Ares warns. Sweat glistens at the base of his throat and at his brow. He stumbles, muscles in his thighs clenching.

Apollo walks forward, arrow still aimed at Ares's head. "Drop the weapon, brother."

"Brother?" He barks a bitter laugh, climbing onto his now healed knee. "We were never brothers."

"We could be now." Apollo rolls his shoulders, then draws the arrow back. "Or you can continue to be my enemy."

Ares rips two more of the arrows free from his flesh. A yelp is plucked from my lips as he rams them, in quick succession, into a Trojan fighting behind him. The man collapses with a choked scream. His skin begins to shrivel and turn black.

Apollo shot plague arrows, I realize.

I can't shove the Amazon away in time. It lodges in the woman's back and she collapses.

With clenched teeth, Apollo throws aside the bow and pulls a sword from his hip.

"No flashy tricks of fire and sun?" Ares's smile widens, white teeth stained with ichor. "Is my father responsible?"

Apollo's face is unreadable.

"He bound your powers, didn't he?" Ares cackles, the sound making me tremble. "Let's see if just your sword can stop me from ripping your darling's heart out."

"Not a chance." I roll, sweeping my legs around and kicking him hard, directly in the kneecap. There's a satisfying crunch, accompanied by his howl of pain. I'm already on my feet, dancing from his wildly swiping blade.

He takes a step forward, then jerks to a halt. He turns to face Hippolyta a dozen yards away, her arm outstretched and a dagger imbedded deep into his spine.

Black ichor drips from the corner of his mouth. "Daughter. I expected familial loyalty from you at least."

He spits, his ichor spraying the sand. The horns of the centaurs echo closer as they crash upon the right flank of the Trojan army.

"I'll be benevolent today." Ares holds his arms wide, turning to face each of us in turn. His grin is wide and maniacal, the dagger falling to the ground as the healing wound pushes it free. "Let's see what is left of you after the Kentauroi take their retribution."

The sand rises around us on a sudden wind, lashing into my mouth and eyes. It rises and rises, spinning in on itself. I cover my face just as Ares steps into the epicenter.

And disappears.

"Bloody coward," Apollo mutters. The sand falls, revealing a line of thirty centaurs powering toward us.

"Why didn't he just kill us?" I ask.

"Nyx is saving us for something worse, no doubt." There's something unsaid in his voice, proving this proclamation for the half-truth that it is.

Exhausted and furious, I nearly lash out at him. Hippolyta comes to my flank.

"We have another enemy at hand," she says.

The centaurs are only yards away. Apollo on my other side, we raise our weapons as one. I brace my body, locking my legs and ready to leap at a moment's notice. I won't be plowed over.

The centaurs dig in their hooves, skidding to a halt. Their leader would be recognizable anywhere, even if I did not know him from last summer.

Eurytion, red hair gleaming in the summer sun, glares down at us from his impressive height. He snorts, more horse than human, and paws at the earth. "I should kill you for what you did."

He speaks to all three of us.

Apollo pulls at the collar of his chiton, revealing a set of pale scars. "Need I remind you that you were the ones who attacked us last summer, not the other way around?"

Eurytion's men pull the strings of their bows tight, a dozen arrows trained on us from head to toe.

"Our commander has forbade me from killing you three. At least until we've completed our negotiations." Eurytion waves a heavily muscled arm to the archers alongside him. "But, believe me, I hope the negotiations fail miserably."

"Have you always been this odious?" Hippolyta rolls her eyes but doesn't relax her stance, weapon still raised.

Another centaur, one I don't recognize, trots up to our standoff. The battle around us has begun to dissipate, Achaeans marching back to the beach as Trojans prepare to gather the dying and wounded they've left behind. A glimmer of relief passes through me.

The new centaur, with the body of a pale stallion, moves between Eurytion and us. His skin is dark, a sharp contrast to the white fur of his other half. His hair is long and pulled into narrow braids that swing past his elbows. His dark eyes look us over before landing firmly on me.

"Are you Daphne Diodorus?" he asks, voice smooth and deep like a sweet, dark wine.

I swallow, throat dry, but nod. I'm no coward.

"You keep curious company, god of prophecy." He looks between me, Apollo, and Hippolyta, before turning to the line of centaurs at his back. "Round up the men."

Eurytion, with a final angry snort, gestures to his men and rears. They turn as a single unit, thundering back across the plain.

The centaur who spoke to us offers an apologetic smile. "Forgive my brother. He has never let go of a grudge in his entire life."

"My brothers are similarly stubborn," I say.

"As are mine," Apollo says, hooking his bow across his shoulders. "It's been many years, Chiron. Have you finally decided to rejoin your kin?"

"My wife implored me," the centaur—Chiron—replies with a lopsided smile. "It seems that we owe Daphne a great debt."

"Your wife"—I stumble forward a step—"the centaur we found in the Sphinx's cave. Chariclo."

"Indeed." Chiron sweeps an arm behind his back and bows low, horse legs dipping. "For which my people and I will be forever grateful."

Hippolyta coughs. "Not grateful enough, it seems." She nods to the army of centaurs now galloping in circles just beyond the bloody plain.

Chiron paws at the earth, digging a blackened hoof into the sand. "Yes, Eurytion has many of my kind at his back. My fellows were quite angry with how many were killed in your escape."

"Maybe they shouldn't have aligned themselves with Nyx"—my lips curl—"and kidnapped us, tortured us, and stole from us. Maybe then we'll take your people's concerns seriously."

The centaur considers me, face unreadable.

"Go back to your fellows, Chiron of the Kentauroi," Apollo says, the command of Olympus in his voice. "Use your famed wisdom to persuade them that Troy is not their enemy."

"The Kentauroi have friends on both sides of this war," Chiron says, voice gruff. "As do I. We owe you and Daphne a great debt for saving my wife. I will try my best."

Without another word, he turns and trots to the centaurs still galloping in the distance. The sun has risen to its apex above us, so hot I can hardly breathe. The air is hazy, making the horse figures look like shimmers now.

I clench and unclench my fingers around my *dory*, palms sticky with blood. Spartan blood. My stomach flips as I remember the men who died beneath my swing. I puke, right then and there, at my friends' feet. Neither looks disgusted, but their pained sympathetic expressions are so much worse.

Apollo glances to the west, where the Achaeans are now building pyres for the day's dead. For the people I slaughtered. "We will have time before the next battle. This was another test."

He opens his mouth, about to say more, but closes it with a flicked glance at Hippolyta, before vanishing in a glimmer of iridescent sunshine.

"If only he'd made us all disappear like that last summer." Hippolyta starts walking toward the city, her feet dragging slightly. "His powers could have helped us out of that mess, just as they could help us win this war."

If he wasn't bound, we could possibly stop this entire war. I don't understand how it is possible for Zeus to have so much power.

Hippolyta looks over her shoulder at the ransacked temples, where Achaeans drink and boast on their steps. "I don't understand why they just take such sacrilege. The gods are supposed to be prideful. Why are they not angry that their temples have been desecrated? Troy, the pride of Olympus, being attacked day in, day out?"

I dip my chin to my chest. "Perhaps it is more entertaining for them to watch this fight unfold. Very little must entertain them after thousands of years."

*   *   *

I make sure Lykou and Helen are with King Priam discussing with the other lords how to barter with the Kentauroi before I make my way to the city's streets. I've barely hit the road before I pull the pipes from around my neck.

I drag a jagged nail over the etchings, the roosters and snakes seeming to mock me, but I don't let myself second-guess my choice.

I bring the pipes to my lips and blow.

As if he had been waiting for me, Hermes steps around a marble column. His braids swing as he saunters toward me.

I raise my chin, staring him down. "I will take you up on your offer."

His wicked grin almost makes me regret the words. "And what makes you think I haven't changed my mind?"

"Because you still desire a place atop Olympus." I roll my shoulders back. "And you owe me a debt."

CHAPTER
27

His is the first of many debts I will call in.

I eye Hermes's sandals, invisible wings fluttering in the sunset-lit alleyway. "Can you take me with you when you travel? Like you did with the Muses?"

"Given up hope of winning already?" Hermes wears an indigo chiton that hooks over a single shoulder, baring half of his muscled chest.

"Just answer the question."

"Yes. Yes." He whips out his *kerykeion*, the golden chalice slashing through the air. "Where would you like to go?"

"Lemnos," I reply instantly.

Hermes's dark skin seems to pale. "There's no bloody way I'm taking you there. He'll kill me the moment I land on that island."

"Then be subtle about it. Or use one of your tricks." I wave broadly at him. "The same ones that keep you from Zeus's sight."

He grumbles, but steps closer. His hand is cool as it comes up to grip my biceps tight.

"Whatever you do," he says softly, "do not look down."

I clench my eyes shut as the world whips from beneath my feet.

Wind rushes in my ears, a hollow roar for a few breathless moments, before I land on unsteady legs. My knees tremble, but I release a solid breath, the wind still crashing around us on a desolate, rocky peak.

Hermes brought me to the mouth of a dark cave, overlooking a red, barren island below. The sea around us is tumultuous and wild, great waves crashing relentlessly into the cliffs.

"Poseidon is in one of his moods," Hermes mutters before turning to the cave. He gives me a not-so-gentle shove. "Well, go on, then. I'll wait out here."

"Afraid, Hermes?" I coo.

"I prefer to be called wise," he hedges, looking into the dark abyss. "I know where I'm not welcome."

"Really?" I start down into the darkness. "Could have fooled me."

"That's not an easy thing to do," he calls after me, sarcasm dripping from his words.

Shaking my head, I descend into the cave's depths. A spiral staircase meets my feet, and I walk down, down, down on sure feet. A steady ringing greets me before the smoke does.

A sea nymph meets me outside a metal archway. Her hair is long and clings to her pale skin, as if perpetually wet. Her eyes are slanted and unnaturally green.

"He's been expecting you for some time," the nymph says, cocking her head. "You may call me Cabeiro."

Ah, yes. Ligeia told me of the nymph that, after being tossed from Olympus in disgrace, sought solace with the god of the forge. I don't understand how a creature of the sea can stand to live beside a forge, but perhaps she stays here because she has to.

"If I leave this mountain, Aphrodite will kill me," she says, answering my unasked question. "Even if the goddess of so-called love has never appreciated her husband, as I do, she is nothing if not jealous."

"Bring her in, Cabeiro," says a gravelly voice.

Hephaestus's forge is bathed in red, the flames licking the walls. The moment I step inside, sweat coats my body, making the sandy folds of my chiton cling to my frame.

The Nereid stops me with a cold, clammy hand on my shoulder. "Though she may not covet what is in this forge, Aphrodite has something that she loves dearly in Troy. Use that."

She leaves me to walk the rest of the way into the rumbling abyss of the mountain alone.

Hephaestus doesn't look up as I approach, too engrossed with hammering away on an anvil at a narrow, golden sword. Ligeia told me as a child that the god of fire was a hideous beast, so horrible to look upon that his own mother threw him from Mount Olympus. But the man I see hunched before me isn't hideous. In fact, he's anything but.

Even atop Olympus when I first met him, I thought his weathered face endearing, the scars upon his knuckles a sign of his fortitude and dedication to his work. His hair is shorn close to his pale, scarred scalp; his eyes are black as coal. He is broad shouldered and tall, made short by the way he hunches over his work.

I scuff the blackened earth at the edge of the forge, clear my throat, and say, "You once promised me armor and weapons."

"And I never break promises," Hephaestus says, still not looking up from the anvil. "But I do not leave my work on doorsteps and hearths for just anyone to find. You must come to me."

I hold my arms wide. "And here I am."

He finally looks up, unsmiling. "When I heard about your fights with Hera and Ares today, I knew you would find me. You need weapons impervious to those of the gods. My work." His voice is harsh, like rough pumice stone. "I must admit I am surprised that you didn't come sooner."

"What use would I have for the legendary work of the god Hephaestus in Sparta?"

"No, that's not it." He squints in the flaring firelight. "You were hesitant to take what *we* owed you. Why?"

There is no malice in the god's face, nor deception and trickery, things I would find lingering beneath any other Olympian's features. So, I answer him honestly.

"Because I wanted nothing to do with Olympus after last year." I incline my head, thinking of Demeter's stone buried in Sparta's field. "Beyond what grace you can give to my people."

"Not your people anymore." He turns back to the gilded sword.

He picks up his hammer as I open my mouth to press, but he cuts me off by powering the tool down, making the metal sing. His voice, like the blow of stone on stone, rings above the power of his own work.

"Return to Troy and your queen, Daphne. Apollo will bring you my work as soon as it's ready."

I dare to ask, "Any idea when that will be?"

He merely shakes his head.

Wordlessly, I leave the great forge, climb the endless stairs, and take Hermes's hand.

"Hephaestus tell you to scram?" Hermes asks when we alight in Troy.

He's brought me to a solitary rooftop, higher than all the others in the great city. The wind is gentle, filling the city with a soft, mournful song from the cornices on the buildings. The sun still lingers, hesitating upon the horizon just beyond the Achaean army. From here, they are mere ants, meandering and marching along that stretch of sand.

"You know Hephaestus better than I, having spent a millennia with him. How do you think he responded?" I walk the edge of the roof, searching for a way down, and grumble when I find none. Around a sigh, I say, "Why did you bring me up here, Hermes?"

"Helen's returned to her room. Fewer questions asked this way." He comes to stand beside me, peering down at a balcony below. "And because I know you're not done with me tonight."

I arch an eyebrow. "Oh? That's news to me."

"No need to grovel or anything," Hermes says, turning to me and sweeping a low bow. "I would be honored to help you train."

A surprised laugh bursts from my chest. "I don't need your help."

"Because you think you're such an amazing fighter already?" Hermes's voice is mockingly sweet.

I glare at him. "No, because I'm already spending my every free moment training with the Amazons."

"I can help with that, too, you know." He steps close, his magic thrumming in the minimal space between us. "The exhaustion you feel after every battle, during every day you practice with Ares's daughters. I can take that away. Even if Apollo can't."

I pointedly ignore his smug look.

"This training I'm offering you is your edge in battle," he continues. "I will teach you things no other warrior in Greece has ever known."

"That would be...helpful." Something like hunger stretches through my veins. I admit, "I'm useless against Ares at his full power."

"Invulnerability from Olympian magic is another thing entirely." Hermes shakes his head. "You do not want to mess around with those curses."

"Why not?"

"I have trained with Ares before," he says, ignoring the question. "I know how he fights. I can show you his weaknesses. The gaps in his armor, if you will."

I frown. "What do you have to gain from helping me?"

"I already told you," Hermes says, spreading his arms wide. "I need you alive."

I guess I could help him. And if he does betray me, I can use the things he teaches me against him.

I hold out my hand. "Deal?"

His smile is wide, teeth glittering in the moonlight. "Deal."

He accepts my hand, his power ripping up my arm like branches of ice. I gasp, nearly letting go, but he holds me tight. When he finally releases me, I stumble backward, almost falling from the roof. He catches me again with a firm arm around my waist.

His smile is a little bit tricksy, coy, and wicked all rolled into one. "Shall we begin?"

CHAPTER
28

Lightning crashes between the trees. Rain floods my vision. Someone throws me backward and I crash into the water.

I'm pulled down into the dark.

The black water surges. I open my mouth to scream and it pours in. I choke and claw for the surface. A howl breaks through, mournful and long.

I jerk awake.

Eos hasn't even risen beyond the city. My room is still dark, the furs intertwined around my bruised body.

A low howl floats through the air. I leap from the bed.

Lykou tosses and turns across the room. Both arms are raised above his head, legs curled as if ready to pounce. His face is slick with sweat, eyes clenched shut and teeth bared. A growl rumbles from his chest, a noise that is far from human. Shivers course up my spine.

Helen sleeps through his fit. I tread softly across the room with both arms outstretched. The silk partition slides over my shoulder as I cross the threshold. The Lykou of before would have woken at the slightest sound. That was before he grew to rely upon wolf senses and before his nightmares dragged him down, down, down into the recesses of Nyx's lair each night.

"Not her," he whispers in his sleep, making me hesitate. His tone takes on a pleading note. "Don't take her from me."

I step closer.

"Hurt her"—Lykou's lips curl back to bare his teeth, so similar to the wolf of before—"and I'll kill you."

Something sharp in me cracks. I reach out to cup his sweaty cheek. His eyes flutter open and recognition dawns in their dark depths.

"Thank you for not attacking me," I say. "I'm not the only one who sleeps with a dagger under their pillow."

"I would know your touch anywhere." He does not pull away from my hand. He takes it in his own and grazes a finger up the underside of my arm.

I cannot return the want, the thirst in his face. Gently, I say, "Shall we patrol the wall together?"

We dress quickly. I wash my face and plait my hair before clipping the red cloak atop my shoulders. Assured that the Amazon warriors outside Helen's door will keep her safe, we make quick, quiet leave of the palace. Lykou walks beside me in the narrow hallways, his arm brushing mine. We take the stone bridge from Priam's palace until we reach the wall. Soldiers march in pairs of two and three atop the impossibly high structure, and we pass them with reverential nods. Lykou is silent, content to walk alongside me.

More Amazons are below, marching along the trenches and wrestling in pairs. Their games are a tradition likely picked up among the Greeks, a funeral rite to celebrate death rather than lose oneself to grief. I look out over the stretch of battle-scarred sand. The Achaean camp is largely silent.

"No funeral games?" I frown.

"Odysseus and his men had a handful of wrestling matches," Lykou says, inclining his head. "But no, the other kings have been silent after each battle."

"Maybe nobody worth celebrating has died yet."

Doubtful, but it is the only explanation I can think of. I purse my lips. The silence makes me itch like I'm wearing an ill-fitting dress.

"It doesn't sit right with you, either," Lykou says.

"No," I say. "I doubt Paidonomos Leonidas leads the army if there are no funeral games. He was very adamant about respecting them."

"When I was on the wall for that first battle, none of the Spartan formations were familiar. Nothing the *paidonomos* ever taught us." Lykou tunnels thick fingers through his hair with a clicking noise of his lips. "Why would Menelaus leave him behind?"

"Perhaps they worry we have given their secrets away and so hoped to try something new?"

"No." My friend shakes his head. "They would use the old formations to lull us into a sense of security and then turn on us."

There are cheers below our feet. Penthesilea has trounced one of her commanders.

I lean over the edge of the wall for a closer look. The sea breeze pulls my hair from its braid to flap behind me with my cloak. A soft sigh over my shoulder makes me turn.

The dawn has started to rise, at long last, painting Lykou's face in delicate light. Longing makes his expression soft. His smile is coaxing and his eyes are imploring. A blush rises up my neck and his smile slips.

"I cannot return your love," I say. The words are barely a whisper but I cannot keep them behind my teeth any longer. "Not in the way you want me to."

"Am I not enough?" His voice trembles.

"You are," I say, taking his hands in mine and squeezing. "You are more than enough. But no amount of searching inside myself will find the love that you hope for. You are like a brother to me."

"You tell yourself that because you cannot bear the thought of losing me." He tears his hands away. "I won't hurt you."

Our love would be pure. It would be painless and without secrets. That isn't what I hunger for, though. I want a love that leaves me restless. One that excites me and has me gasping. Someone who takes the embers inside me and breathes them to life.

I continue walking along the wall, so fast the ground is a blur. My friend jogs to keep up.

"Apollo won't make you happy, Daphne." Lykou's face is no longer soft. Shadows dip into the harsh lines drawn across brow and jawline. "Not forever. Eventually, he will toss you aside as he has all of his lovers."

"This isn't about him," I say, jerking to a halt.

"It's always about him." Lykou pants, waving an arm. "This whole war is about him and his family. They want you to protect this city, but won't even tell you why!"

"Because Helen is Zeus's daughter," I say, with a quick look around to make sure nobody heard us.

"Zeus doesn't give a damn about Helen and you know it." He grabs me roughly by the shoulders. "You and Apollo will never have what we could. Not while his family controls you."

His thumbs dig into my collarbone just above where the Midas Curse dances. Artemis hears everything.

"If you want to turn your back on this, on me"—Lykou releases a shuddering breath—"don't look back and expect me to still be there waiting for you."

I open my mouth to protest—to what end, I don't know—when a clicking echoes up the wall toward us.

I lean over the edge to peer below. Trojans dig a deep trench just at the base of the wall. Some throw objects into the trench, then throw dirt over it, filling the gap back up. I squint. "What are they burying?"

"Animals."

Lykou and I spin around. Paris saunters over. His face is gaunt, as if his sleep was as fitful as ours.

"Why are you burying animals?"

"And what kinds?" Lykou demands. "You'll offend the gods."

"The gods seem to have abandoned us already." Paris waves a hand through the air. "Besides, we're not the ones to kill the creatures. The Achaeans left them at the gates last night."

"That's absurd." My mouth opens and closes. "They wouldn't disgrace the gods, either."

"Judging by their flagrant sacrilege already"—he points to the temples by the beach, where Greeks drink on the steps—"I doubt they care about offending the gods."

"It doesn't make any sense." My friend shakes his head. "Paidonomos Leonidas wouldn't allow it."

"Reports from our spies say that Leonidas is dead. Killed before the Spartan army even left the capital."

My knees threaten to buckle and I reach a hand out for balance. "That's not possible. He's the best commander Sparta has had for centuries."

Lykou's tan face has blanched. "That explains why the battle formations are so different."

"I was going to ask you both if you could tell me anything you

know about them. Anything to give our army an edge in this war."
Paris inclines his head, his voice hollow and unfeeling. "But you just
answered my questions quite succinctly."

I don't know if I would have told him anyway. Fighting against my
people is one thing, but betraying my kingdom's secrets is another
entirely.

That must be written across my face, because Paris says, "It is in
the best interests of Helen that you tell us everything you know. We
can't protect her unless we know our enemies."

The two-pronged blare of a centaur's horn captures our attention
past the wall. A cloud of dust floats above the foothills beyond the city.

Paris says, "The Kentauroi have made their decision."

I swallow. "We should retrieve Helen and go to Priam's council
chamber."

I turn, striding along the wall toward the stairs, and don't look
back to see if either man follows.

Servants drape Helen in a silver chiton threaded with cerulean waves
that flutters behind her as we march to Priam's megaron. We arrive,
pushing in behind Hector and his wife, just before the clip of at least a
dozen hooves echoes down the hallway.

Lykou stands on our queen's other side, refusing to meet my eyes.
He looks toward the entrance, teeth clenched so hard a tic forms in
his jaw. I chew my cheek. Priam's guards straighten as Chiron leads
two other centaurs down the long, red runner to the throne. The Trojan king's knuckles are white as he grips the gilded arms of his throne,
watching the centaurs plod intently toward him.

Chiron stops a casual distance from the throne and bows, his
horse legs bending until his knees touch the floor. The two other centaurs behind him do the same.

"Dear Priam." Chiron stands, holding a hand over his heart. "Forgive our bloody arrival yesterday. Some of my kin are overeager, and you might say that our loyalties are especially knotted as of late."

"Knotted." Priam nods. "An interesting word to describe the Kentauroi who have historically fought the Achaeans, for centuries actually. What makes your kin so loyal to them now?"

I shift slightly when Chiron's gaze flicks in my direction before returning to the Trojan king.

"Old grudges. My kin are notorious for them, actually," the centaur says, mouth a grim line across his face. "But we also take debts just as seriously."

"Oh?" Priam raises a gray, shaggy brow.

Chiron nods. "The Kentauroi have talked long into the night. We would have aligned ourselves with the Achaeans, many of my kin pledged to the goddess of darkness"—a shiver ripples up my spine—"but that pledge does not outweigh the lives of our own."

Now he turns to face me fully, the audience standing apart so that everyone can see who exactly he glances at. I swallow as Helen looks to me, confusion alighting her stunning face. Even King Priam adjusts himself atop the throne, leaning on an elbow to peer at me.

Chiron offers me an apologetic smile. "For the freedom of my wife, lovely Chariclo, kept imprisoned for eight years by the Sphinx, the Kentauroi will not take part in the Trojan War."

The Trojan War.

The title rings throughout my head. These are not mere battles. This is a full-blown war.

The Sparta you know will be gone forever more on the bloody fields of Troy.

"I'm afraid that I cannot offer you anything more, Anax," Chiron continues, "but I am pleased to tell you that we will not be adding another enemy to your number."

Silence stretches broad wings across the great hall, broken only by the rapid thunder of my heart. I look down at my toes, keenly aware of the focus of every person in the megaron. I flex my fingers, pulse rising like an inexorable tide.

Priam finally coughs. "Before you return to your forest, great Chiron, I would have a word with my counselors and generals. I offer you the promise of safety from my armies in return for you leading your kin as far from here as possible."

"If it means that no more of them shall die, then I will gladly accept your offer." Chiron nods to his fellows as Priam whispers to an attendant, waving a hand bedecked with many large rings.

Theseus also wore large rings like Priam's, his entire hand gloved with glittering iron and gold and jewels.

I swallow the pain that rises in my throat like bile. Helen pokes me in the ribs and I turn sharply to her. "Sorry?"

She inclines her head. "The king wants us to join them."

I blink, wordlessly following Helen and Hector to the council chamber atop the palace. Belatedly, I realize it was on top of this room that Hermes took me last night. A flash of moonlight crosses my vision, of the god flinging me aside and a tangle of our swords. The elbow he clipped across my jaw. I touch a finger to the bruise there.

Priam faces off against the centaurs, his arms behind his back. Chiron gives me a sheepish grin when I walk into the room.

"Forgive me," Hector says, glancing between us, "but how exactly do you two know each other?"

"We don't, actually," I say. "I met him for the very first time yesterday."

"The Shield of Helen does not lie." Chiron hooks his own hands in front of his narrow chest, tail lashing the air. "She does know my commanders very well, some of whom would rather bathe the fields below with her blood rather than return to Foloi." He looks to Hippolyta, standing beside her sister. "And yours as well."

"They'd find that I'm rather hard to make bleed," Hippolyta says while digging the tip of a knife beneath her nails with a bored expression.

Penthesilea rolls her eyes. "I apologize for my sister's dramatics, but I don't regret her actions last summer. Your kin stole from us and kidnapped Helen's Shield. Their actions were merely defense, nothing more."

The centaur leader nods. "To which I agree. And now, with all this nasty business behind us, I will gather my men to leave." He turns, but a word spills out before I can stop it.

"Wait." I stumble forward.

He does me at least the courtesy of that. Hoof raised and eyebrows high.

I swallow, keenly aware of the eyes of every important figure in Priam's army currently latched on to me.

"You said that your kin answer to the goddess of darkness." I thumb the hilt of my sword. "What has Nyx promised them for such servitude?"

Chiron considers me, weighing the angry looks of his fellows and the army of centaurs waiting outside the city.

"Power," he finally says, voice soft as silk. "She offered them a new balance of power."

To upend Olympus. That had been her goal last summer. To take from Zeus and his kin what she felt was never theirs, though I don't yet understand how tearing Troy down will help her accomplish this. Perhaps, without the love and devotion of the Trojan people, their powers will grow weaker.

He turns to leave, but pauses on the threshold once more. Chiron turns to Priam and Hector. "You should know that the Achaeans have called in many more allies. You should do the same. This paltry army will not be enough, even with the blood of Olympus offering protection to this city."

*   *   *

I leave the Trojans as they squabble over what allies they have left to call. There are too few, the cities on the Eastern shores of Greece already ransacked by Agamemnon and his allies. I storm the halls toward my room, fists bunched at my sides and cloak whipping behind me.

My jaw trembles, the feeling of my blade slamming into Spartan bodies still echoing through my own.

Prodótis.

That is what I am now, and will be forever. All those years aspiring for Spartan acceptance and I've literally severed the hands that have reached for me. I'm no less a traitor than Ares.

CHAPTER

29

C hiron did not lie.

Too soon, I'm hefting a shield against my chest. My breath fills my helmet with clammy warmth and makes the metal stick to my temples. The fear will never go away, I realize. Not truly. I just need to learn to fight alongside it.

I've been paired with the Thracians, to be lost among their number. I make too easy a target, Menelaus and Agamemnon having ordered their men to single me out among the fray.

Banners flap in the air above the approaching army. I spy the Myrmidon black and Agamemnon's lion. My breath releases in a whistle. Achilles was said to have refused to fight. Either there are defectors among his own men, or something changed among the Achaeans that rallies him to battle now.

They begin to charge. Hooves thunder around me. Roars fill the air.

I join the Thracian charge with a high-pierced scream.

We collide with the Achaeans. I'm slicing, cutting, and slashing my way through the line.

In the back of my mind, Paidonomos Leonidas yells orders.

"*Dive,*" he would tell me.

I slide beneath a Myrmidon's swing.

"*Don't let your back face them.*"

I'm spinning, *dory* jabbing and slicing in quick succession. Blood spurts, spraying my face.

"*Never stop.*"

I keep running. My breath is carefully measured. I've been training for this my entire life.

More of Achilles's Myrmidon banners surge forward, aiming for me in the crowded fold. One cuts through the Thracians with vicious grace. With a single spin, he's cut the back of their knees. My allies fall to the ground. He jabs for me and I parry his swing. His sword thunks into my *dory.*

I nearly lose my grip when he wrenches away. The wood of my *dory* threatens to shatter and snap.

My attacker leaps to his feet just as I do. His movements are a mimic to my own, perfectly honed over twenty-one years.

Pyrrhus.

Myrmidon helmet on his head, his leather armor painted with the teal dolphin of Achilles's army, Pyrrhus angles his sword directly at my neck.

I nearly drop my spear. Despite the chaos reigning around us, I ask, "Why do you wear Myrmidon armor?"

I know his answer before he even says it. "Because, in retribution for your betrayal, Menelaus banished Alkaios and me from Sparta." There is no love in his voice, only cold and hate. "They whipped us both. Burned our homes down. Banished Alkaios's wife and sold her to Agamemnon's men."

My knees threaten to buckle. "I had no choice, Pyrrhus. I had to protect Helen."

"How is helping the Trojans steal her away protecting her?" he roars.

He lunges forward and I have to roll from his swing. The metal hisses in the air above me.

"Bloody hell, Pyrrhus." I crouch. "You could have killed me."

An Achaean aims for me. I deflect the man's wild swing. I stumble backward from his next blow.

Pyrrhus does nothing to stop him, only watching. His chest heaves, fingers tight around the hilt of his sword.

I drop to my knees and slice above my enemy's kneecaps. Blood sprays my chest, coating me in gore. His scream burns into my ears as he falls. I grab the man's head and drag my sword along his neck. He thuds to the ground.

I meet Pyrrhus's wild gaze. His nostrils flare, and I cannot decide if, should he attack me, I would protect myself or let him skewer me.

He leaps across the space again, sealing my choice. The sword slashes, catching my cape. Fabric tears and I'm jerked back. Betrayal flashes through me, a hurt so vivid it's as if he actually managed to stab me.

He pulls back and slices through the air again. I spin as Hermes taught me. My *dory* meets his wrist with a crack loud enough to be heard even above the roaring battlefield.

His face contorted with pain, he switches hands and swings the sword. I ram my shield into his bad arm before he can take a swipe.

"Stay down," I command, but cannot help the pleading tone that edges into my voice. "Wait until the battle dies off and then go back to camp. I'll ask the gods to heal you."

He climbs to his feet. "I don't want anything from them, or you."

I shove him down again. I make sure to hit his bad arm. Yelling and clutching his wrist, he crumples to the ground.

He pants. The pain must be blinding. Even a Spartan can continue through only so much. The bone will be shattered, every movement fracturing it further and pushing it through muscle, skin, and tendons.

"Stay down," I say again. "Or one of these men will kill you, and I won't be around to protect you."

"You're a traitor," he says, spitting at my feet. "I should have thrown you from the cliffs long ago."

I stride forward and yank him up by the cuff of his armor. My face is so close I can smell the wine on his breath. Only a fool drinks before battle.

"And I should have let you remain a stag for the rest of your days."

Even as the words tumble from my mouth, I know I don't mean them.

But they're said and my brother's face hardens. Stone, unfeeling and without even a hint of love.

I drop him and spin, losing myself in the bloody fray. Tears, not from exhaustion or pain, pour down my cheeks.

Every muscle in my body aches. I drag the shield across the sand, limping toward the gates of Troy. I turn for a last look at the retreating Achaeans, kept firmly from ever breaching the line toward the gates, but find no sign of my brother.

His words and curses echo through me, ringing with painful clarity.

I am a betrayer to both Sparta and my family. A sob catches in my throat.

"Why the mournful face?" Lyta jogs across the sand. There's a gash on her upper arm, and her own shield is nowhere to be seen.

"My brother was out there." I raise my face to the sky, fighting back more tears. "He tried to kill me."

She inclines her head. "My father has threatened to kill me. Multiple times now."

I don't mask my irritation. "Did you *ever* have a good relationship with him?"

"No," she allows. "But this is war, Daphne. Not a training yard tussle."

"I always thought that wars were just bloodshed and death," I say. "Not irreparable endings of another kind."

"Wars are messy." She shrugs. Her shoulders sag and a grimace flickers across her face.

I drop my shield. I take her wounded arm and pull it across my shoulders, taking her weight as well as mine. A contented sigh escapes her.

Lykou strides in front of us. His leathers are torn, and his arms stained with blood.

"Wolf," Lyta calls after him. "Black wolf!"

He turns mid-stride, not even looking at me. He gives her a curt nod before continuing to the wall.

"That was meant to sting," Lyta says with a mock wince.

I look down at our feet. "I hurt him far worse."

We're silent for a few moments as we limp across the sand, the only sound the swishing of our feet and the hoplites gathering the fallen weapons around us.

Finally, Lyta releases a long, weary sigh. "They don't talk about love in Sparta."

I glance up. "No. Women are often matched up with those they believe will create the strongest children."

"Spartans are a bunch of stone-headed, piggish oafs," Lyta mutters.

We continue walking, my friend leaning more and more into my side the closer we get to the wall.

"Just because someone loves you, Daphne," she says, voice soft, "doesn't mean you have to love them back."

We pass under the arched gate and I help her down on a set of steps.

"Amazons may not marry for love as well, but that doesn't mean I do not know that particular heartache." She grimaces. "I've lost two lovers to battle. Both were vibrant and ferocious, lovely on the battlefield and off. I lost one woman and thought I would never feel again. Finally opened up my heart to Evandre, only to have her stolen from me by Thanatos."

Her lips tremble.

"Penthe sent me to find the girdle to end my grieving. And then I met you."

She chokes a short laugh. "Don't worry, this isn't some misguided way of flirting."

"Thank you for telling me," I say, rubbing her unwounded arm. "Even with a war raging around us, it is easy to feel alone, especially in matters of the heart."

I let her rest a few moments more before helping Lyta the rest of the way to her palace.

The next morning, the smoke from Achaean burial mounds still spirals into the air, creating a gray haze that stains the horizon. From atop the wall, Lykou, Helen, and I look out on the army gathered below, looting the temples, soiling Troy's once pristine beaches.

"Disgusting." Helen shakes her head, dark hair dancing around her tan face. "Agamemnon is a disgrace to his own kingdom. The laws of warfare mean nothing to him."

The day is hot and heavy already, sweat slicking my skin. Judging from the lackluster movement among the Achaean army, we might have a short respite from bloodletting. Thank Tyche.

"I need to train some more." I swing my arms overhead and dip to the side in a deep stretch. "Will you come down to the training arena?"

"No, but you can go and Lykou will stay to watch over me." Helen shakes her head again. "I'm having breakfast with Hector's wife. I will come down afterward."

There is a hitch in her voice that speaks to the lie in her words, but I don't remark upon it. A moment alone is what she truly wants.

I thud down the palace stairs, an ache to call for Apollo growing in me. He would come, in an instant. It would neither help nor ease the ache, though.

I don't make my way to the training arena, instead pulling the pipes from beneath my shirt once I descend the wall's great steps. Before I can even rest my lips around the instrument, the flutter of Hermes's wings echoes all around me.

Apollo said that this city is protected by the wall, his ichor spilled into every stone. Ares cannot set foot in this city with ill intent unless invited in through the gates. Which is why the Erinyes remained in flight during their attack on the Trojans, and is perhaps why I can actually trust Hermes despite every part of myself screaming otherwise.

His face is mere inches from my own when I turn around. "Your form was sloppy out there."

"I was hoping you could tell me some things."

Hermes groans and throws his hands into the air. "And I was hoping for a bit of a tumble, not some more boring conversation."

"I'll train with you," I allow, and he turns to face me once more. "But I want some answers first. And don't call it a tumble. That—"

He's suddenly pressed against me on the narrow stairway, heedless of the soldiers marching past, his lips nearly touching my own. His fingers brush my cheek, trailing down my neck. "That what? Brings images too hot for your mind to handle?"

My hands rise between us and shove hard against his firm chest. He barely stumbles.

"If you'd let me finish, you would have heard me say that it"—I swallow, suddenly too warm—"that you make it sound like a squabble rather than preparing for battle."

"What is war if not a squabble of epic proportions?" Hermes waves a hand through the air. "All right, all right. Come."

I let him lead me through the bustling, crowded city, to a house close to the center. It has no windows, and only a small doorway. I step through, expecting to find a storage room but instead my feet slosh in a cold puddle. Water drips overhead, falling on my brow and shoulders, and when I look up, blue and green stalagmites reach down toward me.

Shivers wrack my frame, and not from the chill air. "Where did you take me?"

"I didn't take you anywhere, if we're being quite clear." He turns to me and frowns at my face. "We're not in Tartarus. I'll never return there."

I release my breath in a long, shrill whistle. "So where ... ?"

"A cave below Mount Kyllini," he says with an errant wave of his hand. The chill immediately dissipates, the cave brightening at the fissures in the stone around us with a warm, amber light. "I'm the only Olympian allowed here without permission."

"Olympian gifts," I muse, peering into the corners of the cave. Now that it isn't full of shadows, his trinkets are within view. Items from all corners of the world litter the grand space. Not a single one recognizable. The floor around us is covered with a cascade of glittering coins, most I don't recognize, and carpets threaded with vibrant colors. There are also plants, vines winding their way up the wet walls, and lights glowing from painted boxes. No jewels, though, or anything else that would immediately be considered valuable. No, everything here is a curiosity, which is exactly why Hermes added it to his collection.

"Did you take tips from the Sphinx of Thebes on interior decorating?" I wander over to a long oak table at the far end of the cave. "Or is hoarding something that she learned from you?"

"You tease me now, but wait until you try to squirrel away half of my belongings."

I scoff. "Because none of these are stolen?"

On the table, jewelry and weapons gleam in the low light of the cave. Rings and necklaces and amulets are carefully separated and placed on white furs. Swords and spears glow beside them, shined and spotless. None of the metal is aged despite the damp of the cave. My fingers dance above them.

"Tell me about these."

Hermes is beside me in a flutter of wings. His chest puffs out, a smug smile dancing on his lips. "Which ones?"

Softly, I say, "All of them."

He chuckles. "We don't have time for that."

I point to a necklace made of a single ring of amber. "That one?"

"That particular bauble belonged to a powerful woman far, far north of Greece. A trickster friend of mine actually stole it first, so I don't feel guilty for taking it." His mouth quirks to the side. "I left a replica in its stead. The original owner now wears it."

I point to a ring, boring and noteless. It is a single band of gold. "And that one?"

"The Ring of Gyges," he says, matter-of-factly, as if I have any idea what that means. At my blank expression, he puffs up his cheeks and sighs. "It can grant the wearer invisibility."

My eyes widen. It would give me just the edge I need to turn any battle. I reach for it.

Hermes slaps my hand hard enough to make my eyes water.

"Don't touch anything." His voice is stern. "Touch anything here without my permission, and this table is cursed to steal a memory from you."

"That's horrifying." Still, I'm drawn to the table and what each priceless item might represent. The power on that wooden surface practically emanates in waves, making me hungry and thirsty all at once.

"Here." He picks up a plain gray stone. "Since you seem to love wolves so much."

He tosses it to me. The moment the rock lands in my palm, howling erupts around me. They pierce the darkness and echo around the cave, growing louder and louder.

I throw it back to him with a gasp. "What in Olympus was that?"

"This is Gjöll." Hermes slaps it back on the table. "I borrowed it from the same kingdom as that necklace."

"Borrowed?" I scoff, crossing my arms over my chest. "You stole it."

"Semantics."

I mutter a curse under my breath.

Hermes steps in front of me and raises an arm. "How about we look at my garden instead."

He points to a collection of flowers and herbs growing in the single beam of sunlight that filters down into the cave. Bowls with nectar and bushes of fruit reach toward the blue and gray ceiling.

"How many of these did you steal from Demeter and Persephone?" I stroll over to the flourishing patch of green.

"Two or three." His smile is nothing short of smug.

Hermes points to each patch in turn. "We've got haoma, Yao grass, and some peaches that would get me in a lot of trouble if you ate." He turns. "Ambrosia, if you ever want to dabble with immortality. Over here I've got Sanjeevani if you're ever feeling particularly ill. And—"

"Is that my golden apple?" I exclaim, spotting a glimmer of gold.

"It could have been anyone's. Honestly, Daphne. You think I haven't stolen one from the tree before?"

"I can tell when you're lying, Hermes." I snatch it up and shove it into his face. "When did you take this?"

"It was just sitting in your bedroom back in Sparta."

"You sneaky little rat." Indignation makes my skin crawl.

Now it is his turn to cross his arms over his chest. "Did you want Ares to find it after you left? I'm sure his daughter Eris could use it to stir up quite the fuss."

"No. Better here than in his claws." With a resigned sigh, I toss it back into the garden. "How did you even come by all these things?"

Hermes shrugs and begins to walk toward a pair of cushioned *klines*. "Zeus is a paranoid man. He sees betrayers in every corner and doorway. One of my Olympian duties was to travel the world and search for enemies. I collected everything here on such forays."

"Impressive." I don't fail to note the smugness that upturns a corner of his mouth. "And your powers kept you from being caught, as they do now?"

"Well, I'm fast. And..." He points to a patch of white flowers in his garden. They droop, heavy with their petals, stalks a lovely dark green. "That plant keeps me immune to the magic of other gods. Moly, it's called."

I reach for the plant, keenly aware of the Midas Curse now resting on the back of my neck. "I would love that kind of freedom."

He slaps my hand away. "Oh, no, no, no. Moly is poisonous to mortals. Tastes absolutely vile to immortals, too, but not being imprisoned by Zeus is worth a few moments of dry heaving. Although, being immune to their magic will not keep me from getting stabbed in the gut like a skewered goat. That's where my speed comes in handy."

"Are your gifts shared with your siblings? What makes you more or less powerful than any of the others?"

Hermes sits back on one *kline*, the fabric a sea-foam green threaded with silver and gold. "Has Apollo not explained the particulars of our powers yet?"

I take a seat opposite him on a round cushion. "We don't really talk much these days."

He leans back, throwing an arm over his face. "Ah yes, too busy canoodling, I'm sure."

The memories of Apollo's kisses, warm and intoxicating, flash in the back of my mind. A gasp against his lips and his hands entangled in my hair. Our chests pressed against each other. All interrupted before we can get too far. Before I can let myself go too far, rather. I release the fist curled against the pit of my stomach.

"None of that, either."

Hermes sits up, peering at me before shaking his head. "What Apollo has been neglectful in sharing, I guess I can amend. Olympians have many gifts, but we each have our strengths, too. I am the fastest of my brethren, obviously. It is why I was Zeus's messenger. To travel long distances quickly, it would take me a fraction of the power it takes Apollo. Even longer for him when our powers are dissipating as they were last summer, which is why crossing all the corners of Greece took you two so long. But I guess it was hardly comparable to the speed at which a mortal travels." He clucks his tongue and reaches for a small vase that smells strongly of wine. "I have some limited control over the earth, from my mother's side, but nowhere near as much as Demeter or Persephone."

"And Aphrodite?" I try not to sound too curious. "Or Poseidon?"

"If you were trying to deflect from your obvious prying about Aphrodite, you should have picked a different god to name than Poseidon. Everyone knows his gifts. Controller of the sea and shaker of the earth, and all that." He frowns. "Why are you curious about Aphrodite?"

I return his rare honesty with my own. "I was told that she would be willing to do anything to protect something within Troy."

"Her son, Aeneas," Hermes says without hesitation. "She thinks he's a well-kept secret, but the whole of Olympus has known about his existence for the last two decades. Or is it three? I lose track of all the Olympian bastards. She would do anything to protect him, and her gifts are of a much more subtle variety. A turning of the head here, a forcing of the gaze there."

I swish my hands to and fro. "Or a pointedly placed lovers' squabble?"

"She would need a touch of Eris's magic, but yes." Hermes's answering grin is wicked. "Thinking of stirring up trouble, Daphne?"

"And where did these gifts come from?" I ask, ignoring him as I pick up a handful of coins, letting them slip through my fingers and clink to the cavern floor. "You said last summer, both you and Ares, that you didn't deserve your powers. What does that even mean?"

"That is the question everyone seems to want answered." He quirks his mouth and takes on a nasally tone as he repeats, "'*What does that even mean?*'"

"I don't sound like that!"

He ducks as I throw coins at his head. "I've struck a nerve. Or two."

"Or three." I sigh, brushing aside the curls in my face with a frustrated hand. "Do you ever reply with a straight answer?"

"No, always crooked."

This time, he isn't nearly quick enough to avoid the coins I fling at his face. This makes the roosters dancing on his brow and shoulders flare out their wings and open their beaks in noiseless squawks.

I point to the tattoos. "And those? How come only some of you have them?"

"All these questions seem cyclical." Hermes glances at his hand, on which a tattooed snake slithers around each of his fingers. "I, and the others you've seen, got these from a god you have never even heard of. His name is Acat."

The air leaves my chest in a great huff. "Was he banished from Olympus?"

"No," Hermes says. "Because he was never of Olympus. In fact, he has set foot in Greece only once, and that was hundreds of years ago."

"What are you saying? That the gods of Olympus aren't the only ones?"

"That is exactly what I'm saying." Hermes takes a long drink of wine. He licks his lips and sets the jug back down. "I will take a long and insufferable high road now by telling you this. I may have my own squabbles with my brother, but do not blame Apollo for not being honest with you about this, as that golden armor you wear could potentially bring every word you hear and say back to Zeus's ears. Zeus will kill you if he thinks you know too much." He points to my abdomen and smiles, baring perfectly white, straight teeth. "But I've found a way around that. Even if Apollo is too...slow...to yet."

"Too slow?" I arch a brow. "Your insults were much sharper last summer."

"As was your bite," he says tightly. "What happened, between you and Nyx, what it stole from you...I cannot apologize enough." His gaze, steady and unrelenting, doesn't leave mine. "But I would do it again."

It's an effort to keep my voice level. "Why?"

"Zeus does not deserve the power he wields." Hermes snatches up the jug of wine once more and takes a swig. "And neither do his kin."

"Including you," I point out. "Whatever happens to him seems to happen to all. Are you willing to make that sacrifice?"

"To an extent."

I cross my arms over my chest. "Because you actually love the power."

"Of course." Hermes raises a hand and swishes his wrist. The snake leaps from his fingers, a great beast with jade and cobalt scales. It dances in the air, spiraling higher and higher, with each turn another plant blossoming in his cave. "But that doesn't mean I don't feel guilt for how I got these gifts."

"And how was that?"

He snaps his fingers and the snake disappears. It reappears on his arm, slithering around and around before climbing beneath his *chlamys*. I flinch when he leans forward, suddenly planting his elbows on his knees. "Zeus will not hesitate to kill you for the answer. Is it worth the risk to know?"

I raise my chin, trembling slightly. "You tell me."

"That sharpness that Nyx stole from you." Hermes leans back again. "It was replaced with fire."

I say nothing, waiting.

Finally, voice low and deep as though he still fears that Zeus listens, Hermes says, "Before Prometheus found himself chained atop Mount Kazbek and Hades was delegated to the Underworld, the magic of the Hesperides was wild. An uncontained thing, almost as it was last summer if the Muses had been taken from their garden any longer. Some tell of the Hesperides as women. In a way, the Hesperides and the Muses are the same in such stories, but the trees the Muses protect, including the one from which you carry a golden apple, are the true Hesperides. There are three, of which the Muses take much care." He holds up a finger. "The first, Hespere, a tree with golden fruit that bestows life. The second"—another finger joins the first—"is the tree of the seasons. Erytheia never bows, never dies. And the third, Aegle, is the oldest of the three.

"Aegle was born with the dawn of time, when the great powers of the world converged and exploded anew, creating what you and I know today. With its birth came the other two, and magic was born."

Dimly, I'm aware of a war a world away calling to me, but I cannot leave. Not when I still have so many questions.

"And so the magic was shared," Hermes goes on, "spread far and wide. But with all power comes greed. Wars were fought for the power, great beings from all corners of the world converging upon Mount Olympus where the trees first sprang. Zeus rallied his allies, my family, and to secure his victory, he made a deal with the titans. Together, Zeus's family and the titans struck down their enemies, one by one. But before the titans could take their place atop Olympus, Zeus betrayed them and a new war began."

"The war with the titans." I nod. "Ligeia told me of this. The Titanomachy."

"Ah yes, a great clash among titans and gods. There were betrayers on both sides. Nyx aligned with the titans, Oceanus and Themis with the gods." Hermes smiles, a harsh line across his handsome face. "The tales of it you mortals have spun over the centuries are not so far off the mark. You have Prometheus to thank for that, for which he was punished as you saw."

"Ligeia told me he was punished for bringing fire to mortals."

Hermes gives me a disappointed look. "And you actually believed that? No, that was a story spun by Hera to make mortals feel dumber than they actually are. Of course you've always had fire. Prometheus did not like the punishment Zeus chose for his kin. He was a titan himself, remember? One of many that defected from the side of the titans to the side of the gods. He felt betrayed by Zeus, having been promised that his friends and family would not be harmed, and so he brought a different sort of fire to mortals."

"Stories," I say softly.

"Yes." Hermes nods. "And they spread across the world like wild-fire. The allies Zeus made during the great Titanomachy, such as the one who gave me these tattoos, turned their backs on Zeus. They had their gifts from other sources, all over the world. They had no need for betrayers and the paltry-by-comparison gifts that Mount Olympus has to offer."

"And Zeus punished Prometheus by chaining him up on Mount Kazbek."

"Actually, that was all Prometheus's idea." Hermes chuckles. "You've experienced his divine gift. Knowledge. He saw that Zeus would punish him, a fate much worse than his siblings, and instead cursed himself to that lonely crag. None but him know how to break those chains."

"Clever. No doubt Prometheus knew that he would also be stuck there for hundreds of years?"

"Perhaps." A shrug. "But no worse than the fate of his titan kin."

"Who are supposedly in Tartarus." My eyes narrow. "Why didn't I see them down there?"

He shrugs. "Perhaps this brings us back to your first question. Why Troy?"

He snaps his fingers, and I'm thrown from my seat, from the comfortable, cool darkness, to a sunbaked rooftop of Troy. I roll across the clay surface, hissing when it meets my bare skin. The sun beats down upon me, blinding compared to the cavern.

"You are such a wretch," I grumble, climbing to my feet and ignoring the hand Hermes offers me.

"Consider it my retribution for stabbing me in the back," he replies, brushing nonexistent dirt from the front of his *peplos.*

"You deserved it."

"Do you truly believe that?" Hermes stares me down. "After what I told you?"

"Depends"—I cannot meet his eyes—"on if the gods of Olympus are actually any worse than the titans they wrested the power from. On if the titans deserved the punishment Zeus dealt them. And"—I finally turn to him—"on whether you're telling the truth or not."

A breeze stirs, pulling my curls from their plait and whipping them around my face. His own dark, wiry curls, long to his shoulders and now in thin braids, swing between us.

"Do you doubt Apollo as much as you doubt me?" He asks, voice tight.

"The man who could lift my heart or shatter it in a single second?" A gaping maw threatens to open beneath my feet and swallow me whole. "Of course."

Therein lies what keeps me from giving in to the feelings I have for Apollo. The power he and his family have, and how powerless I am against it.

Hermes blinks and steps away. He opens his mouth to say something, then stops, pointing over my shoulder. "Time to don those leathers again."

I turn to see what he points at. On the horizon, glittering beyond the far hills, metal reflects in the high sunlight. It ripples, shifting and slithering like a snake between the foothills. Likely just beyond what the scouts of Troy can see.

"I need to get ready." I turn to climb down from the roof when Hermes catches my wrist.

Compared to the scalding heat of Apollo's touch, Hermes's hand is cold, a balm against the scorching sun above.

"Wait." He reaches for the blade at his hip.

I wrench away, rolling across the roof and leaping into a fighting stance. Hermes only gives me an exasperated look and unhooks the sword. With an easy grace, he flips it, catching it nimbly by the blade and angling the hilt toward me.

"You can have this until Hephaestus gets off his ass to forge you proper armor."

Tentatively, I accept the sword. It is pure gold, iridescent in the light like molten metal. "The Adamantine sword. I thought it was lost with Perseus?" *When he slayed Medusa,* I don't add.

"It can put a target on your head if you're not careful. That sword has made lots of enemies, for an inanimate object." Hermes takes a step back. "But it will withstand any blade Ares might attack you with."

Without a word of goodbye, I turn and begin my descent of the roof toward the army that wants to take my head just as surely as Perseus lobbed heads off with this very sword.

CHAPTER

30

I go to the Amazon palace by the city's northern gate.

"We should surprise them just as they mean to do us," I say, imbuing my words with every last shred of confidence that I have. I brush a hand over the armor I hurriedly donned before running over. "Don't let them make a mockery of us. They hope to take us unawares. We shouldn't let them even leave the hills."

Lyta, who stood when I stormed into the palace, asks, "How many did you see?"

"Three hundred." To my Sparta-trained eyes.

Penthesilea, standing beside her, nods. Her fierce gaze turns to the gate below us. "The question now is are these men fodder, a distraction while they attack elsewhere, or do they truly believe they can take Troy's northern gate by surprise?"

"What were you even doing up there, Daphne?" Hippolyta peers at me.

I'm saved from having to answer by Penthesilea clucking her tongue. She chews on the inside of her cheek before snapping, "Lyta. Tell Hector to meet us at the Northern Gate. We must be quick if we're going to beat them."

Lyta hesitates, body angled to the exit in a blind reaction to her sister's words, but indecision paints her face in stern lines. Her lips pinch, as if she's swallowing back the words she wants to say, the arguments she wants to voice.

"Hippolyta." Penthesilea stands, flicking her wrists out. Two warriors stride over and tie on the queen's vambraces. "Disregard any backtalk that is surely floating around in that stubborn head of yours. Be quick, and tell Hector to use discretion. If we want to take the Achaeans by surprise, we need to leave the city in the dark, hypothetically speaking. We cannot cause a stir."

Without another word, the Amazonian queen turns on her heel and sprints from the room. Lyta motions me to follow her sister. We cut down the stairs, her warriors taking flight behind us, each woman arming themselves in fine leather armor and two swords each. I buckle Hermes's sword to my hip as my heart pounds in my ears, a steady drum that drowns out the sounds of the city.

The people watching us pass merely give us confused looks, and I understand why Penthesilea didn't want to alert the entire army, only Hector. The moment the Trojan army gathers, the people will panic, the horns will blare, and the noise in the city will rise.

Penthesilea doesn't wait for her sister and Hector before ordering the gate open. Unlike the other city gates, which are crowded with markets, this one sits just beyond a horse paddock.

As my hand lands on the red-painted gate, a voice chirps up from behind us.

"Stop!"

Kassandra, looking like a wraith, strides across the paddock.

Horses gallop every which way around her, but she ignores them all. Her eyes are red-rimmed and wide. "You mustn't leave!"

She stumbles the last few steps, and a part of me wonders how she was even let out from her father's palace. Her chiton is only half tied, baring a shoulder and an entire leg. Her hair is only halfway plaited, a single eyelid painted with ochre as she strides right up to the gate and shoves me away.

I'm so startled that I actually fall back a couple of steps.

"Do not sacrifice the warriors of the black banks of the Thermodon," she says breathlessly. She throws both arms behind her as though she can keep these gates shut by sheer force of will. "This field will eat their bodies whole with flame and gold."

She blinks, then stumbles away from the gate. She stares at her hands.

I grab her by the shoulder and peer into her face. "Are you feeling all right, Kassandra?"

She looks to me as if she's suddenly just noticing me. Her pupils dilate, mouth opening and closing. Her thick, dark brows draw together in a frown. "You shouldn't be here, either. Wait with the queen, in the dusty halls of Priam's palace. Do not tread between those foothills to meet the god of death with open arms. You have much blood to let, *kataigída*."

I blink. "How do you—"

"Enough." Penthesilea gives the princess a frustrated look. "None of your fearmongering here on the dawn of a fight. Go back to your palace and silks."

Kassandra recoils as if slapped. "I'm trying to save you."

"My warriors do not need saving." Penthesilea sneers.

Blushing a red so deep her face reminds me of wine, Kassandra steps away from the gate. Her head bows, and Trojan infantrymen stride forward to open the great doors for us.

On hinges so quiet they must be oiled by the gods themselves, the gate is pried open just far enough for each warrior to slink through before shutting firmly behind us. We sprint for the foothills, which are crowded with prickly juniper and vibrant olive trees. The perfect cover from any scouts the Achaeans might have on the crest of the hills.

Hunched low to the ground, we slither among the trees. We don't raise the dust as we pass despite our speed and number, our steps so assured and smooth. We reach a dip between the hills, following the ravine.

Penthesilea jerks us all to a halt with a single raised fist. She glances to the sky, cloudless and still bright with sunlight. Foolish, it seems, to attack the gate in the middle of the day. An itch forms on the back of my neck.

A warm breeze stirs Penthesilea's hair, tugging the ebony strands and grazing her cheekbones with them. A teasing gesture, as though the Anemoi beg for our attention.

Under her breath, so soft I barely hear, Penthesilea says, "Three hundred men, weighed down by little weapons, should have been here by now." Slowly, as dread pools in my stomach like hot oil, she turns to look at me. "Draw your sword."

Before I can even grab the hilt, a scream pierces the air. The breath is knocked from my lungs as a body slams into mine. I'm thrown, tumbling across the sand. Penthesilea's scream matches those of our attacker. She wrenches her two swords free, whipping them in circles. Her warriors draw their blades, metal singing as all three hundred of the Achaeans come running around the hill, from above and below. The Amazons meet them with teeth bared and swords raised.

I stab into the side of a man currently bearing down on one of the Amazons closest to me. He gurgles, blood trickling from his mouth. Before he's even fallen, I'm moving on, sword ripped from his body.

Three hundred Achaeans against forty Amazons. Even if I keep cutting through these men like stalks of grass, we'll never survive unless Hector arrives with the Trojans soon.

Towering above all the others, Ajax thunders through the melee. He carries an *axine* in one hand, a club the size of my body in the other. He swings wildly, knocking both Achaean and Amazon from their feet. A shiver runs up my spine at the sight of him barreling directly toward me. His muscles ripple beneath his black armor with each pounding step, his charge so similar to the Minotaur's.

A *dory* swings for me. I duck and its tip slices my cheek. A searing pain rushes through my face. I deflect the next swing, spinning within the man's reach. Surprise widens his mouth as my sword plunges into his gut.

I don't have time to tear my blade free. A club catches me in the middle. Both me and my victim soar through the air, the wind leaving my lungs when I crash to the earth.

I moan, cradling my ribs as little jolts of lightning tear up my side. I try to push from the ground, but my arms give out and I collapse again. The sun is suddenly blotted out, painting the earth around me gray. With a mouthful of sand, I look up just as Ajax raises his club above his head.

His smile is wicked, his eyes black.

I spit blood at his feet. "No dramatic words, Ares? We all know how much you love to gloat."

The god shows no surprise. "A little weasel like you will take any opportunity to flee. Why wait?"

"So you're not completely dense." I cough. I try to rise again, my elbows trembling. His club cracks into my spine. Even with the Midas Curse, the gold a second armor, his blow reverberates throughout my whole body.

My breath leaves me in a whoosh, and I fall forward.

"Nyx commanded me not to kill you." He bends over, hissing in my ear, "But never said I cannot break you."

A wild scream rips through the air. Ares turns just as Penthesilea leaps forward. Her strong legs propel her impossibly high, the ichor of her father carrying her as she soars.

Penthesilea drives a dagger right into his back. His eyes pop open. She shoves off him, hurrying to my side. Her lovely face is painted with enemy blood. "Can you walk?"

Over her shoulder, I spy Pyrrhus among the fray, standing and watching. He did nothing as Ares nearly killed me.

Another pain, a cold and hollow emptiness like frostbite, floods my chest. My own brother was willing to watch me die.

Penthesilea grabs me roughly by the upper arm and drags me to my feet. "We must continue fighting. We have to hold them off until Hippolyta—"

A dagger's point glints from the center of her chest, stealing her final words.

"No!" I scream, clutching at her arms.

She gasps, patting her abdomen. Blood soaks through her leather breastplate.

Ares's wretched face sneers over his shoulder. "Daughter or not, no ichor spilled of mine will go unmet."

She's wrenched away from me, lifted into the air by Ares. Then, blade and body are thrown aside. With a wild scream, I grab Hermes's sword from the Achaean's body and swing. Ares's hand, the one gloved in black, arcs through the air and thuds beside Penthesilea's prone body.

Ares's roar shakes the very earth. I collapse backward.

"Enough of this," he says, spitting and furious. "I will gut you now, you pathetic little rat."

He takes another step, then dances from the reach of my sword. A smile painted red and black with ichor splits his face. "Hermes gave you his little blade? A traitor to no end."

He moves forward, then jerks to a halt. He looks behind me. I feel it then: the thundering of a thousand hooves shudders through the earth.

My chest heaving, I hold the blade between us. Pain lances through my body with every breath. My arms tremble, struggling for the first time in my life to hold a sword aloft. "Better leave now, Ares." I bare my own bloodstained teeth at him. "Or everyone will know that the gods are pretenders among us in this war."

"Oh, you little fool." He chuckles. "They already know."

He holds his palms up at his sides. The mask of Ajax slips once more over his features as, still grinning, he takes a step back and disappears.

CHAPTER
31

H ector's forces tear through what is left of the Achaean ambush. It wasn't enough, and Hector was too late.

Hippolyta's screams fill the air. Each hollow wail wrenches my soul in pieces. I still lay on the ground, my body battered. My eyes flutter open briefly, tears leaking from the corners as she sprints past me for the prone body of her sister. I turn my head just as she cradles Penthesilea's body in her lap.

She rocks back and forth. A keening wail climbs her spine and bursts from her lips. Just the sight fills me with even more pain. My midriff burns with the fires of Hephaestus's forge.

A cool, gentle touch, like the falling of snowflakes, trips up my side. It dispels the fire, breathing new life into my shattered lungs.

Persephone looks down upon me, frowning. She cups my cheek, and the burgeoning fever retreats. "I cannot heal you too much now, my sister, or they will know." She places the softest kiss on my brow. "I'll come back for you later."

She moves on, leaving behind the scent of pomegranates and wheat. I'm healed enough now to at least rise onto my elbows, though my back still burns. Even Artemis's Midas Curse wasn't enough to hold back the enormity of Ares's rage.

I crawl across the sand to a still sobbing Hippolyta, tears beginning to pour down my own cheeks. She ignores me, rocking and crying. I crouch beside her in silent vigil until the sun falls beyond the bloody foothills.

Once the stars begin to dot the dark purple sky, she finally stands. Penthesilea's bloody body cradled in her arms, my friend shuffles toward the great wall. What remains of the Amazon army falls into line behind her and we march along the sandy path.

Great pyres are already being built. Hades's presence here is as tangible as a hand atop my spine. His wife is no doubt flitting among the crowd, looking for wounded she can marginally heal. At least I have earned the alliance of the Queen of the Underworld, even if I have proven a failure almost everywhere else.

Arms wrapped around my frame, I watch as priestesses rush forward to take Penthesilea from her sister. Hippolyta hugs her body tighter, face screwed up in pain and rage. One attendant, whose face I would recognize anywhere, lays a hand upon my friend's arm.

"Your sister has earned a place in Elysium," Persephone says. Her voice is low and soothing, each word sweeping over Hippolyta until her grip eventually slackens. "You will see her again, there. But first you must set her free."

With one last pain-filled sob, my friend lets go of the Amazon queen.

Persephone scoops up Penthesilea's body and carries her over to the towering pyre built of cedar and pine. The goddess is dressed in simple red, the color of a priestess, her Olympian powers dimmed in this moment to blend among the others. Her dark ebony hair is loose, blowing in the warm southern winds of the god Notos.

Hippolyta accepts the torch Persephone hands her next and, with tearstained cheeks, lights the pyre. Her warriors take up an Amazon *paian*, a solemn battle hymn, their mournful voices filling the valley. My voice cracks as I take up the song alongside them.

Hippolyta's face twists in pain. From the corner of her mouth, eyes still fixed on the blazing fire, she asks, "Who did it?"

Ignoring the burn in my throat, I say, "Your father."

She nods curtly but says nothing.

After the rest of the dead are laid to rest, she and I walk slowly back to the city gates. Her steps drag, her usual grace gone with the sister she sent up in flames. As we walk, she becomes more rigid, her movements clipped. Finally, at the base of the stairs that lead up to her palace, she turns to me and says, "Your secrets will make you a martyr, Daphne."

I take a step back. "What secrets?"

Fury flickers on her features for an instant. "You have the audacity to ask me that? I know of the games you play with the gods. I've seen you walk side by side with Apollo and brawl with Ares in this very war. What aren't you telling me?"

I chew the inside of my cheek. "I haven't been purposefully keeping anything from you, Lyta. I—"

"Enough lies!" She cuts a hand through the air. "If I find out that this war started because of you, it will be your body next on that pyre."

She turns, storming up the stairs without a backward glance.

I stand there, gaping, until my assortment of wounds protest that they cannot keep me on my feet much longer. Bruised, beaten, and with barely enough strength to stand, I drag myself across the city to King Priam's palace. I limp down the hallways, arms wrapped around myself, and jerk to a halt when a tall, dark form steps in front of me. I immediately reach for the Adamantine sword.

"Perhaps you wouldn't be so cautious if you brought your best men with you." Lykou's arms are crossed over his broad chest, his face unreadable.

I lean a wary shoulder against the wall. "I'll remember that next time."

"Be sure that you do." His mask slips, and he rubs a hand over his face before I can read his expression.

A sigh threatens to escape me. "Not you, too."

That's when he snaps. The wolf erased so long ago takes form in his features, a sharp snarl pulling back his lips and twisting his nose. "Not me what, Daphne? Not me angry that you left me behind while you fought and lost a battle? Left me behind again." He steps forward and his arms drop, fists tight at his sides. "I won't ask if you know how it feels to be forced to watch from this city's walls as your people die on the battlefield below."

"I'm sorry, Lykou." Shame weighs atop my shoulders.

"You're sorry?" He makes a harsh sound in the back of his throat and shakes his head. "What about watching as the woman you love slaughters your people left and right? Or how it feels to wonder if she is among the dead herself?"

He jerks forward, forcing me to take an awkward step back.

Close enough now that I can smell the wine lacing his breath, he whispers, "I was your fool last summer and you played me like a lyre. You are no better than them."

The gods. He means that I am no better than the gods.

I clutch a hand on the wall behind me, mouth opening and closing around apologies and promises and other useless words. Because nothing can change the fact that he is right.

Then, as gentle as a moth, he reaches forward and catches the tear now slipping down my cheek as he says, "I am done being your fool, Daphne."

He storms past me, so fast that when I turn around to stop him, he is already gone.

I dread what verbal lashing now awaits me from my queen. I enter our suite, fully braced for her wrath.

But, sitting on the edge of my bed is someone else entirely.

"I was too late," Apollo says. Behind him, strewn across the cobalt furs, is my armor from Hephaestus.

It is gold, as seem to be all my gifts from the gods. I can tell even just by looking at it that the armor will mold to my body like a second skin, matching my every muscle and curve. The shield is black leather and painted with a golden swan.

"What is with Olympian obsession with giving me gold things? A curse, two different sets of armor. A sword." Gold and glittering like the sun just before it sets beyond the mountains on a cloudless day.

"For Helen," Apollo explains, dragging a finger over the domed surface of the shield.

"A bull's-eye for everyone who wants my head, no doubt." I sigh.

Apollo chuckles darkly. "Don't insult Hephaestus. He thought of that as well. The armor will appear the same as whatever army you're fighting for."

I shift on my feet. "I'll have to make sure to thank him profusely the next time I see him."

"I was curious how you traveled to Lemnos, but my answer hangs from your hip." Apollo's eyes drop to the Adamantine sword. "Hermes gave you that."

"He's been more honest with me in a single day than you have in a year." My voice rises with each word until I'm practically yelling in his face. He takes it without blinking. I have no right to be furious over lies. Not after my friends just threw my own falsehoods in my face. Lip trembling, I stab a finger in the air. "No more lies. From me or you."

I look down at my hands, still sticky with blood. I rip free of my leathers, cursing the ties and shredding the cloth beneath in an effort to remove the gore and memory of today. Trembling, I stand naked before him.

My throat bobs. "Just tell me the truth, Apollo. I bloody deserve it." He doesn't say anything, his eyes never leaving my own. His smile has fallen and a pained frown replaces it.

I stride for the pool. The water ripples around me, swirling with red and sand. The delicious cold rinses away most of my aches and pains. I dunk my head and scrub my face.

When I surface, Apollo sits at the pool's edge, legs hanging in the water. "What do you want to know?"

The air leaves my chest in a giant rush. What don't I want to know? I duck my head quickly once more and swim to the edge beside him, resting my arms and chin on the cool marble.

I should pick what is least likely to get me killed for knowing. With a small voice, I say, "Tell me about Koronis."

Apollo gives no reaction, his lovely face impossibly still. He drags a hand through the water, turning to stare at the waves he creates. "She loved the water."

I blink. "If you think that's enough to make me trust you, better think again. I—"

He silences me with an irritated look. He rolls his eyes toward the ceiling. "All this time and you are still as stubborn as that day on Mount Kazbek's slopes. You would have rather fallen to your death than accept my help."

"Can you blame me for it?" I soften the words with an upturned smile in the corner of my mouth.

He does not return the smile. "The princess of Phlegyantis was as lovely as the dawn, and sweeter than honey. A princess has no right to be so perfect. They should all be hindered by some kind of malady or misfortune, but Koronis was absolutely faultless."

Even with hundreds of years passed, his voice is laced with tenderness as he speaks of her. It forms an ache of a different kind deep in my stomach.

"What started as a tentative friendship quickly bloomed into something more. She told me of her desire to form trade ties Greece has never known, encourage the crafts and arts, build a theater, and allow women to join their army. She was loved wholeheartedly by her people, but none more so than myself."

He waves a wrist and the oil lamps around the room flicker to life. Their golden glow paints the sharp line of his jaw, the way his mouth twists in pain.

"Ares told me." I pause, swallowing. "In Tartarus, he told me that she did not return your love."

"He had half of the story." Apollo kicks a spray of water across the chamber. "But that much is painfully true. She instead fell in love with a mortal named Iskhys. He and I weren't the only ones enamored with the lovely princess, though. Tales of her perfection spread across the kingdom and reached the most powerful of ears. Zeus."

The water is suddenly too cold. I climb out, goose bumps prickling my skin. In a blink, Apollo is beside me with a lavender chiton, wrapping it around my wet frame. His thumb grazes the underside of my arm, making me shiver.

"What did your father do?"

"He chased her relentlessly," Apollo bites out, cursing under his breath. "She was pregnant with Iskhys's child and her lover was killed in a storm while out fishing. I have no proof, but I believe with my whole heart that my father and Poseidon are to blame."

"So you stole her away."

He nods. "It was for her protection. If I hadn't, my father would have done far worse if he ever found out she carried another's child. Artemis took her to an island far from my father's reach. For my sister's deception, she was banished to the Taygetus mountain range, allowed freedom only when called upon. For my involvement, I was cursed to centuries of guarding the Muses in the Garden of the Hesperides. And, a lover scorned and vengeful to no end, my father bade Poseidon swallow the kingdom of Phlegyantis whole in an earthquake."

The room is deathly silent, not even a crackle from the oil lamps or murmur from the city below.

"And Koronis?" I reach out, hand shaking as I take one of his. "What happened to her?"

His eyes are rimmed with red. "When she heard of Phlegyantis's fall, she took her own life."

My earlier words sit sour in the pit of my stomach, threatening to make me sick. There are no words I can give him that will ease his pain, so I remain silent and hold his hand tight.

Apollo's callused thumb rubs my palm. "That necklace you wore last summer was my last gift to her. She still had it around her neck when she leaped from the cliffs. I thought she was lost forever, and Poseidon refused to bring me her body. I found out centuries later that her child lived, taken by Hermes to Chiron to be raised in Foloi. The child's descendants were drawn to the sea of their ancestor's undoing, eventually migrating to Eleusis."

Apollo glances to my abdomen, where the Midas Curse spins beneath the wet chiton. He finally meets my gaze again and, voice edged with hatred, says, "Though I have no choice but to fight for my father, I have no love for the man. Haven't since the day Artemis and I were forced to hide Koronis from his claws."

There are no lies in Apollo's words. I know this from the precarious trust we had built between us last summer. Forged from equal bloodshed and tears. And now, hatred simmers inside me, too, a poisonous and oily thing that had already been bred there over a year ago. Not for the god beside me, but for the deity that rules atop his mountain far across the sea.

Apollo leans closer. His mouth, those plush lips, is mere inches from my own. If I dared, I could press high on my toes and kiss him. That sweetness, that underlying spice of his kisses, is intoxicating. It calls to me like nothing ever has before.

The only sound in the room is our own rapid breathing.

"More answers," I say—no, demand—with a ragged voice.

He takes a step back, dropping his hand. "Defend the gates, Daphne. Point Hector's troops toward guarding them day and night. The wall may be magicked, but I do not trust Nyx, Ares, or even Hermes and their tricks."

His gaze lingers on my face before he steps into the shadows. "I won't let you share the same fate as Koronis. Even if it means that my father will throw me from Olympus."

CHAPTER
32

Rain falls upon Troy for the next two weeks, turning the plains into swamps of mud and gore. It is impossible to walk across, even harder to ride horses and steer carriages. Even so, Hector listens to my warnings and has the gates guarded day and night.

My training is brought indoors, banquet halls and megarons commandeered by the armies as our outdoor arenas now flood. I never let anyone finish my healing because, though I should, some small part of me screams that I deserve to suffer alongside these men and women.

A fact I'm reminded of, day in, day out, as Lyta and Lykou shun me.

They each choose different partners, leaving me to train with Hector or Paris, or any number of the other warriors. The Amazons, taking the lead from their new queen, likewise ignore me. I limp and grimace with each bend, my ribs healing slowly. I take each hit thrown my way without protest.

Helen gives me a pitying look as I tumble into my bed across the suite from hers. "Perhaps you should soak in the bath first."

"Tomorrow," I mumble from my furs. Hypnos drags me into the throes of sleep before I hear her response.

I awaken with the blankets tucked around my body and a hand placed firmly over my mouth.

My eyes snap open. Hermes's scent of sweet incense sweeps over me, and my fear lessens just a fraction.

He holds a finger up to his lips and removes the hand from my face. He points toward the ceiling. Understanding his meaning, I nod and take his offered hand.

I'm jerked from the bed and it isn't until I'm standing atop the cold roof, already drenched to the bone, that I remember the deluge outside.

I blink back the spray. "You couldn't have picked a drier place to train?" I have to yell to be heard above the storm. Hermes's grin is as wild as the wind roaring around us. It makes the city sing.

"Where would the fun in that be?"

A crack of thunder makes me jump. "This is insanity!"

"Oh, stop your whining. It's time for some real training." He tosses me the Adamantine sword, a twin of pure black appearing in his other hand.

Before I can even catch the sword, he's charging me. He swings high, then low, forcing me to duck, then jump. My muscles bark in agony. He's relentless, his attacks coming from every angle and almost faster than I can track. I dodge another swing, but take his heel to the gut. The air rushes from my chest and I double over.

"Bastard," I gasp.

"You Spartans rely on your arms too much. What would you do if both were broken?"

"Honestly? Probably die."

"Again?" Hermes dances around me. "Let's teach you how to fight without relying on them."

He leaps, scissoring the air with his legs. I dance backward. He continues forward and I slash out. He pivots on a leg, avoiding my swing, as his other leg kicks, swings out, and catches me in the side.

I stumble. "I could cut your leg off while you do that."

"Go ahead and try."

Another crack of thunder drowns out my yell as I leap forward, slowly. He catches my wrist. I yelp and drop the blade as he twists me around. I'm flung off my feet and slammed face-first into the ground. My jaw screams in agony.

I spring to my feet. "Teach me something new."

His answering grin glitters with excitement. "Finally."

I ignore the fallen sword and raise my fists.

Hermes takes a step back and appraises me. "Do as I do. This will take balance."

He lifts his right knee high, higher, until it is halfway up his abdomen, and I do the same. He straightens his leg, turning as he does until it is a line from right hip and across his chest. It is an effort of will to keep my balance on my left leg. My muscles strain against the roaring wind and rain. He snaps his foot in and out, and I mimic the movement.

"Have your leg directly across the center line of your body. This will engage all of your muscles."

"That's what I'm doing," I say around a grimace. Merely speaking threatens to throw me off balance.

"From here you can either sweep outward to hit your target or sweep inward." He demonstrates, his leg swiping down where it would hit a target with the back of his foot. In the same movement, he switches to his right foot and raises his left leg. It turns in the opposite direction, cutting across his body instead of out.

"Again, how would this be helpful against a sword?"

"Take up your sword and try to attack me."

I drop my leg and collect my blade. Hermes lifts his left leg and I lunge. He twists out of reach and his foot slaps into my side. I spin, swinging again and he jumps out of reach. His foot hits my hand. I cry out, my grip reflexively loosening and the blade falling. I bend to collect it and he rushes forward. I rise just in time for his legs to wrap around my middle, and before I can make sense of direction, his legs grip tight and I'm tumbling through the air.

He holds out a hand and I take it, letting him pull me to my feet. I gasp for breath. "Teach me that."

The moon above is wrapped in cloud and rain as we spend hours going over new moves and ways for me to use my legs in a fight that not even Paidonomos Leonidas would know what to do with. Just as I finally feel like I am getting the hang of fighting with my legs, Hermes takes my wrist. One of his legs sweeps under mine and I'm tumbling through the air. The hand on my wrist jerks me upright, the other catching me around my middle.

I'm pressed into him, chest heaving against his own. The rain feels warm, pouring between our too-close bodies. I can count the raindrops as they fall and slide from his brows to his lips. They're so close the slightest movement would brush them against my own.

"That was cheating," I stutter, keenly aware of his cool arm around my waist.

"So is this." His hand slides up my arm, gently pinching the skin below the bangle Apollo gave me. His thumb rubs over the metal vines. "Has Apollo told you what this is?"

"He said it was for protection." My lips part, my gaze drawn to his mouth.

His eyes shutter. The hand on my back tightens, gripping my drenched chiton. I'm keenly aware of every hard muscle pressed against me, of the rising heat in my core.

Lightning cracks above us and we leap apart.

"He wasn't lying, I suppose." Hermes brushes the front of his *peplos*. He turns to the clouds, roaring and twisting above. "You should get some rest. Hippolyta will pit her finest warriors against you in training tomorrow."

Cold sweeps over me in the absence of his body. "I'm not tired yet."

"That would be your heritage playing tricks on you." Hermes glances at me askance. "The moment we're out of the rain, exhaustion will weigh you down."

Last summer, water had helped me. In small, almost insignificant ways. "Was Peneios my actual father?"

Hermes shakes his head and a glimmer of disappointment goes through me. "No, he was merely your caretaker."

"Where is he?" I venture, stepping into the god's space again. "And my mother."

"They've once again hidden beyond my sight." Hermes looks down at me, his handsome face unreadable. "Be grateful. It means that even your enemies cannot find them."

"I wish my brothers had managed such luck." I bend to collect the Adamantine sword and his black one. I offer it to him and he merely snaps his fingers, the blade disappearing in a blink.

"Where does it go?" I ask, more in an effort to distract myself from the strange ache growing inside me than because I expected an answer. "When you snap your fingers like that. Apollo does the same."

"His belongings probably come and go from his palace atop Olympus, or a hideout similar to my cave. Mine return to Kyllini. I never kept much of my belongings atop that horrible mountain. Besides, I was never there long enough to garner a palace of my own."

He slices a hand through the rain and we're back in my suite, dripping on the marble floor. He looks me over, his face unreadable. "You should dry off. Those furs will stink if you climb into bed looking like that."

Before I can snap a response, he's gone.

CHAPTER
33

The sun refuses to shine on us the next morning. The rain has slowed, but still persists. A mere drizzle now, and not so much a welcome respite from battle as the rain was before. Because, where first I enjoyed my brief pause in bloodletting, I'm now filled with dread for each day.

Our resources are dwindling, as are our numbers. How much longer can this war drag on?

Hippolyta leads us back outside to the arena, despite the drizzle.

"The plains will still have patches of mud for weeks," she barks at us all, with special focus on my bowed head. "Might as well practice fighting in it."

We turn as one to collect our dulled weapons for training.

"Golgotha," Hippolyta says, and the head of the largest in her number snaps up. A narrow face looks up next when she says, "Xene."

I know her next words before they even fall from her mouth. "You two will train with Daphne. Her head was in the mud yesterday."

Anger flares through me. It prickles along my very nerves. Even the shadows that haunt me retreat. My fingers wrap around a *dory*, the weapon of my kingdom, and that anger blooms into something more.

I spin around. "No."

"*Ne?*" There's a bite in her voice that even the language of her homeland can't hide. She yanks a *dory* from the hands of the nearest woman and strides toward me. I brace my legs wide and stare her down each marching step of the way until the point of that *dory* rests against my collarbone.

"Do I need to swipe those legs from underneath you, again?" Hippolyta's eyes are wild. She steps right up to me, her arm raised with the spear high and pressed against my skin.

Everyone in the arena stops what they're doing to watch us.

I dig my toes into the mud. "You can try."

Her nostrils flare. "Get your worthless ass in that pit before I throw you in there myself."

I incline my head. "After you."

I barely have time to duck. Her swing is so fast a viper would envy it. I catch the fist, my palm going to bruise later from the blow, and inch by stubborn inch, I force her hand back down to her side. She allows not even a flicker of surprise in her face.

Biting back a curse, she turns and stomps toward the arena. I follow at a distance and stop across the muddy circle from her.

"I hope your secrets don't weigh you down too much, Daphne of No Kingdom," Hippolyta says, tossing her *dory* from hand to hand.

"Don't say things you don't mean." I smile sweetly. "You very much want me to be weighed down."

She leaps across the space, lance raised. I swipe it aside. Another jump toward me and I deflect. She chases me around the arena, and I let her. She puts every ounce of Ares's blood into each swing. My arms and legs burn within minutes. Sweat drips from my brow and glazes my shoulders.

"Quit fighting like a coward," Hippolyta says. "No wonder Sparta wants nothing but your head."

"Have you forgotten our conversation on the Aegean so soon?" I hit aside another lash of her *dory*.

"Gone with the breeze," she says, bending her knees. Her chest heaves. "Why would I hold on to such fruitless conversations?"

"Not fruitless, exactly."

She leaps forward and I toss aside my weapon to meet her in the air, past her *dory* and colliding directly with her body. Surprise flashes across her features. Her eyes flare wide, mouth opening, so taken aback that my blow is successful. We fall to the earth.

Using my legs as Hermes taught me, I wrap them both around her hips. I grab both her fists and slam them to the mud. She drops her spear and bucks. I'm thrown onto my own back, Lyta collapsing on top of me. I nearly lose my grip, the wet clay making her arms slick. A grin replaces her shock.

I unhook one leg and use it to shove. We flip over and over, wrestling for control until I slam her again into the ground. She bucks, but the leg around her waist tightens. Like a snake, I squeeze and squeeze until—

"I yield." She drops her head back with a sigh. "I bloody yield."

"One small misstep can bring down an entire army," I say, only loud enough for her to hear. "Do you remember that?"

She doesn't answer, only stares at me with those bottomless dark eyes.

I stand and offer her a hand that drips with mud. She takes it, nails digging into my palm as she climbs to her feet.

Wordlessly, she turns her back on me to stride from the arena.

*   *   *

Hector knew exactly who I meant when I asked for Aeneas, and where to find him. As a nephew of King Priam, he has a palace of his own in the heart of the city. Though not as monumental as Priam's, it's still fit for royalty.

I stand at the base of the palace steps, which are tiled and painted with seashells. The lower floor is for servants and the kitchen, the top two for guests and the man himself. Inside is just as resplendent as the stairs outside.

Silk *klines* surround a pool in the center of the main floor. It smells of rose oil as I walk around it. Pink tiles cover the floor, and frescoes depicting the sea cover opposite walls. The palace is empty, though, with not even a servant treading in the hallways.

Curiosity tugs at me. I'm walking around the pool toward the dark archway in the back of the room when a sweet voice says from behind me, "You won't find him."

Aphrodite lounges on one of the *klines*. She wears a sheer emerald dress that leaves nothing to the imagination. She tilts her head, ruby-colored hair catching in the sunlight that filters through the open palace doors.

"I haven't been able to persuade him to leave the city just yet," she says. "He's out there, likely training, as you should be."

I ignore the judgment dripping from her words and take a seat opposite her. "It's a good thing I came here looking for you, then."

She glares and tosses her hair over a shoulder, the locks changing color with the movement from rich auburn to a deep, endless black. Aphrodite notices my attention.

"I'm sure you've heard, rightfully so, that I am the most beautiful woman in the world," she says. "Well, beauty is fluid, is it not? What you might find beautiful is much different than what your brother finds beautiful."

"And can you apply this *gift* to someone else?"

"No need to dandy around words." She waves a hand. "Get to your point, Daphne."

"I need you to cause chaos in the Achaean camp." I lean forward. "Your particular flavor of lovely, romantic chaos."

"Why would I do that?" she asks, though a wicked smile creeps up her face.

"Because you don't want to see this city fall."

"It won't fall." She sniffs. "Apollo's wall ensures that."

"You also don't want to watch your son die on the battlefield."

She stills, inhumanly. Almost a marble statue. "Are you threatening my son?"

Something in me whispers that I should have a dagger in my hands at all times around this viper.

"No." My hands tremble. The stories of Aphrodite's vengeance are nothing to take lightly. "But the Achaeans are. His life is at risk just as any other soldier on that battlefield, especially at Hector's side."

"Ares would never allow it," she says quickly. "He loves me."

"Ares killed his own daughter," I say, voice low. "He wouldn't know love if it bit him in the ass."

"I wouldn't be so sure."

We watch each other. A breeze carries over her scent, of roses and musk, cedarwood and spice. Everything I desire.

"Fine," she finally says, voice curt. Aphrodite unhooks her long legs from under her and stands. Her dress truly leaves nothing to the imagination. "I will do what I can. For Aeneas."

She strides past me toward the entryway, but turns beneath the curved arch. "Remember that I can make you wish you were dead, should you do anything I might consider unwise."

She strides directly into the sunlight streaming through the doorway, then disappears.

Evening has settled upon Troy, oil lamps lit around the city and hearths blazing. I find Helen playing *petteia* with Lykou in a grand room at the center of Priam's palace. A large pool fills the space, the bottom tiled with jade and lavender. Plants I do not recognize hang from the ceiling and climb the walls. This room is a nymph's dream.

"I need to talk with you both," I say, clenching my *peplos*. "Hippolyta as well."

Lykou's mouth opens and closes, eyes as dark as a raging sea at night, but then he says, "Lead the way, Daphne Diodorus."

We find Lyta, still caked in dried mud as she sits on the end of Penthesilea's bed. The furs are tangled, as though Hippolyta has slept there recently or they were never made after her sister fell to Hades's realm.

"Persephone was there," I say, sitting beside her. "When we set the pyre on fire. Persephone herself came to take your sister to Elysium."

A harsh laugh, almost a cough, bubbles up from the back of my friend's throat. "Penthe always said that she would end up there one way or another." She looks to Lykou and Helen. "I should have known that time would come too soon. My warriors are not exactly afforded longevity with our life choices."

A moment of silence passes, broken only by the swirling whisper of a breeze.

"I did not mean to keep anything from you," I finally say, pressing my palm against the rock-hard gold coating my abdomen. "My life is so intertwined with the gods at this point that their secrets have become my own."

She nods. "With a father like Ares, I should have known."

I release a great, shuddering sigh. Despite my sanctimonious attitude toward Apollo, I've become just as bad as him. Too many secrets from the people I love.

Perhaps telling them might lay a curse upon their shoulders, and perhaps such a curse is what Apollo has been protecting me from all along.

They want to know my secrets, though, and I have to trust that they understand what the full price of knowledge is.

And so I tell them.

I start first with the beginnings of my dealings with the gods, Artemis's bargain, and then my journey across Greece, how Theseus died after we left Hippolyta on the plains, and what happened to me in the depths of Tartarus.

I tell them of Zeus's command, the fateful words of the Moirai, and the tangled web of feelings between Apollo and me.

By the time I finish, my throat is dry. Lykou wordlessly hands me a goblet and I take a hearty gulp of the pomegranate juice within.

Helen breaks the silence first. "Why didn't you"—her sinuous voice cracks and she gulps—"why didn't you tell any of us all this before?"

I place my hands palms up on my knees. "Because I am so entangled in the gods' web that I can't differentiate my own lies."

And because I've become the very thing I despised all along.

I meet Lykou's unflinching gaze. The wolf of last summer lingers there, baring its teeth at me. "I have been leaving you out, my dearest, oldest friend," I say, "because every time I look at you, all I remember is how lifeless you felt in my arms and how it was my fault."

I turn to Hippolyta, still sitting on her dead sister's bed. "And you, Lyta. You knew of my involvement with the gods, and have known it all along. Just as Lykou has. But not to the full extent. You did not know of Zeus's command, nor the prophecy of the Moirai. Would you have still taken up my cause if you did?"

I meet Helen's eyes. Something inside me skitters along my heart. Perhaps shame or fear, maybe even pride. "I wasn't honest with you because I was afraid. Of so many things. Of you removing me as your Shield. Of your hatred for my affiliation with your father and his command to protect you."

Silence fills the room, broken only by the crackling oil lamps in each corner. A whirlwind of emotions stir within me as I look to each of my closest confidants, but especially to my queen. The one I am to protect and the one from whom I crave the most validation.

She bites her lip and turns away, wrapping her arms around herself. "I need—I need to be alone. This is a lot to process right now." She looks at me askance. "You do realize that my father never gave a damn about me my entire life, right? Not when men tried to steal me away in the night, or when I was sold like cattle to the highest bidder, when I made perhaps the stupidest choice of all in accepting Menelaus's bid?"

She stomps over to the doorway and braces a hand on the tan stone. Her back is to me as she says, "Or was my stupidest choice following you across the Aegean when I should have returned to my daughter?"

Her absence is like a gaping wound. Each breath leaves a sharp pain in my side. I'm gasping, breathing harder and faster by the second. Hippolyta lays a hand on my bare knee and squeezes.

All my fears and pains and regrets leave me in one great sob. "I'm so sorry. To all of you."

Especially my queen.

"You can make it up to us."

I look up to Lykou. His arms are crossed over his broad chest, voice rough as he says, "Let's get revenge. For the Amazons dead and their queen. Against the gods playing my king like a lyre."

"Yes." Lyta quickly stands and begins pacing. "They will expect an attack soon, once the plain dries. They will expect the full force of Troy's might."

My hands curl into fists. "But they might not expect a few foolish warriors who find that vengeance tastes sweeter than wine."

CHAPTER 34

All that honesty and I feel as though I am naked. Despite the feeling, I wear Hephaestus's armor, black leather that ripples with gold undertones and is dotted with hidden daggers. Twin swords hang from my hips as I stride beneath the moonless sky. Selene's gaze is turned elsewhere, the dark clouds covering her face.

Lyta and Lykou flank me. The latter is as silent as a wolf on the hunt, and the former just as intent. We press against cypress trees along the muddy plain, having exited the city via the smallest of Troy's gates, the southern. The trees have soaked up most of the rain, and the path is drier here, not gripping our ankles like hands reaching from the Styx.

A dark form separates from the trees and stalks toward us. Lyta and Lykou immediately whip out their blades, but I stop walking and raise my chin. I could recognize that gait anywhere.

Apollo stops before us, balancing dual swords like my own. "I will help you."

"We don't need your help," Lykou growls.

Apollo's gaze flicks among the three of us. "The Achaeans have desecrated my temple, and the temples of my family. Agamemnon and his men are due a visit from me."

"But Zeus bound your powers," I say.

"With or without Olympian magic, I'm deadly with a blade."

Of that, I know very well.

Lyta rolls her eyes and marches on. "As long as you're more helpful than you were in Foloi. I had to save you from being skewered by a centaur *twice*."

"In my defense, I was wounded from taking an arrow for Daphne," Apollo says, following.

Guards patrol the reaches of the Achaean camp in twos and threes. We're at the base of a cresting dune, lying on our bellies in the sand. With a wave of his hand, Apollo blends our group into the shadows. We watch them pass for an hour.

"They have no pattern," Hippolyta whispers.

"Makes it harder to infiltrate the line. Cannot predict when the next scouts will pass," Lykou says with equal quiet. "Must be Odysseus's idea. He is the army's strategist, after all."

"When the other kings allow him to have any say, that is." Apollo leans forward, watching as another pair of scouts pass below our dune. "There's been lots of bickering among the kings since they landed on Troy's shores."

"Where were your insights before I lost half of my army?" Lyta's voice cuts through the darkness with deadly calm.

"My father has kept me firmly under his thumb." I can feel Apollo's gaze on me. "But I have my limits."

Hippolyta mutters something under her breath that I do not hear as three more guards patrol beneath us, bearing shields with Ajax's white snake.

Apollo points beyond the men to three temples. "Those are for Hera, Poseidon, and Ares. The Achaeans have stored their food in my brother's temple, thinking that he will protect it from rot and rats. I have infested that building again and again, but the food remains safe. Either my brother's powers have grown substantially since I last saw him, or another goddess aids him. The prisoners are kept in Hera's temple, and I cannot see what they keep inside Poseidon's temple. No doubt they believe that Hera and Poseidon aided them when they crossed the Aegean, so they believe their stores are safe there."

"Are they?" I ask.

Even deep in shadow, I can see a wicked smile pull at the corners of Apollo's mouth. "No."

"You and that sunshine brat can free the prisoners." Lykou points at my face. "Hippolyta and I will take care of the food."

The Amazon grins. "It will be an absolute joy to break into my father's temple and knock over his statue."

Heady pleasure thrums through me at the image, including Lyta smearing Ares's face across the marble floor, snapping his spine beneath my heel.

"Should I worry about that look?" Apollo whispers, grinning.

"We move. Now." Lykou goes first and we follow, careful of our every breath and sound.

We split into two, Apollo on my heels as we flank the southern side of the camp and make a beeline for Hera's temple. Her golden statue is like a beacon in the night, lit by the fires around her.

The deeper into the camp we trek, the more crowded it becomes. There is no laughter in this army, no sounds of happiness or even mourning. As if a sickness swept through.

A slight drizzle has started to fall, plastering my hair to my face.

I press against the canvas wall of a tent as a man passes, followed in quick succession by five more.

"Do these men never rest?" I whisper to Apollo at my side. "Or do they just meander the camp at all hours of the day?"

"There is something dark at work here, even fouler than the meddling of Ares." Apollo leans close, his lips brushing my ear.

A rumble above sounds Zeus's irritation at that very fact. The lightning that cracks across the sea in the distance does nothing to stir the men around the camp. They barely look up, continuing to slog through the muck.

"We should have come up with a plan before barging in here," I say.

Apollo grins. "Not having a plan never stopped you before."

"My point exactly."

I peer around the corner of the tent.

Two men sit in morose silence on a soaked rug, staring blankly at the plates before them. The food on the plates, though fine and not littered with mold, looks untouched.

"What I would give for a soft caress, right now," one says. His hair is dotted with white. Far older than the typical soldier.

"All the lovely ladies are being hoarded by the kings," the other gripes. "But we could fuck the rats that seem to infest this place if we were truly desperate."

I steal one of their cloaks. Apollo's walk is that confident prowl I hate to be on the receiving end of, but it works. Nobody gives us a second glance as we cut through the camp. Nobody doubts our motives, or our attire.

We're mere yards from Hera's temple when Apollo catches me by the wrist and holds up a finger. "Wait."

I open my mouth to ask him why, but he points over my shoulder. I turn and look toward Ares's temple in the distance, on the other side of camp.

"No. Anyone could see us here."

He shakes his head and rolls his eyes to the sky. "Do you have to argue with me about every little thing?"

"I just love when you roll your eyes, Apollo," I snicker quietly as I walk. "What was it you called it? An endearing, mature habit?"

"Glad to know that you at least listen to me, even if you always ignore me."

"Too bad you haven't found a way to break free of your father's bind on your powers. Invisibility would be helpful right now. Or that ring Hermes stole," I say as I look for a place to hide.

Apollo's standing so close I can hardly breathe. "The Ring of Gyges?"

"I think that's what he called it. Let's wait in that tent." I point to a dark one just beyond our goal, the shadows beckoning. "Care to check it first to make sure that Nyx isn't lurking within?"

"You could do that yourself, you know." Apollo eyes the soldiers that pass.

"Her scent." Like a field of overgrown lavender.

There's none of that here, thankfully. I usher him inside and we press into the folds of the canvas. Apollo's body curves into mine in the tight space. Behind us, a set of silk curtains partition what must be the sleeping quarters of another soldier. Hopefully he doesn't come back anytime soon.

"I feel like we've been here before, *kataigída*," Apollo says, voice like silk. He breathes, and the muscles of his abdomen press along my chest. I look up into his face, suddenly breathless.

Swallowing, I say, "I don't think we were ever forced to hide in another man's tent last summer."

"No"—he reaches up and brushes a lock of my hair behind an ear—"but I keenly remember the feeling of your body against mine beneath a dark sky."

"The circumstances were very different." I soften the words with a light chuckle. "How much longer do you think Lykou and Lyta will be?"

"I'm in no rush."

I meet his eyes, the brilliant blue dimmed in the shadows. The barest hint of a beard brushes his sharp chin, the scar I noticed on his cheek barely visible but still definitely there. The mortal Apollo I fell in love with lingers beneath the surface of this god.

"Nothing good ever comes from falling in love with a god," I say. "Please don't ask it of me."

"Not for mortals, no." He cups my face. "But I'll wait."

"What does that mean?"

A barking laugh cuts off his answer, if he was planning on answering. Two men stride past us into the tent. I was so distracted by Apollo that I didn't even notice their approach. What else did I miss?

It would be impossible to miss the next laugh, and the voice that follows it.

"You live in such squalor, Pyrrhus."

"I do not have the luxury of furs and ladies, Patroclus," my brother says. His brilliant red hair shines as he lights the oil lamp in the corner.

Apollo wraps an arm around me, pulling both of us deeper into the shadows of the tent flap's folds. The scent of roses and musk wafts over to our space. As unmistakable as a hand around my throat. Aphrodite's power fills the tent. Curiosity and horror raise the hair on the back of my neck. Of course her help would be two-sided.

"I have offered my own furs many times." Patroclus reaches out and grazes my brother's bicep with a narrow finger. "As has Achilles. Many times."

"I will earn those furs." My brother pats the threadbare cloak he uses for a bed.

"You have, *sýntrofos*. Tenfold." Patroclus's voice is gentle, like my brother is a wild animal that needs coaxing. Which might not be too far from the truth.

He very well might be an animal still. I wonder how much of the stag lingers in Pyrrhus like the wolf in Lykou.

Apollo's arm around me is firm and warm, pressing around my back to pull me against his chest. It's an effort to hold my breath so that my brother doesn't hear us.

"I would be nothing without you and Achilles." Pyrrhus looks down at his callused hands. "A traitor to my country and king."

"The mistakes of your family are not your own." Patroclus's legs tangle with my brother's. "I know that very well."

I catch my lip between my teeth. Heavy footsteps barrel for Pyrrhus's tent. Apollo's grip tightens as Achilles passes us, throwing aside the partition.

"Starting the party without me, lads?" The warrior king's profile is hungry as he looks over my brother and his lover. *Their* lover.

"We would never." Pyrrhus's eyes burn into Achilles.

Heat flames my cheeks as the Myrmidon swoops down to sit between them. His perfect lips capture my brother's with expert ease before next claiming Patroclus's. My mouth pops open, and I slowly turn my face into Apollo's chest.

With Olympian quiet, he whispers, "Perhaps we should have chosen another tent."

I'm saved from spying further on my brother by the acrid stench of smoke. A gray plume begins to fill the tent, suffocating the goddess of love's floral scent.

"What in Hades's realm?" Achilles barks a curse and leaps to his feet.

All three men storm from the tent. A fire roars on the horizon in the unmistakable direction of Ares's temple.

"That's going to infuriate her father," Apollo says.

"I think that was the point."

The temple is living flame, reaching higher and higher into the cloudy sky. It rages hard, the rain barely touching it, and even from here, I can see the hot mist that forms an impenetrable barrier around the temple. Soldiers from every corner of the camp run toward the fire. Commands are shouted, lost in the roaring din.

"Let's go." I lead the way between the tents, pulling my cloak tight.

There are no guards to hinder us when we reach Hera's temple, though. A great boulder has been placed in front of the temple door. I merely nod at Apollo and he begins rolling it away. His muscles ripple in the distant firelight. He clenches his teeth, spitting as the great stone finally moves from the doorway. It tumbles from the promenade, falling to the earth with a great crack.

Thunder rumbles above our heads, blanketing the crash and giving us a moment more. I stride into the temple, sword raised.

Women cower against the painted walls. They are all bloody and haggard. Achaean trophies.

My lips curl around a dozen curses. "May Nemesis burn this entire camp to the ground."

Sword raised above the lock holding all the women's chains in place, I turn to Apollo. "Did my brother know about this?"

Apollo's grim silence is answer enough.

Sparks alight in the cramped temple, illuminating the teal and purple peacocks painted on the walls. The women whimper and huddle together, even when the chain between them goes slack. Their feces are everywhere, these women forced to lay in their own filth. Bruises dot their arms and legs, many sporting blackened eyes and broken lips.

How could Hera just let this happen? Some of these woman are wives, surely. They all have families. She is the goddess of marriage and women. I can't understand how her hatred of mortals, of me, is so strong that she is willing to forsake her own image. Anger rips through me, clenching my muscles and making me grind my teeth. I tuck that feeling away, to use later, and grab the nearest and oldest of them roughly, dragging her to her feet. She cries out, her halo of pale blonde curls oily and flecked with sand.

I cup her face with both hands. The whites of her eyes are wide.

"Listen to me." With my thumbs, I brush away the tears that stream down her cheeks. "We haven't the time to sit and cry. There is no room for fear or pain. We must get these women out of here, *now*."

Her eyes shutter, then go blank. Her lips press in a firm line.

Apollo's hand lands on my shoulder and gives it a firm squeeze. "Let me."

He gets down on his knees before the woman. "Chryseis of Lyrnessus. Sister, cousin, priestess."

She looks at him, her eyes still carefully blank.

"We cannot begin to understand what has happened to you and these women, but I do know that if we wait only a moment longer, it will happen again. My sister cannot protect you. Hera and Athena and Demeter cannot protect you, either. You must protect yourselves now."

I'm keenly aware of the growling army just outside, looking for blood. It won't take them long to check here for those responsible for burning their food stores.

Chryseis blinks, then turns to the women still cowering against the wall. With the command of a queen, she says, "To your feet *now*!"

On weak and bruised legs, the women tentatively stand. I usher them out, but when the god of music moves to follow, I lay a firm hand on his chest.

"I need you to stay."

Hurt flickers in his eyes, gone in an instant.

"Not because I don't want you to follow, but because I have no chance of getting all these women out of here without one last distraction." I press up on my toes and lay a gentle kiss on his cheek. "Make them fear you, Apollo."

"A distraction I will give you, *kataigída*," he says. He pulls free his swords and holds them aloft.

I turn my back on him and hustle the women through the camp. They stumble and fall, but courage seems to have finally taken root in their heels, because nonetheless they fly. We pass empty tents and break through the final line. I usher them over the dunes.

A bloodcurdling scream pierces the night. Three Achaean soldiers charge for us as we crest the sand.

The women break for the line of cypress trees and I whip out my twin swords. The Achaeans meet me on the sandy expanse. I swing out a kick. One ducks, but another doesn't have time. My heel meets his jugular and he goes down. Two to go. I'm a cyclone of black metal, parrying the soldiers' swings and jabbing in the next movement.

One soldier roars as his blade cuts toward my midriff. I spin from his reach and plant my sword in his spine. His roar echoes into the night, no doubt attracting every soldier's attention for miles.

My heart leaps up into my throat, but I swallow it down. The soldier I kicked has finally regained his footing. I aim another blow, this time catching him in the groin. As he doubles over, I pounce for the third and final soldier. His blade meets mine in the air.

A wild scream erupts from behind me. I have just enough time to duck before a sword slices the air above my head.

And imbeds in my opponent's neck.

The man's body thuds to the sand. Hippolyta towers above it, panting. "Themyscira sends its regards."

Lykou runs up after her and grabs my hand. "We have about thirty Achaeans on our tails. Run!"

We sprint, catching up to the straggling escaped prisoners. The thunder of hooves echoes behind us, slowed down by the low branches of the cypress trees and the mud still lingering on the plains.

"Open for Hippolyta of the Amazons," Lyta screams as we cross the final yards to the northern gate.

We reach it as a volley of arrows sing overhead. Men and horses scream from behind me as the deadly tips find their target. The door opens, frustratingly slow. The freed prisoners squeal, trying to force their way through the crack.

I spin around in time with Lykou and Hippolyta, swords aloft and ready to defend them in their final moments of freedom. A man leaps down from his horse and charges us. He is quickly felled. But more men follow, one after another.

My arms ache and lungs burn. The rain has stopped, the air now humid and warm. Lykou's *dory* spins, iron head cracking a man's skull. His blood sprays my feet and legs. We back up as another volley of arrows fly overhead.

"Hurry," Hector yells from behind us. "We won't hold the gate open for much longer!"

"Are all the prisoners inside?" I bark over my shoulder.

Lykou can afford nothing more than a curt nod. He jabs his *dory* at an encroaching soldier and the man dances from his reach.

"Let's get inside, then." I grit my teeth, tasting sand.

We back up, weapons out. I'm the last to pass through the gate. A dozen of Troy's strongest men rush forward and slam it shut, sliding the locks home with a thud of finality.

And I finally allow myself to smile, watching the former prisoners run forward and embrace their loved ones. My elation quickly disappears as Paris strides forward.

"Are you insane?" His face is red with fury, brown hair flaring behind him. He strides right up to my face and jabs a finger into my collarbone, hard enough to bruise. "Your recklessness almost lost us the city. If those soldiers got through the gate…" He spits at my feet. "All the deaths would have been on your shoulders."

"What about Achaean deaths?"

We turn toward Lyta. Something sparks in her eyes, something that I thought had died with her sister.

"What did you say?" Paris is incredulous. "You think that any men you killed on this foolish mission are worth what we could have lost?"

"I don't usually deal with what-ifs." Hippolyta picks her nails with a dagger. "But I was referring to the Achaeans who will die the slow, painful death of starvation now that we've set all their food on fire."

Everyone quiets. Paris takes a step back from me. His finger is still raised, but it curls into a fist that he drops to his side. He turns from Lyta to me, a sneer lingering on his face. "I will talk to my father about this."

He leaves, followed by a battalion of Trojan soldiers. Lykou claps me on the back. His hand rests on my shoulder, gripping it tight. I look up at him. His sharp features are brushed with dried blood. Mud flecks his black curls, which fly as he shakes his head, grinning.

I rub my face and release a shuddering breath. I can't even remember when we first arrived in Troy, or how long we've been preparing for war and fighting it. Has it truly been that long since Artemis brought me to Olympus and Zeus commanded me to fight in Spartan games?

Apollo's face flashes behind my eyes and I sprint for the stairs that run along the wall, taking them two at a time. I'm gasping by the time I reach the top. I spin, looking out over the battlefield to the smoky Achaean camp beyond.

I may have defended Troy all this time, but there was nothing defensive about what I did tonight. All this time, my loyalties have been as hazy as Hermes's. Tonight, though, was a very firm declaration that I fight for Troy.

CHAPTER

35

The next morning, when our forces rally to the city's gates for battle, we find no opponents waiting for us. Smoke still lingers in the air as the Achaeans move to their boats, at least a quarter of the force leaving to find supplies. They've doubled their sentries. Across the line of Trojan soldiers, I flash Lyta a grin before we march right back into the waiting city.

For the rest of the day, Troy celebrates.

Bonfires are lit in every corner of the city, blessings and sacrifices made to the makeshift temples now erected within the walls. I dress Helen for a banquet that Priam hosts in celebration as well.

"We must savor each victory," he said to his people just that morning. "No matter how small and inconsequential they may seem."

"We should be attacking while they're weak. Not partying," I say to Helen, wrapping a silver gown around her frame.

Helen says nothing, her face downturned in a frown. Once lush with curves, her body is now frail, her skin pale and hair limp. As though this war eats her whole.

I rest a hand on hers. "I'm sorry. For all of it."

Her eyes meet mine for a split second in the bronze mirror before she jerks her hand away and stands. "To be sorry means that you would not do it again. But you would do it *all* again, wouldn't you?"

She marches for the doorway, stopping only to place a hand on the frame and say, "Being my Shield wasn't enough for you. You also needed the glory of the gods."

She disappears without another word. With a reproachful look that says he hasn't entirely forgiven me yet, Lykou follows.

My throat bobs. I wonder if she's correct. I drag my fingers over the soft fabric meant for me, the color of seafoam and laced with thunderbolts in yellow. As if the palace seamstresses had known I would be leading the armies not for Helen, but at the behest of Zeus.

That bastard has controlled me this entire time. I screech and throw the fabric aside.

"Perhaps a different color?"

I spin to find Apollo in the doorway, wearing a red chiton so dark it could be black. He stalks forward lazily. Such power, evident even in that simple stride, even with his gifts bound. I turn my head to look up at him when he stops just short of me.

"How did you know that it wasn't my color?"

He smiles and holds up a length of fabric. "You look loveliest in red."

I have a dagger in my palm instantly. It's pressed against his neck before he can even take another breath.

"How did I save you, the night I slashed this very throat?" I shove the blade so that he can feel how sharp the edge is.

Apollo raises his hands so I can see them. His cerulean eyes don't leave mine. "You followed the constellation of Auriga back to

330

the camp," he says, slowly and carefully. "Where you used Dionysus's wine to revive me."

I take a step back, breathing heavily, then drop the knife to my side.

"I had to make sure it was you." I run a frustrated hand through my hair, catching on my knotted curls. "I feel like I'm going mad."

"Understandable that you would be on edge when the trickster has his hand in your bed." Apollo waves to the bed in question, where my armor and weapons lay. The Adamantine sword shimmers there in the torchlight.

I wrap my arms around myself. "If you're jealous, you can—"

"I can what?" He grazes my arm with his fingers. "Leave? Challenge Hermes to a duel? No, jealousy and brutality would never win your affection. I have no interest in squaring off against my brother, nor do I want to stand idly by as he chases after you."

He looks me over, gaze lingering on my lips, the arch of my neck, between my breasts and thighs. I imagine his lips in all those places. Heat creeps from my abdomen to my cheeks.

"No." He meets my eyes. "I will start with what you have asked all this time."

Breathlessly, I ask, "What is that?"

Apollo's mouth quirks to the side. "To prove that you can trust me."

The hand that brushes my arm suddenly stops, gripping me firmly. His face dips, lips brushing my own. My breath catches.

He swallows, then says, "You are so lovely, you make me lose all sense. So strong, I can hardly believe you're real. You're a feast and I am still hungry for more."

I want to turn away from his unflinching gaze. I want to shove him. I want to leave, fight, and even cry. But, most of all, I want to kiss him.

But once you've tasted that heavenly fire, can you really be content with anything less?

I shudder, leaning back on my heels. "About that new dress…"

Apollo blinks, then shakes his head. "Yes. New color." He turns to the fabric he brought into the room. "If not that watery color, or red, and I'm guessing you're getting mighty tired of gold…" He turns his back to me, so I cannot see what he does with his hands. The thought of what his hands could do makes my skin flush.

"What about something simple?" I offer.

He turns and holds a new dress aloft. "It's as if you read my mind."

The fabric is white, shimmering with a pearlescent sheen. I flash him a coy smile. "Would you like to help me put it on?"

His jaw clenches. "Then we'll never leave this room."

In the end, he turns his back to me. I drop my clothes and wrap the fabric around my waist and shoulders. It is as soft as feathers and sits with barely a whisper on my scarred skin.

I let him lead me through the palace hallways. Revelry echoes down the corridors, instruments I've never heard before, laughter and singing. We slip into Troy's crowded streets. Colored lamps have been hung between houses, doorways split by sheets of red and gold and green.

"Troy's colors of celebration," Apollo says, pointing to one. Each is painted with varying animals. Peacocks fan their tail feathers on this one, and snakes slither up and down the next. "And to honor each household's chosen god."

"What do they do with the sheets when not celebrating?" I ask.

Apollo grabs my hand, his fingers warm and callused. "They hang them over hearths in their kitchens, similar to what Ligeia had in your Spartan home."

"Do you think Ligeia was originally from Troy?"

"No. You've visited her birthplace before, actually." He tugs me along. "She was born to a fisherman in Eleusis."

We walk deeper into the city. People dance around the great fires. Food and drinks are passed among all. Spices I could never hope to recognize fill the air, flitting with the smoke and songs.

"Do you know where she and my parents are?" I cannot help the hopeful edge that leaks into my voice.

"No doubt they are hiding." Apollo plucks a hanging flower and threads it through my curls.

"With moly?" I pat the flower self-consciously. It's not the same flower, but a similar color, this one off-white with long, thin petals.

"Is that how Hermes avoids my father's sight?" Apollo guesses correctly. "Perhaps."

He leads me through a market crowded with dozens of food stalls. Each smells more intoxicating than the next. My mouth waters insatiably.

Apollo pays handsomely for a pita stuffed with lamb, feta, and spices. "Your favorite, yes?"

I accept the food with a blush. "You remembered."

"I could never forget how adorable you looked stuffing your face with feta in Knossos."

His golden hue has dimmed, face becoming softer, less burdened with the edges of Olympus and immortality. But his height is still stark compared to the Trojan people, and his beauty beyond compare. People watch us as we flit through crowds.

After we finish eating, Apollo tugs me toward a circle of dancing couples. "Just this once."

"I have all the grace of a fawn," I say and try to pull my hand away.

"I've seen you dance before." He's inexorable. "That's not true."

I don't have time to ask when he's seen me dance before he's pulling me into the throng. My skin is soon slick with sweat, the chiton clinging to my every curve. He rests a hand on the small of my back, the other hooked around my waist to pull me close. Our bodies dip and twist together, hips never parting. His eyes don't leave my own. Hungry, intent, lethal.

Despite knowing the danger lurking beneath that gaze, I don't pull away. We don't stop dancing until Selene's moon has reached the height of the sky. I'm spinning and my eyes are closed.

The Sparta you know will be gone forever more on the bloody fields of Troy.

I stumble, eyes fluttering open with a gasp. Apollo trips with me and we fall from the crowd. People watch us as he leads me toward an empty alleyway.

"What's wrong?" Worry stains his words. He looks me over as if assessing me for any wounds.

I shake my head and clench my eyes shut. "Do you think we are fools to celebrate so prematurely?"

"Fools? No." His voice is husky. He leads me farther from the bonfire, hand still resting on the small of my back. "There is so little joy in the world, especially during times of war, that it is important to grasp it while you can. Otherwise, what is the point of fighting?"

"To survive?" I chuckle dryly.

He returns in kind. "What's the point of surviving without joy, then?"

"In Sparta, joy seemed like a foreign concept. We were supposed to strive for nothing other than the role of Spartiate. Or marriage."

I hook my arm through his and a happy rumble echoes through the god's chest. Our sandals echo down the street, the sounds of revelry slowly fading away. When I look up, a gasp steals itself from my throat.

The great fresco looms before us. The etched faces of the gods look down in varying shades of disapproval and condescension.

"The likenesses are uncanny," I say. "How many hours did you have to sit for this?"

"I did not sit." Apollo shakes his head. "This was crafted from mere memory by a god most haven't even heard of. I haven't seen Kothar-wa-Khasis in centuries."

"Hermes told me of the battle for Olympian power," I say, voice almost a whisper. "Was this god one of the casualties?"

Apollo throws a furtive glance around to make sure nobody—god or otherwise—lingers in the shadows. "Hermes really has no understanding of secrets."

"He's the god of cunning," I say, shrugging. "There's no doubt a reason behind his dispensing of secrets. A method to his madness, so to speak."

"Your nights training with Hermes have given you some insight, eh?" Apollo nudges me with an elbow.

"My…" *Friendship* doesn't sit right on my tongue. "My *partnership* with Hermes has its uses. At least I can expect honesty from him."

A sharp laugh bursts from Apollo. So loud and hard he doubles over, clutching his chest. When he's finished, he points a long finger at the messenger god's image. "Honesty is something you could never expect from him."

I open my mouth to argue but a high-pitched voice cuts through the night.

"Daphne."

Apollo and I turn to face Kassandra. She stands at the end of the alleyway, framed in the refracted firelight. When she speaks, her voice sounds hollow and far away, like at the end of a cave.

"Daphne of Seasara, the Daughter of Ash and Sea." Her eyes are so wide, the white rims stand out. "Helen will be killed."

My hand goes to the sword at my hip. "Are you threatening my queen?"

"Not threatening," Kassandra says, unblinking. "Warning you. If she continues on this path and kneels before the king of Mycenae, he will kill her this very night."

"Are you mad?" I stomp toward her. Everything in my body screams at me to fight her, argue, and toss her aside.

Apollo grabs my wrist and hauls me back. He spins me around to face him, dropping my hand to squeeze my arms.

"Apollo! What are you doing?"

His eyes bore into mine. "Ignore what the princess says and listen to me."

I clamp my lips shut at the urgency in his voice.

"Leave the city. Right now, Helen takes the path you were on just last night. She means to give herself over to Agamemnon to stop this war. She will be unsuccessful."

"What?" My entire body starts to shake. "How do you know?"

"Run, Daphne." Apollo shoves me away. "As fast as you can."

Where everything in my body fought against Kassandra's words, now my entire being screams at me to run.

And so I do. With the wings of Hermes beneath my feet, I flee the city of Troy.

CHAPTER 36

My lungs burn. With inhuman leaps, I'm tearing across the plain. Even in the dark of night, I can make out Helen's figure slipping in and out of the shadows created by the low cypress trees.

My arms pump at my sides and my breath is a sharp hiss. I leap and catch her across the middle. We tumble across the sand. A startled scream bursts from her lips, quickly smothered by my hand. I drag her, fighting and squealing, into the throng of trees.

"Shut up, you fool," I snap. Something inside me bucks at being so rude to my queen, but the fear and rage coursing through me right now quickly squashes it. "They will kill us both on sight."

She freezes against me. I keep my hand over her mouth just in case.

Exactly as I thought, two guards stride over the hill. They peer into the trees. Both of us still. I hardly dare to breathe. They stomp forward, kicking the sand where we just were. I throw a silent prayer up to Hermes, god of deception.

But, in the back of my mind, I know that the goddess of darkness herself works against me.

I glance around, looking for something, anything, to turn their focus elsewhere. They walk even closer and Helen releases a small huff against my palm. I chew my lip raw, the only movement I'll allow. Even my chest stops its rise and fall. The men step into the line of trees.

A screech echoes through the trees above us. Both men jump and whip out their swords. Hawks scream and soar, crashing through the branches before breaking into the night sky. The Achaeans stumble backward, gaping as the birds take flight.

And then dive. They fly right into their faces with wild cries. Both men roar, swinging their arms and running for the dune.

"Thank Tyche," Helen says when the men have disappeared.

"Save your thanks for Artemis, Apollo, and Hermes," I snap, releasing her.

She rips away from me, crawling across the dirt and spinning on her haunches.

"Return to Troy," she says, voice imbued with the command of a queen. "Or come with me to Agamemnon."

"He will kill us both," I say, unable to keep the fury from my voice. "There is no turning back, Helen." I have no titles for her because, in truth, she is no longer a queen.

And I don't know if she ever will be again.

Her face says that she recognizes as much. It crumbles, still lovely even as her heart must shatter in her chest. Her eyes clench shut around the tears that pour down her face.

"I have nothing left but my pride, Daphne." She sobs and throws her hands in the air. "If that. I cannot just stay in that palace, day in and day out, as Trojans die for my mistakes and Spartans die to bring me home."

"Bring you to your death."

"You don't know that." She shakes her head. "You cannot know that unless it is just another secret you are keeping from me."

"It isn't a secret if I'm telling you—"

Fury slights her eyes, snapping her out of her self-pity. She punches the sand. "Don't patronize me."

I release a long, shuddering breath and point in the direction of the Achaean camp. "There are forces at work much darker than vengeful kings. The goddess Nyx is still hungry to bring Olympus to its ruin. And Troy is the start."

"Why Troy?" She flings a handful of sand. "How does destroying a mortal kingdom help her?"

"Even if I knew, I couldn't tell you," I hiss through my teeth. "If I told you, they would kill us both to protect their secrets."

"Who?"

"The gods."

She clutches at her cloak with desperate fingers, pulling it tighter around her knees. "I never understood our blind worship of the bastards. For centuries, they have taken and taken, never truly giving. I am proof of that. Zeus took advantage of my mother and what do I have to show for it?"

"My mother was taken advantage of by a god as well." I huff. "I don't even get the courtesy of knowing which one."

Helen reaches out and runs her fingers through my hair, catching on my tangled curls. Gently, she pries them apart. "Can you give me honesty where they did not?"

I want to ask her if I haven't already, but instead say, "Of course."

"Was our friendship real, at least? It was real to me." She hesitates a moment, chewing on her lip. "I've never had a friend before. I wasn't even close to my siblings. My father put me on a pedestal from the moment I was born, and I think they resented me for it."

I drag a finger through the sand between us, then brush it away with a fist. "It was real."

She takes my hands in her own and squeezes them. "Then you should understand why I want to give myself to them. Even if they kill me. Because we both love Sparta and don't want to see any more of our people die for us."

"Giving yourself over to them won't help." I look to Troy's walls, layered with the blood of the gods.

Helen opens her mouth to press for more, but snaps it closed. Her gaze latches on to something behind me, the color leaching from her features.

I spin just as the hilt of a sword cracks into my temple.

Stars flash across my vision and I fall forward. Helen cries out. A sharp pain flares across my back as someone presses a knee into it. My wrists are wrenched behind me as my chin is dragged up.

Flanked by five soldiers, Odysseus towers above us.

CHAPTER
37

Odysseus's face is speckled with new scars that are not yet healed. They curl under one eye and cross his chin. His glare as he looks down at us is what strikes me the most.

There is no curiosity lingering there as before, only fury and pain.

We're dragged between the tents. No fanfare precedes us, no heckling or cries of victory. Uneasiness flickers inside me. Odysseus should be crowing our capture.

He brings us, bound and gagged, to a tent at the edge of camp. There are little luxuries throughout, like a pile of furs at the far end and a table of maps that are held down by food and wine.

Helen has managed to get the gag out of her mouth. "Most kings would demand a nicer tent, Odysseus."

"Most kings are fools." He waves a hand to us. "Cut their binds. They will not flee."

My arms are jerked painfully, but the binds are indeed cut and my gag removed. I rub my wrists and glare at the offending soldier. He ignores me and returns to stand beside his king.

Odysseus indicates a pair of stools. We quickly sit, though it rankles to be ordered around when I've enjoyed such freedom these last few months. The Ithacan turns to Helen.

"I would call you a fool, but your Shield has already said as much to you."

He continues, "I also heard her tell you that the kings might not be pulling the strings in this war." He turns to the table and gathers up bowls of food. He offers me a grin, the last remnant of the man I met in Sparta. "You may have burned most of the food, but not all of it. So forgive me for not offering either of you ladies what remains."

With a bowl of withered figs cradled in the crook of his arm, he takes the stool opposite us.

"I have been blessed with Athena's protection in this war," he goes on, "and that comes with benefits. Some food for my men, the assured silence of my men, and protection from the gods that meddle with the minds of my fellows." He points to the ceiling. "Any other tent, and the gods would be watching us right now. Athena has assured a steady cover for us, but I do not know what gods seek to undermine that. Or if they are more powerful than even the goddess of war."

"They are."

Everyone in the tent turns to me, and even I'm startled by the sound of my own voice. Zeus will not take lightly to me revealing his enemies or weaknesses. I chew the inside of my cheek a moment before continuing.

"They have to be powerful, or arrogant, enough to believe they can tear down Troy." My words sound hollow.

Odysseus looks at me sharply, pinning me with an unreadable gaze as if he can see right through me.

Helen glances between us. "What my Shield means to say is that there is a reason there have been no victors for each battle."

The king leans back and crosses his ankles. "Well, minus one decisive victory."

"Where Ares himself intervened," I snap.

"Another example of the gods playing us like a game of *petteia*," he says. His voice is like the slither of a snake on a forest floor. Soft and secretive, with just a touch of malice. "I don't deny the benefits of Athena's favor, nor am I stupid enough to question it aloud, but it begs the question: What other gods play in this game and what do they stand to win?"

A question I have asked myself. Apollo has said that the waning love of mortals has made their powers tenuous, held aloft only by the constant workings of the Muses in their garden. Resentments are high among people spending endless days in battle. No doubt the Achaeans have thrown many prayers of late to Ares. Hopefully that number has dwindled after Lyta and Lykou burned down his temple.

No, this has nothing to do with our love or reverence. This has everything to do with what the Trojan wall protects, and whoever wants it.

"You should hear the stories the men spin of you, Helen," Odysseus says around a mouthful of figs.

"They can't be any worse than the stories of my mother," Helen says, voice sharp. "What animals do they claim I make love to?"

"The human variety, I assure you." He chuckles. "Whoever whispers in their ears must work with the goddess Mnemosyne, because the stories are assured to be brilliant plays someday."

"Get on with it, Odysseus," my queen snaps.

His guards shift on their feet, looking around uneasily.

"Well, half of the camp says that Paris stole you away, blinded by your beauty and the promise of Zeus's favor." The Ithacan sweeps his left arm, and then his right. "While the other half claim you left of your own volition. That you seduced the prince and promised him your kingdom, but your own Shield, a *Mothakes* traitor to the Spartans, persuaded you to turn on your people."

A myriad of emotions flutter across Helen's face. Her cheeks flush a violent red, teeth gnashing. Her shoulders hunch as if around a sob that threatens to burst from her chest, and a tear manages to slip down her cheeks. My teeth clack together.

"What do you want, Odysseus?" I fix him with a venomous glare. "Do Ithacans play with their food before they eat as well? Just give us to Agamemnon and be done with it. Or were you never going to hand us over? Is that why you snuck us into camp?"

Helen, face blotchy, looks up. "What do you mean? Are you not going to turn us over to them?"

Odysseus sets aside his bowl and stands. He walks over to the table, dragging a finger along the maps there. "I want nothing more than to return home to my little island, my wife, my son, and even my damn dog. Bringing you to your vengeful husband and his brother won't accomplish that."

"Did you know that the conclave was a sham?" I blurt.

"I had my suspicions." He picks up a bag whose contents I know even before he dumps them onto the rug before us. "One of you play with me. I can't think when I sit idly."

Helen looks like she would rather spit on his face, so I take up the red *petteia* pieces and sit across from him on the rug.

"I'll tell you what." He points in my face. "If you win, I'll share some of my wine with you."

"Answer my questions instead."

He smiles wide, revealing a crooked tooth in the corner of his mouth. He must believe I have no chance of besting him, because his reply is quick. "I will take you up on that deal, but I ask for an answer in return."

I clench my teeth but nod. I know nothing that could potentially cost Troy this war, so I do not fear his question.

We play slowly, carefully, watching each other as much as the pieces. I'm already exhausted from the long night. My feet are sore from my run and the dancing, so I stretch my legs out beside me and flick Odysseus's pieces off, one by one. To no avail, it seems I chip at his flank but recognize my king's inevitable demise.

When our pieces lay scattered beside the cloth board, he looks up at me and asks his question, "Why do you think the gods haven't told you who your father is?"

Something small and insidious twists in my gut. "How would you know that?"

"I heard enough of your discussion with Helen." He begins collecting the pieces and returning them to their bag as he continues, "Do you believe it is because they fear your father? Is there more to you than some bastard of Olympus?"

"Zeus told me that my father isn't of Olympus," I admit, voice soft. "I don't know what that means."

"Well, you're not human. Not entirely at least." He crosses his arms and considers me. "There's a reason they aren't telling you, and it isn't just because of their penchant for secrets. No, the gods fear little more than their own weaknesses, and your heritage just might be one of them."

"Why are you telling us all of this?" I glare at him with suspicion.

"I want to go home." Odysseus inclines his head. "And I do not enjoy being used by the gods."

He stands suddenly and nods to a soldier posted at the tent's doorway. When the man leaves, Odysseus offers Helen a hand to guide her to her feet, and then me.

"My men will lead you back to the wall shortly. I don't wish to give the gods turning Agamemnon's and Menelaus's heads more power than they already have. But." He stops me from turning toward the doorway with a cold hand on my wrist. "There is someone else who wants to speak with you first."

The one whose validation I always craved the most steps into the tent.

CHAPTER
38

Alkaios straightens upon seeing me. Like Odysseus, he comes bearing new scars. They crisscross over his chest, red, glaring lines that shimmer in the firelight. He's haggard and unkempt, his beard long and hair threaded with wispy braids that glare with oil.

None of this surprises me so much as the pattern on his chiton. It's bright blue and decorated with the crest of Ithaca.

My brother notices my gaze. "For what you did, Menelaus had Pyrrhus and me removed from the army and flogged. It would have been until our deaths, but Achilles claimed our brother and Odysseus took me in."

My knees buckle and I'm grateful for the stools in Odysseus's tent. Helen covers her mouth with a trembling hand. Her pale gray eyes are wide.

"Spartans and their melodrama." The Ithacan looks to Helen as he says this. "It would have been a waste of a perfectly good soldier, especially one with a potential foothold into Troy."

I open my mouth to press, but Odysseus cuts me off. "Alkaios was the first to notice the peculiarities."

"Peculiarities?" Helen asks.

"In the kings," the Ithacan says, waving an arm. "Some, like myself, seem untainted. Achilles has the protection of his mother, no doubt, and I of Athena. But Menelaus, Ajax, and Agamemnon. Even Nestor." He shakes his head. "I'm ashamed that I did not notice sooner."

"The desecrated temples. The refusal to have funeral games. The dead animals and chariots. Killing the *paidonomos*. All of them are things no mortal Achaean king would do." Alkaios sighs and runs a hand through his hair before taking a seat across from me. The oily knots catch on his scarred fingers. "It struck me as odd when Menelaus rode a chariot to battle instead of a horse, or marching alongside his men. A Spartan *anax* would never ride a chariot, even one from another kingdom. But then the battle formations he led were nothing I had ever heard of."

I remember the day, that first battle when King Menelaus had called me out in front of the entire battlefield from atop his glistening chariot. The way my enemies had been endless while other sides of the field had cleared within mere hours.

"But then Ligeia's words rang in my ear that night"—a small smile pulls at his lips—"as it always does. Of a battle to the east called the Kadesh."

"You always had the best memory of us three," I say softly.

He ignores me and I try not to think about the twist of sadness in my gut as he continues, "They used chariots to create chaos, surrounding their enemies and sacrificing a few to exhaust the Egyptians. The assailed king at the time called upon his god, Amun, for help, and the god answered. Despite all odds, the Egyptians managed to beat back their enemies. Though they did not win the battle, they still managed to survive."

"And this is relevant because?" Helen raises her narrow brows. Exhaustion paints dark circles beneath her eyes.

"Because the gods themselves intervened." My brother's shoulders are hunched, but his gaze is sharp. "The king went back to Egypt and the love of their gods grew. They proclaimed a victory though there was none, and the people revered the gods for it. The king went on to be quite powerful."

"What gods help the Achaeans?" Helen's voice is high-pitched, balancing on the edge of hysteria. "And what hope do the Trojans stand of holding them at bay?"

"Well, you can thank that wall for keeping you safe." Odysseus points over his shoulder. "It is magicked to keep those who wish Troy ill from breaching the city unless invited in. But a combined might of gods might be enough to tear it down."

Alkaios crosses his arms. "That is not the only advantage the Trojans have. Daphne is touched by the favor of Apollo and Artemis."

Both of whom have been incapacitated, Apollo bound by his father, and Artemis flounced easily by Hera.

Odysseus continues, "As for which gods control the Achaean kings? Your Shield probably has the answer to that question."

Everyone in the tent turns to me expectantly.

"Ares fights for the Greeks." I grimace. "As do the Erinyes, likely Eris and Nemesis, and"—I hesitate, my throat dry—"anyone else who supports Nyx."

A heavy silence blankets the tent. It's broken only by the mournful camp army beyond the canvas walls, the wails of wounded men, and the wretched coughing of the sick and weary.

Odysseus stands after a long, tense moment, breaking it. "That explains things. It's no wonder Zeus does not end this squabble. If the stories of Nyx's hatred toward him are true, then this war will have the opposite effect of the Kadesh War. It will not inspire love for the gods, but rather hate. Zeus and his family likely wait until the exact moment to turn the tides and win the favor of the people."

"We are nothing more than pawns to them." Helen's eyes are far away.

She's not wrong. Despite always knowing and proclaiming as much, the truth of her words stings no less. I rub my arms as a chill suddenly sweeps over me from head to feet.

Alkaios coughs, straightening and crossing the distance between the two of us. "What of Hermes?"

I blink. "What about him?"

"He was your enemy." My brother takes another step. "Does he fight for the Achaeans or the Trojans?"

I answer honestly. "I don't know."

Alkaios squints, as if trying to see through my words. He takes my chin between his fingers. "You're not lying." He releases me as if stung. "But you're not being honest, either."

"Hermes has visited me." A shuddering breath escapes me. I swallow, unable to look at Helen. "Once or twice."

Alkaios's lips curl back from his teeth. "Does he kiss you as sweetly as Apollo?"

My fist cracks against his jaw. His entire body jerks back.

When he straightens, rubbing his chin, he says, "You two should return to Troy. Nyx will soon know you are here, and that Athena protects something in this tent."

Odysseus lifts an arm toward the entrance. "My men will see you to the edge of camp. May whatever gods you answer to protect you from there."

I wrap an arm around Helen's trembling shoulders and guide her toward the entrance of the tent.

"Wait."

I turn to face Alkaios. His impressive height now claims the space in the tent. I clench my teeth as he walks toward us. War has engraved his face with weary lines.

"When you fled with Helen, you didn't just betray Sparta. You betrayed Pyrrhus and me." Hatred laces his words. "I bet you didn't even think of us. What would happen to your own blood?"

Bile climbs up my throat. "There wasn't time, Alkaios. Another moment and they would have killed us both."

"You faced all the odds last summer and bested them." He shakes his head. "You're not our sister anymore. But I guess you never were. Olympian bastard."

"Then she will be *my* sister." Helen tugs on my hand. She glares up at Alkaios.

"Before this war ends, ask yourself, Daphne, who you answer to. Your people or your queen?" He looks down his narrow nose. "Your family or the gods?"

Helen and I flee wordlessly back to Troy. Away from the Achaeans or the accusation in my brother's words, I cannot say.

CHAPTER

39

W e need to stop this war."

We're in the grand bathing chamber, the air humid and making our clothes stick to our skin. Hippolyta stalks around the giant bath. Lykou's face is unreadable.

After returning to Troy, Helen and I immediately sought them out and dragged them from their beds. Granted, Lykou was already wide-awake with worry when we reached him.

"I thought you weren't going to keep any more secrets from me," he said, rolling from the auburn furs.

"That's why I'm rudely waking you up."

Now at the pool, I lean down and drag a hand through the crystal-clear water. The movement immediately eases the aches in my arms. I snatch my fingers back. I have no interest in using the heritage of a god in any way.

"Priam won't see reason," Lyta says, kicking up a spray. "Or at least, there's no way we can make him do so without looking like fools."

"We have to at least try." Helen stands with her arms crossed.

Lykou walks over to me and sits. "What did your brother say to you?"

I shake my head. "Nothing important."

The lie festers between us. We both know it.

"Remember when I told you, not so long ago, that I don't deserve your lies." My friend grabs my hand, and then a small smile tugs at the corner of his mouth. "And that you are beholden to no one."

I nod, lower lip trembling.

"That includes your brothers."

My gaze snaps to his.

"Why did Alkaios say that about Hermes and Apollo?" We both look up at Helen, her arms still crossed over her chest.

"Apollo and I…" I swallow. "I have a complicated history with the gods."

"She loves the god of prophecy," Lykou says. There is no judgment or reprimand in his voice. "Alkaios knows that."

Helen turns toward the room's entrance, in the direction of the Achaean camp beyond the walls. "I guess I cannot fault you for that, Daphne. We cannot control who we love."

Lykou's hand tightens around mine.

"And yet we can control who we save." Hippolyta marches toward the doorway. "Let's go stop this war."

Before we meet with Priam, Lykou helps me pull on Hephaestus's armor. The leather is snug, sitting comfortably without pinching or pulling at my skin. It is also light, but I have no doubt that it is stronger than all other armor that awaits me on the battlefield.

My friend's touch lingers on my shoulders and hips, and I let it. The touch is a comfort, if nothing more.

We walk slowly to the audience chamber, waiting as farmers and lords make their complaints. When our turn arrives, Helen steps forward. She's draped in green Trojan silks and her eyelids painted with teal. With her wavy mahogany hair and the stubborn set of her jaw, I cannot help but think she looks so much like Artemis.

There is nothing delicate about my queen. She is as fierce and wild as the goddess of the hunt.

"My *anax* Priam," she says, bowing low with reverence. "May I beg a private audience?"

The old king leans forward on his throne, steepling his fingers and resting his chin upon them. "If by private, you mean with your bodyguard and that Amazon entourage, I think you've misunderstood the definition of the word."

I resist the urge to roll my eyes.

Helen is much more polite than I would be. She gives him a demure smile. "Yes, my *anax*. I would like to meet with you, my people, and yours to discuss this war."

He considers her a moment. A hiss of skirts lets me know that Kassandra has come to stand behind us. I flash her a quick look, but she is watching her brothers. Hector and Paris walk up to their father, standing on his either side. Too quiet for us to hear, they confer with hunched shoulders and backs turned to us.

After a long, tense moment, Priam nods to Helen and stands. His red *peplos* sweeps behind him as he marches from the megaron, followed by his sons, his guards, and our measly entourage.

The mapped floor is freshly mopped when we enter, the ground still glistening. It makes my sandals squeak as we follow and I immediately feel more on edge. Priam leans a hand against the sole table in the room and turns to us.

"You wish to stop this war," he says without preamble.

Helen nods, not betraying even a glimmer of surprise on her lovely face. "We can bargain with them. Do whatever we must to end the needless bloodshed."

"Even give yourself over to them?" Paris asks. His face is unreadable.

Lykou and I step forward at the same time.

Helen casts her eyes down. "I would if I thought it would help, but we know that despite rumors, I'm not the true reason for my husband's declaration of war."

"You think we haven't gathered as much by now? Achaeans do not care for honor." Priam shakes his head, the glass beads woven into his graying hair tinkling. "No, now it is a matter of pride."

"Your pride?" Lyta glares at the Trojan. "My women will not turn their backs on you, but you would be expending their lives needlessly."

"We will quash down the Achaeans like the rats they are," Paris says, slamming a fist on the table.

Hector, ever the pacifist, steps between all of us. "This war will not last forever. We ask only for a few battles more, to cut down enough of them to have them turn tail and flee."

"My husband"—Helen's chin trembles and her hands curl into fists—"will drag out this war for a decade, until there are only two left standing, and even then he will leave and come back with more."

"Then perhaps it is your husband we should kill first." Paris's eyes glint, his mouth a hard line.

Helen matches him glare for glare. A *salphinx* sings in the distance. An Achaean rallying cry.

"The Greeks demand more blood spilled," Priam says, waving a hand toward the city below. "And we shall answer in kind."

I turn to Hippolyta, face beseeching, but she can only shake her head. If we withdraw, we will be labeled as cowards. If we do not fight, we will be killed as traitors.

*   *   *

I march onto the battlefield, Hephaestus's armor snug on my skin. Lyta squints, standing next to me, and looks me over.

"Something is different." Her gaze roves from my sandaled feet to my helmet. "One blink and that is the Amazon armor my sister gifted you with, and the next it is black."

"A gift from Hephaestus."

"Think he could outfit our entire army?"

"You'll have to ask him yourself." I look down at the girdle sitting around her waist. "What abilities does that girdle have?"

"It helps me see through deceptions." Hippolyta's eyes gleam. "If only my sister had been wearing it, and not me."

"She would never." I turn forward to face our common enemy. "She would want you to have every ounce of protection available."

"I miss her." Lyta's lip trembles.

The Achaeans march ever closer, the sounds of their drums and horns filling the plains. Dread seeps into my bones, filling me with a queasy ache. I don't think I'll ever leave behind the fear that sweeps through me at the start of every battle. This time, though, it is but a mere itch.

Just as Alkaios said, the Achaean kings ride forth in chariots with spiked wheels.

There is no fanfare, no pronunciations or sweeping battle cries. They come charging and they do not stop. I angle my sword high, pointed toward the men who run in my direction. A scream claws from my throat as the front lines are broken and the Achaeans power forward.

As one, Lyta and I move in a sweeping motion. Lykou takes up the rear with dual swords. Blood sprays around us as our blades cut through armor and flesh. The Adamantine is an extended limb, cleaving appendages as no other blade could.

I ignore the symbols painted on my enemies' armor. I don't need the shroud of guilt around my shoulders. I need speed and strength.

Hermes's training takes me by force. I kick a spear aimed for my thighs and balance on the wood to swing my other foot around. My heel clips my assailant's jaw and knocks him out, and then a blood-curdling cry catches my attention from above.

Furies dive with wild screams. Trojans and their allies are ripped from the battle, then dropped from staggering heights into the fray. They fall with sickly thuds all around me. Archers atop Troy's walls fire volley after volley. The Furies expertly avoid the arrows.

I spin and slide across the sand. The *dory* is a familiar weight in my hand as I scoop one up. Another man is yanked from the field, and even from yards away, I can see the whites of his eyes blaze with fear. I heave the *dory* back and let it soar.

My throw is short, the weighted butt bringing it down. I can only pray to Nike that it hit a Greek and not one of my allies. As I turn and search for another spear, an Achaean charges for me, but the Adamantine sword is ready. I meet his swing and his blade shatters. Pieces of bronze litter the ground around us, and shock blanches his features in the instant my sword slices his gut. I don't wait to watch him die.

I'm sprinting across the plain for another spear. It's in my hands and soaring through the air—it misses the nearest Fury by scant inches. I slice the kneecaps of the next Greek and I fling his sword at the nearest demon soaring above me. She banks and her hideous face turns in my direction.

Fear like I've never known before skitters through my bones.

All three women begin flying toward me. They swoop, claws

missing my face and arms as I roll away. Their wings will forever beat in my nightmares.

"We have a fate worse than death for you, Shield of Helen," they say as one.

The Furies have been said to inflict madness upon their victims.

Thundering footsteps power in my direction. I turn and cover my eyes as a spray of sand blocks the women from my view. A gasp wrenches from me.

Apollo, breathing heavily, stands between the Furies and me.

His bronze tresses are pulled back with a chaplet of golden leaves. His tan face is severe, the sharp angles of his jaw pulled into a look of absolute fury. Fire blazes in his blue eyes.

"You stand in the way of retribution, Son of Zeus?" they ask as one.

The god stands straighter, twin falchions appearing in his hands. "For her? I will stand in the way of anything."

His swords lash out, impossibly fast. The blades cut and jab, tearing their pale skin and spraying black ichor all around us. Each cut heals instantly. He holds out a fist. Light flashes from his curled fingers, flutters, and then dies.

The grins do not fall from the Furies' faces. This is a game to them, a chase. We are the mice and they are the hawks about to flay the skin from our bones.

I spin and hack at the nearest arm reaching toward me. She rises just above my blade with a preternatural swiftness. Her hand latches on my wrist. Fire and fury overwhelm me as I scream. Tears spill from my eyes and my knees buckle. She wrenches my other arm behind me. A cold fills the limb, my swords falling to the sand.

Apollo yells, gold flaring around him. The Furies hesitate. The light blinks away and he staggers with a furious roar. An Erinys pounces onto him and they both fall to the sand in a tangle of limbs.

My helmet is ripped away. The two other Furies grab my arms, with one grabbing my face. My teeth clash together. The Erinys gazing into my face is calm despite the war raging around us.

"For you, a curse I place with utmost glee," she says. Her voice is a claw raking down my spine.

"Curse her," Apollo says, voice like rage incarnate, "and I will rip the wings from each of your backs."

The Erinys clenching his arm behind his back grins, so wide I can make out the blood staining her teeth.

"We can kill you. Remember, son of Zeus?" says the Fury holding my face. "We are gods just the same as you."

Turning to me, she says, "You, Daphne, Daughter of Ash and Sea, we curse you."

"Go ahead," I hiss.

I spit in her face, fighting against the flame and chill and fear to look her in her eyes. They are black and emotionless. Her brow drips with my spittle.

Magic will not help me here. No power of Olympus can save me. Her lips curl back to reveal teeth stained with blood. This is going to hurt. "We curse you with—"

I ram my forehead into her nose. Bright light flares behind my eyes. Ichor sprays between us. The Erinys screams. My eardrums threaten to burst. My cry mingles with hers. As her hands release me, feeling returns to my limbs. I jerk free of her sister's grip.

The Erinyes release a wild war cry and leap for me. I meet one in the air and hook my legs around her waist. Throwing my weight down, I fling her with my legs across the sand. The other is too startled to immediately react. Apollo rips free from his captor and rolls to his blades.

He meets the Furies with a roar, blades a cyclone of singing metal and pulsing golden light.

The Amazon war horn sounds behind me and I spin around.

Hippolyta rallies her remaining warriors into a phalanx. A line of chariots bowl through Trojan hoplites around them.

One chariot stands out among the others. It's painted a red so dark it could be black, its rider taller than any mortal man. Ares leads the line of kings on their wheeled steeds. His horse is black like midnight.

I sprint toward them. My swords are lost behind me. The only weapons I have left are the daggers on my thighs.

A primeval smile splits Ares's face. He tips his spear forward and aims for his last remaining daughter. The chariot blazes forward.

My arms pump at my sides as I cross the plain in inhuman lengths, the strength and speed of whatever god sired me imbuing me.

But it is the Spartan in me that grabs one of my daggers. My years of training bring me to a stop at just the right distance. I may have missed the Erinyes, but I will not miss this target. I fling the dagger. End over end it soars through the sky.

And embeds in Ares's eye.

He's flung backward. The god of war tumbles from his chariot. Riderless, the horse stumbles and the spoked wheels bounce, and then tip. The other chariots lose formation. They break and then flee.

I don't pause. I'm running again, another dagger already in my hand. I leap the final distance and straddle the god of war. His body is solid rock between my sweat-soaked thighs. I do not think twice about the consequences of taking a god's life. Ares's one eye blinks just as my second dagger rams into his throat.

A gurgled gasp escapes him, black ichor spurting between my fingers. His lung collapses around a final breath.

The adrenaline rushes from me. I stagger to my feet, reeling.

I killed Ares.

I killed the god of war.

I'm blasted back in a flare of lavender light, landing in a tangle of twisted limbs. Sand whips around the plain, blinding and furious.

I spin around, but the Amazons are gone in the storm. Even Troy's walls have disappeared from view. I cover my eyes against the sting.

Hera steps from the storm raging around me. She is lovely and flawless. The sand seems to avoid her as if a barrier of wind protects her from its touch. She levels a long finger at me.

"You may have avoided justice once today," she says, voice dripping with rage. "You will not do so again."

The storm rises and I'm swept from the bloody fold.

CHAPTER

40

I stumble across a flawless marble floor. I'm in the pantheon—again—and covered in sand and blood. The sand has dried and makes my skin itch, but I dare not reach to brush it from my skin. Not when the gods stare me down.

Poseidon looks as if he wishes to kill me with his gaze alone. Good luck to him. Dionysus's pillar is empty. Demeter's face is unreadable, as is Hades's. Very well. It is one thing to save Olympus, and another to kill a god, even one that had betrayed them. Above the pantheon, the sky is still a vivid blue. No clouds, no hint of Zeus's wrath—yet.

"You." Hera's shrill voice cuts through the air. She marches toward me with a finger pointed at my chest. "You killed my son."

Aphrodite stands. Her soft pink *peplos* is wrinkled, so unlike the pristine clothes of the gods around her. "How is that even possible?"

Her question hits me like a punch to the gut. The judgment in her words and how it truly isn't misplaced. I shouldn't have been able to kill Ares.

"It isn't possible." Hera says. "Only a god can kill a god."

"She's taken down Ares on her own before." The god of music leans back on his pillar, a forced nonchalance. Apollo is immaculate in a red chiton and looking for all the world as if he didn't just face down the Furies.

"When we were weakened." Hera's face is hideous in her fury and despair. Her tan face is a valley of wrinkles and age spots. In her agony and rage, she's releasing the ageless mask and channeling her powers elsewhere. Likely to skewer me. "Not at the height of our power."

"Your son was willing to kill all of you," I bite out.

"My son is dead." Hera's voice cracks. "But you obviously don't understand the bonds of family, having so quickly thrown your own to the wolves."

Her words hurt worse than any whip ever could. I stagger a step back. My teeth clench so hard they threaten to shatter.

"I will not apologize for doing what I failed to do last summer." My hands curl into fists. "He has tried to kill me, time and time again. He was going to kill everyone I care about."

"We did not send you to defend your friends," Poseidon says, voice dripping with disgust. He stands and walks toward me. "We sent you to protect Helen. How did killing our kin help you accomplish that?"

"Because Ares is still aligned with Nyx," I say around a sneer. "And you are all fools if you think she won't exact her revenge on Helen, or Sparta, or even Troy. Unless you think that I have no reason to believe she wants something inside the city?"

The goddess of wisdom and war assesses me, Athena's blue armor shimmering under the pearlescent light of the sun above. The tattoo of Glaukopis takes flight from her brow and lands on her shoulders, tan feathers ruffling.

"I think," she says, gaze latched on to my armor, "that we should instead ask where you got your weapons from."

My face is unyielding stone. "Hephaestus can tell you where I got them."

"Oh, he already told us where your armor, daggers, and one of your swords is from." Athena braces both hands on her pillar and shoves off. "He did not know how you reached his forge, or how you came by *this* sword."

Glittering gold and black, the Adamantine sword appears in her hand.

"A single lie," Poseidon says, "and I will wipe Troy from the earth."

"You disgust me." I glare and turn back to Athena. "Hermes gave it to me."

"You mean to tell us that you have been colluding with one of the gods who tried to destroy us?" Athena steps closer.

I look up into her eyes. I am tall, but not nearly so much as she. She towers over me. Glaukopis's talons are pitch black and primed to strike my face.

"You still owe me an answer for saving Athena's power last summer." I turn toward the bird.

The pantheon goes deathly silent. Athena's lips curl back over her wide mouth.

"Glaukopis doesn't answer to you," she says.

"What gods aid the Achaeans in the Trojan War?" I ignore her and continue talking to the owl. "Your master promised me an answer from you last summer."

Glaukopis clicks his beak and flares his wings wide. His voice is melodic when he says, "You already know that Nyx has swayed the Achaeans to fight for her. She controls them in ways you do not yet understand, but will soon. You also already know that she is aided by the Erinyes and Ares, and the goddesses Eris and Enyo. It is why the

Trojans have yet to make a truly decisive victory against Menelaus and those who fight for him." The pantheon of gods and goddesses lean forward to hear what other names he has to say.

"Nyx is aided by Eros," the owl continues, ignoring Aphrodite's gasp, "and Nemesis."

Athena sighs through her nose, but Glaukopis continues, "Poseidon, Hera, and my master, Athena, have aided the Achaeans as well."

Hera's mouth opens in a voiceless protest. Zeus leaps to his feet while Athena turns just as a silver trident materializes in Poseidon's hand. Apollo is behind me, his arms firm as they encage and haul me away. I don't have time to cry out before the trident soars. It impales the owl against a marble pillar.

Athena's wild cry could shatter the world. The floor shudders. With a frenzied growl, she clenches a deep blue spear in her fist. Poseidon barely has time to duck before the spearhead pierces the air where he just stood.

"Enough!" Zeus steps between them and catches his daughter's fist.

"You did this." Hera's voice shakes as she points to me. "You are nothing but chaos."

There's a blinding lavender light and searing pain in my temple. I spin to the floor with a short gasp as green light bursts around all of us. Hera's scream is drowned out by Apollo's roar, and then it all goes black.

CHAPTER 41

Gentle hands pry me from the floor. I recognize Demeter's mint and fruit scent without having to open my eyes. Black coats the inside of my eyelids.

A rumble grows beyond me and my eyes flutter open. There's a slash in my bicep that beads with blood. It runs in rivulets down my arm, dripping on the floor. My limb starts to go numb, but my focus is dragged inexorably away.

Apollo crouches above me. If looks could kill, his would blast the gods from the earth.

"Touch her again," he growls, "and I'll rip out your throat."

"You dare threaten me?" Hera steps within my line of sight. Her dress is torn, her hair ripped from its braid.

Behind Hera, Glaukopis twitches, still pinned to a column. His eyes are blank as black blood drips to the floor.

I ignore the sound he makes and turn to a heaving Poseidon. There are slashes down his cheeks, blackened ichor matching the dying owl. The handiwork of Athena no doubt.

"Why would you help the Achaeans?" I step forward, unflinching despite the power radiating from the god.

He looks down at me with stormy eyes and says simply, "Because they worship me more than the Trojans."

Fury courses through me like a typhoon waiting to be unleashed. My teeth gnash. "Are you truly so proud that you would be willing to watch the city fall, despite knowing that your downfall is behind those very gates?"

Every god turns to me fully now. Artemis coughs, and Demeter takes a step away from me. Apollo looks me over, aghast.

Slowly, as if weighing each word, Zeus asks, "What are you implying?"

Thunder rumbles overhead.

"I know why Apollo spilled his own blood into the walls of Troy. What you seek to hide there." Zeus's face whips toward his son and I raise a fist. "Don't look at him. He told me nothing. It was just another secret that you forced him to keep from me. Just like my parentage."

Poseidon takes a deliberate step forward. "Watch your tone, mortal."

Athena cradles Glaukopis's body to her chest. Her hands glow with an eerie blue light. Her voice strangled and raw, she asks, "Who told you what those walls protect?"

"Who do you think?" Hera sneers. "Hermes manipulated her against us."

Doubt flickers in my mind, but I force my face into a stubborn frown. "Hermes didn't have to do anything. Your callous behavior—all of yours—did that."

"So you admit that you're against us?" Poseidon's voice has dropped to a lethal quiet and calm. The slow drawing back of a wave before it threatens to wipe a city from the earth.

"The only ones I'm against are those who wish my queen harm." I flick my gaze from Poseidon to Zeus. "I'm not fighting this war for you any longer, or your mad family. I'm fighting it for Helen of Sparta."

"Always fighting for someone new." The look Hera bestows upon me is nothing short of complete disdain. Her lips curl back from her teeth. "When will you learn that your loyalty means nothing if not for the right people?"

"Better to fight for a queen who actually loves her people," I say, raising my chin, "than for a goddess who abuses them."

A lavender sheen begins to glow on her skin. Her hair rises, a dark cloud stretching wide.

I don't give her the satisfaction of my fear.

"Are you going to hurt me?" I cock my head and ignore the itch in my fingers to reach for my sword. A sword that isn't there anymore.

"Hera will take a seat." Demeter's hand lands on my shoulder, her fingers warm but firm. "There's been enough violence."

Hera cocks her head. "What is the loss of one more useless girl?"

"If you strike her," Artemis says, taking a stand on my other side, "it will be the end of this pantheon."

The cosmic energy of gods swirls behind me, great and glorious. I can feel their presence, warm and electric. Without turning, I recognize Persephone's joyous warmth and the calm reserve of her love, Hades.

"Her blood may not be Olympian, but the ichor is still there. No matter what you all fear." Persephone steps forward, placing me firmly behind her. "The same laws that rule the pantheon apply to her. She cannot be punished for Ares's death."

Hera's face contorts, eyes blackening. "He was my son, and I will take my vengeance."

"You owe Daphne your life," Apollo says, words like the lash of a whip.

"I owe that mortal nothing! Only a god can kill a god," Hera says. "You all know this. We will not bend our own laws to her. Do not let your hearts turn mortal for this fool."

"She is not mortal, though." Hades's voice makes everyone jump. "And we must stop pretending such. Although not a god, either, she is bound to our laws, which she, albeit unintentionally, upheld by killing Ares. He was a traitor to Olympus and the foundations of our rule."

A click echoes through my head. My mouth drops open.

Shock fills me. "If not mortal, then what am I?"

All the gods turn to me. None of them reply, making me more furious than ever before.

"Damn ungrateful Olympians and their egos the size of the sea." A splitting pain forms in my temple, but I ignore it. "Tell me! If I'm not a god, and I'm not a mortal, what am I?"

The answer is all over their pale, horrified faces. Sweat forms at Poseidon's temples. Hades shifts uneasily and his wife reaches a hand for him, to either steady him or herself.

"You fear my father?" My hands curl into fists. "That's why you won't tell me who he is? Because you fear him?"

Demeter gives me a long, sad look. "We do not fear your father. We fear what he is."

"What does that fear have to do with why you won't tell me his name?"

"We fear nothing because we are gods!" Aphrodite strides forward to plant herself between our two sides. "You all squabble like pathetic mortals. Send her back to Troy. Living will be punishment enough."

Her smile, painted with cruelty and promises, will live in my nightmares forever.

CHAPTER 42

This time, when I walk through Artemis's palace, I'm brought to the halls of Troy and not the Taygetus forest. I would have much preferred the press of pine trees and their comforting smell to the spices that linger in the palace air. Helen is just leaving her suite when I stride through the doorway.

She catches me with a hand on my wrist. "Where have you been?"

A huff escapes me. "Where do you think? Someone needed to pacify the gods after that battle."

Like children fighting over a single toy.

The gods have something they wish to protect within this city, but their petty hearts might just betray them. I'm not only fighting against the might of the Achaeans and the gods who aid them, but also the gods who are willing to let their egos ruin them.

Helen's chest rises and falls with rapid breaths. "Hector killed Patroclus in the battle yesterday."

I nearly stumble at her words, following as she leads me through the palace.

"Achilles stayed out of the battles until now," she continues. "No wonder we'd had such luck. His mother has Poseidon's ear, and she would have turned him against us. But now, with Achilles calling for Hector's blood, we can only guess what Poseidon will do next."

Her silk *peplos* is baggy, looser than I've ever seen it. I can't remember if she's been eating, or even exercising since we arrived. She'd always been lean, as if carved from marble—being gifted with divine grace having helped substantially—but the stress has eaten away at her.

"No need to guess," I say. "Poseidon has already made it perfectly clear who he supports."

Helen starts to speak but then clenches her teeth.

"What aren't you telling me?" I press.

"The Achaeans sent a message last night. I've been looking for you since." Her eyes flick down the hallway. "Achilles challenged Hector to a duel. For his lover's blood."

I double over as surely as if punched square in the gut. "His lover?"

Not Pyrrhus. Not my brother. No, no, no...Great, shuddering gasps wrench from me.

Her mouth pops open and she grabs me by the shoulder. "You were close with Patroclus?"

Patroclus of Locris. A third to the lovers' entanglement I witnessed in the Achaean camp. I cannot even begin to imagine the pain Achilles must be in, losing his lover. Just thinking about losing Apollo makes me feel unsteady. My heart thunders, but my breathing steadies.

I cough and straighten. "Hector won't stand a chance. He's a brilliant fighter, but Achilles has divine ichor within him." I catch Helen's hand, small and cold, within my own. "You're blaming yourself right now. Don't. This war was inevitable."

There's a hard edge of finality to my voice that keeps her from protesting, but—"That's not all, Daphne. Priam has already agreed. He had no choice. The people would riot if he didn't."

"The king is selling out his own son to Achilles's revenge fantasy?"

She actually stops walking, turning to face me in the narrow hallway. Her tan face is gaunt in the shadows, her once luscious hair limp.

"Menelaus also challenged you."

A hollow ringing begins in my ears.

"What?" I blink.

"If you beat him, the Achaeans will leave. They will even give up any qualms of the Hellespont and return my daughter to me." A hunger, fierce and unbroken, alights behind her eyes, then blinks out like a dying ember. "But if you lose, the Trojans will return me to Sparta."

Only the Fates can tell what would come of her then.

My knees threaten to buckle, and my stomach twists. The corridor seems to spin.

"A challenge you'd be stupid to take up." A cool, familiar voice echoes down the hallway. Hermes's face is unreadable as he strides down the hallway toward us. "I can get you both out of this city tonight. Within the hour, even."

I lean back against the cool wall, suddenly exhausted. "You know I can't take you up on that offer."

Hermes glances between Helen and me. "I also know that Daphne has probably told you far too much for me to bother playing coy with my words around you both. God of trade, at your service."

"Also the god of thieves and trickery." I rest a cheek against the wall.

"Semantics."

It's all too much. Ares's blood still stains my hands. I'm still wearing Hephaestus's armor, and gods only know if whatever gifts he imbued it with still linger after Hera declared me her number one enemy. And then there's this.

A battle to the death.

To decide a war.

"Where did you get that?"

My eyes flicker open to find Hermes standing close and deathly still. I follow his gaze. The wound Hera so kindly bequeathed me still gapes, the blood crusted and blackened around the edges.

"Who gave you that?" he asks. This time his voice is soft, like the unforgiving flat of a blade hiding a sharp edge.

"I got it out on the battlefield," I say through my teeth. As the god of lies, he should see right through the falsehood, but I have no wish to worry Helen further. I turn to her, leaning my bad arm against the wall to cool the flame currently licking beneath my skin. "Tell Priam I will accept Menelaus's challenge."

Without giving either an opportunity to question me, I turn on my heel to prepare for my own death.

I'm peeling off my armor, grimacing as the blood coated beneath it pulls at my skin, when Hermes appears on the foot of my bed. He reclines, kicking up his feet and assessing me.

"Which of them gave that to you?" His voice is deceptively calm, but he's coiled like the snakes tattooed on his skin.

I sigh, reaching for a sarcastic response, but find my reservoir of wit drained along with my energy.

"Hera." I don't meet his eyes. Instead, I continue to remove the stained armor. "She was quite cross with me."

"Expectedly. Ares was her favorite son." Hermes springs to his feet. He's grabbing my arm before I can blink. I hiss, even if his touch is surprisingly gentle. "Your dear Apollo couldn't spare the time to heal this before sending you back?"

A cool tingling, so unlike the warmth of Apollo's gifts, courses through the arm. The gash knits itself back together. I don't have the strength to pull away once he's finished, letting him continue to hold my arm as I remove what remains of my armor.

"He was a bit preoccupied with the politics up there." Only when I'm naked do I finally wrest my limb from his grip and begin to stumble to the bath.

His gaze follows my every step but Hermes doesn't move after me. He sits back, eyes heavy-lidded. Warmth floods through me, starting at my core and rising up my neck.

"Nudity is as common as breathing in Sparta." I watch him over my shoulder. "Don't make me regret undressing in front of you."

Hermes meets my gaze. "So you didn't just strip down in front of me as a distraction from your lover's negligence?"

"Apollo isn't my lover."

"Yet." The god peers around the room. "Were you in my cave recently?"

Surprise flickers through me. "No. How would I have gotten there?"

"I've taken you through the doorway."

"So anyone can just waltz right into the cave you said is completely safe?"

"Not just anyone." He continues sniffing around my room. "I told you that mortals, or immortals with my permission, can enter."

"Perhaps some mortal took the wrong doorway."

He barks a laugh, as if the idea is completely preposterous. His tone is serious, though, as he says, "Don't go in there without me."

I refrain from rolling my eyes. "Yes, mother."

"I guess you'll similarly ignore my warnings about this duel?"

I reach for a vase of oils. "You know me so well."

He drags a hand over his face. "And you understand that Nyx will be there? You didn't just kill Hera's favorite son. You killed the goddess of darkness's commander. And this isn't the first time you've interfered with her plans."

"I've fought her before."

My reflection in the water shifts. I hardly recognize myself. War has made me gaunt. Any softness in my face and body is replaced by raw strength. Someone capable of killing a god.

I lean closer, peering at my features. I search for any sign of the ichor that the Olympians claim is in my veins. All I see is a girl, too brutish to be considered a classical beauty, and weighed down by her past.

The oil is snatched from my hands. I blink and Hermes is in the water with me. He's still fully dressed, but I keep my gaze up with a firm chin. He grips my arms and shakes, making the water splash from the bath.

"She will kill you, Daphne." His brown face is pulled tight.

"If I was worried about my own fate, I wouldn't bother to fight." I cup his cheek with a gentle hand. "I'm doing this for my queen."

"What about your friends?"

Unlikely. Lykou and Lyta will be furious.

I lie, "They'll understand."

"Am I not your friend?" He steps closer and my heart stumbles. "I don't want you to die."

"I don't want to die, either," I admit.

His lips press together, face pulled into a frown. I shudder a deep breath, then take a step back.

"Anyway." I snatch the oils away from him. "As another of Nyx's former commanders, shouldn't you be talking me into fighting for her, not fleeing from her?"

"Do you think that I've been trying to win you over to her side this entire time?" His voice is sharp.

"I don't know what you've been doing," I admit. I rub my body with the oils, washing away the grime and magic.

He's silent for so long that I wonder if he's disappeared. I turn around.

Hermes still stands in the pool. "You still don't trust me?"

"I don't trust anyone." My words ring with a truth so sharp it could cut to the heart.

And it does. I see it in his face, the light fracturing behind his wicked, beautiful eyes that are so like Apollo's.

"That will get you killed someday," he says, voice ragged.

He waves a hand and the Adamantine sword appears at the edge of the pool. "Don't lose this again."

Hermes disappears before I can retort. Though even if he'd waited, I wouldn't have anything to say.

I meant what I said before in the pantheon. When I declared that I would fight this war for Helen and no one else, that means this battle, too.

The morning of the duel, both Helen and Lyta help me prepare. Lyta murmurs little tips and pointers, flaws in Menelaus's fighting techniques, as Helen laces up my freshly cleaned armor. I don't accept Hephaestus's armor this time, setting aside the black and gold leather for the worn Amazon attire that Penthesilea gave me long ago. It still fits my body like a sleeve as if made for me.

"Mycenaeans fight heavy on their feet," Hippolyta says. She hands me the Adamantine sword. "He will use brute strength. But don't let that deceive you. He's also fast. Never stay in the same place."

I swallow and nod. My throat is so dry the movement hurts.

They follow me to the city's western gate but leave me there.

"We will watch from atop the wall." Helen squeezes my hand. "You have my faith, Daphne. I wouldn't trust anyone else, not even the gods, to protect me."

With that and one last tearful look, she lets Lyta lead her away. Lykou comes next. Wordlessly, he scoops me in for a hug. He buries his face in the crook between my neck and shoulder. I likewise wrap my arms around him. His scent is so painfully familiar.

Finally, he releases and holds me at arm's length. "Not that I don't have faith in your abilities"—a fake smile is plastered on his tan face— "but promise me that, if you die, you'll continue fighting even in the Underworld."

"Not even Hades could keep me from returning to you," I say, and I swear the god himself stands behind me, chuckling. "But..." I grip his shoulder and force him to look me in the eyes. "If anything should happen to me, I need you to protect Helen with your life. I don't give a damn about honor. You call down Apollo and have him take her somewhere safe. He can retrieve Hermione, too, if that's what it takes to get her to leave with him."

She would choose to stay for this city that protected her, but at least I'll die knowing that she has a chance.

Lykou nods. He leans in, quicker than I can react, and kisses my cheek. His sigh is sweet as he leans back, presses his forehead against mine, and jerks away.

I don't have time to say anything more before Hector marches forward. He's flanked by Paris and Kassandra. Helios drags the sun high above them, so dawn's light frames the three heirs of Troy in gold and white.

Paris does nothing but give me a stern nod. His focus is on his brother, who he must know will perish on that field. Kassandra turns to me.

Her white dress is rumpled; dark crescent moons linger beneath her eyes. "A shadow will overturn your victory, Daughter of Ash and Sea. Do not stray from the touch of the sun."

She blinks once, then turns to her brother. "Achilles has an aim that is true. No shield can keep his blade from piercing your heart."

Hector claps her on the shoulder. "It is a good thing then that he fights with a spear."

Lykou takes Kassandra's hand and leads her up the stairs to the top of the wall. I watch them go. She grips his fingers until her knuckles are white. The hem of her chiton dances around his legs in the rising wind. A pair they make. Hopefully they can find comfort in each other if Hector and I don't return from this fight.

The gates creak open, crying out as if already mourning the loss of their prince.

Raising my chin, I follow him onto the field.

CHAPTER
43

Menelaus and Achilles stand apart on separate halves of the dusty terrain. The rising sun behind me paints their faces in shades of yellow and brown. Hector and I share one last nod before moving to our opposite sides.

My sword is already in my hand and my shield hefted high in the other. I will take no chances.

A *salphinx* sings. There are no proclamations, no threats or boasting. We know the true weight of this fight.

Menelaus leaps forward with a spear hooked beneath an arm. He covers the distance in inhuman bounds. A god imbues his steps.

I run to meet him. His spear swings wide. I slide beneath it and slash at his knee but he jumps before my sword can kiss his skin. He spins around, his spear jabbing the earth where I just stood.

The sun is now to his back. It's blinding, but I don't let him take advantage. I leap to the side and avoid his next swing. Before he can try a third time, I jump within his reach and slam my shield into his. He stumbles backward.

"Moves I should expect from a traitor to her own people," he says. He bends, feet crossing over each other as he circles me. "I always said that Sparta should never allow women to train with their men."

"Because we'll toss you all on your backs?"

"Because women and betrayal go hand in hand." He lunges.

I dodge the point of his spear and grab it, yanking him forward. I slam my forehead into his own. Stars erupt between my eyes. His nose spurts and blood sprays between us. He spits at my feet and stumbles away.

Achilles and Hector's fight is wild. They lunge and dive toward each other. They're mere feet from our own duel now. Spears clash in the air. Hector sweeps Achilles's legs and sends him tumbling, but he rolls away before pouncing to his feet. Hector hooks a foot under Achilles's *dory* and kicks it away.

Menelaus lunges for me again. I beat aside his *dory* with my shield.

"You're a traitor to Sparta," he bites out. "To your people."

"But not to my *anassa*." I clip his jaw.

He's relentless. Slashing and jabbing, again and again. I barely have time to deflect. Sweat drips into my eyes and soaks the back of my neck. But I'm younger and stronger.

He strikes. This time, instead of beating away his swing, I drop my shield and grab on to the spear. He lurches and I yank. He falls to his knees as I rip the *dory* from his hands. He doesn't have time to cry out before I spin it in the air and slam his temple with the butt.

He drops like a bag of rocks.

Something barrels into me and I'm flung into the air. My back collides with the ground hard enough to knock the wind from my lungs.

Hector and Achilles duel where I just stood. Both have lost their weapons. They grip each other by their forearms, yanking and pulling. Hector wrenches from the Myrmidon's grip, then Achilles leaps, spinning in midair to catch the Trojan prince across the jaw with his heel.

I knew Achilles was an incredible fighter, but nothing like this. Hector stumbles backward and picks up my shield. Achilles stoops and picks up my sword. I clench my hands into the sand and horror dawns on me.

"No." The word is a whisper.

The Trojan leaps to the side to avoid the next swing and Achilles takes a step back. His face is painted with fury and pain when he leaps forward. The Adamantine sword drives right through the shield and plunges into Hector's chest.

With a roar that can be heard all the way to Atlantis, Achilles lifts both shield and Hector's twitching body and flings them aside. Wails erupt from the wall.

I choke and climb to my feet. Rules of combat keep me from attacking, but an image of my nails gouging out his eyes fills my head. He stares me down in a wordless dare.

Wild laughter erupts and we both turn. Menelaus rises, his body swaying and head hanging. His back heaves with the insane, keening laughter. Ignoring Achilles, still standing over Hector's lifeless body, I march over.

"I'm sorry." Tears prick my eyes. I grit my teeth and wrench free the sword.

When I turn, Menelaus now stands tall.

Achilles has disappeared. I spin, but he's nowhere to be seen. When my gaze lands on my once king, I gasp.

Shadows reach long tendrils from his back. They arc higher and higher, snuffing out the sunlight, city, and sky, until all that remains are him and me and darkness.

"You thought it would be so simple?" This time, when my opponent speaks, his voice has lost its deep timber and is now sweet like over-ripe pomegranate seeds. And when he raises his face, his eyes are no longer brown.

They're red.

Nyx's full lips part in a wide, terrifying smile.

CHAPTER

44

Under my breath, I say, "Ready to kill each other again?"

"Only one of us was successful in that endeavor last time." With a toss of her long, ebony hair, Nyx sheds the disguise of my former king. Menelaus is gone, and in his place stands the goddess of night. "You're more useful to me alive, in any case. But you don't need all of your limbs. One hand will do."

I don't let myself feel a trace of fear. "Will do for what?"

Her shadows lash out. They come from all angles. I move in a large sweep, the Adamantine cleaving through them like stalks of wheat. Her darkness sweeps a wide net around me, trapping me in a sea of crawling black.

So I let the darkness rise in me, like calling to like. It claws from the depths of my battle-weary soul. Through my battles and journeys and scars, a storm has grown inside me, waiting to erupt.

I fling myself through the shadows, swinging wildly in an arc. I cleave through the air like a living blade. Her ruby eyes go wide.

I'm atop her and we tumble through shadow and sand. Her claws dig into my arms and pierce me to the bone as we roll. A scream bursts from my chest but I wrench from her grasp. My blood sprays between us. My blade slices her gut and I fall backward. Without hesitation, she surges after me, but I roll and spring to my feet.

"You're even more reckless now than when you were on death's doorstep." She sounds almost proud.

"The venom slowed me down last time," I say, angling my sword at her. Blood runs down my arms, making my grip slick.

She leaps forward and I throw myself away from her reach. I'm dancing with death.

The darkness surrounding us pulses, lightening for mere moments before suffocating us once more.

"Apollo is trying to come to your rescue." She walks slowly around me.

"I don't need him to save me."

"Maybe not." Nyx inclines her head, black hair spilling over her shoulder. Dark wings spring from her back and feathers along her arms.

I blink the sweat from my eyes and the feathers dart through the air toward my face. Diving to avoid their touch, but not nearly fast enough, one pierces my hip. It bounces off harmlessly.

The Midas Curse swoops, sheathing my arms, torso, and legs. It's a golden second skin.

Nyx laughs, a piercing sound like the cry of a hawk. "Can't do anything without their protection."

"What can I say? They must like me a lot." I twirl my sword. "How can you resist this adorable face?"

"The scar on your arm says otherwise." She points with a long nail at the wound Hermes healed.

She spins across the distance, arms wide and claws reaching an impossible length. They slice through my uniform and glance off the Curse encasing my ribs. My swing goes wide.

Through gritted teeth, I say, "I can only aspire to be as much of a pain in their asses as they have been in mine."

Nyx straightens, appraising me. "Your father was just as much a thorn in their side during the Titanomachy."

I nearly drop my sword. "My father?"

"Have they not told you who he is yet? They wouldn't, would they?" Her claws retract. "It could very well be their undoing."

My heart flutters, with trepidation or fear I cannot say. Or is it a challenge despite the fact that I can't trust a word she says, rising in me as surely as the darkness? "Will you tell me, then?"

She grins. "I thought you would never ask. You are no mere mortal, nor god. You are the daughter of a titan and the oldest being to walk this very earth. Ruler of all fresh water."

"A titan." My grip on the sword slips. I feel as if I've been punched square in the gut. "Oceanus."

Somewhere beyond our ball of shadow, thunder rumbles. Nyx waves and her features melt into the shadows. Out crawls the rough-hewn edges of Menelaus's face.

Her voice, a sweetness that will forever haunt my nightmares, still emerges from his lips. "I hope you survive Zeus's wrath, Daphne, daughter of the traitor Oceanus."

The darkness dissipates, revealing a sky tinged with gray, roiling clouds.

It's Menelaus's voice that speaks next. "If only to kill them yourself."

He turns to the crowd formed on the walls of Troy, and the line of Achaean soldiers surrounding us. He sweeps his arms wide and says, "I forfeit this duel."

A resounding silence greets his proclamation. Many soldiers drop their shields and spears, and the Achaean kings looking on have gone blank-faced. Achilles, still towering over the body of Hector, spits and turns to drag the corpse away.

I can't even protest for the sanctity of Hector's remains. Shock holds me immobile, from both winning this duel and the circumstances of my victory.

A hiss from the crowd, a symphony of crickets and snakes, begins to grow around me, from both the wall and the army watching on. Hushed whispers, weeping, and cheers. Exclamations, but above all, the wail from behind the wall grows. Kassandra, Queen Hecuba, and Hector's wife all lean over the battlements. They cry and wave their veils as Hector's body is dragged away. In the arms of Hector's wife, a baby begins to screech. Still, Achilles walks on.

This is the price of war. It is a hungry beast, making meals of us all. War cares not who wins and loses, only that the blood is spilled.

CHAPTER 45

I don't understand why Nyx would challenge me, with an entire war at stake, with no intention of ever winning. I shake my head. My hair catches on my lips, the strands heavy with sand and sweat.

Nyx would not have told me the name of my father if it didn't go against the interests of Olympus.

Oceanus.

If her word can be trusted—no, it really can't be—I don't understand how he can be feared by Zeus. Oceanus was one of the titans to betray his own during the Titanomachy. He helped Zeus take the Olympian throne.

She wanted me to know my father's name to put a target between my shoulder blades. She won't need to kill me because Zeus will do that for her. One thing is for certain—he knows. I rest a hand on the gold now sheathing my rib cage. Artemis will have heard what Nyx told me, and Zeus will pry that from her lips no matter the cost. I've heard enough stories and have been privy to enough Olympian squabbles to know that nothing can keep his wrath at bay.

My mind is awhirl as I walk through the streets, hardly registering the celebrations all around me. But with celebration comes mourning. Many cry and scream, still watching over the wall as the body of the crowned prince of Troy is dragged away to the Achaean camp.

I'm forcibly knocked from my thoughts when Helen flings herself at me. She wraps her thin arms around my chest and squeezes tight. Tears spring from her eyes. "We couldn't see anything from atop the wall. It was like you and Menelaus disappeared into the air. Hermes told me you had survived and I couldn't believe it. Not until I saw you with my own eyes."

"Hermes was with you?" I let her continue to hold me as we hobble through the city's narrow alleys.

"He cloaked himself. I don't know how you trust him after all that conspired last summer, but"—she bites her lip—"I will follow your example."

Perhaps you shouldn't, I think, then I turn my gaze upward, tracing the coral-colored roofs and buildings as they reach toward the clouded sky. At this point, I can trust none of the gods, not even Apollo at the behest of his father. Though Apollo might kill himself before Zeus even had the chance.

The very thought fills me with a pain so intense I nearly double over. I brace a hand on the wall beside me and stop.

Worriedly, Helen looks me over. "Are you wounded?"

Even Apollo, with the powers of Olympus behind him, is no match for his own father and the gods who align with him. The gods who want the secrets of the Titanomachy to stay in the dark.

But one god has been able to avoid the touch of Zeus's fury.

*   *   *

Less than an hour later, I sit on the sunbaked roof with my feet dangling over the edge. Anyone in the city could look up and see me. Perhaps even the gods see me, yet I don't care.

I bring the pipes to my lips and let out a little trill. Hermes is sitting beside me before I can even blink.

"That was a sorry excuse for a duel down there." He squints against the sun's glare and kicks his legs back and forth like a child. The god pouts. "You didn't even use any of the techniques I taught you."

Below marches a mourning procession. They wear varying shades of dark blue, black, and green. Priam and his wife are carried in a *lectica* as Paris and his siblings follow. Prolific is the king of Troy, for over fifty children of Priam wear the *meander* on their clothes. Helen, guarded closely by Lykou, walks alongside Lyta with their heads bowed.

"Perhaps you could teach me something more useful." I turn to the god of trickery. "Like how you have managed to avoid punishment from Olympus."

"Haven't we gone over this ad nauseam?" Hermes groans. "Why do you still think I deserve to be punished?"

"This has nothing to do with what I think you deserve," I snap. "This has everything to do with what you know."

He tenses.

"I want you to help me avoid their reach." I rest a hand on the Midas Curse swirling atop my thigh. "The moly you grow in your garden. Is it how you keep Artemis from spying on us? How you keep them from tracking you and torturing you with their powers?"

He considers me, handsome face unreadable. "Once, I was mortal like you. Boring and unremarkable."

"You and I both know that I am many things, but boring is not one of them."

His mouth crooks to the side. "I was always curious, though. And far too nosy for my own good. My mother and Zeus were lovers. He had many, so many that at this point they must be faceless. I found her alone and crying one day, her eyes so red and puffy she could hardly recognize me. Zeus had tired of her. He preferred them younger and without many thoughts. Seeing my mother cry"—his jaw clenches— "it hardened something in me. Something that would not soften even when I became a god.

"It was Hecate who discovered the powers of the Garden of the Hesperides. That each plant at the base of the great trees had a different magic. A different gift to bestow upon us." He cocks his head to the side. "Or curse, depending on which way you looked at it."

He takes my hand and squeezes my fingers. "Can I show you?"

Slowly, hesitantly, I nod.

Hermes releases a long, shaky breath, and then I'm suddenly pulled below the cold, dark sea.

"I climbed to the top of Mount Olympus, intent on murdering Zeus. He'd made my mother cry too many times."

Hermes's voice is far away, but I see him.

He walks up a barren mountainside. The ground is dotted with patches of snow. The harsh wind blasting down the mountain rips at his threadbare cloak. He grimaces into the frigid spray of wind and snow.

There are no tattoos across his dark brow, and his black hair is knotted and unkempt. This is the mortal Hermes before he ascended into godhood.

He strides right past me, sandaled feet digging deep in the snow.

His toes must be in agony, if he can even feel them. He looks right past me, gaze intent upon the high reaches of Olympus.

I follow, my teeth chattering.

We climb for many hours. Hermes curses whenever he slides on the snow, falling on his hands and knees so many times, his skin starts to turn purple and bleed. We reach a layer of clouds, so thick it is impossible to see past them, and press on. Once we step past their soft touch, the air suddenly warms. I breathe a soft sigh of relief, following Hermes as he cuts through the now flourishing bushes. His march has become a crawl as he tries to soften his footsteps.

There are no palaces yet. Only three peaks of overgrown forest. The power of the mountain emanates all around me. It pulses, tugging at my skin and hair. Hermes hunches over, peering through the trees.

Three great trees stretch from the earth in the center of a glen. The gods stand around them, linked hand in hand. Some I do not recognize while others are as familiar to me as my brothers. None, I notice, are yet made immortal.

Ares is still alive, his hair shorn short and his face impossibly innocent. He holds his mother's hand. Hera wears a deep purple chiton and her smile is more lovely and honest than I've ever seen in godhood.

Beside the now king of Olympus are his two brothers, blond and pale. They all grin and laugh. Across from the Olympians are the men and women who must be titans. A tall, broad-shouldered man with blond curly hair stands with another man, likewise tall and long-limbed, but with dark skin and even darker hair. And to that one's left...

Nyx, youthful and grinning, takes up his hand. She barely reaches his waist. From Hermes's hiding place in the trees, I can just barely make out the color of her eyes. They are not red yet, but instead a beautiful pale blue. The love with which she looks up at the man beside her means that he could only be her consort, Érebos.

A woman with black hair and pale white skin walks around the circle. She bends to pluck plants, handing select flowers and herbs to the surrounding people.

She stops at the god standing in front of where Hermes and I hide in the forest. His hair is still that lovely metallic mix of red and brown, a burnished bronze not even the powers of Olympus can take credit for. His back is firm, deeply tanned muscle.

"Apollo," the pale goddess says. "This flower will give you light and music."

I cannot see his face as he raises the plant to his lips and swallows. All the others follow, then immediately crumble. Some scream and moan. Others roar and the entire earth trembles. Lightning crashes and the wind rises. The trees sway and the moon and sun threaten to collide above us.

Hermes curses. A pale, sweaty sheen covers his brow. He crawls backward on his hands and knees. The earth trembles and we both fall to the forest floor. Pine needles bite into my skin.

And then the earth stops moving. A great stillness sweeps through the glen. Each of the gods pant and gasp. Then, slowly, they begin to stand.

Zeus rises first and grins. Lightning dances across his fingers.

"Impossible," Hermes whispers beside me.

Poseidon stands next and pumps his fists. Each movement makes the earth roil. I cling to the roots of a tree. As the gods and titans all rise around the three trees, Hermes's face pales. His mouth opens and closes. The knife he held clenched in his fist the entire trek up Mount Olympus falls to the ground.

It lands among a patch of small white flowers that seem to droop.

The moly plant that grew in his cave below Mount Kyllini. He bends, and instead of picking up his knife, he reaches for one such flower. My heartbeat slows to a death march. My eyes are wide, searching Hermes's face.

I can only watch as he raises the flower to his mouth and swallows.

His eyes glaze with euphoria, and then he collapses at my feet.

I'm flung through the air. The sun blazes above me, burning my shoulders and the bridge of my nose. The palace roof is firm beneath my feet once more. I blink, my vision focusing and then becoming hazy again.

"That's how you became gods," I gasp out.

Hermes steadies me with a hand, the dancing creatures once more tattooed across his brow. "The moly gave me my powers. It is another reason I was selected to be the messenger god. I can relay news, good or bad, without fear of retribution in the form of Olympic power."

"What fools mortals are." I shake my head. "To believe the stories about all of you."

"When we took those plants from the Garden of the Hesperides, we disrupted the natural balance of life. It took us many decades to finally gain control of our powers. Even then, it took the Muses cultivating the garden to channel the gifts the Garden provides. Otherwise the ebb and flow of magic became too much, too unruly and chaotic for even the strongest among us to control." He gazes down at the mortals below. "Many humans died when we lost control of our powers."

My mind reels from what I just saw, what Zeus would no doubt kill me for knowing. "And yet you were willing to let that happen last summer when you took the Muses away."

"Don't remind me of my mistakes, Daphne." He turns to me, searching my face. "I'm reminded of them every day."

The breeze between us is warm, a firm reversal from the blasting winds of Mount Olympus. His hand still grips me, and I trace the snake coiling up his arm.

"Can you give me the same powers?" I ask.

"What?" Hermes rips his arm away. "Did you learn nothing from what I just shared?"

"I've heard the stories. Of mortals bequeathed with gifts from Olympians. Have I not earned this? To be invulnerable from their magic?"

"If you've heard the stories of their gifts," he says slowly, "then you've also heard of their curses. Often, the two are one and the same."

"Let me make the choice for myself." I raise my chin. "Give me some moly and I will gladly eat it."

"That would do nothing but poison you." Hermes scoffs and shakes his head. "No, I won't do it. I can't. The risks are too great, and if Apollo didn't want to murder me already, if I do as you ask, he will hunt me down for the rest of my immortal existence."

"And stealing the Muses from Olympus wasn't risky? Betraying your entire family?" I step close so that he can see the depths of my gray eyes. "If you don't do this, Hermes, Zeus will kill me for what I know."

His lips are a firm line. "Nyx told you who your father is."

I give him a curt nod. We're both breathing heavily. Lips pressed in a firm line, he reaches for my hand again. A chill sweeps up my fingers, starting from beneath my nails and creeping up my arm.

"This cannot be undone."

My heart thunders in my ears. "I know."

White light pierces the back of my eyes. My head feels like it might shatter. A scream catches in my throat, but no sound escapes me. I fall to the roof, hard enough to bruise my knees. Hermes's grip on my hand remains firm. Cold sweeps through my entire body like the rough barbs of hoarfrost. I clench my teeth so hard they might shatter.

Then it's over. I open my eyes again and Hermes looks upon me, cerulean eyes glistening. There's a crack of metal at our feet and I glance down.

A chunk of gold wobbles there. The Midas Curse has dropped from my leg.

Dark clouds swirl overhead, blotting the sun. This is not Nyx's power. Zeus is furious.

Purple and black swirl above, broken by blasts of white lightning. It whips my hair around, stinging my cheeks and neck. Another blast nearly knocks me from my feet.

Hermes's voice cracks as he says, "What have we done?"

I'm nearly knocked from my feet again, but not by the wind. The earth roars, a great shudder ripping through Troy and to the beach beyond.

The gods are angry. I have outwitted Zeus. His Curse, his way of spying on me, is no more. This war has proven fruitless for them. The land beyond Troy will be stained with Achaean blood for centuries. Their temples have been desecrated. The faith in them has waned.

The earth continues to shake. The pillars of the palaces groan. I grab Hermes, holding on to him for balance. Rain falls in sheets, so hard I cannot see. It's ripped to and fro by the blasting wind. Another crack of lightning arcs across the sky.

Their egos will be their ruin. The power of these walls cannot keep the entire world at bay, and one day their hubris will be the reason they fall, and whatever they seek to protect within will finally be found and destroyed.

Hermes yells something, but I cannot hear him over the gale. I cannot hear my thoughts, either. Perhaps that is my fury, the storm inside me finally unleashed.

Then, with one last blast of lightning, the tempest dissipates. With a great rush of wind and rain that drenches me through, the dark clouds drift apart.

Surprise makes me take a step back.

"Now that is the last thing I expected to see." Hermes's voice is filled with awe.

Towering above the western gate of Troy, with the sun shining high above our heads and on the wood-paneled surface, stands a great horse.

CHAPTER
46

I leave Hermes atop the roof, still staring dumbly at the horse, without a word.

The Horse, the people of Troy call it. They whisper of it, like the hissing of snakes all around me, as Helen and I march along the wall.

Beyond, nothing but abandoned firepits remain of the Achaean camp.

No doubt the gods aided in their quick escape. Below, a line of horses, real and with riders astride, thunder through the gate and across the plain. Mud tears beneath their hooves. Twelve in all for every direction, the scouts disperse to search for any sign of the once-great army that tried to bring Troy to its knees.

"What tricks has your husband concocted now?" Priam asks without preamble as Helen and I make our way over to him.

He wears a black *peplos* and his face is still lined with utmost grief. There is a touch of blame, fleeting yet undeniable, in his gaze as he looks the two of us over, for the loss of his son and the many other children killed on the field below. Belatedly, I realize that Hector's body must have disappeared along with the Achaean army. Priam cannot give his son a proper burial. The pain must be as keen as losing one's limb.

Paris cannot even deign to look at us. He leans against the balustrade, hair pinned back with a golden circlet. It had been his brother's, I distantly recall.

"I'm afraid, Anax Priam, that I have no idea what mischief my husband has concocted this time," Helen says primly.

"Mischief." Paris snorts. "That's a word for it."

The wooden horse is painted in varying shades of green, red, blue, and yellow, with designs and pieces of each kingdom's sigil. The patterns are disjointed and jarring.

The eyes of the Horse are two different colors, and two different shapes. One is green and the other red. The eyes of ships.

Helen notices this at the same time I do. "The belly of the Horse is made from their ships."

"Then they couldn't have gone far if not by sea, and in such a short amount of time. Their camp still stood before that storm." Paris nods to nearby soldiers. "We'll catch them in no time."

"And then what?" Helen doesn't sound sad, merely tired. She gives him a bored look beneath long, thick eyelashes. "You'll challenge them to another duel? My Shield has already won this war for us." She waves a hand in my direction. "Daphne beat Menelaus in combat, and rules of the duel declared the victor of this entire fruitless war."

"We will make them pay and bring my brother's body back to the city where it belongs." Paris stomps over, face stormy. He stabs a finger in my direction. "She didn't win anything. You both have been nothing but a plague upon this city."

Outrage soars through me. Helen has been little more than a prisoner this entire time, and me a battering ram that has given body and blood to defend Troy. I press my lips together to keep from saying anything I might regret, then turn back to the Horse.

The colossal structure is taller even than the wall, so high the snout is within reach. Below, over a dozen chariot wheels have been attached so that it could be dragged from the beach over to the wall, but the storm has washed away any tracks.

"How did they gods-damn manage to build this thing in a single day?" Priam reaches out and runs a hand over the snout.

Helen points to the Horse's rump. "With the help of Athena, no doubt."

There, painted with black ashes and between the woven grass holding the entire thing together, is the outline of an owl. I don't know if she managed to revive Glaukopis, but not a mortal alive other than myself is sure to know of Poseidon's attack on Athena's pet.

Except, perhaps, the mortal sitting atop one of the Horse's wheels.

"I see you've found the great bloody contraption the Achaean cowards have left you," he calls up to us. He frowns, tan face pulling into a sour expression. "It would be rather hard to miss."

"Some might say it would be impossible to miss," Priam calls down to the man. "Who are you and what is this thing?"

"What does it look like?" The man's voice is rather peevish for someone without a single ally for miles. "Those bastards left this behind, and me with it. It's a tribute to Athena, as if the big ol' owl plastered across its rear end wasn't obvious enough." He sniffs. "And as a gift to Troy."

"A gift?" Paris blinks, nonplussed and unimpressed.

"That's what I, Sinon of Delphi, said." He heaves a great, exaggerated sigh. "Though I'll admit that I have no idea what you should do with it once it's inside."

"Once it's inside?" Priam rests his elbows on the wall.

"Yes, once it's inside. It's like talking to a fool," Sinon mutters, words carried up the wall by the warm southwest breeze of the god Libonotus. "It is a gift, and given in the name of Athena. To leave it outside the city would be to turn your prim noses up at her."

Priam's counselors, crowding the wall alongside us, begin to mutter. The king takes a step back and begins to march down the wide steps. We follow, forming a line, and the gates are swung open. Kassandra marches up alongside me, ignoring the frown Paris tosses in her direction.

She gives me a curt nod. "Shield."

I return it. "Princess."

A battalion of guards accompany us, all bearing fresh scars and looking for all the world like they've aged an entire decade during this single war.

"A gift," Sinon says as we walk up to him. He leaps off the wheel. His legs are long and skinny, not a warrior but perhaps an adviser. I recognize him from Odysseus's tent that night when they caught Helen and me. He continues, "A token of peace, if you will."

"A foolish gift." Priam's voice is raw, grief still lingering.

The Trojans would make the Achaeans pay for the loss of his son once they are caught, even if it drags out this war a hundred more years.

"To shun this gift is to shun the goddess Athena," Sinon says, voice edged with warning.

My neck aches as I lean back to look up at the great statue. Curiosity mingles with distrust, creating a rising tension at the base of my spine that has nothing to do with the awkward angle.

Helen speaks my thoughts. "Agamemnon never would have willingly left without his prize. He would die before fleeing."

"Then where is he? Hidden under the dirt." Paris's voice drips with sarcasm.

I barely refrain from snapping the man's head back with a punch across the jaw. My hand curls into a fist, but I keep it hidden behind my back.

"Burn it."

We all turn, some gasping, to Kassandra. Her eyes, though fixed on the Horse, have taken on a faraway look.

"On great wheels, the doom of Troy will be borne inside." There's a faint tremor in her voice, as if she fights against the prophecy. "In the belly of the beast, deception lurks."

My heart thunders in my chest. I blurt, "Burn it."

Surprise at my own outburst registers in the back of my mind. Kassandra is mad, but where once I assumed her ramblings thoughtless and deluded, now a quiet panic overtakes me as the truth of her words sings.

Sinon pales, mouth dropping open in outrage. "You would turn the gods against all of us if you took a torch to this Horse."

"Ignore her," Paris says with a harsh scoff. "My sister is insane. She's prone to fits and hysteria."

"Perhaps we should ignore you, Prince Paris." Helen walks in front of me, her green gown sweeping in the breeze. The sunlight catches the golden mesh in her brown curls, and her lovely face pulls into a frown. She turns to Priam and says, "Listen to your daughter and my Shield. Do not bring this thing into the city." She points to Sinon. "That man is an adviser to Odysseus, one of the craftiest men I've ever met. This Horse is a trick."

"And risk the ire of the gods for what?" Priam shakes his head. "What could this statue actually do to us if we bring it into the city?"

The belly of the Horse draws my gaze like a moth to a flame. A frown pulls my brows together. My pulse roars in my ears. *In the belly of the beast, deception lurks*, Kassandra said.

"They're inside it," I say. Everyone spins to look at me. "They're in the Horse. The Achaeans."

Everyone peers at the Horse with renewed interest, but most shrug.

"Don't be absurd. We will not burn this Horse," Priam says, a hard edge of finality, the tone of a king, in his voice. "Paris speaks the truth. My daughter is very ill. Do not take her words to heart and damn us all to the wrath of Olympus."

"Then let me," a steel-sharp voice says from behind us.

Lyta, flanked by her warriors, marches up to the statue and plants her fists on her hips.

"I don't fear Olympus," she says. "Let them try to punish me and let the world see how foolhardy that is."

She stretches out a hand, arm unshaking. Without question, one of her soldiers brings forward a torch.

Before it can be lit, Priam rushes forward. His jaw trembles, the gold woven into his braided beard dancing. "No. Don't curse us all."

Hippolyta looks from Kassandra to Helen, Paris, and finally to me. Our eyes meet, and she nods.

"I'm going to save us all."

Sparks spit into the air as the torch is lit. The flame reaches high, as if begging for a taste of the Horse.

She reaches forward and finds my gaze again. "If you and the Princess Kassandra speak true, then whoever waits inside this statue better show themselves now. Better to face my sword than to die by fire like cowards."

The torch dips. It ignites instantly on the dry grass and aged wood. The wheels light first, the fire ripping around them.

Nothing happens from within the horse. Nothing stirs. There is no movement.

"You arrogant fool," Paris barks out, before turning to his soldiers. "Get some water. We need to put the fire out."

"No." Hippolyta's arm whips out, and her own warriors stop them. "Wait."

The fire climbs higher and higher. It follows the twisting grass and wood. I hold a breath, not daring to speak or move, my eyes glued to the belly of the Horse.

There's a dull thud. The entire Horse rocks. A wheel cracks and the statue begins to wobble.

And then the belly opens and a rope drops.

Swinging down, man after man falls to the earth. The people watching on the wall begin to scream. Trojan and Amazon warriors whip out their swords and spears. The gates are slammed shut behind a battalion led by the last of Troy's allies.

There are fifty in total that climb from that belly. They cough and rub at eyes that water like waterfalls. Their skin is sooty and hair singed as they stumble free of the burning statue. Alkaios, hair shorn to the scalp on either side, swings down behind Odysseus. Pyrrhus drops down next, tumbling across the dirt. His *himation* is black and singed by the flames.

My body jerks forward of its own volition. Lyta's firm arm catches me across the middle, keeping me from running to my brothers.

More men climb free, coughing and waving away the smoke that springs tears in their eyes. The last to drop lets out a short screech as his armor catches fire. He lets go of the rope and falls into the burning base. His screams will forever echo in my memory, just as the smell of roasting flesh will reside there.

When he blessedly stops crying out, cut short by death and the touch of the god Thanatos bringing him to the Underworld, we finally give our undivided attention to the Achaeans.

Odysseus kneels at the forefront, the hem of his armor singed. Menelaus stands beside him. Neither man looks regretful for their attempted deceit. In fact, Odysseus smiles ruefully and Menelaus simply glares.

Directly at me, I don't fail to notice.

With a cackle, Lyta tosses aside the torch. "I believe apologies are in order."

The Mycenaean king of Sparta spits at her feet. "I will never—"

She cuts him off with an impatient look and a raised hand. "I wasn't talking to you, prisoner." She turns to Paris. "What did you call me earlier? A fool? Well, who's the fool now?"

Priam steps forward. "Kill them all."

"No!" Helen yells at the same time I do.

Everyone looks to us, brows raised with surprise. After all, we should want these men dead more than anyone else.

Odysseus's bare neck is pale despite the relentless sun of Troy. It's bared to us, his head still bowed. He expected us to kill him, and yet he still chose to climb from the Horse. Or perhaps he knew that I would protest. It is impossible to say what goes on in that tricky mind, but I do know that both Helen and I owe him our lives.

"If we kill them, we lose our leverage," I say, and sheath my sword as an example, the sliding home of metal firm. "Should Agamemnon and the other kings return, they will want their allies back, despite how dishonorable the whole lot of them seem."

The Ithacan looks up. His eyes are glassy from the smoke. Recognition of a debt returned.

Paris opens his mouth to protest but Priam ignores his heir and begins to bark orders at the Trojan soldiers. The prisoners are chained and led inside. I watch them all carefully for any signs of gods or goddesses hiding beneath mortal facades. Despite finding no immortals among them, I cannot help but feel as though I have let in a wolf among the sheep as they are dragged into the cellars beneath the Trojan city.

Celebrations rock the very earth that night. Music rumbles from every corner of Troy. The farmers have returned the horses to the fields outside the city and the markets' stalls once more line the walls. People celebrate the victory while nothing more than embers of the Horse linger outside. Helen and I are as still as statues, overlooking the city from the balcony of our suite.

The room no longer feels like a prison, but instead a new home. For where can we go now that the war is over if not Sparta or any other Achaean kingdom? I have no doubt that Hippolyta would readily accept me into the Amazon ranks. Helen has no place there, though.

She stands beside me, arms wrapped around her narrow frame. "What do you think Hermione is doing right now?"

I start at the mention of her daughter. Helen hasn't said the girl's name since we arrived on the shores of Troy. My queen's lip wobbles.

"Dancing." I offer her a warm smile. "The princess loves to dance."

She chokes back a sob. "Menelaus would never let her. If Agamemnon does barter for his brother's freedom, my daughter will never dance again once he returns to Sparta. Marrying her off will probably be one of the first things he does when he gets back to that dark palace on the hill. He'll excuse it as paying for his losses at war."

"My father has agreed to negotiate for her freedom."

I whip around, Adamantine sword outstretched.

"Whoa, whoa, whoa!" Paris holds his hands up.

I squint, trying to see through any possible godly deceptions, but find none. I have no strength or patience left for politeness. "What do you want?"

"I've come for Anassa Helen." Though the title is nothing more than courtesy at this point, he still gives her a reverential dip of his chin. "The king would like to speak with you about your place here in Troy, and your daughter's if we are able to negotiate with your husband."

Helen trembles but shows no fear. "And what place will that be?"

"That is for you to decide." Paris glances down to his sandaled feet, no doubt oiled and rubbed just an hour ago. No longer the unwitting soldier, but again the pampered prince. "Would you like to celebrate with me? The finest entertainment Troy has to offer is on full display tonight. It would be good for you to get to know the people you might one day rule."

The words, though unspoken, sit as heavy as gold in the room. He holds out a hand.

Helen might no longer be Queen of Sparta, but Paris is willing to take her as his wife, Queen of Troy, someone who might hope to broker peace with Sparta once Hermione comes of age and inherits her mother's former title.

After a long moment, Helen places her hand in his. "I would love another tour of Troy." Without looking, she says over her shoulder, "Daphne, you would do well to enjoy the city's delights."

A dismissal, for now. And meaning I should get to know our new home.

I don't have to wait long after Helen leaves, not even enough time to gather my thoughts, prepare my words, before he bursts into the room.

Apollo's eyes are wild, searching with a quiet panic until he finds me sitting on the edge of my bed. He stops short on the other side of the great hearth.

"What did you do?" He reaches a tentative hand and I let it cup my cheek. "How? How did you remove the Curse?"

"None of the gods can use me now." I still wear the armor from my battles with Nyx and Menelaus; my hair is still wet from Zeus's storm and skin still crusted with sweat and sand. But that's who I am, until the very end. A warrior who has earned the title and her freedom. "I will choose who I fight for from now on."

"If there wasn't a target on your back before"—Apollo shakes his head, curls falling before his eyes—"there sure is now."

"We can protect each other." I stand, drawn to him as if pulled on a gilded thread. "You have kept secrets from me in a misguided attempt to protect me, from your father, from Hera and Poseidon, from whatever you are all so desperate to keep hidden in this damned city. You can be honest with me now."

I reach out with shaking hands, betraying the fear that stirs in my core at what I did and what's to come, and take his arms. His skin is scorching beneath my palms.

A warm breeze stirs between us, rippling the water of the bath and making the flames crack and hiss. We stare at each other, looking nowhere but the depths of our eyes. My heart pounds, a drumbeat in my ears. Apollo's breathing hard, his chest mere inches from my own.

We've been here before, this same impasse again and again. Kept apart by time, history, fate, and, above all, myself. Because I could never let myself be with a man I feared could control me.

Now, I don't need to fear his retribution, or the painful touch of his father's lightning. Hera, Nyx, Aphrodite, Poseidon, none of them can touch me with their power. I reach up and brush a lock of hair away from Apollo's brow.

"No more tricks," I say, voice barely a whisper. "No more secrets."

Before I can say another word, Apollo's warm hands are cupping my cheeks, pulling me close for a kiss. His touch is searing, his lips piercing. My hands explore his chest, his hips, and he pulls me down to the bed.

"Daphne," he whispers, his voice husky in my hair. "Oh, my *kataigída*."

I say nothing, claiming his lips again and again until he's moaning. With his deft fingers, my armor is gone. His hands can't find purchase. They travel every inch of me. Filling me with an insatiable heat and longing.

I claw at the ties of his *peplos* until it falls away and I lean up.

He's naked beneath me, all hard panes and tan skin. An ache burns in my very core, resounding with need.

His eyes flash with worry, threatening to defuse the moment. "Do you regret this? We can stop."

I trace the line of his jaw and chin. "I could never regret any time spent with you, Apollo." Slowly, hands still trembling, I pull the ties of my chiton and let it fall around us. He grips my thighs, eyelids heavy with hunger.

I pull away the leather thong at the base of my neck. My braid is unbound, and I lean down, claiming his lips again. My curls become a golden curtain about our faces. With each kiss, I claim another piece of my strength from the gods that controlled me.

I am his, and he is mine—for better or for worse.

A steady clipping of sandaled feet eventually wakes me. Celebrations are still in full swing outside, evident by the cheers and singing that fill the dark sky. I can't have slept for very long. Apollo slumbers beside me. In his sleep, he's not nearly so warm, as if the magic of Olympus disappears with the rise of the moon.

Something in me whispers to get dressed. Slinking like a cat so I don't wake the god, I climb from the bed and pull on my chiton. I look down at him, tangled up in furs, one arm stretching high above his head. I want to reach down and kiss his brow, smell again the musk of cedarwood, but the whispering continues in the back of my mind. I grab the Adamantine sword before leaving.

The cold dread rising in me makes the hallways feel longer than normal as I softly tread down them. The shadows are deeper, and they echo with wailing and whispers. What disturbs me most is that these are real sounds, not the tricks of the gods who are hell-bent on bringing me down, because I am no longer affected by their magic.

I turn a corner, the wall decorated with a fresco of Elysium, and come to a dead stop. I press into the shadows.

Kassandra tugs against Lykou's grip. Her face is splotchy and red.

"I have to warn her," Kassandra says, her voice low and scratchy, as if she has spent the better part of the afternoon in tears. "I may be too late already."

"Warn me of what?" Both jump and turn toward me when I step out of the shadows.

"Of what comes." Kassandra rips her hands away from my friend. Her eyes, so dark in the dim light, take on a faraway look. "The arrows of Olympus will rain upon you, Daphne, daughter of Oceanus. While you may have protected yourself from their piercing touch, you have left others vulnerable. Tossed aside the cloak, you have." She stumbles forward, mouth gaping open. Her eyes blink, and she recognizes me for a mere moment before they go dark again. "The wolf will roam once more."

My heart thunders in my chest. A quiet panic overtakes me as the truth of her words sings. The air suddenly reeks of lilies and the sea.

"Lykou," I say. "Find Helen and leave Troy. Get out of here."

Confusion flits across his face. Maybe Hermes can take my friend away. I pat my body, searching for his pipes. I've left them with my armor.

Hera sashays around the corner. Her long, dark hair is bound up high in a twisting tower above her head. She wears a magenta chiton, laced with gold, and carries her dreaded scepter.

She points the silver staff at me, the peacock atop it gold with wings extended. "You thought you were so clever. Mortals always think they are so much smarter than us, with their few years and misplaced confidence. Fools."

"Run, Lykou. Take Kassandra and go!" I turn, arms outstretched to take any blow Hera might make.

Lykou grabs Kassandra's arm and turns, prepared to bolt, but we all jerk to a halt.

Poseidon leans against the wall behind us with his muscled arms crossed. His beard, a shade darker than his bright hair, is threaded with sea glass that catches the lights of the oil lamps when he smiles.

He straightens and his trident appears in one hand, made of cerulean sea glass and spun with threads of silver. "You may be invulnerable," he says to me, "but they are not."

He lunges at the same time I do. I leap forward, but arms of steel jerk me back. Hera's Olympic strength no longer affects me, and I fling the queen of Olympus over my head. She crashes into the wall just as Lykou's sword rings against Poseidon's spear. I tear across the space and fling Kassandra behind me, both our backs firmly to the wall.

Hera climbs to her feet, face splotched red with fury. She sprints toward us. The Adamantine sword cuts through the air and catches her scepter. Lykou yells behind me. How have people not yet come running at the noise we're making?

That's when I hear it, a steady roar outside the hallway. The people of Troy still celebrate. The cheering and songs of mourning join together and rise to deafening heights.

Hera's strength is now nothing compared to my own. I shove down her scepter until it hits the floor. The stones crack in a rippling circle from the impact and a rumble echoes around us.

"Dammit, Apollo," I say between gritted teeth. "Even that had to have woken you up."

"Oh, I'm sure he's awake by now," Hera says sweetly. "But he's a bit preoccupied at the moment."

The image of Athena wreaking havoc in my suite right now fills me with cold dread.

I spin, cracking Hera in the ribs. She stumbles backward, gripping her stomach. Lykou yells again and I turn, my fist and sword jabbing in quick succession. I clip her jaw and slice the wrist that holds her scepter. She drops it with a scream. I kick it down the hallway and turn to my friend.

Poseidon holds him aloft in the air with a single hand around his throat. Lykou's legs kick in vain.

A wild scream wrenches from me. My fist cracks into Poseidon's chin at the same time my knee finds his groin.

He drops Lykou like a sack of grain. I shove my friend back toward a cowering Kassandra.

She's screaming. The noise cuts to a short screech.

I spin around with my sword aloft.

Hera holds Kassandra against her chest, a knife pressed to the princess's throat. A bead of blood wells there and drips down the coppery blade.

"The magic in Troy's walls dictates that I can't kill this princess," Hera says. Her eyes are wide, wild even, and her once-pristine hair is a tangled mess about her shoulders. "Even now, I feel it tugging me away as I threaten her."

I slowly lower my arms. "So let her go."

Lykou pants beside me with fists at his sides.

Her grin is catlike. "Fine."

Before I can react, Hera shoves Kassandra toward me. I catch her, spinning her behind me, our backs firmly to the wall. Poseidon climbs to his feet. He levels me with a glare that could flay a man. With careful steps, watching me as if I might pounce, he walks to the goddess's side. Lykou likewise comes to mine and we form a wall before the Trojan princess.

Poseidon's face is unreadable, but tension radiates from him in waves, making the narrow corridor feel even more cramped. It's matched by Lykou, as if he knows what must come next.

Because, while the gods cannot harm a Trojan, I've heard nothing about the magic of the wall protecting a Spartan within the city.

I angle my shoulder so that I half cover my friend. "Don't you touch him."

"Maybe next time you will consider what it means to be under our protection," the god of the sea says. "And what it means to be without it."

He raises a fist and Lykou crumples beside me.

"No!" I scream.

Lykou's mouth is open in soundless agony. The grooves along his spine snap and thud, twisting my own gut as he turns over, wrists bent at unnatural angles and legs curling into his stomach. Long black hair erupts from his arms and legs.

Kassandra begins a keening wail behind me, and then Lykou's back snaps in half.

I drop to my knees, gaping in horror. My friend is gone in a blink, replaced by a great, black wolf.

"Not again," I say under my breath. "Not again. Not again. Not again."

I reach for the wolf's face and hold it between my hands so that I may look in his eyes. They are a warm brown and painfully human before they close and he collapses. His chest rises and falls, letting me know that he is at least alive. But that doesn't keep the guilt and horror that churns in my stomach at bay. Instead, I heave.

There is nothing inside me to puke on the floor, but great, wrenching gasps escape me nonetheless.

"Do allies mean nothing to you if they're not Olympian?" The words come out in a strangled screech. "He almost lost his humanity for you once already. I *died* for you."

Hera only sneers. "Maybe you should have stayed dead."

Something wild builds within me, begging for release. I would tear down this entire palace if it meant destroying the two of them right now. I would call upon a typhoon and blast them from the very earth.

Poseidon sees something in my face that makes him take a step back. "Think again before standing against us, Daphne. Next time we will not be so kind."

He disappears in a blink and the scent of the sea wafts over me. Hera stays and, as I watch, her hair coils itself back up high atop her head. The cut on her cheek heals, and her clothes straighten.

She brushes the dust from her chest with a sigh. "It's sad really, the lengths you have gone to disrespect us. We made this world."

"You didn't make anything," I spit out. "The Hesperides did, and you control its power. I know what you did to the titans."

She flinches as if struck. "Apollo should have kept his mouth shut."

"He didn't tell me." I stand. "But now he doesn't need to fear telling me the truth because your magic is useless against me. And for every friend, every person that I love, that you hurt?" I raise my sword and point it at her. "I'll hurt you in kind."

She looks down the blade at me. The goddess reaches out and drags a finger along it. It slices her skin and black ichor drips on the floor.

"Apollo doesn't need to fear telling you the truth?" She cocks her head and her gaze turns to Kassandra cowering behind me. "Then why hasn't he told you what he did to *her*? What he took from the Princess of Troy?"

Hera's gone, disappearing in a blink of lavender mist and the pungent stench of lilies.

There's a clapping of sandals down the hallway and Apollo comes sprinting around the corner. He jerks to a halt when he sees us. His nose curls at the lingering smell and he searches my face.

Horror blankets me, for both the wolf at my feet and the princess behind me.

"What did you do, Apollo?" My heart is being stabbed. "What did you do to Kassandra?"

CHAPTER
47

Apollo's chiton is torn and a gash stretches across his abdomen from shoulder to navel. The ichor has already stopped dripping, the wound healing itself before my eyes as the god straightens.

He strides forward and I take another step back. Kassandra presses against my spine as he grabs my hands. "The princess was once my lover."

I tear my hands away. I asked for honesty, and I have it, but the reality of it is like a slap in the face. "Of her own volition?"

Now it is Apollo's turn to look as though slapped, but he knows the stories I've heard, of him and his kin. Too many to ignore, even in the face of my own feelings.

"Yes." He turns to Kassandra.

Finally, she speaks from behind me. "I asked him for a gift, and instead he gave me a curse."

Apollo's face twists. "Just as you asked Hermes for a gift, the effects of which we don't know the true weight of, Kassandra asked for one as well. But there is a price to pay for the gift of prophecy, and it is a price that no mortal body can pay."

I turn as he reaches around me and brushes a knuckle across Kassandra's cheek. "I wish I had known that at the time."

"Don't lie," Kassandra says, spitting. "You cursed me."

"I did not mean to," Apollo insists. He takes another step forward.

Kassandra yanks me backward. Lykou rumbles from the floor, blinking blearily as he rouses from his stupor. His legs wobble as he attempts to stand, and then he collapses again.

I turn to the god in question, fully aware of the pain coloring my expression.

"Please." He holds out his hands. "Let me explain to both of you."

"You've done enough," Kassandra says, continuing to pull me away.

Apollo winces.

"She's right," I say, my heart wrenching as his face crumbles. "You've said and done enough."

Lykou climbs back up onto his legs and bares his teeth at the god.

"I said it before, and I'll say it again, Apollo." My lip wobbles, and tears stream down my cheeks.

"Then don't say it." In a blink, Apollo swoops in to take my hands. His grip is warm, but not inhumanly so.

"As much as everything in my body screams at me to, I can't ignore your history." A sob chokes me, and I clench my teeth around it even as tears stream from my eyes. I rip my hands away. "I cannot let you destroy me, too."

"I would never hurt you, Daphne." Apollo's own face crumples with pain.

"Did you mean to hurt Kassandra?" I wave a hand in the princess's direction, and even though it will kill him, I also ask, "Did you mean to hurt Koronis?"

A myriad of emotions cross his face. Pain and fury, fear and remorse. "No."

"I don't know if I believe you," I say, trembling. Not from fear, but a pain keener than I've ever known.

His bronze curls flicker with gold and a light passes behind his eyes, there and gone in an instant, before his face falls and his usually bright gaze goes dark.

"If that's how you feel"—he swallows—"I should have heeded your words before, truly listened to them."

My heart cracks, even as I tell myself that this is the right choice. The right path for us both. Even with my titan heritage, I am nothing more than a mortal, and he a god. Even if I could forgive his history someday, that wouldn't change the fact that my lifetime is a mere blink in his.

He steps forward, back stiff and jaw clenched hard.

"Tell me you hate me," he says, making me blink in surprise.

My mouth pops open. "What?"

He steps forward, right up against me. "Tell me you hate me. Tell me this was nothing and that you want nothing more to do with me."

"Apollo—"

"Tell me"—he cuts me off, his face so close his lips brush my own—"and mean it."

I release a long, shuddering breath.

"Otherwise I will not walk away, *kataigída*." His eyes drop to my mouth. "I cannot."

"I want..." I swallow. "I want you to..."

"Say it," he says, voice rough.

I shake my head, a single tear spilling down my cheek. With a gentle finger, he catches it on my jaw and grazes the back of my cheek with his hand.

"*Kataigída.* Daphne." Hearing my name upon his lips makes my heart crack anew. "I understand. I will leave. And you don't have to worry about me hurting you as I have so many before you."

He stills, eyes looking over my shoulder and widening.

A low rumble spills from Lykou's maw, fangs bared.

Slowly, I turn.

The Moirai, bedecked in shimmering red armor, march down the corridor.

CHAPTER
48

The Fates' power fills the hallway, a simmering cloud of fate. It brushes against me, then recoils, as tangible as misting rain. Kassandra whimpers from behind me, gripping my arms and digging her nails into my skin.

"Come to impart some more terrible wisdom?" I ask with a drawl. I'm calmer than I have any right to be.

Lykou barks at the Moirai. His hackles are high. Their faces remain unchanged as each hefts a bronze club. One, the closest in appearance to her mother, points to my chest.

"You have tangled the web of fate, Daughter of Oceanus." Her hair, dark and wiry, rises about her shoulders.

My eyebrows rise. "I did not know I was so powerful."

"If you have come to punish Daphne, take me instead."

Surprise makes my mouth fall open as Apollo steps in front of me, though it is quickly snuffed out.

"I don't need you to take my punishment," I say, yanking him back. "I don't need you for anything." I turn to the Moirai. "Promise to leave Lykou and Kassandra alone, and I will do whatever you ask."

The youngest in appearance scoffs. "We are not here to punish. Our gifts, our threads, are worthless now on you. Whatever you touch, you unweave."

"How?" The question falls from my mouth.

"You are now immune to our gifts," says the third. "The future is carefully woven, and with your every step you cleave it in two. The Olympians helped the Achaeans create the Trojan Horse with the intention of fostering love for the gods once more. Troy was meant to fall to the men in that Horse. The Achaeans would take the city in the night, and thank Olympus for their victory."

"Only fools would actually lug that thing into the city," I mutter.

"Fools, the righteous, those under the sway of curses and gifts," Klotho says, her voice hollow. "All reside here in this city, and each was to play an important part in Troy's downfall."

"At the behest of your mother, no doubt."

"We met your mother, too," Lakhesis says. Her ruby eyes gleam when I start. "Normally, we visit a mother three days after a child's birth, but yours was different. You've seen the day, heard her screams thanks to Prometheus. We were there. Did Ligeia ever tell you what wisdom we shared with your mother before she died?"

"If I say no, will you get to the point?" Weariness weighs down my shoulders like a shroud of stone. Tears from only moments before are still wet on my cheeks. Lykou, still a wolf, leans against me. He bares his fangs at the Moirai.

"You may be obstinate like your father, but that will not endear you to him," Klotho says, keeping her finger pointed at my face. "No, in fact it will have the opposite effect."

"We don't need to weave that into your fate." Atropos laughs softly.

"Fate has never controlled me."

The women laugh. Apollo gives me a pleading glance, but I ignore him.

"Nor need we worry about the fall of Troy." Atropos leans back. She's so like her mother that I tremble just to see her. Her dark hair falls into the flames, but does not burn. "There are some fates even we cannot weave."

A chill snakes down my spine. I reach for the sword at my hip. "What do you mean?"

"There is nothing you can do to save this city," Atropos says. "Troy will fall tonight."

Kassandra gasps. "No!"

There's a dull roar in my ears. "But that's not possible. Nothing remains of that damned Horse but cinders."

As one, bodies disappearing in a great rush of smoke that makes me cough, they say, "The downfall of Troy has been inside the city this entire time."

CHAPTER

49

The Moirai vanish in a blast of heat and smoke. I cough, waving a hand, and by the time it dissipates, nothing remains of the Fates. Nothing but every part of my body screaming at me to run.

The music hasn't stopped, and neither have the joyous cheers, both echoing through the hallways. A dull roar begins in my ears, like the rising of a summer storm.

"Lykou," I say. "We need to check on the prisoners. Kassandra, go warn your parents."

The princess sprints away, and I am forced to hope she will follow my orders, whether they believe her or not.

I dash for our rooms, grabbing Hermes's pipes and a pair of daggers on the way and strapping them to my thighs.

"Let me help you." Apollo reaches for my hand.

I spin and slash his wrist. He bites back a yelp.

"I don't need your help," I say, pouring as much loathing and disgust as I can into my voice. It isn't enough. "You and your family have done enough damage." To add salt to the wound, to match the stinging of my fractured heart, I add, "Besides, you'd be useless to me as powerless as you are."

His face crumples. I jog from the room, Lykou on my heels. I don't look over my shoulder to see if Apollo follows.

"Go find Lyta," I command as we run from the room, pointing down the hallway. He lunges into the shadows and I do the same in the opposite direction.

I go over my mental map of Troy as I sprint down stairs and alleyways. I take a corner so hard I slip, slamming into the wall. My arm barks in pain, but I don't stop. I'm thundering down the streets, ignoring the curious stares that trail me.

Just outside the prison, there's an enormous celebration. Trojans burn wooden effigies of gods as they dance, passing amphoras of wine and bowls of food.

I arrive at the barracks to find it heavily guarded, but no one looks alarmed. In fact, they all look at me as if I'm deranged when I demand, "Where are the prisoners?"

Whether it be from newfound respect or being truly unbothered, none of the Trojan guards protest when I march inside. The cells are belowground, down a cracked, narrow stairway, but not so far down that my skin prickles with cold or the memory of Tartarus.

The Achaean prisoners are crowded into a single chamber no larger than my suite, all fifty of them. A murmuring starts when I arrive.

"*Prodótis*," some whisper as I pass.

Some spit through the bars of the cage, leering and telling me in great detail how they would mutilate my body. Most largely ignore me, simply shaking their heads and turning away.

My heart hammers in my chest, so intense I can hardly breathe. I cannot find my brothers in the crowd despite my gaze normally being drawn to Pyrrhus's auburn hair. The Spartans are easiest to pick out by their glares and the way they sneer as I stalk past.

The men part for Odysseus when he walks slowly forward, every step measured.

"What can we do for the Shield of Helen?" He waves to the meager space left in the cell. "I'll admit that this is a fair bit roomier than the Horse we were all crammed inside. I could ask Teucer to scootch over and make space for you."

I don't laugh, much too panicked for even a crack of a smile. "What are you planning?"

He cocks his head. "Other than rotting in here until Agamemnon returns and bargains for our freedom? Nothing really. Maybe relieving myself a few times in each corner and teaching the men an Ithacan dance I'm quite fond of. You might like it, actually. It involves—"

I silence him by yanking him forward by the cuff, slamming his chin into the bars. "Quit toying with me, Odysseus. What are you all plotting?"

Several of the men perk up.

The Ithacan merely frowns. "We were plotting to climb from the Horse in the dead of the night after you all brought the damned thing inside, but I expect nothing remains of the statue except cinders and we're all stuck behind bars now so..." He whistles and grabs the bars, leaning back to stretch out his arms. He grunts in satisfaction when both elbows pop.

I grab the bars as well and give them a firm shake. Neither budge. Marching down the line, I try each to the same effect. I should have expected Troy to have the finest cells this side of the Aegean.

"Which of the gods helped you create that wooden monstrosity?" I peer into the crowd, frowning.

Menelaus leans against a wall in the back of the room, staring at the ceiling and ignored by everyone around him. He's not possessed by Nyx any longer, if she was ever inside his head. Perhaps he was always just a craven and cruel man.

No doubt the soldiers despise him. Multiple failed efforts to take the city, and many lost Spartans. Still no sign of Alkaios, though.

"Athena for starters," Odysseus says, "but I'm sure you knew that from the great big owl Nestor insisted we add." He begins ticking off names on his fingers. "Poseidon, Hera, and some of the lesser ones. Thetis, Angelos, and Enyo. We never saw them, but they left us gifts, hints. It was Athena's idea to build it using ships. We started in the water, and Poseidon aided us unseen. Then that great storm arrived and the contraption was lifted out."

"Their hubris will be their own downfall one of these days." I shake my head.

"But that's the thing," the king says, voice light for someone trapped in a cell. "The gods may be proud and deceitful, but they are not stupid. If there truly is something within these walls that they want to protect, why would they help us?"

"Perhaps they wanted you within the walls to protect it. Or to control you all. They don't fear us mortals. Not truly." I inhale through my nose. "None of you spoke with them directly?"

"Well, one of us did." Odysseus's grip on the bars tightens. His knuckles are white in the dim light. "How do you think we knew you would spot our battalion in the foothills that day, in order to ambush you?"

"Someone knew I was with Hermes on the roof." Cold dread splashes over me like a pail of water. "Alkaios. He asked about me. What the messenger god meant to me."

"The battles were even because a god spoke through your brother." Odysseus's brows rise. "Someone who understood your god of tricks."

"Where are my brothers?" I ask quietly.

*   *   *

Alkaios and Pyrrhus are loose in this city, no doubt under the influence of Nyx. Troy is lit with wine and joy, making the citizens wholly blind to any dangers. I cannot wait for Lykou and Lyta to get here before I start looking. With a sharp order to the Trojans that two of their prisoners managed to escape, I dive into the unruly crowd with single-minded focus.

I slip between people, searching for Pyrrhus's long red hair. He eludes my gaze, everywhere I turn. He has the entire city to hide in. I should be trying to understand his goal, not searching randomly.

Alkaios was trained with the same instincts as myself. A hunter's focus has always guided both of our movements. Pyrrhus had always been the more rash of us all. Alkaios has the silent gait, the uncanny ability to meld into any shadow and avoid being seen by any creature.

Both have reason to want to watch this city and me burn. Bile rises in my throat, threatening to choke me.

I force myself to squash my panic and think rationally. It would be useless to simply leave the city. No, Alkaios would feel he owes Odysseus a life debt, and would do anything to help him escape. Or, at least that's what he would have done if not influenced by gods unknown toward some other purpose.

I shake my head, trying to rearrange my thoughts in a useful order. As Odysseus said, the gods may be proud but they are not fools. No, an enemy of Olympus likely helped the Achaeans. And likely the same one who is hiding my brothers in the shadows right now. Pyrrhus, rash and impulsive, is more susceptible to godly influence. Nyx could get in his mind. They have to be searching together for whatever it is the walls of Troy protect.

The wealth of Troy does not immediately lay in its treasure, but rather in the ingenuity of its people.

I'm just thinking in circles. Cursing under my breath, I stomp past another bonfire and narrowly avoid colliding with a celebrating Amazon, her wine spraying the ground and splattering across my feet.

I wrack my mind through everything I've seen in this city. The markets and palaces, the megaron and fields where horses roam free. The statues and temples just beyond the walls, and the frescoes on every corner.

I jerk to a halt. That fresco of the pantheon that I first saw when the Erinyes attacked the city.

"This fresco was made by the gods themselves," Kassandra once said.

I break into a sprint again, dashing around revelers and corners. My breath burns up my throat as I run faster than I ever have before. Passing the courtyard where Apollo and I once danced, I slam into another corner. The air knocked from my lungs, I stumble only once before taking off again down the last alleyway to the fresco.

The art looms high before me. I'm sliding across the ground, knees and hips barking in protest. Above, Selene has brought the moon high, full, and whiter than bone. Nobody else lurks in the alley.

Doubt settles along my spine like a clawed touch. I turn every way, peering into the shadows, but nothing lurks and there is no lingering scent of lavender prone to be left behind when Nyx uses her magic.

The fresco arches above my line of sight, the paint unblemished despite the elements and age. At my feet, Trojans have left gifts to thank the gods for their victory. Laurel for Apollo, bowls of cow's blood for Zeus, and perhaps sheep's blood for Hades, olive branches for Athena, and bread for Demeter. More gifts for the other gods line the ground. I nudge the bowl for Zeus aside with a toe, careful to make sure none of it splashes out onto my feet.

A whisper of the celebration's music flits in the air. Not Hermes, not Apollo's lyre. Troy's *paian* song. The city celebrates in blissful ignorance to the danger lurking in the streets while I stand here and gape at a giant painting.

But I just can't look away.

The stones shimmer in the moonlight, though not from magic or impurities. The small cracks catch my eye again, arcing in a semi-circle just higher than the reach of my arm. My hands curl into a hesitant fist for the barest of moments before I place my palm on the crack slicing Apollo's face in two.

A boom so loud it makes my ears ring echoes into the night. I jump back. Not a cloud in the sky, no hint of Zeus's lightning. No, the sound came from the wall. From within the wall. Then a rumble begins to form. The bowls of blood shiver. Olives roll down the street. I take another step back, mouth falling open.

The cracks widen. They peel and roll backward with little clicking movements until, finally, a doorway appears.

CHAPTER

50

I've stood at the edge of the abyss before. Many times.

Above the labyrinth, the entrance to the Underworld, in Arachne's lair, and even in Tartarus.

But I've never felt such cold, sinking fear like I do now.

The alleyway has gone deathly silent, as if all the mice and crickets have fled for another city altogether. Even the sounds of Troy's celebration are nothing more than a dull murmur in the distance.

Everything screams at me to leave, to continue my search for my brothers and Nyx. Instead, I take a step toward the darkness. Pulling the Adamantine sword from its sheath, I take another step. Then another, until the shadows swallow me whole.

Unlike the wet filth coating the walls of the labyrinth, this place is pristine. Untouched. Not even a layer of dust coats the immaculate marble walls of the corridor I march down. My steps do not echo here. No, the air is tight. I find it hard to breathe.

When I stop, the shadows press closer around me as if curious. I force myself to take a deep, steady breath. Rolling back my shoulders, I continue on with more speed to my steps.

This is no labyrinth or twisting abyss. There are turns, yes, but no real choices. There is one path, with the only choice being: continue on, or turn around while you still can.

On and on, deeper into Troy I traverse. The jet-black marble hallway has a downward tilt. The air is somehow warm, not colder, the farther down I walk. Soon, I'm sweating, clothes clinging to my body and hand slick around the hilt of my sword until, finally, I arrive.

I've seen this room before. Prometheus brought me here. When I step into the tomb, oil lamps in every corner burst to life with purple flames. At the far end, a single *pyxis* stands tall on a pillar of onyx marble. The walls are more frescoes, this time painted in only black and white. I don't have to peer close to see what image they form.

The Titanomachy, starting with the titan Cronus killing his own father, Uranus, with a sickle. His blood sprays far and wide, and everywhere it lands a new titan is born. As Uranus dies and Cronus takes up the mantle of King of the Titans, his father makes one last prophecy: that all Cronus's children will rise up to overthrow him.

So the new king eats his children, one after the other, until none remain, save for Zeus, whose mother, Rhea, has taken to a cave. Once the god of lightning comes of age, he overthrows his father and frees his siblings.

Cronus lived on, and a war raged. Zeus and his siblings versus the titans. When enough of their own kin defected, eventually the titans were struck down, trapped in Tartarus while the gods claimed their thrones atop Olympus.

But that can't be right. I was in Tartarus, and the titans most definitely were not.

The other side of the room paints a much different story. It starts with the birth of the Hesperides, as Hermes told me. Three trees become one in an explosion of white and black tiles.

Titans and gods form a circle around the now interlocking trees. The next panel shows the birth of the world as I've been told, and yet a new beginning entirely. The sun rises and Helios chases it. The trees bloom and Demeter arrives to cultivate the fruit instead of nurturing it to life. The sea stirs, a great storm rising above an island, and both Oceanus and Poseidon rise to hold it at bay. Two titans I cannot name stand above a crowd of mortals.

And set them all aflame.

I gasp, covering a hand with my mouth.

Then the next panel shows the gods gathering together. Poseidon and Athena meet a nameless titan atop a sea cliff.

And drown him together.

Next, the gods form a circle, even Apollo with his unmistakable shoulders and face. I could recognize him even in a sea of a thousand people. Hermes stands at one side of him, Artemis at his other. They are joined by gods I don't recognize, and a few titan allies. They lock hands as the remaining titans lash out with weapons and elements. The following panel is all black, and I hurry on to the next one.

The circle of gods remains, with a few titans taking up their hands, but in the center stands a tall, narrow jar.

Exactly like the *pyxis* beside me.

Horror creeps up my spine.

The wall wasn't meant to protect what the gods had hidden in Troy. It was meant to contain it.

"You understand now, don't you?"

I spin, sword raised.

Nyx, with skirts made of shadow and long claws extending from each finger like daggers, blocks the entrance of the tomb.

"Understand what?" I dare to ask.

She gives me a disappointed look. "What is inside Pandora's jar. It wasn't the evils of the world, nor hope, as Zeus had Prometheus proclaim." Nyx cocks her head. She's not even looking at me. Instead, she focuses on the jar hungrily. "But, rather, my family."

"The gods are your family, too," I choke out.

"Though these panels paint a cleaner picture than the stories Zeus likes to let the mortals believe, they are also not the complete truth. I bet Hermes told you a fair amount." Her shoulders seem to sag, and her nails retract to normal, mortal size. "Gods and titans from all over the world came together at the Hesperides. We were once all mortals ourselves, and the trees gave us the very powers we wield today. But some gods got greedy. Some, as Hermes also no doubt told you, did not see the mortals as merely a lesser species. We saw them for what they truly are."

"You used us as playthings," I spit, grip tightening on the sword. "You would torture and kill all of us. We were nothing but slaves."

"Yes, Helots with little value other than to serve us." Her laugh is nothing sweet.

"Why here?" I wave to the tomb.

"Zeus thought he was so clever hiding them here." Disgust curls the goddess's lips. "He cursed that doorway you so stupidly opened, so that it could only be opened by one with titan blood."

I blanch. "That's why Apollo would never tell me who my father was." My hands and cheeks feel numb. "Because, if Zeus thought I knew how to open those doors, that I had the power to, he would have killed me."

She nods, the movement strangely sage with her maniacally

twisted face. "Going to Hermes to make yourself immune to Olympian magic was either a stroke of genius or luck." She considers me. "Probably the latter."

I'm only slightly offended.

"Now that you've done the hard part of finding the tomb and opening it—for which I am truly grateful—I need you to get out of my way." She points over my shoulder. "It is time to reunite with my family."

"I don't agree with Zeus's methods," I say, angling my body so that it is firmly between her and the *pyxis*. "But neither will I let you free the titans."

They will kill the Olympians in revenge for their imprisonment and turn on the mortals who have forgotten them. It will be complete carnage on every plane of this world.

"No, I didn't expect you to hand them over to me." She straightens. Her hair becomes shorter, more curled and lightening in color to a warm brown. Her eyes fade from red to gray and her pale skin darkens to a tan. The image flickers, at war with the gift I received from Hermes that allows me to see through the gods' deception.

Helen's voice leaves Nyx's lips at the same time as her own. "But you will give it to him."

A ring, small and gold, appears in the shimmering air beside her. I blink, and then my brother appears. He holds the Ring of Gyges.

CHAPTER
51

With trembling arms, I raise my sword between my brother and me.

"That's not who you think it is," I say, nodding to the goddess behind him.

"Helen told me everything." Alkaios levels a *dory* at me, the spear made from a shimmering black metal exactly like the Adamantine sword. "How you manipulated her. Stole her from Sparta and tricked her into betraying her own kingdom. All at the behest of the gods."

"That's not Helen," I say, lip quivering. "Helen wasn't the one manipulated. You are."

He lunges forward. The spearhead strikes where I just stood. I spin and deflect it. The strike makes my entire arm reverberate, and a hollow ringing fills the space.

"I will bring you to Agamemnon and Menelaus," Alkaios says,

panting slightly. His eyes are wild, dark at the edges. "Or, for my *anassa*, I will kill you."

This isn't the Alkaios I've trained with for fifteen years. The brother who taught me how to use a sword, spear, and bow was meticulous with his every attack, ruthless, and fought with a mask that kept me from ever guessing his next jab. Now, his movements are wild, erratic even, as he swings haphazardly at me. I'm deflecting from all angles. I roll beneath a swing and my elbow clips the ground. There's a burst of sharp pain, then the entire limb goes numb.

"Please, Alkaios," I say, switching the sword to my other hand. "This isn't you. Family above all else."

"You betrayed us first, remember?" He lunges again.

I step back and the spearhead clips the *pyxis*. It dances on the pedestal. My stomach drops. The jar stops its spinning, but the distraction costs me. The spearhead goes straight for my face.

I turn away just as it slices my cheek.

Blood pours down my neck. I don't stop moving. With my bad hand I whip out a dagger. I complete the circle and raise both weapons. With the hilt of the sword, I hook the spear from my brother's grasp and I slice his wrist.

His grip loosens and I fling aside the spear. It cracks on the wall behind me.

"Remember when I nearly drowned in the Eurotas. You and Pyrrhus saved me." My voice trembles.

"Another lie." Alkaios punches the air with his good fist.

"The Ring of Gyges," I say desperately. "It took the memory when you stole it from Hermes."

"Your parents tried to stop her from taking me," Nyx as Helen says, her voice raw and bleating. "And she killed them, too."

"Liar!" My swing goes wide.

"Here, my soldier." Nyx throws something black through the air.

My brother catches it. The black elongates and splits into a metal star. He jabs and I stumble back from his reach. My spine collides with the marble pillar. The *pyxis* holding the fate of the world rattles.

The metal star hooks under my arm. It slashes my wrist at the same time his fist catches my chin. I drop the dagger with a gasp.

"I'm your sister," I say, not recognizing the desperation in my own voice.

"You murdered our parents."

"I did not!"

He goes on, not caring or not hearing, lost to Nyx's power and the madness of war that overtakes us all. "You betrayed our kingdom and kidnapped Helen. You're not my sister. You're just the monster that killed my mother."

He leaps forward, both hands wrapped around the star. I swing up to catch the many-edged blade. It snaps in two before I even touch it. The sword catches a half above my head, and I can't react in time as his other hand punches me directly in the stomach.

I don't feel anything at first. Then the air blows out of me in a great rush. I stumble, slipping on the warm liquid that now coats my feet. Horror blankets me and I cradle my midriff.

He holds the two halves aloft, one coated in my blood and the other now sweeping for my neck. I raise the sword just in time and both blades screech. I twist with all my remaining strength. The blades wrench free and fall to our feet. I step backward as Alkaios raises the second half.

He leaps forward and punches toward my heart. I barely raise the dagger in time.

It rams into his stomach.

Awareness eddies into his gaze, while blood coats my hands, warm and sticky. I let go as if burnt.

Confusion flits across his face. He looks around, as if just now recognizing where he is. "Daphne, why?"

"No, no, no," I say, tears streaming down my face. He collapses into my arms and we both crash to the floor.

My hands flutter uselessly over the wound. Numbness has begun to flood my own limbs when I paw at my chest and rip Hermes's pipes from my neck. He has to heal my brother.

But when I raise the instrument to my lips, no sound comes out. I press it so hard against my mouth, it threatens to splinter. Black spots fill my vision.

"Work, damn you," I scream at the pipes.

"Prometheus once told me that our magic is a gift that seems valuable at first, but is really a curse." Nyx's lavender scent coats my nose before I see her. She towers over us, her edges hazy in my failing vision. "Those pipes won't work for you anymore."

"Then how did I open the doorway?" I cup my brother's face. His eyes flutter, struggling to stay open. "Stay with me, Alkaios."

"It was imbued with the power of the titans, not Olympus. A curse so strong no Olympian could break it. The blood of my family went into the very stones of that doorway." She steps over me, toward the *pyxis*. "And now they're going to tear the whole city down."

"No!" I try to climb to my feet, but my legs don't work. I can barely raise myself even to my knees.

She considers me a moment, hands still outstretched. "You should want this as much as I do. They're your kin. Your father may be free, but your uncles and aunts are trapped in this very jar."

"And if you release them, they will kill every single person in this city." A sob claws from me.

"True." She drops a hand. "But I never gave a damn about Troy."

Before I can cry out, she shoves the *pyxis* from the pillar. Time seems to slow. Singing echoes down the long hallway, broken only by a mournful wail of the wind along Troy's walls.

The jar shatters on the floor and darkness erupts all around us.

CHAPTER
52

The entire earth rumbles, the pieces of the *pyxis* trembling. My eyes flutter open. I'm not dead yet, but I wish I was.

Gone are Troy's songs. Screams fill the halls, from above and below, the Trojans fleeing whatever monsters wreak havoc in the city. My hands are outstretched, reaching in vain for the brother gasping for breath across from me. I lay beside him, my arms entangled with his.

"Stay with me," I beg. "Apollo will be here soon."

He has to come. He has to. I know this as surely as I know that my heart still longs for him.

My brother's eyes are open, but unseeing. His mouth opens and closes.

"If I could take your pain and put it in myself, I would," I say around the tears that fall down my cheeks. "If I could take my life and give it to you, I would."

"I know," Alkaios says.

"I would do anything for you," I say through clenched teeth. I can't feel my arms now. Blood pools between us. Mine and his. "I would do anything for you and Pyrrhus."

"I know, Daphne." His eyes fall shut as a soft sigh escapes his lips.

"Stay awake! Stay bloody awake."

I can't force my legs to move, my body to crawl closer to him. I can only watch as his chest rises, falls with a shudder, then stills.

A scream so wild it could tear down the walls wrenches from my chest. It bursts from me with the last of my strength. The blood slows, then stops. Only mine continues to pour as great, heaving sobs claw from me.

I don't know how long I'm lying here, begging him to come back to me, fighting my own demise, and praying for it to come claim me at the same time. The ground shakes endlessly, and a great roar echoes down the hallway, but it is nothing compared to the dull ringing in my ears.

The room is frigid now, darker than the depths of Tartarus. Then a wave of golden light sweeps over me.

"Daphne!" Warm arms scoop me up. "Where are you wounded?"

I don't have the strength to answer. My limbs are leaden, my eyes falling shut as my head droops into his strong chest.

"Daphne, don't you dare let go."

"Apollo," I say, voice so soft. "How did you find me?"

"Thanatos came to get me. He saw you with your brother."

When the god of death came to claim my brother's soul for the Underworld.

Another sob bursts from me, but turns to a cough. Blood coats my lips.

"Don't you dare go to him," Apollo says, voice ragged. "Don't you dare leave me."

I don't have to ask who. Thanatos, the god who brings souls to

Hades, stands at the periphery of my vision. His hair is black and his eyes are red. Like his mother, I recall dimly.

My eyes open one last time. I nod. "It's okay. I'm ready to take my shame with me to the Underworld."

"You should be ashamed of nothing," Apollo says. His entire body trembles beneath me, or is Troy still shaking?

With the last of my strength, I raise a hand to his cheek. My palm leaves a bloody handprint there.

His secrets. They were always to protect me. If I had known I was key to Olympus's downfall, I might have eventually sought it out. From curiosity, fury, or even pride, I cannot say. I know I would have, though.

Sobs wrack his chest. "I will tear the entire Underworld apart to return your soul to me."

"I"—a cough wrenches my entire body—"I forgive you."

My hand falls and darkness sweeps over me. I should tell him how I really feel, the love that swells within me, and that I've never been able to quash. There's no strength left in me to say those three simple words.

"I can't heal you," he says. He clenches my body to his, rocking back and forth. "I can't heal you."

Thanatos reaches a pale hand toward me.

Apollo's hand flutters over my arm and then stills.

I'm dimly aware of him pulling the bangle from my arm, its stones gleaming in the purple firelight.

Another part of me, my soul perhaps, rises. I step above Apollo, watching him clutch my body and gaze at the bracelet with a determined gleam in his eyes.

Thanatos drops his hand, features blanching.

The god of prophecy plucks one of the stones from the silver metal as easily as if plucking a grape. Not a stone, I realize. A seed.

"It's the only way," he says.

Then he places the seed between my lips.

CHAPTER 53

Syrup coats my tongue. My eyes flutter open, chest rising and fall-ing. The room is dark, purple lights dim. I have no idea how long I was unconscious. Apollo has disappeared, but my brother's body remains.

Cold and still.

I don't have the strength to rise yet. My hands flutter above my abdomen, searching for a pain that must be there. The only ache that remains is the slow fracturing of my heart.

Alkaios's lifeless eyes watch me.

I roll over with a grimace, unable to look at him any longer. The simple movement should be agony, but I feel nothing. Frowning, I finally glance down at where Alkaios stabbed me in the gut.

The chiton is still torn, dyed red with my blood that darkens at the edges, but beneath...Beneath is smooth, unblemished skin.

I remember nothing after Apollo passed that seed between my

lips. Not light or darkness, pain or pleasure. Nothing between now and then.

I pat my cheek. No gash remains, but blood still coats the side of my face and hair. Hope soars through me and I shove myself over to Alkaios.

His skin is cold. Another strangled cry escapes me as I grab up the bracelet, discarded by Apollo in the puddle of our blood, and snap off one of the seeds.

My brother's eyes are unseeing as I tilt his head back and force the opalescent stone into his lifeless mouth. I wait with held breath, cupping his face and hugging him close. His chest remains still.

"Breathe, damn you." I punch his chest with a fist. "Don't leave me yet."

In my heart, I know he's already gone. A strangled noise claws through my clenched teeth. A wild, fractured tempest rises in my chest, threatening to burn this entire world down. Nyx could have just killed me, but she wanted to punish me instead. I'll show her exactly how calamitous a *kataigída* can be.

Another rumble makes the pieces of the *pyxis* rattle, and screams echo down the long halls. Wails and the stench of burning flesh drag my attention inexorably to that dark entryway.

And then there it is, the thunder of footsteps. They hurtle down the corridor. I cradle my brother's body close and await their arrival with tearstained cheeks.

Odysseus steps into view first, the shadows peeling away like a cloak as the Ithacan king strides into the tomb. He sees me, then Alkaios in my arms, and his jaw drops.

"Shield of Helen," he says, voice rough. "What have you done?"

My voice has abandoned me. I can do nothing but stare up at him with a haunted expression, still stained with my brother's blood.

A steady line of soldiers file in behind him, led by Agamemnon.

The burly king's face splits in a wicked smile. His teeth are rotten and stained. "Thought you could hide down here from us, *prodótis*?"

I finally find my voice. "How did you get into Troy?"

"You haven't seen how we've rearranged this city?" He places his fists on his hips. "You have yet to see the Achaean masterpiece."

He nods to a pair of soldiers and they jerk me to my feet.

"No," I cry out, holding my brother firmly to my chest. He's almost weightless when he should be leaden in my arms.

One soldier marches forward and tries to rip away his body. He grunts, fingers digging into my skin. I let one arm fall away only to slap his face. He jerks back, entire head swinging to the side, and stumbles into his fellows. They catch him, roaring with laughter.

"You're really going to let that traitorous bitch push you around?" one asks.

With a wild growl, the man spins, fist flying. I watch it, as if in slow motion, flying toward my face. I let it. It's the least I can do for the pain I've caused this world.

It hits my nose. Lightning should have cracked across my entire face. Pain should have exploded behind my eyes. Instead, a dull ache forms along the crooked ridge of my nose and base of my teeth.

The man hisses, whipping his hand back.

I'm too startled to protest when two more sets of arms rip mine apart and take Alkaios from me.

"I'll give him the proper burial he deserves," Odysseus says, as if that should assure me and not shatter my heart even more.

I let them drag me up the dark hallway. Something inside me whispers that I should fight them and they could do nothing to stop me.

I don't.

A cool presence presses against my spine. I'd recognize his scent anywhere.

"Don't say anything," Hermes whispers from under a Spartan helmet. "Don't fight. I'll get you out of here."

I stumble, but we continue up the hallway.

"No," I say, so low nobody else can hear me but someone with a god's hearing.

Now it is Hermes's turn to trip. "What? Let me get you out of this city. They will kill you otherwise."

Let them, I want to say. *Let them kill me for what I did to Alkaios.*

Instead, I say, "Find Lykou and Lyta. Help them and Helen get out of this city." I bite my lip. "Kassandra, too. Anyone else you can."

I will not have their blood on my hands, too.

Hermes opens his mouth to protest, but it snaps shut behind me. The scent of the man suddenly changes, his grip tightening on the wrist behind my back. The messenger god has disappeared. Hopefully my friends are still alive for him to find.

Bright light spills down the hallway as we stomp up toward the entrance. The harsh light hits my face and I blink back tears as I'm thrown to the ground in the alleyway.

It's an alleyway no longer, though.

The buildings around the fresco have been annihilated. Nothing remains but tan rubble and torn cloth streaming over stones and...

Bodies.

Trojans, marked by their straight black hair and painted faces. A gasp bursts from me and the tears threaten to come anew. I want to search the dead, to assure myself that Helen and my friends are not among them.

I blink against the relentless sun. Menelaus towers above me, four men and women flanking him.

Their clothes are so threadbare they could be naked. One is a tall woman with wild green hair and pale skin. She glares down at me with a mixture of hate and revulsion. Beside her is a man as tall as a tree, with long dark limbs and even longer, dark braided hair. His eyes are red and they bore into me as if he could read my very thoughts. On Menelaus's other side, a pair of men with matching blue eyes and red hair stand; one is broad and burly, the other as slim as a reed.

I recognize them from Hermes's memories. The power pulsating off all of them makes me tremble.

"*Titans*," I say, the word tumbling from my mouth like a curse.

"So you know who it is we can thank for capturing this city." Menelaus waves a hand to the destruction.

"And you're the one we can thank for our freedom," the tall red-haired man says.

I toss my head back. "You can actually thank Nyx. That bitch has been nothing but a thorn in my side since—"

I'm cut off by his rough fingers yanking my face by the chin. He rubs a long, broken nail against my lower lip. "You are one of us. I can taste your ichor in the air."

I jerk from his grip and spit at his feet. "I'm nothing like any of you."

"She is the daughter of Oceanus," the woman says, hissing. "We should kill the traitor's bastard."

"Yes, yes." The tall dark man claps his hands with glee. His breath reeks of carrion. "We can make a game of it. We can each claim a piece of her."

The one who touched me considers it. "It would be a shame if something so lovely went to waste."

"As long as I can have her spine." The burly man steps forward. He looks me over hungrily. "It will be fun to break."

"You can try," I snarl. "But I might break yours first."

A cough draws their attention from me. A glimmer of fear, small but obvious, twitches at the corner of Menelaus's eyes. He says, "I would like to claim this woman for punishment. She has been the source of my people's troubles. The very cause of this war. I will take great pleasure in burning every drop of fight in her."

I meet his gaze, glare for glare. I am not afraid of him.

The titans consider him for a long moment, before the woman finally says, "You may try." She turns to me. "Something tells me that she has awoken, and nothing you can do will succeed in hurting her."

The burly man laughs, a sound like rumbling thunder. "We can wait."

Menelaus nods to two soldiers and they drag me to my feet. They don't get me the length of ten yards before Odysseus calls out from behind them.

"I claim her!"

He runs and grabs me roughly by the upper arm. He yanks but the soldiers refuse to let go of me.

Agamemnon marches forward to stand by his brother's side. "What nonsense is this, Ithacan? Menelaus has already claimed her punishment as his prize."

Odysseus's fingers tighten. "Of which my debt to her supersedes." He nods to Menelaus. "His as well."

"What debt?"

"If not for Daphne's intervention, both you and I would be dead." Odysseus straightens. "Unless you don't remember the Trojans calling for our blood when we climbed from the Horse. They were ready to kill us then and there. It's because of this woman that we can stand upon the conquered ruins of this city." He tugs on my arm again. "And I will claim my debt."

"Do you know," the Spartan king growls, "how long I've hungered to kill her?"

"Perhaps you should have better spent this war actually strategizing." Odysseus raises a hand in apology as Menelaus's face goes white with fury. "No offense meant, but we wouldn't have won this war without certain divine intervention."

Menelaus looks as if a bucket of cold water would turn to steam if flung upon him. He and Odysseus stare each other down, one with daggers in his eyes and the latter with cool assurance.

Agamemnon's hand claps down on his brother's shoulder, making us all jump. "Easy now, little lion." He nods to the titans still watching us down the alleyway. "The battles have just begun."

I'm wrapping my head around his words when Menelaus shoves me. I stumble and slam into Odysseus's chest. The king of Sparta spits at our feet, then stomps off.

"I will take it out on my wife instead," he says with no small amount of anger and disgust.

I move to follow and make sure he doesn't hurt Helen, but the Ithacan pulls me against his chest and holds me firm.

"Easy, girl," he says against my ear. "We still have to get you out of the city in one piece."

Or what's left of it.

He drags me through Troy's ruins and my heart sinks.

Not a single building remains standing. Whatever happened up here was colossal enough to wipe an entire city—the greatest city this world has ever known—from the earth. Strong enough to tear down Apollo's wall and leave hardly a single soul alive.

"What happened?" My eyes are wide, voice small.

Odysseus grimaces. "The titans were released from their slumber and they decided to take out their anger on this city. Once the gates were opened for Agamemnon, whatever power was imbued by the gods in the wall gave way. Troy didn't stand a chance."

Beyond where the walls once stood, dozens of pyres burn high.

I'm almost afraid to ask, but, "Were there any survivors?"

He shakes his head. "Not enough."

We climb over the remains of the wall, Odysseus clenching my arm the entire time. His warriors flank us, some with prisoners of their own. Pretty girls, handsome boys, children, and weaponry. Trophies, the whole lot of us.

We pass by the pyres on our way to the beach. They line what used to be the edge of the Achaean camp, and the closer I get, the more I see. Hundreds of them. So many, the air is filled with smoke enough to begin gathering in the sky and blocking out the sun. The stench of burning bodies would normally make me gag, but I remain emotionless, my face a statue of marble. For if I show any emotion now, it will not be grief for my enemies, but instead for the friends and family rotting in the fallen city behind me.

We pass a great golden fire, grander than all the others. I recognize the men crowded around the bursting flames. One turns when we pass, as if drawn to me.

Pyrrhus's face lights up, then crumples. Then I see the body at his feet, with arms crossed over his chest and coins already placed over his eyes. The lifeless form of Alkaios waits to burn next.

My brother begins to run toward me. His arms pump at his sides as he bounds across the soot and sand.

Odysseus quickens his steps. We are so close to the line of crashing waves. Already, his boat waits for us.

Pyrrhus clears the space between us and, as his body crashes into mine, there is no love on his face.

His fists are flying. They crunch into my nose, my eyes, and my throat. Blow after blow. I don't have time to cry out before another jab to my throat steals the last of my breath.

"You killed him!" he roars. "You killed our brother!"

I barely feel the blows, despite the carnage they must be doing to my face and body. He pummels me into the sand and I let him, shutting my eyes and clenching my lips shut. The inside of my mouth fills with blood, but it quickly vanishes. Before I can think on it, I'm hauled to my feet and Pyrrhus is thrown aside.

"Enough!" Odysseus barks. "You have touched what is not yours. Do it again, and you will lose those hands."

Pyrrhus looks as though he is willing to lose all his limbs to beat the life from me. So I finally say, "Don't, Pyrrhus." My eyes are already swelling and I can barely see through them enough to stare my brother down. "Save it for another day. You'll bring me to justice then."

"I hate you." He trembles as he says the words. "Alkaios was right; you are a curse on this world." He levels a bruised fist at my chest. "I will rip your heart out and feed it to the crows the next time I see you."

There's a dull ringing in my ears when Odysseus drags me away, onto the ship's gangplank, then I turn. Somehow, despite the pummeling my face received, I am able to open my eyes enough for one last look at Troy.

Gone is the city of beauty and art, where song rang even during the darkest times of war. The lovely buildings and gardens have been destroyed. The famed horses are all dead or claimed as war prizes. The streamers that hung between buildings blow across the bloody ground.

All that remains of the city is ruin. A hollow *paian* flits on the air, and one last sob is wrenched from me. I hope Lykou, Lyta, and Helen managed to flee. I hope Kassandra is with them, safe in my friend's arms, and that Hermes has squirreled them to safety.

A great shadow rises above the ruins. Titan power, like a heavy shroud, bears down upon the land. It swoops high and suffocates the sun, drenching the plain in black. It's the last thing I see before I'm shoved belowdeck.

They chain me to the walls. Water slaps against the sides of the ship and, as if in a dream, I blearily wonder if Oceanus knows where I am. If he's known all this time what his daughter has been doing.

What havoc and ruin she's been causing.

Curses echo above me from the soldiers and sailors. The ship left the shores of Troy long ago, but time is nothing to me now.

A sudden wave tilts the floor and I topple into the sodden, stained wall with a yelp. Surprisingly, the movement doesn't hurt despite the beating I received from Pyrrhus. Nothing hurts, in fact. More waves crash from every angle, making it impossible to steady myself. I go limp against the chains, swinging back and forth. I hang my head and my stomach heaves once, then stops moving.

The entire ship stills. The sounds above disappear, no more shouts, stomping, or rolling of water. Sandals nudge into my line of sight.

"Apollo," I cry, my head whipping up.

I cannot keep the disappointment from crumpling my face.

"No," Artemis says, one corner of her mouth pulling down. "You'll never see him again."

The ship sways. "What do you mean?"

"He will die protecting Olympus from the titans. The Moirai have fated it."

"No. Damn fate." My heart thuds. I bare my teeth. "Free me, and I can help fight them."

She drags a finger along my chains. "I'd free you, but you're probably safer here."

"Let me decide that for myself!"

She ignores my proclamation and looks me over with unbridled curiosity. "The ambrosia seed worked. I bet you can feel it awakening inside you."

"Feel what awakening?"

"You'll see." The goddess looks around the belly of the ship, at the treasure looted from Troy, the motionless, frozen prisoners.

I raise my weary brows. We've played this game before. The back and forth, half answers, and testing each other. She told me so little, that day in the glen. Did she know who my father was even then, before or after she branded me?

As if reading my mind, she finally says, "I'm sorry. For cursing you, I mean. The Midas Curse was meant to help you, but it just kept you in the dark." She cuts off, head tilting toward the deck. She leans an ear high as if listening to something beyond the boat.

When Artemis speaks next, her words are fast, tumbling out of her mouth. "Pyrrhus let the Achaeans into the city. When the titans were freed, they made a deal with Agamemnon and Menelaus. Or so the mortal kings believe. The titans will turn on them when the time comes, as they have all races, and they will..." She chews on her lip. I've never seen Artemis remotely worried before, and it makes dread curl in the pit of my stomach. She holds out her hands. "We won't be able to help them this time."

"You can't abandon them." I strain against my chains and the wall seems to groan. "You can't just abandon all of them."

Sparta will not just stand down. They will never bend or bow to the titans.

They will be annihilated.

"I'm so sorry, Daphne." Tears form in her lovely green eyes like rain upon leaves. "The titans have arrived at Olympus's gates. I must go."

"No." I jerk against the chains and the metal sings. "Take me with you. I'll help you fight them."

"You're not ready yet." She shakes her head. Her body is hazy, fading before my eyes. "Avenge us, daughter of Oceanus. Avenge your people."

She's gone and the sound of the sea returns. It's wild outside, accompanied by the clap of thunder and the shouts of Odysseus's crew, and the sound of my own wild thoughts. They're a storm, a raging tempest in my heart and head.

I have no people left, because I betrayed them. I have no family, because I murdered them. And now I have no gods, because I failed them.

I failed everyone.

I sag against the chains. There are no tears left to fall. Only pain. Pain to wrench from my very soul. Like a tsunami, it rips from me with a wild roar.

A void of silence greets me. The very earth stills.

Then the walls of the ship cave in and the water explodes around me.

EPILOGUE

AEAEA

For hopefully the last time, I awake upon a beach with sand clinging to my lips and hair.

Exhaustion, like none I've ever felt before, even in the grips of the god of death, weighs me down. I can barely flutter my eyes open. The orange sky of an autumn sunset greets me with purple clouds, while the waves push me farther and farther up the beach. There's coughing and exclamations from beyond my line of sight. I don't even have the energy to find out who speaks.

"We should have never left Troy in such a rush," a man yells. "We should have waited for the squalls to pass."

Troy.

Just hearing the name is like a punch to my gut. Pain wrenches me from the ground, my back arching and eyes clenching shut. A wild roar begins to build. The wind, as if in answer, rips my hair from my face and sprays water everywhere.

Men and women begin to scream, but their cries are lost in the din of the rising storm.

Then cold hands clap my cheeks. They squeeze my face painfully.

"Open your eyes, Daphne!"

I don't recognize the voice, sharp and reedy. The wind continues to build, rocking my entire body and lifting it from the earth.

"I command you to open your eyes!"

They snap open of their own accord. There's not a single light in the sky, only a dark, unrelenting storm. The wind rages, and I cough against the swell that has dragged me back out to sea.

A cold body holds me. Her hands still cup my face. Waves rock, tossing us around. I swallow a mouthful of water and choke.

Her hair is white and her skin pale green. Her features are so familiar, though. Determined and furious. The woman's nails dig into my skin, and I feel blood begin to pour down my face.

"Do not let this storm control you," she says. "You *are* the storm."

"I don't know how," I say. My voice is hollow and raw, as if the squalls have ruined my throat.

"Think of a sunset that brought you happiness," she says. "Of a time when the clouds disappeared and joy blossomed within you."

I remember pillow-soft kisses, wet sand beneath me as Apollo pulled me close. The setting sun alighting the world with flame as our lips met and everything else ceased to exist.

The wind dies as suddenly as it burst to life, and the clouds flee the piercing magenta rays of the sunset. We're swept back to shore. I hit the sand with a gasp. My knees bark as the tender skin is torn by broken shells and driftwood.

The woman is standing immediately. She sweeps a hand through her sodden white hair, which hangs past her knees, and it dries instantly. Her clothes do the same, whipping in the breeze and pressing against her thin frame.

"You are Circe," I say. "Ariadne's aunt."

I would recognize her features anywhere. The pert nose and tiny mouth. The lovely, upturned eyes amid a serious face.

"I am." She nods. "And such a demonstration of power could only belong to the daughter of Oceanus."

"That was me?" I cough and the remaining water hurls from my lungs.

She leans down and hauls me to my feet with surprising ease for someone so thin. Godly strength, no doubt. Only when I stand do I finally look around.

Odysseus's men and prisoners have washed ashore, the boat nothing more than broken pieces strewn across sand and rocks gleaming with mussels and many-legged starfish. The island is unlike any I'd ever known in Greece. The beach boasts large rocks, while trees I do not recognize hang over walls of shifting sand. Atop a high hill, a house of beechwood glares down at us, the open doorway a dark abyss. Long ago, Ligeia told me of the plight of the goddess Circe, exiled to the island Aeaea. A daughter of the titan Helios, feared for her great and unwieldy power. Or perhaps that is only what the stories would have me believe.

"You were never exiled." Not a question. "You're the daughter of a titan. You could open that doorway, too."

"My mother sent me here, to Aeaea, to protect me the moment Zeus learned of that door's weakness."

Ligeia also told me that Aeaea was far beyond Greece to the west. On the opposite side of the Aegean as Troy.

I stagger, feet slipping on the wet rocks. "How did we get here?"

"You brought them here," Circe says simply, shrugging a shoulder. "My magic called out to yours, it seems. I was just spelling the island against the turmoil I felt stirring in the east, and you barged right through all my enchantments and hexes as if they were nothing more than cobwebs. That curse from Hermes no doubt."

"But why here?" I watch in horror as Odysseus's men hurl their guts up on the sand. They likely did not pass the distance in a blink of an eye as I did.

I follow as Circe turns and walks toward the men. "You wanted an escape. You'll find nothing of the sort here."

I jerk to a halt. "What do you mean?"

A smile pulls at her thin lips. "I will help you."

"Help me what?"

"Learn how to use your powers." She waves to the sea. "To save Olympus."

Shock jars me, but it is met in kind by a fierce hunger. I turn toward the water, and it seems to shudder under my attention. The ocean stretches beyond my line of sight but the pull of Olympus is undeniable. It's there. Waiting for me.

The wind rises around me, fluttering the hair on my shoulders and stirring the hem of my bloodstained dress.

I will save not just Olympus.

I will also save my people.

AUTHOR'S NOTE

A tale as old as time.

When I hear that expression, I think of *The Iliad*, a story first passed down orally, and then shifting like the sands every time it was transcribed and translated over thousands of years. When I sat down to begin drafting *Blood of Troy*, I read multiple variations of *The Iliad* and *Odyssey*, and watched various TV shows and movies about it, too. Each had their minor and major differences from one another.

It was important to me to do many things when drafting this story: cherish the characters in ways that are authentic while bringing originality to a tale that has been passed down for thousands of years, flip readers' preconceived notions, and respect the history and the character of Helen. As I said in my previous author's note in *Daughter of Sparta*, history has been written by the winners, each finding is up to interpretation, and nobody knows what the truth is. Which begs the question: What is the true story of Helen of Troy?

At one point in *Daughter of Sparta*, Apollo tells Daphne that she will never truly know him, and that much is true of any Greek myth, particularly the Trojan War. In actuality, we do not know much about the Trojan War, other than that archaeological evidence points to a war between the Achaeans (known then as *Ahhiyawa*) and Troy (known then as the city of Ilius/*Wilusa*), and that the famous city was on the northern banks of ancient Turkey. This is a time and place steeped in both magic and realism, when science wasn't yet developed enough to offer rational explanations for things, so people spun the myths we hear today to explain the phenomena they were experiencing. It is also important to consider who would be spinning such tales. Even *The Iliad* changes depending on the translator. It is also important to recognize the liberties I have taken with the story while acknowledging that perhaps these are not liberties at all but much closer to the truth than we know, with our limited knowledge of what actually befell people on the shores of Troy and the heights of Mount Olympus.

And so with *Blood of Troy*, I sought to create a story that was both authentic and original, that does not diminish the myth that has persevered for many millennia, and that would still be a new experience for readers. To do so, I accrued a stack of sources almost as tall as I am. In addition to the (what felt like endless) list of books and articles I used for reference in *Daughter of Sparta*, I can thank the insight and wisdom found in *Strategy: A History* by Lawrence Freedman; *The Trojan War: A New History* by Barry Strauss; *Helen of Troy: The Story Behind the Most Beautiful Woman in the World* by Bettany Hughes; *A War Like No Other: How the Athenians and Spartans Fought the Peloponnesian War* by Victor Davis Hanson; *The Histories* by Herodotus; *Women at War in the Classical World* by Paul Chrystal; *The War That Killed Achilles: The True Story of Homer's* Iliad *and the Trojan War* by Caroline Alexander; *Warfare in the Classical World: An Illustrated Encyclopedia of Weapons, Warriors, and Warfare in the Ancient Civilizations of Greece and Rome* by John Warry; and *Battles of the Greek and Roman Worlds: A Chronological Compendium of 667 Battles to 31 BC, from the Historians of the Ancient World* by John Drogo Montagu.

GREEK GLOSSARY

Achaeans—the collective name for the inhabitants of Ancient Greece

agon—competition

agora—designated part of the city where merchants could sell wares and civic announcements were made

amphora—two-handled vase used for storage

anassa—queen

anax—king/emperor/tribal leader

Anemoi—gods of the wind

axine—battle axe

ballista—crossbow

bdelyròs—bastard

Carneia—festival in Sparta held in honor of Apollo

chaplet—headdress or diadem in the form of a wreath made of leaves, flowers, or twigs

chiton—a single rectangle of woolen or linen fabric that is either wrapped or tied around the body

chlamys—a short cloak that was draped over the tops of one's arms and pinned at the right shoulder; most commonly worn by men

dory—a three-meter-long spear used by the infantry of Spartan soldiers;

commonly made with wood, it often had an iron spearhead, and a bronze butt-spike

ephor—an elected Spartan politician

Erinyes—also known as the Furies, female chthonic deities of vengeance

fresco—art; a wall painting created by applying pigments to wet plaster

gymnasion—the gymnastic school in which Grecians practiced a number of physical activities and trained; mostly found in Sparta

Helot—subjugated population ruled by Spartans; sometimes slaves, though often they worked in Spartan agriculture

himation—a heavier, much larger cloak than the *chlamys;* worn by both sexes; could be used as both a cloak, or in the absence of a chiton, wrapped around the body and over shoulders

hoplite—heavily armed foot soldier

kalyptra—a thin headdress worn as a veil

kataigída—storm; tempest

kerykeion—a caduceus/staff

kerykes—herald; announcer

kline—couch, much like a lounge chair

kylix—a wine-drinking cup

lambda—the letter (Λ), standing for Laconia or Lacedaemon, which was painted on the Spartans' shields

lectica—a raised litter held up by servants for travel; commonly used by Greek nobles

lyre—a small U-shaped harp with strings fixed to a crossbar

Mana Mou—term of endearment for a mother figure; "My Mother"

meander—also known as the "Greek Key"; a pattern typically found among frescoes, jewelry, or along the hemlines of clothes worn by royalty megaron—great hall in ancient Greek palace complexes

Moirai—the three goddesses of fate

Mothakes—social class of people in Greece; "Non-Spartan"; not allowed many of the same civil rights as full Spartans, but still allowed many liberties

ochre—powder makeup for the eyelids and cheeks

paian—battle song

paidonomos—the headmaster of Spartan military training

pantheon—domed, circular temple

peplos—full-length dress that hangs loosely around the shoulders and is tied loosely around the waist

petteia—game similar to checkers, chess, and backgammon

phalanx—a formation of heavily armed hoplites drawn in close order with overlapping shields and spears

prodótis—traitor

pyxis—a cylindrical box with a separate lid

salphinx—trumpet

Spartiates—males of Sparta with full citizenship

suagroi—person with a romantic attachment to pigs

sýntrofos—comrade

xiphos—a double-edged, one-handed straight short-sword

ACKNOWLEDGMENTS

There are so many thanks I need to share, and never enough pages to do so.

First and foremost, I want to thank my family. Living in Vermont, I am halfway across the world from my parents, on either side of the globe. To my family in Scotland, particularly my mum, Scott, and Charlotte, thank you for being my greatest support, the ones I can always call. To my family in Alaska, particularly my dad, for being my cheerleaders. To Grandma and Nana, with so much love.

Next, I want to thank both my friends and family for showing me what strength is. It's what helped me write this draft. Daphne and I appreciated having all of you in our corner. To Remy and Noodles, my marketing support duo. To my CPs far and wide, Ellie, Carly H., Diana, the 21ders, and fellow authors. To June, Adalyn, and Katy for taking a chance on *Daughter of Sparta* and giving me the best blurbs I could ever ask for. To Molly, Guapo, Natalia, Autumn, Jeannie, Tori, Dexter, and Amy, and all my wonderful friends far and wide, too many to name here. I am so grateful for you all.

An enormous thanks to my team at Little, Brown Books for Young Readers. This book wouldn't be in your hands without the incredible Alvina Ling, Tracy Shaw, Bill Grace, Andie Divelbiss, my publicist Shivani Annirood, Andy Ball, Annie McDonnell, and Savannah Kennelly and the entire team at The Novl. I wouldn't have gotten the opportunity to even write this beast without the hard work of T. S. Ferguson and Hallie Tibbetts, who fought for my story and had faith in me from the beginning. This story would also not be possible without my tireless editor Caitlyn Averett, who sprinted headlong with me on a marathon of revisions. Your insights were so appreciated.

A very emphatic thank-you to my team at Dystel, Goderich & Bourret, LLC. To Lauren Abramo, for bringing my books into the hands of readers all over the world. A massive, all-encompassing thank-you to my wonderful, thoughtful, determined agent, Amy Elizabeth Bishop, the champion Daphne and I are so grateful for. Also Z, of course.

Lastly, home is where the heart is. Infinite thanks to my loving partner, Zachary. My champion and rock, warm arms and heart. Nizhoni and Tuff deserve all the thanks and pizza too.

Claire M. Andrews

was raised in both Alaska and Scotland but currently lives in Vermont; when not writing, she can usually be found outside, swimming, skiing, or hiking across the state's famous Green Mountains. She is the author of *Daughter of Sparta* and *Blood of Troy*, and can be found on Instagram and Twitter at @cmandrewslit.

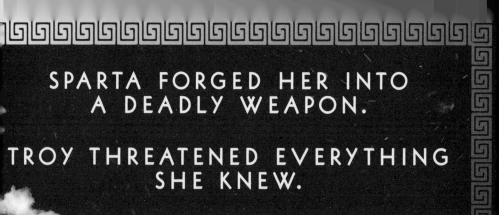
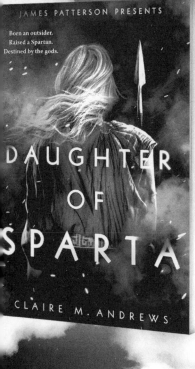
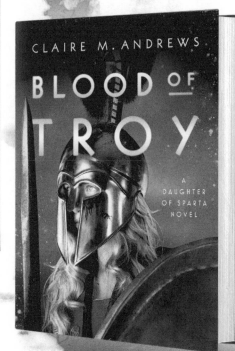